Alexander Kent writes:

I suppose the days of fighting sail and the independent seamen of the eighteenth/nineteenth-century Navy have always fascinated me, perhaps even from my childhood, when I walked around Nelson's *Victory* and tried to picture the fury of a sea-battle.

During the last war, in spite of belonging to an Army family, I joined the Navy without hesitation. It seemed the right thing to do, as if it was expected of me. I served in the battle of the Atlantic and in the campaigns of the Mediterranean and Normandy, but through it all I never lost my affection for those far-off days when only the 'wooden walls' stood between Britain and her enemies.

Ten years after becoming a professional author and novelist, I fell in with Richard Bolitho and his own life and times. Now, as I research the material of his exploits with my Canadian wife Kim, who is also a writer, I feel we can really share the memories of those fine, brutal ships, and the men who by choice or enforcement served and died with them.

Beyond the Reef

Alexander Kent

PAN BOOKS
IN ASSOCIATION WITH
WILLIAM HEINEMANN

First published 1992 by William Heinemann Limited

This edition published 1993 by Pan Books Limited
a division of Pan Macmillan Publishers Limited
Cavaye Place London SW10 9PG
and Basingstoke
in association with William Heinemann Limited

Associated companies throughout the world

ISBN 0 330 31957 4

1 3 5 7 9 8 6 4 2

A CIP catalogue record for this book is available from
the British Library

Printed and bound in Great Britain by
Cox & Wyman Ltd, Reading, Berkshire

For Kim, my Tahiti girl –
with love

Contents

1

Band of Brothers

The normally sheltered waters of Portsmouth Harbour seemed to cringe under the intensity of a biting north-easterly which had been blowing for some twelve hours. The whole anchorage was transformed into an endless mass of cruising whitecaps with lively catspaws to mark its progress around the many black-and-buff hulls of moored men-of-war, making them tug violently at their cables.

It was late March, a time when winter was still reluctant to release its grip and eager to display its latent power.

One of the largest ships, recently warped from the dockyard where she had suffered the indignities of repairs to the lower hull, was the second-rate *Black Prince* of ninety-four guns, her fresh paintwork and blacked-down rigging shining like glass from blown spray and a brief rainsquall which even now had reached as far out as the Isle of Wight, a dull blur in the poor light.

Black Prince was one of the most powerful of her kind, and to anyone but a true sailor she would appear a symbol of sea-power, the country's sure shield. The more experienced eye would recognise her empty yards, the canvas not yet sent up to give her life as well as strength. She was surrounded by lighters and dockyard longboats, while small armies of riggers and ropemakers moved busily about her decks, and the clatter of hammers and the squeak of tackles were evidence of the work being carried out in the deep holds and on the gundecks.

Alone by the packed hammock-nettings *Black Prince*'s captain stood at the quarterdeck rail and watched the comings and goings of seamen and dockyard workers, who in turn were supervised by the ship's warrant officers, the true backbone of any warship.

Captain Valentine Keen tugged his hat still tighter across his fair hair but was otherwise oblivious, even indifferent, to the biting wind and the fact that his flapping blue coat with its tarnished sea-going epaulettes was soaked through to his skin.

Without looking, he knew that the men on watch near the deserted double-wheel were very aware of his presence. A quartermaster, a boatswain's mate and a small midshipman who occasionally raised a telescope to peer at the signal tower or the admiral's flagship nearby, a sodden flag curling and cracking from her main truck.

Many of the men who had served the guns around him when they had fought and all but destroyed the big French three-decker off the coast of Denmark had been taken from his command while the ship had undergone repairs from that short, savage embrace. Some for promotion to other vessels, others because, as the port admiral had put it, 'My captains need men *now*, Captain Keen. You will have to wait.'

Keen allowed his mind to stray back over the battle, the terrible sight in the dawn when they had gone to assist Rear-Admiral Herrick's *Benbow* in his defence of a twenty-ship convoy destined for the invasion of Copenhagen. Shattered, burning hulks, screaming cavalry horses trapped below in the transports, and *Benbow* completely dismasted, her only other escort capsized, a total loss.

Mercifully *Benbow* had been towed to the Nore for docking. It would be too painful to see her here every waking day. A constant reminder, especially for Vice-Admiral Sir Richard Bolitho, whose flag would soon break out again from this ship's foremast. Herrick had been Bolitho's oldest friend, but Keen had been more angered than saddened by Herrick's behaviour both before and after *Benbow's* last fight. It might well *be* her last too, he thought grimly. With the many ships they had seized from Copenhagen to bolster their own depleted fleets and squadrons, any dockyard might think twice before committing itself to such a programme of repairs and restoration.

Keen thought of Bolitho, a man he cared for more than any

2

other. He had served him as midshipman and lieutenant, and with him in the same squadron until eventually he had become his flag-captain. Keen imagined him now with his lovely Catherine, as he had done so often since their return to England. He had tried to close his mind to it, not to make comparisons. But he had wanted a love like theirs for himself, the same challenging passion which had captured the hearts of ordinary people everywhere, and had roused the fury of London society because of their open relationship. A scandal, they proclaimed. Keen sighed. He would give his soul to be in the same position.

He walked to the small table beneath the overhang of the dripping poop and opened the log at the place marked with a piece of polished whalebone. He stared at the date on the damp page for several seconds. How could he forget? March 25th 1808, two months exactly since he had put the ring on the hand of his bride in the tiny village church at Zennor, which had given her her name.

Like the battle which had preceded his wedding by four months, it seemed like yesterday.

He still did not *know*. Did she love him, or was her marriage an act of gratitude? He had rescued her from a convict ship, and from transportation for a crime she had not committed. Or did his uncertainty stem from the fact that he was almost twice her age, when he believed she could have chosen anyone? If he did not contain it, Keen knew it would drive him mad. He was almost afraid to touch her, and when she had given herself to him it had been an act without passion, without desire. She had merely submitted, and later during that first night he had found her by the embers of the fire downstairs, sobbing silently as if her heart had already broken.

Time and time again Keen had reminded himself of Catherine's advice when he had visited her in London. He had confessed his doubts about Zenoria's true feelings for him.

Catherine had said quietly, 'Remember what happened to her. A young girl – taken and used, with no hope, and nothing to live for.'

Keen bit his lip, recalling the day he had first seen her, seized up, almost naked, her back laid open from shoulder to hip while the other prisoners had watched like wild beasts, as if it had been some kind of savage sport. So perhaps it was, after all, gratitude; and he should be satisfied, as many men would be merely to have her.

But he was not.

He saw the first lieutenant, James Sedgemore, striding aft towards him. He at least seemed more than pleased with his lot. Keen had promoted him to senior lieutenant after the tough Tynesider Cazalet had been cut in half on this same quarterdeck on that terrible morning. The enemy ship had been the *San Mateo*, a powerful Spaniard sailing under French colours, and she had crushed the convoy and its escorts like a tiger dispatching rabbits. Keen had never seen Bolitho so determined to destroy any ship as he had been to put down *San Mateo*. She had sunk his old *Hyperion*. He had needed no other reason.

Keen often found himself wondering if Bolitho would have held to his threat to keep pouring broadsides into *San Mateo*, which had already been crippled in the first embrace at close quarters. *Until they strike their Colours*. Thank God someone still sane enough to think and act in that hell of iron and screaming splinters had brought the flags tumbling down. But would he have continued, without mercy, otherwise?

I may never know.

Lieutenant Sedgemore touched his hat, his face red in the stinging air. 'I shall be able to get the sails ready for bending-on tomorrow, sir.'

Keen glanced at the Royal Marine sentries by the hatchways and up on the forecastle. With the land so close there were always the reckless few who would try to run. It would be hard enough to get more hands, especially in a naval port, without allowing men the opportunity to desert.

Keen had much sympathy for his men. They had been kept aboard or sent directly to other ships to fill the gaps, without any chance to see their loved ones or their homes.

Keen had spent more time than was necessary on board, simply to show his depleted company that he was sharing it with them. Even as it crossed his mind, he knew that too was a lie. He had stayed because of his fear that he might make Zenoria openly reject him, unable even to pretend.

'Something wrong, sir?'

'No.' It came out too sharply. 'Vice-Admiral Bolitho will be coming aboard at noon.' He looked across the nettings at the shining walls of the dockyard and harbour battery and on to the huddled buildings of Portsmouth Point, beyond which the Channel and the open sea were waiting. Bolitho might be over there already; at the old George Inn, perhaps? Unlikely. Catherine would be with him. He would not risk a snub or anything else which might distress her.

Sedgemore kept his young features impassive. He had never really liked his predecessor, Cazalet. A fine seaman, admittedly, but a man who was so coarse in his speech and behaviour that he had been hard to work with. He watched the bustling figures at the tackles, swaying up more bales and boxes from one of the lighters alongside.

Well, *he* was the first lieutenant now, in one of the navy's newest and most powerful three-deckers. And with an admiral like Sir Richard Bolitho and a good captain like Keen, there would be no stopping them once they were at sea again. Promotion, prize money, fame; there was no end to it, in his mind anyway.

It was the navy's way, Sedgemore thought. If a dead man's shoes were offered, you never waited for a second chance.

Keen said distinctly, 'Tell my cox'n to prepare the barge, and have the crew piped at six bells. Inspect them yourself, although I doubt if Tojohns will leave anything to chance.'

He glanced at the open log again where the midshipman-of-the-watch was writing something, his tongue poking from one corner of his mouth with great concentration. Another picture crossed his mind. His coxswain, Tojohns, on his wedding day only two months ago, supervising the garlanded carriage which had been towed by the midshipmen and petty officers of this ship, his ship, with himself and his young bride inside.

He turned aft and stalked away beneath the poop to seek the one place he could be alone.

Sedgemore watched him go and rubbed his chin thoughtfully.

A post-captain – what Sedgemore himself would be one day if everything went well for him, and he managed to avoid Cazalet's fate.

To be captain of a ship like *Black Prince* . . . He looked up and around him. There was no higher reward for any man. He would want for nothing.

He saw the midshipman staring at him and rasped, 'Mr M'Innes, I'll trouble you not to waste your time, sir!'

It was uncalled for; but it made him feel more like a first lieutenant.

Lieutenant Stephen Jenour caught his breath as he turned the corner above the shining dockyard stairs which led directly down to the landing stage. After two months ashore either working for Vice-Admiral Sir Richard Bolitho or visiting his parents in Southampton, he felt at odds with the sea and the bitter wind.

He thrust open a small door and saw a blazing fire shining a welcome across the room.

A uniformed servant asked coldly, 'Your name, sir?'

'Jenour.' He added sharply, 'Flag lieutenant to Sir Richard Bolitho.'

The man bowed himself away, muttering something about a warming drink, and Jenour was childishly pleased at his ability to command instant respect.

'Welcome, Stephen.' Bolitho was sitting in a high-backed chair, the fire reflecting from his gold lace and epaulettes. 'We have a while yet.'

Jenour sat down and smiled at him. So many things had changed his young life since joining Bolitho. His parents had laughed at him for vowing that one day he would serve this incredible man who had been, until Nelson's death at Trafalgar less than three years ago, the youngest vice-admiral on the Navy List. Now he *was* the youngest.

He never tired of recalling each separate incident, even that stark moment when *Black Prince* had been about to leave Copenhagen in search of Herrick, and Bolitho had turned on him in pleading desperation and confirmed his worst fears. 'I am losing my sight, Stephen. Can you keep a secret so precious to me?' And later when Bolitho had said, '*They must not know*. You are a dear friend, Stephen. Now there are other friends out there who need us.'

Jenour sipped the hot drink. There was brandy in it, and

6

spices too, and his eyes smarted but he knew it was from that memory and nothing else.

A dear friend, and one of the few who knew the extent of the injury to Bolitho's left eye. To be entrusted with such a secret was a reward greater than anything he had believed possible.

He asked carefully, 'What will Captain Keen's answer be, Sir Richard?'

Bolitho put down his empty goblet and thought of Catherine, imagined he could still feel the warmth of her body in his arms as they had parted this morning. She would be well on her way to London now, to the house she had bought by the river in Chelsea. Their private place as she had called it, where they could be alone together when they were required to be in the capital.

It was strange to be without Allday, but his coxswain – his 'oak' – had gone with Yovell, his secretary, and Ozzard his little servant, in the same coach. Catherine was fearless, but Bolitho felt safer on her behalf knowing that she travelled with such a staunch escort.

He thought too of his last interview with Lord Godschale at the Admiralty, and Godschale's attempts to soothe him whenever he touched on a point which might provoke controversy.

'Their lordships *insist* that you are the best choice of flag-officer to go to Cape Town. You had, after all, a vital part in taking it from the Dutch – our people know you and trust you accordingly. It should not take long, but it needs your handling to establish regular patrols of smaller craft in the area, and perhaps to send more of the major men-of-war back to England. When you have installed a post-captain in overall charge there – acting-commodore if you like – you can return too. I will offer you a fast frigate, and do everything possible for you.' He had given the great sigh of one overburdened with responsibility. 'Even while Admiral Gambier and your own squadron were in Copenhagen preparing the prizes for their passage here, Napoleon was already busy elsewhere. God damn the fellow – twice he has attempted to seize the Danish fleet, and he has even provoked Turkey to turn against his old ally the Tsar of Russia. As fast as we seal one door, he explores another.'

7

It was difficult not to admire Napoleon's ever-changing strategy, Bolitho had often conceded. Shortly after Herrick's hopeless fight to save his convoy, the French army had invaded Portugal, and by November was in Lisbon, with the royal family in flight to their possessions in Brazil. It was rumoured in Whitehall that Spain, another ally if an unwilling one, would be Napoleon's next target. He would then become a ruler of overwhelming strength, a threat once again with all the riches of Spain to support him.

Bolitho had said, 'I think that this time he may have overreached himself. He has turned Portugal into an enemy, and will surely incite Spain to rise against him. It will be our one chance. A place to land an army where it will find friendship, and be treated as a liberation force.'

Godschale had looked distant. 'Perhaps, perhaps.'

Another secret. Jenour knew; so did Yovell and Allday. Bolitho had refused to take passage in a frigate and had seen Godschale's heavy features go almost purple as he had exclaimed, 'Do you mean to say that you are going to take Lady Catherine Somervell with you on passage to Cape Town?'

Bolitho had been adamant. 'A ship of war is no place for a lady, my lord. Although I am sure Lady Catherine would accept without hesitation.'

Godschale had mopped his face. 'I will arrange it. A fast packet under Admiralty warrant. You are a damned difficult fellow to deal with, Sir Richard. What people will say when they discover – '

'We shall simply have to ensure they do not, my lord.'

When he had told Catherine she had been surprisingly excited about it.

'To be there with you, dearest of men, instead of reading of your exploits in the *Gazette*, to be part of it all . . . I ask for nothing more.'

The door opened and the servant peered in at them. 'I beg your pardon, Sir Richard, but it is reported that your barge has just left *Black Prince*.'

Bolitho nodded and remarked to Jenour, 'I'll wager Captain Keen will be surprised to find that I am not staying aboard.'

Jenour followed him from the snug shelter of the senior officers' waiting room.

He knew that Keen cared for Bolitho as much as he did himself. Would he leave *Black Prince* in exchange for some obscure position in Cape Town as captain in command of all local patrols? It would mean a broad pendant, and the real possibility of promotion to rear-admiral after that, if everything went well. But it would also mean leaving his bride behind so soon after their marriage, as well as severing his close links with the man who was even now standing at the top of the dripping stairs, peering across the tossing array of whitecaps.

I am fortunate that the choice is not mine. Not yet, in any case . . .

Bolitho pulled his boatcloak around his body and watched the green-painted barge pulling lustily across the choppy water, the oars rising and falling as one, the bargemen very smart in their checkered shirts and tarred hats. Keen's coxswain would be in charge today, and Bolitho was suddenly uneasy, knowing that Allday would not be there.

He thought of Catherine's happiness at the prospect of their journey, when before, when he had told her about Cape Town, there had been only anger and despair. 'Is there nobody else they can send, Richard? Must it always be you?'

When Godschale's acceptance of his request that she accompany him had been delivered to Falmouth, she had thrown her arms about him like a child. *Together*. The word which had become a symbol to both of them.

Ever since Keen's wedding they seemed to have spent days on the terrible winter roads: London, Falmouth and London again.

He thought of their last night at a small secluded inn Allday had recommended; as, seated in the waiting room before Jenour had arrived, he had stared into the fire, remembering it. The need of one for the other, until they had lain by the fire in the inn's private room, unwilling to waste the night in sleep.

The bargemen tossed their oars and sat stiffly facing aft while the bows were made fast to the stairs. The first lieutenant stepped lightly on to the wet stairs and raised his hat, his eyes everywhere, puzzled as he realised there was no chest or luggage to be stowed aboard.

'Good day, Mr Sedgemore.' Bolitho gave a brief smile. 'As you see, mine is a short visit this time.'

He and Jenour settled themselves in the sternsheets and the barge cast off, shipping water over the stem as they quit the shelter of the wall.

'Repairs going well, Mr Sedgemore?'

The lieutenant swallowed hard. He was unused to casual conversation with a vice-admiral.

'Aye, Sir Richard. It will be a month or so yet, I'm told.'

Bolitho watched the passing dockyard boats, and a yawl towing a new mast for some ship undergoing refit. If Napoleon did invade Spain, the naval blockade would have to be tighter than ever until they could put an army ashore to meet the French in open battle. He thought sadly of Herrick. Even his poor, battered *Benbow* might be sent back into the fray.

He heard the distant crack of a musket, and saw figures running on to *Black Prince*'s forecastle; he guessed that a marine had just fired on a would-be deserter.

Sedgemore said between his teeth, 'I think they got him.'

Bolitho looked at him calmly. 'Would it not be more useful to put your pickets on the foreshore and catch them if they swim there? A corpse is little use for anything, I'd have thought.' It was mildly said, but Jenour saw the first lieutenant wince as if he had been hit in the face.

The next few moments put all else from his mind. The climb up the slippery side, the trill of calls and the stamp and crash of the Royal Marines' guard of honour. Then Keen, his handsome features full of welcome as he stepped forward to greet him.

They shook hands, and Keen guided him aft to the great cabin.

'Well, Val?' Bolitho sat down and looked at his friend. 'You will not be hampered by me again just yet.'

He watched Keen pouring claret, noting the lines around his mouth. Strain of command. The many, many difficulties of completing a refit and putting right the wounds of battle. Making up a depleted company, storing, taking on powder and shot, preparing new watch-bills to eke out the experienced

10

hands among the volunteers and pressed men. Bolitho had known all these challenges even in his first command, a small sloop-of-war.

'It is good to see you.' Keen offered him a goblet. 'Your visit sounds something of a mystery.' He smiled, but it did not reach his eyes.

'And how is Zenoria? Missing you, no doubt?'

Keen turned away and fumbled with his keys. 'There was a despatch delivered on board this morning, sir. It came by post-horse from the Admiralty.' He opened a drawer and took it out. 'I forgot, in the excitement of your arrival.'

Bolitho took it and glanced at the seal. Something was wrong. Catherine had hinted as much.

He said, 'I am ordered to Cape Town, Val, to ensure there is no further complacency. We need more local patrols than ever now that the anti-slavery bill has been passed in Parliament. Slavers, pirates, privateers – they will all need seeking out.'

Keen stared at him as if he had not heard properly.

Bolitho added quietly, 'They require an experienced post-captain to command there. He will have the broad pendant of commodore for his pains. I will return to *Black Prince* eventually, but if you accept this appointment, *you* will not.'

'I, sir?' Keen put down his goblet without seeing it. 'Quit *Black Prince*?' He looked up, his eyes full of dismay. 'And leave you, sir?'

Bolitho smiled. 'This war is coming to a crisis, Val. We must put an army into Europe. We shall need our best leaders when that time comes. You are an obvious choice – you've earned it ten times over, and the fleet will need flag-officers like you now that Our Nel is dead.'

He recalled the general he had met just before they had managed to retake Cape Town. *Despite all the triumphs at sea, they will be as nought until the English foot-soldier plants his boots on the enemy's own shores.*

Keen walked to the spray-streaked stern windows and stared down at the distorted waves beneath the counter.

'When might this be, sir?' He sounded dazed by the sudden turn of events. Trapped.

11

'Soon. *Black Prince*, I am assured, will be in dockyard hands for some while yet.'

Keen turned. 'Advise me, sir.'

Bolitho took a knife and slit open the thick envelope. 'I know what it means to be parted from a lover. But it is the lot of every sea-officer. It is also his duty to seize any opportunity for advancement, to which he is truly suited, and from which his country may benefit.'

Keen looked away. 'I would like to accept, sir.' He did not even hesitate.

Bolitho read quickly through the neat lettering and said gravely, 'You have a further duty while you hold command here, Val.' He tossed the letter on to the table. 'There has been a court of enquiry at the Governor's house here in Portsmouth. Their lordships have decided that Rear-Admiral Herrick must stand trial at a court-martial on the prescribed date.'

Keen picked up the letter. 'Misconduct and neglect of duty . . .' He did not continue. 'My God, sir.'

'Read on. The court-martial will be held here in *Black Prince*, your command and my flagship.'

Keen nodded, understanding at last. 'Then I am eager for the Cape, sir.' He finished with sudden bitterness, 'I will not be needed here.'

Bolitho took his hat from the cabin servant. Then he said, 'When you are ready, Val, please tell me . . . tell *us*. It is what true friends are for.'

Keen seemed to search his face for something.

'That I shall never forget.'

'I am depending on it.' He hesitated, hearing the marine guard stamping into line at the entry port. 'Your pain is mine, as mine has too often been yours.'

Ebenezer Julyan, the sailing-master, was loitering by the wheel, and Bolitho guessed he had been waiting purposely to see him. As though it were yesterday, he recalled Julyan's grin of pleasure as they had sailed to meet the towering *San Mateo*, when Bolitho had given him his own gold-laced hat to wear to make the enemy believe that *Black Prince* was a Danish prize.

He called, 'Did you give that hat to your boy, Mr Julyan?'

The man laughed. 'I did that, sir. It made a rare stir in th' village! It be good to see 'ee again, Sir Richard!'

Bolitho looked round at other familiar faces, who had also faced death that day. He thought too of Keen's bitter comments; then he touched the silver locket through his shirt, the one she had fastened around his neck this morning as she always did when they were to be parted, even for a few hours.

May Fate always guide you. May Love always protect you.

With Keen so downcast, it seemed wrong to think of all the happiness she had given him.

Catherine, Lady Somervell, walked to the window with its small iron balcony and looked out across the swirling Thames. The city had been wide awake by the time her mud-spattered carriage had clattered to a halt outside this small, elegant house in Chelsea, the streets full of traders and carters from the various markets hawking meat, fish, vegetables, all a reminder of the London she had known as a very young girl; the London she had shown in part to Bolitho.

It had been a long hard journey on that appalling road, past leafless trees stark against a cold moon, and splashing through a downpour an hour later. They had stopped every so often to eat and drink, but not until Bolitho's portly Devonian secretary Yovell had inspected each inn to make certain it was suitable for her to enter. Several times he had climbed back into the carriage, grimly shaking his head to signal Matthew to drive on.

They had looked after her wonderfully, she thought. They had refilled her copper foot-warmer with boiling water at each stop, and ensured that she had been well wrapped in rugs as well as her long velvet cloak, and independent though she was, she had been glad of their company.

The house felt strange after Falmouth, damp and unfamiliar, and she was thankful for the fires blazing in most of the rooms. She thought of the grey Bolitho house below Pendennis Castle, and was still strangely surprised that she could miss it so much when she was away from it. She heard Allday laugh in the kitchen, and somebody, probably the faithful, silent little Ozzard, putting logs on one of the fires.

Once during the journey on a comparatively smooth stretch

of road, when Yovell had fallen asleep and Ozzard had been outside on the coachman's box, she had engaged Allday in conversation, listening intently as he had answered her questions and spoken of his early days with the man she loved. The ships and the battles, although she knew he had skirted around the latter. He never tried to shock or impress her, and he seemed to feel free enough to speak with her on equal terms, almost as a friend.

When she had asked him about Herrick, he had been more wary.

'I first knew him as one of the Cap'n lieutenants in the old *Phalarope* – back in eighty-two, it was.' He had given his lazy grin. ''Course, I didn't exactly *volunteer*, so to speak.' It seemed to amuse him. 'When the Cap'n finally left *Phalarope* he took us with him, me an' Bryan Ferguson. Then I became his cox'n.' He had shaken his head like a big shaggy dog. 'Lot of water since them days.'

Then he had looked at her very directly. 'Rear-Admiral Herrick is a stubborn man, begging your pardon, m'lady. An honest gentleman, an' that's rare enough these days, but . . .'

Catherine had watched his uncertainty. 'Sir Richard is deeply concerned about him. His oldest friend, would you say?'

It had given Allday the time he needed. 'Next to *me*, m'lady! But folk don't change, no matter what their circumstances. Sir Richard never has. A flag-officer he may be, a hero to most people he certainly is, but he's no different to the young cap'n I saw in tears at the death of a friend.'

'You must tell me that too, Allday. There are so many gaps I want . . . I need to fill.'

The carriage had lurched into a deep rut and Yovell had awakened with a startled grunt.

'Where are we?'

But Allday had looked at her in that same level way, as he had at English Harbour when her husband had been alive, and Bolitho had become her lover again after their stupid separation.

'I'll tell you, m'lady, don't you fret. This passage we're makin' to the Cape will show you the man *we* sees, not the one who comes home from the ocean. The King's officer.'

She heard herself laugh. 'I do believe you are filling in your own gaps about *me*, Allday!'

Now for a few more moments she was alone in the room where they had loved so demandingly, as if they were trying to make up for the lost years.

She thought of Valentine Keen, his troubled face when he had spoken to her of his hopes and fears for his marriage to Zenoria. Another mystery: so close a band of brothers – poor Oliver Browne's 'happy few' – and yet there was a coldness between Herrick and Keen. Because of Bolitho, or because of Zenoria?

She had never mentioned to Richard what she had seen in Adam's face at Keen's wedding. She might after all have been mistaken. In the same heartbeat, she knew she was not; she was too experienced not to recognise that Adam, Richard's nephew and the nearest to a son he would ever know, was in love with Keen's Zenoria.

But Adam was a captain now, albeit a very young one, and his first frigate, the *Anemone*, was somewhere at sea with the Channel Fleet. It was just as well, at least until things settled down again.

She tossed away her cloak and gazed at herself critically in a tall mirror. A woman envied, admired and hated. She cared for none of it.

She saw only the woman who was loved by England's hero. The man. She smiled, remembering Allday's sage-like confidences. Not the *King's officer*.

She was waiting for Bolitho when he reached the house in the late evening, although she had had no forewarning of the time of his arrival. He strode through the doors and gave his hat and cloak to the new maidservant, before taking Catherine in his arms.

They kissed, and he studied her for several seconds.

'Thomas Herrick is to be court-martialled.'

She put her arms around his neck. 'My news is not good either.'

He held her away, searching her face anxiously. 'You're not ill, Kate? What has happened?'

She said, 'There was a woman here today.'

'Who?'

'She left a card.' Her voice was husky, almost despairing. 'It was "expected" that you might be here, she said.' She looked at him directly. 'Your daughter is unwell. The person sent as messenger would tell me nothing further.'

Bolitho stared at her, expecting bitterness or resentment. There was neither. It was more an acceptance of something which had always been there, and always would.

Catherine said, 'You will have to go, Richard. No matter what you feel for your wife, or for what she connived at with my late husband. It is not in your nature or mine to run away.' She touched the cheek near his damaged eye, her voice a whisper so soft that he could barely hear it.

'Some may call me the vice-admiral's whore, but such fools are to be pitied rather than scorned. When you look at me as you are doing now I can barely let you go. And every time you enter me it is as the first time, and I am reborn.' She lifted her chin and he saw the pulse beating in her throat. 'But stand between us, my darling Richard? Only death will ever do that.'

She turned away and called to Allday, whom she had sensed to be waiting in the hall. 'Stay with him – you are his right arm. Under these circumstances I cannot go. It would only harm him.'

The carriage had returned to the door. Bolitho said, 'Wait for me, Kate.' He looked strained but alert, his black hair still dishevelled from travel, with the single loose lock above his right eye almost white where it hid the terrible scar on his forehead. A youthful, sensitive face; he might still have been the captain Allday remembered and described so vividly, in tears for a fallen friend. Then she moved against him and touched the old family sword, seen in all those portraits in Falmouth.

'If I had a wish in the world it would be to give you a son to wear this one day. But I cannot.'

He held her closely, knowing that if her reserve broke he could not leave her, now or ever.

'You once said of me, Kate, that I needed love "as the desert needs the rain." Nothing has changed. It's you I want. The rest is history.'

As the door closed she faced the stairway. Yovell was

standing there, anxiously polishing his small gold-rimmed spectacles.

She said aloud, as if Yovell were not even there, 'If she tries to hurt him again, I will surely kill her.'

Yovell watched her pass. Distress and anger could not diminish the beauty which turned so many heads. He thought of all the immediate obstacles. Herrick's court-martial, the rumours he had gleaned about Captain Keen's marriage, and now this.

Perhaps it was as well they were all sailing for the Cape.

2

Strangers

Even though it was dark, the quiet and exclusive square was
exactly as Bolitho had remembered. Tall, elegant houses, most
of which seemed to have every window ablaze: light even
reflected from the wet, bare trees where, within weeks,
nursemaids would be wheeling their charges and loitering to
gossip about their households.

The carriage pulled up on its brake and Bolitho saw Allday's
features quite clearly as he leaned over in the glare of one of
its lamps. Bolitho climbed down and stamped his feet to
restore the circulation, giving himself time to compose his
thoughts.

There was a mews at the end of the nearest houses where a
brazier glowed in the damp air, almost hidden by the various
grooms and coachmen who would wait, all night if required,
for their lords and ladies to call for them from lavish supper
parties or from the gambling rooms across the square. It was
the other London, which Bolitho had grown to hate. Arrogant,
thoughtless. Without pity. As different from Catherine's
London as these mindless fops were from Bolitho's sailors.

'Wait nearby, Matthew.' He glanced at Allday's massive
shadow. 'Stay with me, old friend.'

Allday did not question him.

The door swung inwards even before the echo of the bell
had died. A footman stood outlined against the chandeliers,
his features invisible in shadow, like a wooden cut-out in some
fashionable shop.

'Sir?'

Allday said harshly, 'Sir Richard Bolitho, matey!'

The footman bowed himself into the splendid hallway, which Bolitho noticed had been completely redecorated with new claret-coloured curtains instead of the others he had seen on his last visit. Those had also been new at the time.

He heard the murmur of voices and laughter from the dining-room upstairs – hardly what he had been expecting.

'If you will wait here, Sir Richard?' The footman had recovered his confidence a little. 'I will announce your arrival.'

He opened a door and Bolitho remembered this room too, despite more expensive alterations. Here he had confronted Belinda about her connivance with Viscount Somervell, Catherine's dead husband, how they had planned to hold her under false charges in the notorious Waites prison until she could be deported, disposed of. He would never forget Catherine in that filthy jail, filled with debtors and lunatics. Catherine could never be caged; she would have died first. No, he would not forget.

'Why, Sir Richard!'

Bolitho saw a woman standing in the open doorway and somehow knew she was the 'messenger', Lady Lucinda Manners, presumably one of Belinda's close friends, who had left the brief note at Catherine's Chelsea house. Piled fair hair, a gown cut or pulled so low it barely covered her breasts . . . She was watching him, an amused smile on her lips.

'Lady Manners?' Bolitho gave a curt bow. 'I received your letter on my arrival in London. Perhaps – '

'Perhaps, Sir Richard, I will suffice as your companion until Lady Bolitho is free to leave her guests?' She saw Allday behind the door for the first time. 'I thought you would be alone.'

Bolitho remained impassive. *I can well imagine*. The delicious predator: another attempt at compromise.

'This is Mr Allday. My companion. My friend.'

There was a tall-backed porter's chair in the hallway and Allday sat down in it very carefully. 'I'll be in range whenever you gives the word, Sir Richard.' One of the chandeliers shone briefly on the brass butt-plate of the heavy pistol concealed under his coat.

19

Lady Manners had seen it also, and she said a little too brightly, 'You have nothing to fear in this house, Sir Richard!'

He looked at her calmly. 'I am glad to know it, ma'am. Now, if you would hasten this interview I would be equally grateful.'

The murmur of voices overhead stopped, as if the house itself were listening, and Bolitho heard the hiss of her gown against the banisters as she descended the beautiful staircase.

She stood two steps from the bottom and regarded him in slow examination, as if looking for something she had missed.

'So you came, Richard.' She offered her hand, but he remained where he was.

'Let us not pretend. I came because of the child. A matter of – '

'Duty, were you about to say? Certainly not out of affection.'

Bolitho glanced meaningly at the opulent surroundings. 'It seems that my protection is rather more than adequate, let alone deserved.'

The chair squeaked and she exclaimed, 'I would prefer not to discuss this in front of servants, yours or mine!'

'We speak a different language.' Bolitho found he could look at her without hatred, without any of the feelings he had expected. To think she had even chided him that he had married her for the worst possible reason, because she had looked so much like his first wife, Cheney.

'Allday has shared all the dangers and furies of this damned war – he is one of the men your so-called friends would spurn, even though he daily risks his life to keep you in comfort.' He added with sudden anger, 'What about Elizabeth?'

She seemed about to return to the attack, then gave it up. 'Follow me.'

Allday leaned forward to watch until they had disappeared on the curving staircase. He would not worry too much, he decided. Bolitho had a great deal on his mind, but he had shown his steel to her ladyship and the other bitch with the bare shoulders and the glance that would sit fair on a Plymouth trollop.

He reflected on the passage to Cape Town. It would be like no other, he thought. With Lady Catherine, Captain Keen and young Jenour in company, it would be more like a yacht than a voyage on the King's business. Allday considered Lady Catherine. How different from the sluts he had seen in this house. Tall, beautiful; a real sailor's woman, who could turn a man's heart into water or fire just by looking at him. She even cared about the Bolitho estate in Falmouth and had according to Ferguson, the steward and Allday's good friend, done wonders already with her suggestions and advice on how to make it pay again, to restore the losses incurred when Bolitho's father Captain James had been forced to sell much of the land to settle his other son's gambling debts.

Now they were all gone, he thought grimly. Apart from young Adam, to whom Bolitho had given the family name: there would be no more of them. It made him uneasy to imagine the old grey house empty, with none of its sons to come home from the sea.

It was something he shared with Bolitho, and a preoccupation he worried about in private. That one day the enemy's steel or a blast from the cannon's jaws would separate them. Like the master and his faithful dog, each fearful that the other would be left alone.

Upstairs conversation was returning to the dining-room. Bolitho barely noticed as they stopped outside an ornate gilded door.

Belinda faced him coldly. 'As Elizabeth's father, I thought you should know. Had you been at sea I might have acted differently. But I knew you would be with . . . *her*.'

'You were right.' He returned the cold, steady stare. 'Had my lady caught the fever from poor Dulcie Herrick I think I would have ended my life.' He saw the shot go home. 'But not before I had done for you!'

He thrust open the door and a woman in a plain black gown, whom he guessed was the governess, scrambled to her feet.

Bolitho nodded to her, then looked at the child who lay fully dressed on the bed, partly covered by a shawl.

The governess said quietly, 'She is sleeping now.' But her eyes were on Belinda, not him.

Elizabeth was six years old, or would be in three months' time. She had been born when Bolitho had been in San Felipe with his little sixty-four gun flagship, *Achates*. Keen had been

21

his flag-captain in *Achates*, too, and in that battle Allday had received the terrible sword-thrust in the chest which had almost killed him. Allday rarely complained about it, but it sometimes left him breathless, frozen motionless with its recurring agony.

Belinda said, 'She had a fall.'

The child seemed to stir at her voice and Bolitho was reminded of the last time he had seen her. Not a child at all: a miniature person, all frills and silks like the lady she would one day become.

He had often compared it with his own childhood. Games amongst the up-ended fishing boats at Falmouth, with his brother Hugh and his sisters and the local children. A proper life, without the restrictions of a governess or the remote figure of her mother, who apparently only saw her once a day.

He asked sharply, 'What kind of fall?'

Belinda shrugged. 'From her pony. Her tutor was watching her closely, but I'm afraid she was showing off. She twisted her back.'

Bolitho realised that the child's eyes were suddenly wide open, staring at him.

As he leaned over to touch her hand she tried to turn away from him, reaching for the governess.

Belinda said quietly, 'To you, she is a stranger.'

Bolitho said, 'We are all strangers here.' He had seen the pain on the child's face. 'Have you called a doctor – a good one, I mean?'

'Yes.' It sounded like *of course*.

'How soon after it happened?' He sensed that the governess was staring from one to the other, like an inexperienced second at a duel.

'I was away at the time. I cannot be expected to do everything.'

'I see.'

'How can you?' She did not conceal the anger and contempt in her voice. 'You care nothing for the scandal you have caused with that woman – how could you hope to understand?'

'I will arrange a visit from a well-appointed surgeon.' Belinda's tone left him quite cold. This was the woman who had left Dulcie Herrick to die after pretending friendship to

22

her, who had used Herrick's revulsion at Catherine's liaison with her husband, and who had discredited Catherine and eventually deserted her in that same fever-ridden house. He tried not to think of his old friend Herrick. He, too, would die or live in dishonour if the court-martial went against him.

He said, 'Just once, think of somebody else before yourself.'

He moved to the open door and realised he had not once called her by her first name.

He was in time to see somebody peering curiously out of the dining-room.

'I think your friends are waiting for you.'

She followed him to the head of the stairs. 'One day your famous luck will run out, Richard! I would I could be there to see it!'

Bolitho reached the hallway as Allday lurched up from his porter's chair.

'Let us go back to Chelsea, Allday. I will send a letter in Matthew's care to Sir Piers Blachford at the College of Surgeons. I think that would be best.' He paused by the carriage and glanced at the street brazier, the dark figures still hunched around it. 'Even the air seems cleaner out here.'

Allday climbed in with him, and said nothing. More squalls ahead. He had seen all the signs.

He had seen the look Belinda had given him on the stairs. She would do anything to get Bolitho back. She would be just as glad to see him dead. He smiled inwardly. *She'd have to spike me first, an' that's no error!*

Admiral the Lord Godschale poured two goblets of brandy and watched Bolitho, who was standing by one of the windows staring down at the street. It irritated the admiral increasingly that he should always feel envy for this man who never seemed to grow any older. Apart from the loose lock over the deep scar on his forehead which had become suddenly almost white, Bolitho's hair was as dark as ever, his body straight and lean, unlike Godschale's own. It was strange, for they had served as young frigate captains together in the American war: they had even been posted on the same date. Now Godschale's once-handsome features had grown heavy like his body, his cheeks florid with the tell-tale patterns of good living. Here at the

Admiralty, in his spacious suite of offices, his power reached out to every ship great and small, on every station in His Britannic Majesty's navy. He gave a wry smile. It was doubtful if the King knew the names of any of them, although Godschale himself would be the very last to say so.

'You look tired, Sir Richard.' He saw Bolitho dragging his mind back into the room.

'A little.' He took the proffered glass after the admiral had warmed it over the crackling fire. It was well before noon, but he felt he needed it.

'I heard you were out late last night. I had hoped . . .'

Bolitho's grey eyes flashed. 'May I ask who told you I was at my wife's house?'

Godschale frowned. 'When I heard of it I cherished the thought that you might be returning to her.' He felt his confidence ebbing under Bolitho's angry stare. 'But no matter. It was your sister, Mrs Vincent. She wrote to me recently about her son Miles. You dismissed him from your patronage, I believe, while he was a midshipman in *Black Prince* . . . a bit hard on the lad, surely? Especially as he had just lost his father.'

Bolitho swallowed the brandy and waited for it to calm him.

'It was a kindness as a matter of fact, my lord.' He saw Godschale's eyebrows rise doubtfully and added, 'He was totally unsuited. Had I not done so I would have ordered my flag-captain to court-martial him for cowardice in the face of the enemy. For one who enjoys spreading scandal, my sister appears to have overlooked the true reason!'

'Well!' Godschale was at a rare loss for words. *Envy.* The word lingered in his mind. He considered it again. He was all-powerful, wealthy, and beyond the risk of losing life or limb like the captains he controlled. He had a dull wife, but was able to find comfort in the arms of others. He thought of the lovely Lady Somervell. *God, no wonder I am still envious of this impossible man.*

Godschale pressed on grimly. 'But you were there?'

Bolitho shrugged. 'My daughter is unwell.' *Why am I telling him? He is not interested.*

Like the mention of the midshipman. It was merely another probe. He knew Godschale well enough by reputation, both past and present, to understand he would hang or flog anyone who put his own comfort in jeopardy, just as he had never shown the slightest concern for the men who month after month rode out storm and calm alike, with the real possibility of an agonising death at the end of it.

'I am sorry to know it. What can be done about it?'

'Lady Catherine is with a surgeon at this moment. She knows him quite well.' He felt his injured eye prick suddenly as if to reveal the lie, the real reason she had gone to consult the heron-like Blachford.

Godschale nodded, wondering why Bolitho's wife was allowing such interference.

Bolitho could read his thoughts as though he had shouted them aloud; he recalled Catherine's voice, while she had lain at his side in the darkness. They had talked for much of the night, and as usual she had seen everything more clearly than he.

'You care so much, Richard, because you still feel responsible. But you are not. She made the child what she is. I've seen it happen all too often. I shall visit Sir Piers Blachford – he is one of the few I would trust. I am sure he will be able to help Elizabeth, or find someone who can. But I will *not* see you destroy yourself by going to that house again. I know what she is still trying to do . . . as if she has not already taken enough from you.'

Bolitho said, 'In any case, I am quite certain you did not bring me here merely to discuss my domestic situation, my lord?'

Strangely, Godschale seemed content to leave it at that. Until the next time.

'No, quite right. Quite right. I have completed all the arrangements for your visit to the Cape. My aide will give you the full details.' He cleared his throat noisily. 'But first, there is the court-martial. The date is set for the end of next week. I have sent word to your flag-captain at Portsmouth.' He looked at him challengingly. 'I did not choose *Black Prince* for the court-martial out of spite. You will be more private in her. Dockyard work can be held up during this beastly affair.'

Bolitho asked quietly, 'Who is the President to be?'

25

Godschale shuffled some papers on his ornate table as if he could not remember.

He cleared his throat again and answered, 'Admiral Sir James Hamett-Parker.'

Bolitho felt the room spin. In seconds he had seen the man. Dour, uncompromising features, a thin mouth: a man more feared than respected.

'I shall be there to give evidence, my lord.'

'Only if you are asked – as a witness after the fact, so to speak.'

Bolitho turned from the window as a troop of dragoons clattered past.

'Then he is already condemned.' Then he said sharply, surprised that he could still plead, 'I must do something, my lord. He is my friend.'

'Is he?' Godschale refilled the fine goblets. 'That brings me to the other matter . . . The court was prepared to allow *you* to defend him. It was my idea, in fact. The whole affair can do nothing but harm to the fleet – to all senior officers who are far from support, and who have only their own judgment to sustain them. With our army poised on the threshold of Europe every officer from admiral to captain will need all the confidence in the world if this great venture is to succeed. If we fail, there can be no second chance.'

He had voiced the very opposite view at their last meeting, Bolitho thought, but it no longer mattered.

'Do you mean that Rear-Admiral Herrick rejected me as his defence?' He recalled Herrick's face the last time they had met, the blue eyes stubborn, hurt, bitter. 'Whom did he choose?'

Godschale glanced at the clock. It would be better if Bolitho was gone before his sister arrived to add to the general problem.

'That is the point, Sir Richard. He will have nobody.' He studied him, heavily intent. It was not like Godschale to risk anything which might dislodge his position of power. Was it really true what they said about this man, he thought uneasily. Had Bolitho's charisma touched even him?

'There is something you might do.'

Bolitho saw his inner struggle and was surprised by it. He

26

had never known Godschale in this mood before. 'Yes. Anything.'

Godschale was beginning to sweat, and it was neither from brandy nor the heat of the fire.

'Rear-Admiral Herrick is at Southwark. He will be met there by the Marshal to take a coach to Portsmouth the day after tomorrow. You will need all your discretion; many sea-officers come and go on the *Portsmouth Flier* and might recognise you. It would embroil you even further . . . there might even be an attempt to smear you with collusion.'

Bolitho held out his hand. 'I thank you for this, my lord – you may never know what it means. But one day I may be in a position to repay you. And have no fear. I heard nothing from you.'

Godschale attempted to give a rueful grin. 'Nobody would believe it in any case, not of me, that is!' But the grin would not show itself.

Long after the doors had closed behind Bolitho, Godschale was still staring at the window where his visitor had stood. He thought he would already be feeling regret, but if anything he felt strangely uplifted.

His secretary opened the doors with a flourish as Godschale rang the little bell on his table.

'My lord?'

'Send for my carriage. Now.'

The man stared at the clock, bewildered by his master's behaviour.

'But Mrs Vincent will be here in an hour, my lord!'

'Do I have to say everything twice, man? Send for the carriage!'

The man fled and Godschale poured another goblet of brandy.

Envy. Aloud to the empty room he said abruptly, 'God damn you, Bolitho, you put years on me! The sooner you get back to sea the better, for all our sakes!'

It was already dark again by the time Bolitho's carriage arrived at the inn at Southwark. After they had rattled over London Bridge to the south bank of the Thames, he imagined he could smell the sea and the many ships lying at anchor, and wondered if Allday had also noticed it, and was thinking about the passage to the Cape.

He heard Matthew curse from his box and felt the wheels jar savagely against fallen stones. He rarely swore, and was the best of coachmen, but this carriage had been borrowed for the journey. Secrecy would be impossible if the Bolitho crest was there for all to see.

They slowed down to pass a big mail coach standing outside the famous George Inn, from which place so many sea-officers began their long and uncomfortable journey to Portsmouth. Without horses it looked strangely abandoned, but ostlers and inn servants were already loading chests and boxes on top, while the passengers consumed their last big meal, washed down with madeira or ale as the fancy took them. The George was the one place in London where Bolitho was most likely to be confronted by someone he knew.

A little further along the road was the smaller Swan Inn, a coaching and posting stop with the same high-galleried front as the George. But there the similarity ended. The Swan was used mainly by merchants, somewhere to break their journey or discuss business without fear of interruption.

In the inn yard shadowy figures ran to take the horses' heads, and a curtain twitched as someone peered out at the new arrival.

Allday's stomach rumbled loudly. 'I smell food, Sir Richard!'

Bolitho touched his arm. 'Go and find the innkeeper. Then eat something.'

He climbed down and felt the bitter air sweeping from the river. Upstream in the little Chelsea house Catherine would be looking out at this same river, imagining him here.

A bulky lump of a man appeared in the light from an open side door.

'God swamp me, Sir Richard! This *is* a surprise!'

Jack Thornborough had begun life as a purser's clerk during the American Revolution, and later when discharged he had obtained work in the nearby naval victualling yard at Dept-ford. It was said unkindly of him that he had robbed the yard so successfully with the connivance of ships' pursers that he

had made enough to purchase the old Swan lock, stock and
barrel.

'You can guess why I'm here, Jack.' He saw the man's bald
pate shine in the shaft of light as he nodded like a conspirator.

'In 'is room, Sir Richard. They'm comin' fer 'im day arter
t'morrer, so they says, but they might come earlier.'

'I must see him. Nobody should know about it.'

Thornborough led him through the door and bolted it. He
beamed at the plain black hat and unmarked cloak which
Bolitho had donned for the occasion. 'Yew'm more like a
gentleman of the road, beggin' yer pardon, than any flag-
officer!'

He felt his stomach contract and realised that, like Allday,
he had not eaten since first light.

'See to my people, will you, Jack?'

Thornborough touched his forehead, just for an instant a
sailor once again.

'Leave it to me, Sir Richard!' He became serious. 'Up them
stairs right to the top. You'll not meet a soul, nor will anyone
see you.'

A very private room then. For highwaymen perhaps, or
lovers unaccepted by society. Or a man he had known for over
twenty-five years, who was facing disgrace or death.

He was surprised to find that he was not even breathless
when he reached the top of the creaking stairs. So many walks
with Catherine, along the cliffs at Falmouth or through the
fields where she had described what she and Ferguson had
planned for the estate. She had, moreover, won the respect of
Lewis Roxby, who had always had an eye on the Bolitho land,
and had acquired some in the selling-off of property to settle
Bolitho's brother's debts. Roxby was after all married to
Bolitho's favourite sister Nancy. It was good that she and
Catherine were friends. Unlike Felicity, who seemed so full of
hate.

He rapped on the dark, stained door: years of smoke from
the inn's many grates, from encounters in the night with those
who did not wish to be seen. But Jack Thornborough would
not let him down. He had been serving in the same frigate as
Bolitho's dead brother Hugh, and despite Hugh's treachery
had always spoken kindly of him. As others had often

remarked, the navy was like a family; sooner or later you met the same ships, the same faces. Even the ones who fell were not forgotten. Bolitho rapped again and for a moment imagined that the room was empty, the journey wasted.

A voice said, 'Go away.'

Bolitho let out a sigh. It was Herrick.

'Thomas, it's me. Richard.'

There was another long pause and then the door opened very slightly. Herrick stood back and waited for Bolitho to enter. The small, poorly-lit room was littered with clothing, an open sea-chest, and incongruously on a table amongst some letters lay Herrick's beautiful telescope, Dulcie's last gift to him.

Herrick dragged a coat from a chair and stared at him. He was stooped, and in the candlelight his hair seemed greyer than before. But his eyes were bright enough, and there was only ginger beer on another table, no sight or smell of brandy.

'What are you doing here, Richard? I told that fool Godschale not to drag you into it . . . I acted as I thought best. They can all go to hell before I'd say otherwise!' He walked over to get another chair and Bolitho was further saddened to see that he still limped from his wound. He had been cut down by a jagged splinter on *Benbow*'s quarterdeck, with his marines and gun crews strewn about him like bloodied bundles of rag.

'You'll need help, Thomas. Someone must speak for you. You know who the President is to be?'

Herrick gave a tight smile. 'I heard. Killed more of his own men than the enemy, I shouldn't wonder!'

Wheels scraped over the cobbles and harness jingled in the inn yard at another arrival. It seemed as if it came from another world; but suppose it was the Admiralty Marshal? There was only one stairway, and not even the impressive Jack Thornborough could hold him off forever.

Herrick said suddenly, 'Anyway, you'll be called as a witness.' He spoke with savage bitterness. 'To describe what you found after the battle. As a witness you'd not be allowed to defend me, even if I wanted it.' He paused. 'I just thank God my Dulcie is not here to see this happening.' He stared at the shining telescope. 'I even thought of ending it all, and damn them and their sense of honour.'

'Don't talk like that, Thomas. It's not like you.'

'Isn't it? I don't come from a long line of sea-officers like you.' It was almost an accusation. 'I started with nothing; my family was poor, and with some help from you I gained the impossible – flag rank. And where has it got me, eh? I'll tell you: probably in front of a firing-squad, as an example to the others. At least it won't be my own marines – they all bloody well died.' He waved a hand vaguely, like a man in a dream. 'Out there somewhere. And they did it for *me* – it was my decision.'

He stood up stiffly, but instead of the rear-admiral Bolitho could only see the stubborn and caring lieutenant he had first met in *Phalarope*.

Herrick said, 'I know you mean for the best, Richard . . .'

Bolitho persisted, 'We are friends.'

'Well, don't throw away all you've achieved for yourself because of me. After this I don't much care what happens, and that's the truth. Now please go.' He held out his hand. The grip was just as hard as that lost lieutenant's had been. 'You should not have come.'

Bolitho did not release his hand. 'Don't turn away, Thomas. We have lost so many friends. We Happy Few – remember?'

Herrick's eyes were faraway. 'Aye. God bless them.'

Bolitho picked up his plain cocked hat from the table and saw a finished letter in the light of two candles. It was addressed to Catherine, in Herrick's familiar schoolboy hand.

Herrick said almost offhandedly, 'Take it if you like. I tried to thank her for what she did for my Dulcie. She is a woman of considerable courage, I'll grant her that.'

'I wish you might have told her in person, Thomas.'

'I have always stood by my beliefs, what is right or wrong. I'll not change now, even if they allow me the opportunity.'

Bolitho put the letter in his pocket. He had been unable to help after all; it had all been a waste of time, as Godschale had hinted it would be.

'We shall meet again next week, Thomas.' He stepped out on to the dark landing and heard the door close behind him even before he had reached the first stair.

Thornborough was waiting for him by his busy kitchen.

31

He said quietly, 'Some hot pie to warm you, Sir Richard, afore you leaves?'

Bolitho stared out at the darkness and shook his head. 'Thank you – but I've no stomach for it, Jack.'

The innkeeper watched him gravely. 'Bad, was it?'

Bolitho said nothing, unable to find the words. There were none.

They had been strangers.

3

Accused

Captain Valentine Keen stood by *Black Prince*'s quarterdeck rail and watched two unhappy-looking civilians being swayed up from a boat alongside, their legs dangling from boatswain's chairs.

The court-martial was to be held in the great cabin, which had been stripped of everything, the dividing screens removed as if the ship was about to go into action.

The first lieutenant came aft and touched his hat. 'That's the last of them, sir.' He consulted his list. 'The wine bills will probably be enormous.'

Keen glanced at the sky. After the longest winter he could recall, it seemed as if April had decided to intervene and drive it away. A clear, bright blue sky and perfect visibility, with only a hint of lingering cold in the sea-breeze. The great ship seemed to tremble as the wind roused itself enough to rattle the rigging and halliards, or to make lively patterns across the harbour like a cat ruffling its fur. In days, perhaps, Keen would be gone from this proud command, something he still found hard to believe when he had time to consider it.

The members of the court, spectators, clerks and witnesses had been coming aboard since morning, and would soon be seated in their allotted places according to rank or status.

'You may dismiss the guard and side-party, Mr Sedgemore.' He took out his watch. 'Tell the Gunner to prepare to fire at four bells.' He looked up at the great spars overhead, the sails now in position and neatly furled, Bolitho's flag at the fore. 'You know what to do.'

Sedgemore lingered, his eyes full of questions. 'I wish we were away from here.' He hesitated, trying to judge his captain's mood. 'We shall miss you when you leave with Sir Richard Bolitho . . . It is rumoured we may be going to Portugal's aid before much longer.'

'I think it most likely.' Keen looked past him towards the dockyard. The green land beyond, the smells of countryside and new growth. Sedgemore was probably already planning his next step up the ladder, he thought. He took a telescope from the midshipman-of-the-watch and levelled it on a spur of jetty. He had seen the bright colours of women's clothing but as they leaped out of the distance he saw they were merely a handful of harlots waiting for easy prey.

He thought of Zenoria's eyes when he had told her of his mission with Bolitho. What had he expected? Opposition, resentment? Instead she had said quietly, 'I knew you were a King's officer when I married you, Val. When we are together we must enjoy our lives, but once apart, I would not stand between you and your duty.'

It was like being lost in thick woodland, not knowing which way to turn or what to do. Perhaps she did not care; perhaps she was even relieved that he was going, to break the tension between them.

He saw a captain of marines passing below him with a sword carried in a cloth: Herrick's sword, a necessary part of this macabre ceremony. When the court had made its decision the sword on the table would tell Herrick if he was found guilty or innocent. What malicious mind had thrown up Admiral Sir James Hamett-Parker as a suitable president? He had been known as a tyrant for much of his service. Just eleven years ago when the fleet had erupted in the great mutiny at the Nore and Spithead, Hamett-Parker had been one of the first senior officers to be ordered ashore by the delegates. He would not forget that; nor would he allow anyone to interfere with his judgment. As flag-captain Keen had met most of the others. A vice-admiral, a rear-admiral, and six captains. All of the latter held commands either at Portsmouth or in the Downs squadron. It was hardly likely they would want to annoy Hamett-Parker, with the war about to spread into the enemy's own territory.

Sedgemore said shortly, 'Sir Richard is coming, sir.' Then he was gone, probably still wondering why Keen should exchange this proud ship for some vague huddle of small vessels in Africa.

Bolitho said, 'A fine day, Val.' They walked to the side to be away from the watchkeepers. 'God, I wish it was all over.'

'Shall you give evidence, sir?'

Bolitho looked at him. There were shadows under Keen's eyes, tension around his mouth.

'I shall be there to explain our deployment on that morning.' He seemed to hear Herrick's bitterness. *To describe what you found after the battle.* 'It seems I am barred from asking questions. A witness *after* the event.'

Keen saw the ship's gunner standing by as a crew loaded and then began to run out a twelve-pounder. When it was fired, and the Union Flag was run up to the peak, everyone would know that the trial had begun. When the flag flew from there, and only then, did it tell outsiders what was happening. The court-martial Jack would bring memories to some, pity from others, and indifference from the many who did not have to risk their own lives at sea.

'I wanted to speak with you, Val, about your views. You were there also – you saw it, and the aftermath.' Bolitho glanced around the upper deck. 'We too lost some good men here that day. But for the enemy swallowing the bait, and our false Danish flag, it might have gone very differently.'

Keen regarded him steadily. 'I have known Rear-Admiral Herrick for much of my life. As a first lieutenant, a captain and now a flag-officer. In those early times I came to appreciate both his courage, and I think, his sincerity.'

Bolitho sensed his uncertainty, his search for an explanation which might not be painful, or worse, come between them.

'You can speak freely to me, Val.'

Keen bit his lip. 'I think he has always been surprised at being given flag rank sir.'

'That is shrewd of you. He has often said as much to me.'

Keen made a decision. 'But I cannot forgive or forget that he was about to stand me in the very predicament he now finds himself in. He would listen to no reason; he was guided only by the book. But for your intervention on my behalf – ' He

35

stared across at Portsmouth Point, the sea lapping below it as if the land itself were on the move. 'So I am afraid I do not see his actions in quite the same light.'

'Thank you for telling me, Val. It meant much to you, and now it means a great deal to me.'

Keen added, 'I once said that I thought I knew what you would have done if committed to the same circumstances – ' He glanced round sharply as a lieutenant touched his hat from the foot of the ladder. 'What is it, Mr Espie?'

The lieutenant looked at Bolitho. 'I beg your pardon, Sir Richard. The Judge Advocate sends his respects and wishes you to know that the Court is about to assemble.'

'Very well.' To Keen he remarked, 'I understand that your dear Zenoria is meeting with Catherine today while we are thus employed. I am glad they are close by.' He saw Keen's face suddenly laid bare, the inner anxiety as plain as if he had called out aloud. He touched his sleeve. 'We have seen many storms and have weathered them, Val. We are friends.'

The words mocked him. He had said the same thing to Herrick at the Swan Inn. He turned and walked aft to the companionway.

Minutes later the air reverberated to the crash of a single charge, while from aft, perfectly timed, the court-martial Jack broke to the breeze. It had begun.

The great cabin was barely recognisable. Even two of the twenty-four pounders had been hauled and handspiked around to make more room for the many lines of chairs. Bolitho seated himself and handed his hat to Ozzard, who scurried down the narrow aisle between the mass of figures without apparently noticing any of them. The little man's sense of outrage, perhaps, at seeing his personal domain, where he served and cared for his vice-admiral, demeaned by what was happening.

Bolitho had seen many heads turn to watch his entrance. Some would know him, may even have shared his exploits. Others would only savour the scandal, his open affair with Lady Somervell. Those who knew him very well would appreciate his feelings today, and his concern for a man who had known the same dangers, and shared similar perils.

They all rose respectfully as the members of the Court came

along the same narrow aisle and seated themselves in silhou-
ette against the tall stern windows, Hamett-Parker at the
centre of the table, with his fellow members paired off on
either side of him in strict order of seniority.

He gave a curt nod to the Judge Advocate, a tall, heavy
man who had to stoop between the deckhead beams, and who
looked more like a farmer than an official of Admiralty.

'Be seated, gentlemen.'

Bolitho saw Herrick's sword for the first time, glittering
faintly in the reflected sunlight, lying before the President.
Then he realised that Hamett-Parker was looking straight at
him. Recognition, curiosity, perhaps dislike; it was all there.

He said, 'You may bring in the accused, Mr Cotgrave.'

The Judge Advocate bowed slightly. 'Very well, Sir James.'

Bolitho touched the locket beneath his shirt. *Help me, Kate*.

He stared hard at the stern windows and concentrated on
the shimmering panorama of moored shipping and blue sky.
At these windows he had sat and dreamed or planned. Had
watched Copenhagen burning under the merciless bombardment of artillery, and the huge fireballs from the Congreve
rockets.

He heard Herrick's limping step and the crisp click of boots
from his escort.

Then he saw him, to one side of the table, regarding the
men who would judge him with little more than a mild interest.

The President said, 'You may be seated. There is no point
provoking the pain from your wound.'

Bolitho found that his fists were so tightly clenched that they
hurt. With relief he saw Herrick sit down on the proffered
chair. He had expected he might refuse, and so set the tone of
the whole proceedings.

Herrick's blue eyes turned and then settled on him. He gave
a brief nod of recognition and Bolitho recalled his own anger
and hurt when they had met at the Admiralty; it felt like a
thousand years ago. Bolitho had shouted after him, stung by
Herrick's rebuff over Catherine. *Are we so ordinary?* It had
been a cry from the heart.

Hamett-Parker spoke again in the same flat tones.

'You may begin, Mr Cotgrave.'

Herrick's escort, a debonair captain of marines, leaned forward but Herrick was already on his feet again. He had attended enough courts-martial to know every stage of the procedure.

The Judge Advocate faced him and opened his papers, although Bolitho suspected he knew them as a player knows his lines.

'In accordance with the decision made by their lordships of Admiralty, you, Thomas Herrick Esquire, Rear-Admiral of the Red, are hereby charged that on diverse dates last September as stated in the Details of Evidence, you were guilty of misconduct and neglect of duty. This is contrary to the Act of Parliament dated 1749, more commonly called the Articles of War.'

Bolitho was conscious of the great silence that hung over his flagship. Even the footfalls of the watchkeepers and the occasional creak of tackles were faraway and muffled.

Cotgrave glanced at Herrick's impassive features before continuing, 'Contrary to Article Seventeen, whilst you were appointed for the convoy and guard of merchant ships, you did not diligently attend to that charge. Further, you did not faithfully perform that duty, nor did you defend the ships and goods in said convoy without diverting to other parts or occasions, and if proven guilty shall make reparation of the damage to merchants, owners and others. As the Court of Admiralty shall adjudge, you shall also be punished criminally according to the quality of the offences, be it by pains of death or other punishment as shall be adjudged fit by the court-martial. God Save the King!'

Admiral Sir James Hamett-Parker's thin mouth opened and closed like a poacher's trap.

'How plead you?'

'Not guilty.' Herrick's reply was equally curt.

'Very well. Be seated. You may presently proceed, Mr Cotgrave, but before doing so I would remind you that there are some persons present who have no experience of sea fights and strategy other than what they . . . read.' This brought a few smiles despite the seriousness of the moment. 'So it may be required from time to time to explain or describe these terms and variations.' He pressed his fingertips together and stared at the assembled people. 'So be it.'

*

Bolitho leaned forward and watched intently as the Judge Advocate described the various positions of Herrick's convoy, the North Sea Squadron, and the major fleet commanded by Admiral Gambier, who had been in control of operations at and around Copenhagen.

It was the second day of the court-martial, the first having been made up mostly of written evidence and sworn statements. There had also been a dying declaration, which had been further testimony to the ferocity of that battle. A junior lieutenant in Herrick's *Benbow* had managed to make it under oath after a second amputation of his crushed legs.

Bolitho had sensed the moment, not here in the great cabin, but on that terrible day when the enemy ships had bombarded *Benbow* until she had run with blood, and her masts had been torn out of her like rotten sticks. The lieutenant had died even as he had been describing how he had run aft from his division of upper-deck guns, where most of his men had been cut down or dragged below to the surgeon. He had called on Herrick to strike in the name of pity. *We were all dying to no purpose*, he had said. He had claimed that the rear-admiral had clutched a pistol in one hand and had threatened to shoot him if he did not return to his station. Then the main-topmast had fallen and crushed his legs. But he persisted in his claim that Herrick's answer had stayed with him. *We shall all die today*.

One of the clerks had peered at Herrick as if to compare the man on trial with what he was writing.

Another sworn statement had come from *Benbow*'s surgeon, who was also in hospital. He had stated that he had been unable to deal with the great flood of wounded and dying men. He had sent word to the quarterdeck but had received no reply. The Judge Advocate had looked around the court. 'We must keep in mind of course that the ship was fighting for her life. The man sent aft with the message, if indeed that was the case, may well have been killed.'

It had been very damning, all the same. There had followed a short pause for a meal and some wine, the senior officers and important guests to Keen's own quarters, the remainder to the wardroom.

After that, Captain Varian, at one time in command of the frigate *Zest* in Herrick's squadron, and himself awaiting the convenience of a court-martial, gave evidence on what he had come to expect under the rear-admiral's flag. Bolitho had listened with contempt. This was the man who had failed to support *Truculent* in which Bolitho had been taking passage from Copenhagen, having been sent on a secret mission to parley with the Danes in a futile attempt to avoid war. *Truculent* had been shadowed by French men-of-war, a trap from which there had been no escape. Only the arrival of Adam's *Anemone* had saved the day. But not before *Truculent*'s captain, Poland, had been killed and many of his men with him.

On that occasion, as now, in the great cabin Varian claimed that Herrick never gave any scope or initiative to his captains. He had only been obeying instructions as Rear-Admiral Herrick would have demanded.

At length the President turned to Herrick. 'You are entitled to question this witness. You refused a defence, so it is your privilege.'

Herrick barely glanced at Varian's pale features. 'I do not care to discuss this matter with a man already facing a charge of cowardice.'

He said it with such disgust that it had brought a gasp from the assembled visitors. 'He is a coward and a liar, and but for the intervention of others I would have had him arrested myself.'

It had all been much like that. An old carpenter who described the state of *Benbow*'s hull, with the pump barely containing the intake of water and only wounded men available to use it.

The last witness to be called, even as dusk made it necessary to light all the lanterns in the cabin, had been Herrick's servant, Murray. A rather pitiful little figure against so much gold lace and glittering regalia.

Under examination he had admitted that Herrick had been drinking very heavily, which had been more than just unusual.

The Judge Advocate had said, 'Just what you know, Murray – opinions have no place here.'

He had glanced at Herrick, who had replied, 'I *was* drinking more than usual, he is quite right.'

As the little servant had hurried gratefully away, John

Cotgrave had rustled through his papers, gauging the time to a second.

'Of course, I had overlooked the fact you have only recently lost your wife.'

Herrick had seemed oblivious to everyone else there. 'She was everything to me. After that – ' He had given a tired shrug.

'So it might be suggested that because of grief and personal distress you threw everything into a fight you could not win against overwhelming odds, with a total disregard for the lives in your care?'

Herrick had stared at him coldly. 'That is untrue.'

Today had begun with more professional witnesses. Three masters from merchant ships in the convoy, and written testimonies by others who had managed to survive. Several of them had claimed that they could have outsailed the enemy had they been allowed to quit the convoy.

Herrick denied this. 'We had to stand together – the enemy had frigates as well as line-of-battle ships. It was our only chance.'

The President leaned forward. 'I understand that Admiral Gambier suggested in his dispatches to you that you might release your only frigate to his command for the attack on Copenhagen? Did he not leave it to your discretion?'

Herrick faced him. 'It seemed urgent. In any case I thought I would meet up with the North Sea squadron for the final approach.'

The Judge Advocate said, 'The squadron commanded by Sir Richard Bolitho?'

Herrick did not even blink. 'Just so.'

Cotgrave continued, 'Now we reach a vital part of the matter, prior to your meeting with the enemy.'

Hamett-Parker tugged out his watch. 'I trust it is not a lengthy business, Mr Cotgrave? Some of us would wish to take refreshment!' Somebody laughed but stopped instantly as Hamett-Parker's cold eyes sought him out.

Cotgrave was unimpressed. 'I will try not to waste the court's time, Sir James.'

He turned to his clerk. 'Summon Commander James Tyacke.' To the great cabin he added, 'Commander Tyacke is serving in the brig *Larne* of fourteen guns. A most gallant officer. I must ask all those present to try and show him respect rather than sympathy. It is a matter of . . .' He got no further.

Something like a sigh of dismay came from all sides as Tyacke's tall figure strode aft beneath the deckhead beams. In his early thirties, he had been with Bolitho at the Cape, when he had taken a fireship to destroy anchored enemy supply vessels and so cut short the siege of the town and harbour. In doing so he had seen his beloved command, the little schooner *Miranda*, sunk by the enemy. Bolitho had personally promoted him and given him the brig.

Tyacke would have been handsome, as his profile suggested, but one complete side of his face had been scored away to leave it like raw flesh; how the right eye had survived was a miracle. He had been at the battle of the Nile as a lieutenant on the lower gundeck of the old *Majestic*. They had come up to the big French *Tonnant* and had continued close-action until the enemy had hauled down her colours. Had the French captain known the true state of the English third-rate he might have persisted. The dead had been everywhere; even her captain, Westcott, had been killed. Tyacke had been flung across the deck, his face seared and torn, although he could never remember afterwards precisely what had happened. An exploding charge, an enemy wad through a gunport; he simply did not know, and there had been nobody near him left alive to tell him.

He faced the court now, his terrible wound in shadow, a private man, a man of courage. He had nothing but his ship. Even the girl he had loved had turned away from him when she had learned what had happened.

He saw Bolitho, and smiled faintly in recognition. No, he was not quite alone any more. He had come to admire Bolitho more than he could have believed possible.

The Judge Advocate confronted him, angry with the court and perhaps with himself for trying to avoid Tyacke's impassive stare.

'You were the first to sight the French vessels, Commander Tyacke.'

Tyacke glanced at Herrick. 'Yes, sir. We came on the ships quite by accident. One of the big three-deckers was unknown to me. I discovered much later that she was in fact Spanish, taken into the French command, so we had no cause to recognise her.' He hesitated. 'Vice-Admiral Bolitho knew her, of course.'

One of the court leaned over to whisper something and Hamett-Parker said, 'She was the *San Mateo*, which destroyed Sir Richard's flagship *Hyperion* before Trafalgar.' He nodded irritably. 'Continue.'

Tyacke looked at him with dislike. 'We beat as close as we could but they were on to us, and gave us a good peppering before we could show them a clean pair of heels. Eventually we found the convoy and I closed to report to the rear-admiral in charge.'

One of the captains asked, 'Had the frigate already left the convoy?'

'Aye, sir.' He paused, expecting something further, then he said, 'I told Rear-Admiral Herrick what I had seen.'

'How did he receive you?'

'I spoke through a speaking-trumpet, sir.' He added with barely concealed sarcasm, 'The enemy were too close for comfort, and there seemed some urgency in the air!'

The Judge Advocate smiled. 'That was well said, Commander Tyacke.' The mood changed back again. 'Now it is very important that you recall exactly what the rear-admiral's reply was. I imagine it would have been written in *Larne*'s signal book?'

'Probably.' Tyacke ignored his frown. 'As I recall, Rear-Admiral Herrick ordered me to find Sir Richard Bolitho's North Sea squadron. Then he changed his mind and told me to report directly to Admiral Gambier's flagship *Prince of Wales* off Copenhagen.'

Cotgrave said quietly, 'Even after seven months, during which time you must have had much to occupy your attention, the fact that Rear-Admiral Herrick *changed his mind* still seems to surprise you? Pray tell the court why.'

Tyacke was caught off guard. He replied, 'Sir Richard Bolitho was his friend, sir, and in any case . . .'

'*In any case*, Commander Tyacke, it would have been sensible, would it not, to find Sir Richard's squadron first, as it was only in a supporting role against the Danes at that time?'

The President snapped, 'You will answer, sir!'

Tyacke said evenly, 'That must have been what I was thinking.'

Cotgrave turned to Herrick. 'You have a question or two perhaps?'

Herrick regarded him calmly. 'None. This officer speaks the truth, as well as being a most gallant fighter.'

One of the captains said, 'There is a question from the back, sir.'

'I am sorry to interrupt the proceedings, even delay refreshment, but the President did offer to have matters explained to a mere landsman.'

Bolitho turned round, remembering the voice but unable to identify the speaker. Someone with a great deal of authority to make a joke at Hamett-Parker's expense without fear of attack. Dressed all in black, it was Sir Paul Sillitoe, once the Prime Minister's personal adviser, whom Bolitho had first met at a reception at Godschale's grand house near Blackwall Reach. That had been before the attack on Copenhagen.

Sillitoe was thin-faced and dark, with deep hooded eyes, very self-contained; and a man one would never know, really know. But he had been charming to Catherine on that occasion when the Duke of Portland, the prime minister at the time, had attempted to snub her. Standing amidst so many now, he was still quite alone.

Sillitoe continued, 'I would be grateful if you would clarify the difference 'twixt two seafaring terms which have been mentioned several times already.' He looked directly at Bolitho and gave the briefest of smiles. Bolitho could imagine him doing the very same while peering along the barrel of a duelling pistol.

Sillitoe went on silkily, 'One witness will describe the convoy's possible tactics as being "scattered", and another will term it "dispersed". I am all confusion.'

Bolitho thought his tone suggested otherwise, and could not help wondering if Sillitoe had interrupted the Judge Advocate for a different purpose.

The latter said patiently, 'If it pleases, Sir Paul. To scatter a convoy means that each ship's master can go his own way, that is to say, move out from the centre like the spokes of a wheel.

To disperse would mean to leave each master to sail as he pleases, but all to the original destination. Is that clear, Sir Paul?'

'One further question, if you will bear with me, sir. The ships' masters who have claimed they could have outsailed the enemy ships – were they all requesting the order to *disperse*?'

Cotgrave glanced questioningly at the President and then replied, 'They did, Sir Paul.'

Sillitoe bowed elegantly. 'Thank you.'

Hamett-Parker snapped, 'Then if that is all, gentlemen, this hearing is adjourned for refreshments.' He stalked out, followed by the other members of his court.

'You may dismiss, Commander Tyacke.'

Tyacke waited until most of those in the cabin had bustled away and Herrick had left with his escort. Then he shook Bolitho's hand and said quietly, 'I hoped we would meet soon, Sir Richard.' He glanced at the deserted table where the sword was still shining in the April sunlight. 'But not like this.'

Together they made their way out to the broad quarterdeck, where many of the visitors had broken into small groups to discuss the trial so far, all to the obvious irritation of watchkeepers and working seamen alike.

'Is everything well with you?' Bolitho stood beside him to stare at a graceful schooner tacking past; he guessed Tyacke was comparing her with his lost *Miranda*.

'I should have written to you, Sir Richard, after all that you did for me.' He gave a great sigh. 'I have been appointed to the new anti-slavery patrol. We sail for the African coast shortly. Most of my men are volunteers – more to escape from the fleet than out of any moral convictions!' His eyes crinkled in a grin. 'I never thought they'd get it through Parliament after all these years.'

Bolitho could agree with him. England had been at war with France almost continuously for fifteen years, and all the while the slave traffic had gone on without hindrance: a brutal trade in human beings which ended in death from the lash as often as from fever.

And yet, there were many who had voted against its abolition, describing the traders and plantation owners in the Caribbean as loyal servants of the Crown, men ready to defend their rights against the enemy. Supporters usually added the extra bait for their cause, that a plentiful supply of slaves would continue to mean cheaper sugar for the world's market, as well as releasing other men for active duty at sea or in the army.

This new patrol might suit Tyacke very well, he thought. The private man with a small company which he could educate to his own standards.

Tyacke said, 'I fear I did little good for Rear-Admiral Herrick's cause just now, Sir Richard.'

Bolitho replied, 'It was the truth.'

'Will he win the day, do you think, sir?'

'We must.' He wondered afterwards if Tyacke had noticed that he had not said *he*.

Tyacke remarked, 'Ah, here comes your faithful cox'n.'

Allday moved effortlessly through the chattering groups and touched his hat.

'Begging your pardon, Sir Richard, but I thought you might want to take your meal in the Master's chart-room.' He gave a grim smile. 'Mr Julyan was most firm on the matter!'

Bolitho answered readily, 'That would suit very well. I have no stomach for this today.' He glanced around at the jostling, apparently carefree people who were waiting to be called to their refreshment, seeing instead this deck as it had been on that dismal September morning. The dead and the wounded, the first lieutenant cut cleanly in half by a massive French ball. 'I do not feel I belong here.'

Tyacke held out his hand. 'I have to leave, Sir Richard. Please offer my best wishes to Lady Somervell.' He glanced at Keen, who was waiting to see him over the side to his gig. 'And to you too, sir.'

Keen had known what it must have cost Tyacke to go all the way to Zennor to see him marry Zenoria, to experience again the shocked stares and brutal curiosity to which he would never become accustomed.

'I thank you, Commander Tyacke. I shall not forget.'

Tyacke raised his hat and the marines' muskets thumped in salute, a cloud of pipeclay floating from their crossbelts like smoke. The calls shrilled and Bolitho gazed after him until the gig was pulling strongly away from the ship's great shadow.

'Join me in the Master's quarters, will you, Val?'

Someone was ringing a bell, and the small tide of visitors began to flow towards the temptation of food, brought on board, it was said, from the George Inn itself.

Ozzard had prepared a meal which seemed to consist mostly of several kinds of cheese, fresh bread from Portsmouth, and some claret. He had learned very well what Bolitho could and could not take when he was under great strain.

Keen asked, 'What do you think, Sir Richard?'

Bolitho was still thinking of what he had observed before entering the chart-room. Near the big double-wheel the Judge Advocate had been in close conversation with Sir Paul Sillitoe. They had not seen him, but had separated before continuing up to Keen's quarters.

'If only he had called someone to defend him. This is all too personal, too cleancut for outsiders to understand.' He toyed with the cheese, his appetite gone. 'I think it will be over quite soon. This afternoon Captain Gossage will give evidence. He can say little of the battle because he was wounded almost as soon as *Benbow* engaged. But it will depend much on his earlier assessment, his guidance as flag-captain when the truth of the situation was apparent.'

'And tomorrow?'

'It will be our turn, and Thomas's.'

Keen stood up. 'I had better be seen to welcome the senior officers to my quarters, I suppose.' He did not sound as if he liked the prospect.

'A moment, Val.' Bolitho closed the chart-room door. 'I have a suggestion – or rather, Catherine put forward the idea.'

'Sir? I would always be guided by that lady.'

'While we are away on passage to the Cape, we think Zenoria should be offered the use of our house in Cornwall. You have rented one here, I believe, while *Black Prince* is fitting out, but in Cornwall she would be with people who would care for her. There is another reason.' He could sense Keen's instant guard; it was so unlike him. Matters were worse than they had feared. 'Zenoria once told Catherine she would take it as a great favour if she could make use of the library there. It is extensive . . . it was built up by my grandfather.'

Keen smiled, his eyes clearing. 'Yes, I know she wishes to

educate herself more, to learn about the world.' He nodded slowly. 'It was kind of Lady Catherine to concern herself with this, sir. Zenoria's first time alone as a married woman . . .' He did not continue. He did not need to.

'That's settled then.'

Later when the court convened, Bolitho ran his eyes over the seated spectators, for that was what they had become. Like onlookers at a public hanging. There was no trace of Sir Paul Sillitoe.

Herrick looked tired, and showed considerable strain. He too must be thinking of tomorrow.

The Judge Advocate cleared his throat and waited for Hamett-Parker to offer him a curt nod.

'This court is reassembled. Please call Captain Hector Gossage.' He glanced around at the intent faces as if expecting another interruption. 'He was flag-captain to the accused at the time of the attack.'

Herrick turned and looked directly at his sword on the table. It was as if he expected to see it move, or perhaps he already imagined it pointing towards him.

Gossage's entrance was almost too pitiful to watch; he seemed to have shrunk from the bluff, competent captain Bolitho had met on several occasions. Now his face was lined, and one cheek was pitted with small splinter scars; one sleeve of his dress coat was empty, pinned up and useless, and he was obviously still in great pain. A chair was brought and Gossage assisted into it by two orderlies who had accompanied him from the hospital here at Haslar Creek.

Hamett-Parker asked not unkindly, 'Are you as comfortable as we can make you, Captain?'

Gossage stared around as if he had not properly heard. So many senior officers and guests. 'I should be standing, sir!'

Hamett-Parker said quietly, as if daring anyone to so much as cough or move, 'You are not on trial here, Captain Gossage. Take your time and speak in your own words. We have studied the Details of Evidence, heard the opinions, for they were little more than that, of many witnesses. But *Benbow* was the flagship and you were her captain. It is *your* story we wish to hear.'

It was then that Gossage seemed to see Herrick opposite him for the first time.

He began brokenly, 'I – I'm not her captain any more. I've lost everything!' He tried to move round so that Herrick could see his empty sleeve. '*Look what you've done to me!*'

Hamett-Parker gestured to the surgeon and snapped, 'The court is adjourned until the same time tomorrow.' To the surgeon he added, 'Take good care of Captain Gossage.'

As the little group shuffled toward the rear of the cabin, Hamett-Parker spoke to the Judge Advocate, his tone severe. 'That must not occur again in this court, Mr Cotgrave!' But when he glanced round Bolitho saw only triumph in his eyes.

4

Revenge

The house, which was of medium size and owned by the Admiralty, was situated just outside the dockyard gates. It had a permanent staff, but was entirely without any kind of personality; it was merely a place where senior officers and Admiralty officials could stay temporarily while conducting their business with the dockyard or the port admiral.

It was not yet dawn but already Bolitho could hear the comings and goings of carts and waggons, and during the long night he heard the occasional tramp of feet and the clink of weapons as the press-gangs returned from yet another search of outlying villages for men who were without any official protection.

The last time, when he had been awakened from a troubled sleep, he had heard a woman's voice, high-pitched and pleading, although he could not make out the words. She had been calling out long after the gates had clanged shut, her man taken from her side to help fill the depleted ranks in the fleet. Her pleas would fall on deaf ears, especially with the war about to expand still further. Fit men, sometimes *any* men would suffice. Even those with the written protection, fishermen, sailors of the HEIC, prime hands whom the navy needed more than any, kept out of sight at night when the press were about. It was useless to try and right a wrong if you awoke with a bruised head in some man-of-war already standing out into the Western Approaches.

Very gently he lifted Catherine's head from his bare shoulder and eased it on to a pillow. As he did so he felt her long, tumbled hair slide from his skin, their bodies still warm from their embrace.

But it had been a night without passion or intimacy, a night when they had shared an even deeper love, knowing their need and support of one another. With great care he climbed from the bed and walked quietly through to the adjoining room. The fire was dead in the grate but already he could hear a servant, or perhaps the loyal Ozzard, re-laying another downstairs.

This room, like the house, felt damp and unlived-in, but it was still a haven compared to the alternative: a local inn, prying eyes and questioning glances. Everyone would know about the court-martial. This was a naval port, the greatest in the world, but gossip flourished here like a village.

He stared from a window and after some hesitation thrust it open, admitting the cold air of dawn, the strong tang of the sea, freshly-cut timber, tar and oakum, the stuff of any Royal dockyard.

It was today. He stared hard at the dark shadows of the buildings beyond the wall. Allday and Ozzard would have prepared his best dress coat with its gleaming epaulettes, each with a pair of silver stars to display his rank.

He would not feel the familiar weight of the old family sword against his thigh; he would wear, instead, the lavishly decorated presentation sword given to him by the people of Falmouth in recognition of his service in the Mediterranean and at the Battle of the Nile. For here he was authority, the vice-admiral again; not 'Equality Dick' as his sailors had so often called him, not even the hero who brought admiring grins from the ale-houses and coffee establishments because of his liaison with a beautiful woman. It made him feel like a stranger to himself. He could not forget Herrick's bitterness at Southwark, when he had gone to plead and reason with him. *Don't throw away all you've achieved for yourself because of me.* He was what his father would have wished, a flag-officer like all the others in those portraits which lined the stairway and gallery in the old grey house in Cornwall.

He heard a girl laugh somewhere, probably Catherine's new maid servant, Sophie, a small, dark creature whom Catherine had said was half-Spanish. She had taken her as a favour to an old friend in London; at a guess the girl was about fifteen. It had happened quite suddenly, and Catherine had not yet had time to relate the full story. She had been concerned only for him, and what might be the outcome of today.

There had been a letter sent from London by postboy, from Lord Godschale. The packet which was to carry them to the Cape had left the Pool of London and was making her way down-Channel to Falmouth, where she would await Bolitho's arrival. A strange change of plans, Bolitho had thought, more secrecy, in case there should be fresh scandal about Catherine's going with him. Godschale had cleared his own yardarm by suggesting that Catherine pay her own fare and expenses for the voyage.

She had given her bubbling laugh when he had told her. 'That man is quite impossible, Richard! But he has a roving eye and a reputation to support, I am given to understand!'

They had also discussed Zenoria. She had left in the Bolitho carriage the previous evening with Jenour and Yovell for protection and company. She had seemed eager to go, and when Bolitho had said, 'She will be able to say goodbye to Val at Falmouth,' he had not sounded very convincing, even to himself.

The only good news had also been from London, from the heron-like Sir Piers Blachford. Elizabeth's injury was neither permanent nor serious, now that she was under proper care. Bolitho had not told Catherine that Belinda had sent word that he himself was expected to pay all the necessary costs: she had probably guessed anyway.

He waited for the first hint of daylight, then covered his uninjured eye with his hand and stared for so long that the eye pricked painfully and began to water. But there was no mist, no failing vision this time; perhaps the three months ashore, with occasional trips to Portsmouth and London had worked in his favour.

Without turning he knew she had entered the room, her naked feet soundless on the carpet. She came up behind him and put a coat around his bare shoulders.

'What are you doing? Trying to catch a cold, or worse?'

He put his arm around her body and felt her warmth through the plain white gown, the one with the gold cord around her throat which if released could bare her shoulders or her whole being.

She shivered as he ran his fingers over her hip. 'Oh, dear Richard – soon now, and all this will be over.'

'I have been poor company of late.'

Catherine turned in his arm and looked at him, only her eyes shining in the faint light.

'So many thoughts, so many worries. They strike at you from every side.'

She had read Herrick's letter aloud to him, and he had been moved that she had shown more regret than anger. In it, Herrick had thanked her for staying with his wife to the end. A letter between total strangers. He ran his hand under her long hair and kissed her lightly on the neck.

She covered his hand with hers. 'Much more of that, Richard, and I will forget the importance and the formality of this day.'

She looked out at the paling sky and the last weak star. 'I love everything we do, all that we have found in one another.' He tried to turn her towards him but felt her strong supple body resist him; she would not, could not face him. 'When you are away from me, Richard, I touch myself where you have touched me, and I dream it is you. The climax is matched only by the disappointment when I know it is . . . just another fantasy.'

Then she did turn, and embraced him so that their faces were almost level, her breath mingling warmly with his, her body pressing against him.

'So when you come back to me, be the navigator and explorer once more. Seek out every mood and every part of me until we are joined again.' She kissed him very gently on the cheek. '. . . and again.' She stood against the light, so that he saw her body through her pale gown. 'Now go and prepare yourself. I will further shock the servants by preparing some breakfast for *my man*!'

Bolitho stared after her, then sighed as the drums began to rattle to beat up the marines at their barracks.

A glance; a word; a promise. They could not dissolve the immediate problems. He straightened his back and touched the crudely mended wound in his left thigh, a legacy of eight years ago, and his mind lingered on what she had told him. Dissolve, no; but once again she had made him feel restored. He was ready.

John Cotgrave, the Judge Advocate, stood up and faced the seated officers in the great cabin.

'I am ready, Sir James.'

Hamett-Parker grunted. 'Proceed.'

Cotgrave said, 'Captain Hector Gossage has stated that he wishes to complete his evidence, and the surgeon has assured me that he will be able.' He glanced briefly at Herrick's set features. 'However, with the Court's indulgence, I would suggest that Captain Gossage's appearance be made later, when he has been examined again.'

Hamett-Parker asked, 'How is this to be managed, Mr Cotgrave?' He sounded irritated by the sudden change of tack.

'May I suggest, Sir James, that the last witness for today be called first? I do not intend to summon Captain Keen of this ship; it would merely be to corroborate this important witness's testimony.'

Bolitho saw the quick exchange of glances. Gossage would be the final witness, so any previous evidence of an indifferent nature, or testimony which might be in Herrick's favour, would be forgotten. Gossage was hostile – a broken man, but one whose ability to hate was clearly unimpaired.

The officer of the Court next in seniority, Vice-Admiral Cuthbert Nevill, asked mildly, 'It is all rather unusual, surely?'

Hamett-Parker did not even turn. 'The case itself is more so, what?'

Cotgrave faced the assembled visitors. 'The next witness is an officer well known to all of us and to every loyal Englishman. At no time was he consulted on the strategy used to defend the convoy, and only arrived . . .' He hesitated and allowed his words to sink in '. . . in this very ship at the scene of the battle, when all was lost. The convoy of twenty ships sunk or captured, the remaining escort, *Egret* of sixty guns, also destroyed, and overwhelmed by a superior enemy force as we have heard described here.'

Bolitho heard the shuffle of feet and the creak of chairs as the assembled visitors peered around the great cabin. It would be hard for landmen to visualise this powerful three-decker cleared for action, from these same stern windows to the foremost divisions of guns. Harder still to see death here, or imagine the roar and crash of artillery, the screams of the wounded. The captains present would see it differently, however, and be reminded, if they needed a reminder, that the final responsibility was theirs, or lay with the man who flew his flag above all of them.

Cotgrave continued, 'I would ask Sir Richard Bolitho, Vice-Admiral of the Red, to come aft.'

Bolitho stood up, his mind suddenly like ice, recalling Catherine's words when they had lain awake in the night. *Remember, Richard, you are not to blame*. And this morning when he had looked from the window over the darkness of the dockyard. *Just a man*. Was it only this morning?

'Now, Sir Richard, if you would care to be seated?'

Bolitho replied, 'I prefer to stand, thank you.'

Hamett-Parker asked, 'Are you not satisfied with the way this Court is being conducted, Sir Richard?'

Bolitho gave a short bow. *This man is an enemy*. '*Black Prince* is my flagship, Sir James. Had I not been called to give this testimony, something which my own flag-captain is well able to offer, I might have been a member of this Court. A more useful and profitable role, surely?'

The vice-admiral named Nevill muttered, 'Quite agree.'

Cotgrave said, 'Let us continue, Sir Richard, for all our sakes.'

'I am ready.'

'For the benefit of the Court, Sir Richard, tell us what happened when the brig *Larne* arrived off Copenhagen with the news of the convoy's predicament. Not too fast for my clerks, if you please, and for the gentlemen from the newspapers.'

Bolitho said, 'I was summoned to Admiral Gambier's flagship *Prince of Wales*, where, after discussing the "predicament" as you choose to call it, and hearing of it from Commander Tyacke, I pleaded to be allowed to go to Rear-Admiral Herrick's assistance.'

'It was night-time, was it not?' Cotgrave singled out a sheet of notes. 'I am given to understand that when the dangers of navigating the Narrows in the dark were pointed out you stated that you had done it before, under Nelson?'

'That is true.'

Cotgrave smiled gently. 'Very forceful. You were guided through eventually by the brig *Larne* and followed by *Nicator*, an elderly seventy-four from your own squadron?'

Bolitho said, 'We might have been in time.'

'In the event, you were not.' He continued smoothly, 'Now please describe the scene when daylight found you on that particular morning.' He wagged a finger like some church schoolmaster and added, 'May I remind you, Sir Richard, there are landsmen present – we have not all shared your own wealth of experience, of which we have heard much over the years.'

There was absolute silence in the cabin, so that even the slight patter of rain against the tall stern windows seemed an interruption.

'I had had the ship's sailmaker create a false Danish flag. It was my intention to lure the largest enemy ship, the *San Mateo*, into close range, to make her captain believe *Black Prince* was a Danish prize.' He hesitated over the enemy's name, and guessed it was not lost on many present. 'For we, too, were outnumbered. But for the ruse I fear we might have shared *Benbow*'s fate.'

'By this time, the *Benbow* had become a dismasted onlooker, I believe?'

Bolitho saw Herrick lean forward as if to interrupt and answered, 'Hardly that. *Benbow*'s guns were still firing, and even though her steering had carried away and her masts were gone, she did not strike.'

Cotgrave looked at the intent faces of the Court. 'After you had forced the enemy to submit, and the prize crews of the surviving ships were ordered to lay down their arms, you then boarded the *Benbow*. Tell us what you found.'

Bolitho looked steadily at Herrick. 'There were more dead than alive in view, and the afterguard, helmsmen, gun crews had all been cut down by chainshot and canister at close range. She was so badly damaged that it was all we could do to rig temporary steering, and eventually take her in tow.'

Hamett-Parker commented without feeling, 'It seems likely she will remain a hulk until her final disposal.'

Cotgrave nodded gravely. 'Of course, Sir Richard, you and the accused have been friends for years. I imagine he was more than relieved to see your ships and most of all, yourself.'

Bolitho turned towards the rain-dappled windows, a shaft of watery sunlight glinting on the Nile medal, which he always wore with pride.

'It was a scene from hell. We had little time to speak with one another, and the rear-admiral's wound required immediate attention.'

He looked once again at Herrick, recalling that morning, the bitterness in his voice. *It will be another triumph for you.* Like an accusation.

'In that case, Sir James?' Cotgrave started as Herrick rose to his feet and gripped the chairback for support.

Hamett-Parker snapped, 'You have a question?' He seemed surprised.

Herrick nodded, his eyes still on Bolitho. 'I do, Sir James.'

'Very well.' To Bolitho he said, 'Remember, Sir Richard, you are still under oath.'

Herrick said quietly, 'It is not a point of evidence.' He was speaking to the court, to everyone here, and to those who would never come back to speak of anything. His eyes, his whole being was directed at Bolitho.

'I am ready.'

'I want to make something clear. I would like to know, had *you* been in my position that day, would you have acted as I did?'

Cotgrave said hastily, 'I hardly think – '

Hamett-Parker waved his challenge aside. 'I see no wrong in it. Please answer, Sir Richard – we are all attention!'

Bolitho faced the officers but could feel the intensity of Herrick's eyes. 'There are several ways to defend a convoy, Sir James, even if the escort is insufficient, as it surely was that day. Sometimes you can signal the vessels in the convoy to draw together to add their own artillery in the defence of all. It is a well-known tactic of the Honourable East India Company. Likewise you can order the ships to disperse, leaving the slower ones to be sacrificed.'

They all stared at Herrick as he said calmly, 'It is not what I asked.'

Cotgrave bit his lip. 'That is so, Sir Richard. You must answer.'

Hamett-Parker snapped, 'Even if the reply might damage the circumstances of a friend. You are a man of honour, sir. We are waiting!'

He tried to read Herrick's mind, divine the intention behind this. *What are you doing? What are you making me do?* There was something else there too. It was almost amusement, a mocking challenge. *Another triumph for you, Richard!*

Bolitho replied quietly, 'I would not.'

Hamett-Parker pressed his fingertips together and put his head on one side like a bird of prey.

'I believe that some here present may not have heard, Sir Richard.'

Bolitho looked at him coldly. 'I said: *I would not!*'

Herrick sat down and said, 'Thank you. A man of honour.'

Bolitho stared at him. Herrick had forced him into answering the one question which would surely condemn him. It had been deliberate, brutal in its intensity.

Hamett-Parker nodded very slowly. 'If there is nothing further, Sir Richard?'

Bolitho said, 'I can only say that the accused is a gallant and loyal officer. I have served alongside him many times and know all his qualities. He has saved my life, and he has given his to the service of his country.'

Cotgrave cleared his throat. 'Some might suggest that you are biased, Sir Richard.'

Bolitho turned on him angrily. 'And why not? *In God's name, what are true friends for?*'

Hamett-Parker interrupted, 'We will adjourn until after refreshment, gentlemen.' He looked at Bolitho. 'By which time Captain Gossage will be present to continue with his assessment of the rear-admiral's intentions on that day.'

Bolitho waited for the great cabin to empty, and sat alone, his head in his hands. Where was the vice-admiral now?

Keen joined him and said quietly, 'I was at the door, Sir Richard – I heard everything. They will demand the most severe punishment of all.'

He was shocked to see Bolitho's face when he looked up at him: the tears in his eyes.

'He has just executed himself, Val. And for what?'

For a long, long moment the question seemed to hang in the air like an epitaph.

Lady Catherine Somervell stood beside a window, one hand toying absently with a curtain. The roofs of the nearest dockyard sheds were wet with rain, but already there was a promise of sunshine, and of some warmth. She saw and cared for none of it.

She was thinking of *Black Prince*, out there somewhere unseen behind the tall buildings. The court-martial would have recommenced, and this afternoon Richard would try to defend his friend, even if he could only offer help through personal evidence.

She looked over her shoulder at her new maid Sophie. In the filtered sunshine, with her dark hair hanging down to her eyes as she smoothed out one of her mistress's gowns ready for packing, she could have been fully Spanish. Her mother had married a trader of that country who had vanished shortly after the Revolution in France; he had never been seen alive again. There had been three children, and Sophie was the youngest. She had gone to work for a tailor in Whitechapel, and within a year had proved herself a quick learner and an excellent seamstress, but her mother had become ill and had asked Catherine to take her into service. She had known she was dying and used her earlier friendship with Catherine as the only escape for her remaining child: London was no place for a girl like Sophie to be left to fend for herself. If Sophie grieved for her mother, she did not show it. Perhaps, Catherine thought, when she knew her better, she might share the rest of the story.

'I wonder if they will fire another gun when the court-martial is finally over.' She wished she had asked Richard before he had left this morning. But she had not wanted to distract him, to offer him hope when there might be none.

Sophie paused. 'Don't know, me lady.'

Catherine smiled at her. Sophie's voice had the accent of

the streets, an aspect of London Catherine had known at her age, and earlier. It helped in some way, a reminder.

Catherine thought of the dawn when she had awakened with something like panic when she had found him gone. She turned the beautiful ring on her finger, which Bolitho had put on her left hand after Keen's wedding at Zennor, and tried to take some reassurance from it. But what of the next time they were parted, when Bolitho was once more at sea with his men and his ships, a target for every enemy sharpshooter as poor Nelson had been?

She shook her head, as if he had just spoken to her. There was the long passage to the Cape and back. It might be uncomfortable, but she would enjoy every second they could still be together.

When Richard returned this evening or later perhaps, whatever the outcome, she would make him forget. *She must*. Then she turned the ring again to the shaft of sun which had at last penetrated the low clouds over the Solent, and watched the play of light across its diamonds and rubies. She could recall the exact moment, when all the others had left the church for the wedding celebrations: Richard taking her hand. *In the eyes of God we are married, dearest Kate*. It was something she would never forget.

There was a rap at the door and one of the resident servants entered the room and gave a clumsy curtsy.

'There be a gennelman downstairs, m'lady. He begs an audience with you.'

Catherine waited and then replied, 'I can sometimes read your thoughts, my girl, but I need a little help now.'

The girl gave her a cow-like stare, and eventually produced a small envelope from an apron pocket.

Catherine smiled. The Admiralty house did not apparently run to a silver tray for such purposes.

She tore it open and walked to the window again. It was not a note, there was only an engraved card inside. She looked at it for several seconds until a face seemed to form there. Sillitoe. Sir Paul Sillitoe, whom she had met at Admiral Godschale's reception by the river.

She was still uncertain whether he was a friend or another

potential danger to Richard. But he had shown her kindness in his strange, withdrawn manner.

'I shall come down.'

The hall was empty, and the door still partly ajar; she saw a smart phaeton with a pair of matching greys outside in the road. Sillitoe was standing in the small drawing-room, feet apart, hands behind him.

As she appeared he took her proffered hand and touched it with his lips.

'Lady Catherine, you honour me too much, when I have given you so little warning of my arrival.' He waited until she had seated herself and said, 'I have urgent business in London, but I thought I must see you before you depart for the Cape of Good Hope.' He grimaced. 'An unfortunate name, I think.'

'Is anything wrong, Sir Paul? Are we not to go after all?'

'Wrong?' He was watching her now, his hooded eyes full of curiosity. 'Why should there be?' He walked past her and hesitated by the chair; and for an instant she expected him to touch her, place a hand on her shoulder, and she could feel her body stiffen in readiness.

'I was merely thinking that you might find the prospect of a longish voyage, hemmed in by foul-mouthed sailors, unpleasant. It is not what I would choose for you.'

'I am used to ships.' She glanced at him, her eyes flashing. 'Sailors too.'

'It was merely a thought, one which disturbed me more than I would admit to anyone else. I experienced a moment of delusion, wherein I imagined your staying behind, with me to guide you around the town, and offer you – if only temporarily – my companionship.'

'Is that what you really came to tell me?' She was astonished at the calmness in her voice, and equally by the man's cool impudence and declaration. 'For if so it is better that you go at once. Sir Richard has enough on his mind without suffering the added burden of unfaithfulness. I should say, *how dare you*, Sir Paul, but then I already know how men like you dare.'

'Ah, yes, Sir Richard.' He looked away. 'How I envy him –' He seemed to be searching for words without losing her attention and tolerance. 'I wanted to know, Lady Catherine – I believe he calls you Kate?'

'Yes – and *only* he does.'

Sillitoe sighed. 'As I was saying before I was again distracted by your lovely presence – I will always be available as a friend, more if you should ever need that. That is what I came to say.' He moved towards her as she made to rise from the chair. 'No, please stay, Lady Catherine. I must lose some miles before dark.' He took her hand, forcefully as she did not offer it, and held it, his eyes locked with hers. 'I knew your late husband, the Viscount Somervell. He was a fool. He deserved what he got.' Then he kissed her hand and released it. '*Bon voyage*, Lady Catherine.' He swept his hat from a chair. 'Think of me sometimes.'

It was growing dark in the street outside, and long after the phaeton had clattered away, Catherine still sat in the damp, empty room looking at the door.

Like the words she had spoken to Richard this morning. *They strike at you from every side*. Sillitoe's visit had put another edge to them.

She stood up, startled, as a dull bang echoed across the harbour. They did fire a gun, after all.

She stared at herself in a mirror with something like defiance. Richard would have to be told about the visit. There were others who would be only too willing. But not all of it. Another duel, as Belinda had once flung in her face? She shook her head very slowly and saw the confidence returning to her reflection.

Only death would ever come between them.

Admiral Sir James Hamett-Parker settled himself once more in his chair and glanced briefly at his companions. He was still savouring the taste of fine cheese and the liberal glasses of port, finer than any he had lately enjoyed. It seemed to sustain him in this time of confrontation with his final duty, unpleasant though it would be. His mind lingered on it. *But necessary*.

He realised that the Judge Advocate was watching him patiently. The stage was set. He glanced at the accused, but the stocky rear-admiral's face gave nothing away.

The men from the London and Portsmouth newspapers

were present; the marine officer was behind Herrick's chair, as if he had never moved throughout the whole trial.

He said, 'Mr Cotgrave, I would like to be assured that Captain Hector Gossage is indeed fit to give his evidence.'

Cotgrave regarded him impassively. 'The surgeon is here, Sir James.'

A surgeon from Haslar Hospital bobbed to the table. 'I have presently examined Captain Gossage and am confident there has been an improvement, Sir James. He begs me to apologise for his behaviour before this Court, and I agree that he had been given too much to reduce his pain, and was not himself.'

Hamett-Parker gave a rare smile. It reminded Bolitho, who was watching every move with growing despair, of a fox about to pounce on a rabbit.

Hamett-Parker nodded. 'Then we shall proceed.'

Captain Gossage walked from the rear of the visitors and barely needed the support of each row of chairs as he passed. He did not even seem to notice the curious stares which came from every side. Pity, understanding from his fellow captains, impatience too from those eager to see it finished one way or the other.

He bowed slightly to the officers of the Court and sat down gingerly in the same chair as before.

Bolitho watched as he shook his head to the offer of help from a hospital orderly.

The Judge Advocate asked, 'Are you comfortable, Captain Gossage?'

Gossage moved painfully to hold the stump of his severed arm clear of the chair. 'I am, sir.' Then he faced the admiral. 'I can only ask the Court's pardon for yesterday's behaviour, Sir James. I barely knew what I was doing.'

The vice-admiral named Nevill nodded. 'Only time can mend what you have suffered.' Some of the other officers beside him murmured in agreement.

Hamett-Parker said, 'Then we will continue?'

Bolitho heard the sharpness in his tone. A man who obviously hated anyone else to offer an opinion.

A messenger came up the aisle between the chairs and placed some books on a table within Gossage's reach.

He said, 'My ship's log and signal book, Sir James. Each

portion of the engagement is recorded until we came to close-action.' His face was like stone. 'When there was nobody left on the quarterdeck to attend to it. Even the admiral's flag-lieutenant had fallen by then.' He pouted, as Bolitho had seen him do in the past. 'And I had been carried below to the orlop.'

Bolitho saw his remaining hand clutch his chair, reliving the nightmare, the agony, the sounds of hell itself.

Cotgrave said gently, 'In your own words, Captain Gossage. The details of the log are already recorded.'

Gossage leaned back and closed his eyes. 'I am able, thank you.' There was a bluntness in his tone. For these moments anyway, he was no longer a cripple; he was the flag-captain again.

'After making contact with the brig *Larne*, and knowing the approximate position and bearing of the enemy, we decided to make all sail possible.'

Cotgrave prompted, '*We* decided?'

Gossage nodded and winced. 'As flag-captain I was always consulted, naturally, and you will already know that the same wind which brought Sir Richard Bolitho's ships to our eventual relief, was opposing us and our convoy.'

Cotgrave darted a glance at his clerks; their quills were dashing back and forth across their papers. 'And then, on the day when the enemy made its appearance, what was happening?'

Gossage replied, 'There was a mist, and the convoy had become scattered overnight. But we had made good progress, and I knew that *Larne* was fast enough to pass word to the admiral.'

'Were you as surprised as *Larne*'s commander that it should be passed to Admiral Gambier, rather than to Sir Richard, the accused's friend?'

Gossage considered it. 'Admiral Gambier was in overall command. I can see no other alternative.'

Cotgrave turned over another paper. 'Was there any discussion as to whether the convoy should scatter or disperse at this point?'

Gossage dabbed his face with his handkerchief; the pain was making him sweat badly.

'Yes, we discussed it. We had no frigate, the wind was against us; if the convoy had been broken up I believe it would have been destroyed piecemeal. Most of them were slow, deep-laden – an ill-matched collection if ever I saw one.' He did not conceal his bitterness. 'Even the poor old *Egret*, our remaining escort, was a floating relic.'

Hamett-Parker snapped, 'You cannot say that!'

Cotgrave gave a mild grin. 'I am afraid he can, Sir James. *Egret* was a hulk even before the war began. She was refitted for less demanding duties.'

Gossage repeated, 'She was a relic.'

Bolitho watched Herrick's expression. He was staring at Gossage as if he could not believe what he had heard.

'And then?'

Gossage frowned. 'Rear-Admiral Herrick ordered a gun to be fired to hasten the convoy into a manageable line again, to keep station on one another. Then he insisted that I should order the signal to be spelled out, *word by word*, so that each master would know and understand the nearness of danger.'

'And what of your superior's demeanour at that time?'

Gossage glanced at Herrick, his features completely empty of expression. 'He was calm enough. There was no other alternative but to stand together and fight.' He lifted his chin slightly. 'The *Benbow* has never run away. Nor would she.'

Bolitho watched Herrick's face working with sudden emotion. Once he shook his head, but when asked if he wished to put a question to his past captain he wiped his eyes and remained silent.

Bolitho felt the tension rising around him like steam. Gossage's simple, almost resigned words had changed everything. He was the man of the moment, the only man who had known what had really happened. Bolitho's own description of what he had found when he had boarded the shattered flagship had acted like an introduction. Gossage had ended it.

Cotgrave folded his papers and cleared his throat. 'I believe it is time for the Court to adjourn, Sir James.'

Bolitho looked over and saw Hamett-Parker staring at him, like that first time. There was no hint of justice being done. If anything, there was only fury.

'Remove the accused!'

Then the Court filed out.

Keen entered and found a seat beside him. 'I still cannot understand! I am not deceived, am I, Sir Richard?'

Bolitho was glad he was with him. 'You were not, Val. Gossage made no prior statement, he was too ill at the time. Perhaps this is his way.'

Keen still watched him with surprise. 'But he owes Rear-Admiral Herrick *nothing*, Sir Richard!'

'Have you never heard of revenge, Val?'

Someone whispered hoarsely, 'They're coming back.'

Gossage was standing in the shadows, drinking from a goblet which someone had brought for him. He looked tired and sick, yet unable to leave.

Hamett-Parker said flatly, 'Marshal, do your duty.'

The Royal Marine officer picked up Herrick's sword and after a small hesitation, laid it down again. It brought a great roar of gasps and excitement from the craning visitors. The sword's hilt was toward Herrick's chair.

'Bring in the accused.'

The footsteps halted abruptly beside Bolitho's seat, and when he glanced round he saw Herrick, as white as a sheet, staring at the table as if he had been stricken by some terrible disease.

Cotgrave said, 'Rear-Admiral Herrick, you are discharged. The charges brought against you are dropped. They cannot be recommitted.'

Herrick stared round until he saw Gossage, then he said tonelessly, 'Damn you to hell, Gossage. *God rot you*.'

Gossage raised the goblet in salute and leaning on the orderly's arm, allowed himself to be guided to another door.

Keen said, 'I must see the members of the Court to their boats, Sir Richard.' He turned anxiously. 'Wait for me, please.'

But Allday was here, massive and frowning, his hat beneath his arm.

Bolitho touched Keen's sleeve and shook his head.

To Allday he said, 'Take me ashore, old friend. It's all over.' He looked back at Herrick and saw some officers around him, their faces beaming with congratulations.

He could not see Herrick's expression. He was still holding the sword in his hands like a man who had been cheated, and betrayed.

5

The Hand of a Lady

Bryan Ferguson opened the doors of the big grey house and beamed with pleasure.

'Captain Adam, of all people! When I saw you ride in just now I thought, well, for a moment . . .' He shook his head admiringly. 'What a pity John Allday is not here to see you!'

Captain Adam Bolitho walked into the great room, his eyes taking in everything, noticing small changes. The hand of a lady.

He said, 'I hear he has been in Portsmouth, Bryan.'

'You know of the court-martial, sir?'

Adam walked to the great fireplace and touched the family crest above it. Remembering. Remembering so many things. How, when only fourteen years old, he had walked all the way from Penzance where his mother had died, with a scrap of paper and the name of the one man who would take care of him. This home was like his own. Sir Richard Bolitho had made certain it *would* be his one day, just as he had given him the family name.

He remembered what Ferguson had asked him. 'Aye, the whole fleet must know by now.' He changed the subject. 'I saw my uncle's carriage in the stable yard. Is he here yet?'

Ferguson shook his head. 'He will be sailing from Falmouth soon, so he sent his flag-lieutenant on ahead to attend to things. Yovell came with him.'

He watched Adam as he moved restlessly about the room. He had looked so like Bolitho when he had ridden in. But the young man with hair as black as his uncle's was only twenty-seven with the single epaulette of captain on his right shoulder.

Adam saw the look and smiled. 'It will be a pair this year, Bryan, if all goes well. I shall be posted in the autumn.'

Ferguson approved. So like his beloved uncle, he had gained his first command at the age of twenty-two or three. Now he captained a fine new frigate named *Anemone*.

Adam said, 'I am ordered to the Irish Sea. There is privateer activity in those waters. We might call a few of them to action.'

Ferguson asked, 'Can you stay until tomorrow? Sir Richard should be here by then – he sent word by postboy this morning. I can tell Mrs Ferguson to prepare one of your favourites if . . .' He saw Adam's eyes widen suddenly with surprise, or even shock.

Zenoria stood in the curve of the stairway and looked at him for several seconds. 'Why, Captain Bolitho!' She laughed; she had seemed a young girl again when she had been frowning at the sound of voices. 'What a family for surprises!' She offered her hand and he kissed it.

He said awkwardly, 'I did not know, Mrs Keen . . .'

She smiled. 'Please call me Zenoria. Lady Catherine has taught me the informality within this family.' She threw back her hair and laughed at his intent features. 'Does *command* make that difficult?'

Adam had recovered a little. 'Captain Keen must be thanking God every day for his good fortune.'

She saw him look towards the stair and said, 'He is not yet here. Perhaps the day after tomorrow. He is sailing with Sir Richard.'

'Oh, I see.'

Ferguson said, 'Mrs Keen will be staying with us, Captain Adam.'

She walked into the adjoining room and gestured towards the tall ranks of leather-bound books. 'Unlike you, Adam,' she hesitated over his name, 'I had little education but what my father gave me.'

Adam smiled, but his tone was sad as he answered, 'I lived in a slum until my mother died. She had nothing but her body, which she gave to her "gentlemen" in order to keep us alive.'

He dropped his eyes. 'I – I am so sorry, Zenoria, I did not mean to be offensive. I want anything but that.'

She touched his arm and said quietly, 'I am the one to apologise. It seems that life was hard for both of us at the beginning.'

He looked at her hand on his cuff, Keen's ring shining dully in the bars of sunshine.

He said, 'I am glad you are to stay here. Perhaps I might call, if my ship is in harbour?'

She walked to the windows and gazed out at the garden and beyond to the hillside.

'How can you ask?' She turned, framed against the trees, her eyes laughing at him. 'It *is* your house, is it not?'

Ferguson left the room and found his wife, the housekeeper here, discussing vegetables with the cook.

'How is he, Bryan? Will he stay awhile?'

The cook made some excuse and went back to her kitchen and Ferguson said, 'I think he *will* stay, Grace.' He turned and heard the girl laughing, for girl was all she was. 'I just hope Sir Richard comes soon.' To himself he added, and Lady Catherine. She would know what to do.

His wife smiled. 'All together again. A proper home once more. I'll go and see to things.'

Ferguson stared after her plump figure, remembering how she had nursed and cared for him when he had come home from the war with an arm missing.

If only it could be as Grace believed. But one day, inevitably, the news would come. He glanced up at the nearest portrait by the stairs, Captain David Bolitho, who had died fighting pirates off the African shores. He was wearing the family sword. It had been new then, and made to his own design. Like all the other portraits, he was waiting for the last Bolitho to join them. It saddened Ferguson greatly, but perhaps he would not live to see it. He followed the voices to the library and saw Captain Adam offering Zenoria his arm as a prop while she stood on some small steps to examine books which had probably not been disturbed for years.

My God, he thought, they look so right together. The realisation shocked him more than he had believed possible.

Adam turned and saw him. 'I *shall* be staying awhile, Bryan. My worthy first lieutenant can use the experience!'

Ferguson could say nothing to Grace; and anyway she would not believe him. She saw good in almost everybody.

Allday, then? But he would not be here to offer advice or reassurance once the ship had sailed for the Cape.

Adam did not even see Ferguson leave. 'As you are already wearing riding habit, may I take you up to the castle? It will give us both an appetite suitable for Mrs Ferguson's table!'

Footsteps came through the hallway, and he saw Lieutenant Jenour staring at him uncertainly.

Adam shook his hand warmly. 'You look weary, Stephen!' He waited for the girl to put a book back on its shelf, his eyes never leaving her. 'But you are my uncle's flag-lieutenant so you do not have to explain. I was that too, some years back.'

He called, 'Come, Zenoria, I'll fetch the horses!'

She paused by Jenour. 'Is everything settled, Stephen?'

'I think so. It is rumoured that Rear-Admiral Herrick has been discharged, cleared of all the accusations. I still do not properly understand.'

She put her hand on his. 'I am glad, if it is true – for Sir Richard's sake especially. I know he was very disturbed about it.' She raised her riding crop and called, 'I'm *coming*, Adam! You are all impatience, sir!'

Jenour watched them leave, his young mind busy on several matters at once. But one thing stood out like a navigation beacon on a cliff. He had not seen Keen's wife so happy before.

Yovell appeared through a small door, his jaw working on something he had borrowed from the kitchen.

'Ah, there you are, Yovell . . .' The little vignette of the girl and the young captain vanished from his thoughts. A flag-lieutenant never had enough time in any day to keep his admiral's affairs in motion.

Allday paused on a narrow track and settled down with his back against a slate wall. When he was home from sea and had a spare moment he often came to this quiet place to be alone with his thoughts. He gave a tired grin. *And with a good stone bottle of rum.* He began to fill his pipe, and waited for the sea-breeze to soften before lighting it. He could see the whole span of Falmouth Bay from here; it was not that far from the farm where he had been working as a sheep-minder when the press-gang from Bolitho's ship *Phalarope* had eventually caught up with him, and, although he had had no way of knowing it, changed his life forever.

They had been back from Portsmouth for two days, and it was no surprise to find that the news of Herrick's court-martial was already common gossip. He swallowed some rum and wedged the bottle carefully between his legs. Now it was off to sea again. Strange to wake up each day without the squeal of calls, the Spithead Nightingales as the Jacks called them. No gun and sail drills to send the feet stamping and the topmen clambering aloft, one mast racing the next for the best performance. He would be a passenger this time. The thought might have amused him, but for the other sadness which hung heavily upon him. He had told Bryan Ferguson, his oldest friend, about it; but nobody else. It was strange, but he had had the feeling that Ferguson had been about to confide in him in turn about something, but had decided to let the matter drop.

Allday had seen his son John Bankart on his return from Portsmouth. He had once been so proud of the lad, especially as he had not even known of his existence for years. When his son had been appointed as Captain Adam's coxswain, Allday's pride had expanded even further.

Now Bankart was out of the navy, and Captain Adam had arranged it; he had said that he had known he would be killed if he remained with the fleet. But there was worse to come. His son had got himself married. They had not waited for Allday to come home. They had not even written to him. He could not read at all well, but Ozzard would have read a letter for him. Allday listened to the breeze as it hissed through the long grass, while some gulls wheeled and screamed against a clear sky. The spirits of dead sailormen, some said.

He had lost his temper when his son had added insult to injury by telling him that he and his bride had been offered work and security across the Western Ocean in America.

'Life's fresher, different over there.' He had exclaimed

angrily, 'A new chance – somewhere we can raise a family without a war raging at our gates year in, year out!'

Allday swallowed another wet of rum and swore under his breath. 'We had to fight them buggers once, my lad, and by God we'll be doing it again one o' these days, you just see!' He had left their cottage with one last shot. 'You, a Yankee? An Englishman you was born, an Englishman you dies, an' that's no error!'

The rum and the warm air were making him drowsy. He shook himself and began to refill his pipe. Young Adam's *Anemone* would be under way by now. She would make a fine sight when she tacked around Pendennis Point. He grinned, impatient with himself. Must be moonstruck or something. How could he still get excited at the sight of a rakish frigate after all the things he had seen?

He thought suddenly of Lady Catherine. He did not know how she had done it but during the long haul from Portsmouth she had brought some light back to Bolitho's grey eyes again.

It would be strange to be sailing with them . . . just as well Ozzard and Yovell were going too. All mates together. Who would have thought it could ever happen to him? His head lolled and his pipe fell across the rum bottle and broke in pieces.

His skull grated against the rough wall and he struggled up into a sitting position again.

The sea was still bright and empty, and the gulls as querulous and noisy as before.

Then he was on his feet, his head bent like an old dog as he strained his ears, ready for when it came again.

Not gulls this time. It was a scream. A woman terrified for her life.

Allday loped along the wall, his head down, cursing himself for being unarmed without even a toy dirk.

There was a loose piece of slate, heavy and sharp, like some ancient axe-head; he seized it as he passed.

The scream came again. Allday clambered over the wall and stared down at the narrow lane that wound towards the bay like a little gully.

There were two men, and they did not even hear him. A cart loaded with boxes and personal possessions drawn by a small donkey was stopped in the lane, and the woman was being held by one of the men, a tall, bearded ruffian who was twisting her arms up her back while she struggled. The other one, who had his back to Allday, was equally rough and dirty, but there was no mistaking his intentions as he said harshly, 'Now let's see what else she's got, Billy!' He began to pull at the front of her clothes while his companion twisted her arms still further, so that she screamed again.

'Not *now*, matey!' Allday waited until the man swung round, judging the exact moment. The heavy piece of slate hit the man's forehead just above the eye and Allday heard the bone crack like a rotten nut. He had a vague picture of the other man taking to his heels while the woman tried to cover her breasts, her eyes wide with terror and stunned disbelief.

'S'all right, m'dear.' He bent over the inert shape and hit it again. 'Gallows bait.' But it was not all right. The pain thrust through his chest like red-hot iron, so that he could neither breathe nor cry out.

Suddenly she was bending over him, lifting his shaggy head on to her knees while she gasped, '*What is it? I must help!*'

He wanted to calm her, to make it safe for her. *Of all times.* His mind cringed as the pain stabbed again, worse than before. He could see it as if he was still there on that bloody island. The Spanish sword, and Bolitho trying to fight off his attackers.

Not here. Not this way.

He looked up at her. A nice face. A real woman. He tried to speak again, but the pain tightened its grip. She repeated, 'I must get help!'

He lifted one hand and watched it come to rest on her shoulder. She was trembling. Then he heard himself mutter, 'Behind that wall . . .' To his own ears he sounded quite as usual, but he was not, and she had to bend right over him to hear. She smelled of lilac, he thought stupidly. '*Rum.*'

She backed away, avoiding the body with the outflung arms.

Allday tried to stare at the sun. The Cap'n must not know. He would make him come ashore, leave him on the beach while he went off somewhere.

She was back, and he felt her bare arm under his head, lifting him. Her eyes were anxious, unsure.

74

Allday swallowed hard and she dabbed his mouth with the hem of her dress. 'Better,' he managed to murmur. 'A nice wet. Nelson's blood, they're calling it now.'

She gripped his shoulder and whispered, '*Horses*.'

Allday felt the tall shadows pass over him and saw the gleam of buttons. Authority. Two coastguards making their way to town.

One of them dismounted and bent down on the dirt lane. 'John, you old rogue, what've you been up to this time?' But his eyes were troubled. 'Are you all right, ma'am?'

She knelt beside him, staring at Allday's face. 'He saved me. There were two of them.'

The coastguard observed her torn clothing and the laden cart with professional interest. 'Footpads. Deserters most likely.' He loosened a pistol in his belt. 'Ride to the squire's house, Ned, it's nearer. I'll stay here in case that vermin comes back.'

His companion watched from his horse as he stooped over the body.

'Dead, is he?'

His friend grinned. 'No. The squire *will* be pleased. Someone else for him to dangle at the roadside!'

The mounted man called, 'There goes the *Anemone*, Tom. What a sight, eh?'

It seemed to rouse Allday, and he gasped, 'Must see. Must get up!'

The other coastguard spurred his horse into a trot. 'I'll be off then.' He looked down at Allday as the fight went out of him. 'And *you*, John Allday, behave yourself until someone comes. I'd not dare face Vice-Admiral Bolitho if owt happened to you!'

The woman held up an apron to keep the sun from his eyes.

'John Allday.' She sounded dazed. 'I know of you, sir. My late husband served in your ship.'

Allday sensed it was important. 'What ship, ma'am? I expect I'd remember him.'

But he already knew. The ship that would not die.

In a small voice she said, 'The one they still sing about. The old *Hyperion*.'

*

Lady Catherine Somervell watched while Ferguson supervised the loading of chests and boxes into a carriage outside the front porch. By the cold fireplace Bolitho was scanning yet another official letter from the Admiralty, his features giving nothing away. She could watch him for hours, she thought, sharing his concern for so many things, the warmth of his company when they were alone together. His love for her above all else.

She said, 'The postboys must be wearing out every horse between here and Whitehall.' She crossed to his side. 'What is it?'

He looked at her but his eyes were distant, absent in thought. 'Thomas Herrick. It seems they have offered him an immediate appointment in the West Indies. It does not say exactly where, but they certainly wasted no time.'

She slipped her hand through his arm. 'That is good, surely. For him, I mean.'

He smiled. 'It is often said that a court-martial will either make or break a man.'

She heard Allday laughing in the courtyard. He seemed entirely changed, his earlier gloom dispersed, but as yet she did not know the reason for either of his moods.

'Why did Herrick act as he did? I still cannot understand.'

Bolitho recalled Captain Gossage's slow, deliberate evidence, his apparent support for everything Herrick had done.

He replied, 'I believe it was Gossage's revenge. To make Thomas live with his guilt, rather than see him destroyed, or allowed the peace only death could bring him.'

He sensed her surprise and said gently, 'He is not the man I once knew.' He looked up at the portraits. 'Nor would I be, without you.'

She guided him to the window. 'I shall miss this place, Richard. But it will be here . . . waiting for us. We shall not be separated this time.' She thought of her dismay when she had seen Adam walking with Zenoria, when they had finally reached Falmouth. She glanced at Bolitho's profile and embraced his arm with hers; he still suspected nothing. Adam had left to rejoin his ship almost immediately. Now Keen was here, although she had barely seen him in any attitude of intimacy with his bride.

Bolitho asked, 'What is it, Kate? Are you troubled?'

She laughed, letting it break the tension that these last days had given her. 'I just want to be gone, my love. Before something else bursts in to disturb you!'

Allday passed the door and saw them embrace by the window. He found Yovell checking one of his lists, making sure that nothing had been overlooked.

'D'you recall a master's mate named Jonas Polin?'

Yovell peered over his small spectacles. 'Yes, I do. I used to pass the time with him. A Devon man like myself.' He frowned. 'Why does his name come to mind? He went down with the old ship.'

Allday sat on a chest while Ozzard forced down the lock.

'I met his widow yesterday. A trim little craft, an' no mistake.'

Yovell eyed him severely. 'I heard about you going to someone's rescue on the cliff lane. Tom the coastguard was full of it. They caught the other man, by the way – the dragoons ran him to earth. He told me something else too, John. About *you*.'

'If you dare to squeak a breath of it to Sir Richard, I'll . . .' He grinned, knowing that Yovell would say nothing about his collapse on the road.

'Tell me about poor Jonas Polin's widow.'

Allday said, 'She was going to Fallowfield. Don't know it meself.'

Yovell smiled. 'I'm the foreigner here, and I'm the only one who seems to know where places are!' He folded his arms across his rotund body and looked at Allday thoughtfully. This was special. Serious too.

'It's on this side of the Helford River, near Rosemullion Head. Tiny place, just farm folk and a few fishermen. Why would she be going there? Old Jonas was a Brixham man, good Devon stock.'

Allday said cautiously, 'Nice little inn in Fallowfield, the Stag's Head, to all accounts.'

'Was, more like. The place has been almost derelict for a year or so.'

'It won't be no more, Daniel. She's bought it. Going to

77

bring it to life again.' Her words still echoed in his ears. *You will always be welcome, Mr Allday*.

Yovell folded his list and put it in his pocket. 'She could do that. It's a long, long march to the Royal George in the next village.' He seemed to make up his mind, and to Allday's surprise he crossed over to him and gripped his hand.

'I wish you luck, John. God knows you've been hurt often enough, and I don't necessarily mean by the Frogs.'

Ozzard looked up from his knees, but he said nothing and could not smile. The thought of a woman's body brought the memory back instantly, its horror as stark as ever. The room in Wapping. The screams, the blood: hacking and hacking until there was only silence.

Ferguson left them to it and went back into the house, wiping his forehead with his sleeve. He had seen Keen crossing the garden alone, and turned away to avoid him. He kept telling himself it was nothing to do with him, or with anyone else, but the thought only made him feel more guilty.

A little later Tojohns, Keen's own coxswain, came through the door and touched his hat to Bolitho.

'Beg pardon, Sir Richard.' He avoided glancing at the admiral's lady and swallowed hard. Being here in the same house, sharing it all with the two people who were the talk of London and most seaports, was like being with royalty. 'Word's come from the town. The ship is about to anchor in Carrick Road.'

Bolitho smiled. He was suddenly excited, sharing it with her, like some midshipman with his heart on his sleeve.

'We shall board her tomorrow. Ask Stephen to deal with it.'

He looked round as Keen climbed the worn stone steps. What was he thinking? Was he already regretting handing over *Black Prince* to another? Was he measuring the value of promotion against leaving his young bride here in Falmouth?

Bolitho said, 'Tomorrow, Val.'

'I'm ready, Sir Richard. A captain without a ship, but still . . .'

'Did someone say that the ship is here?' Zenoria came in from the library. Her eyes immediately went to her husband.

Bolitho said kindly, 'It will not be forever. But I think Val is doing the best for his future, and for yours. A hard choice.'

He looked at Catherine. 'But it always is. Only the unhappy find no pain in parting.'

Zenoria stared from one to the other. 'I am sorry, Sir Richard, but I did not know it was his choice. I thought my husband was under orders to take this appointment upon himself.'

Bolitho said, 'It is the navy's way, Zenoria.' To break the sudden tension he said to Keen, 'Will you walk with me a while, Val? I have had more news from the Admiralty.'

When they were alone Catherine put her arm around the girl's shoulders, and said softly, 'Try to love him as he loves you. He needs to know, to be told. All men do. He is a good man, decent and trusting . . . he must never have that trust tarnished.'

Zenoria said nothing but faced her. There were tears in her eyes. 'I am trying, Catherine. I have tried so hard . . .'

Catherine heard more footsteps as boxes were hoisted in readiness for loading into the carriage.

'Go to him now. Care for your man as I care for mine.' Her fine dark eyes were suddenly blurred. *I love him so much I fear for his every move. Those he has tried to help turn their backs on him, and his true friends are fathoms deep in one ocean or another. But it is his life, and so I knew when I gave myself to him. And yet . . . there are times when I awake and find him gone, and I think my heart will break . . .*

She saw Allday watching them and said brightly, 'And what is this I am hearing about *you*? A secret love, the rescue of a maid in distress?'

Allday grinned. He did not know how he knew, but he realised he had arrived at just the right time.

Valentine Keen walked through the shadows, his shoes slipping on damp grass. There must have been a heavy dew overnight, he thought, but now the garden was alive with birdsong at every level. It would be dawn quite soon, whereas the land beyond this place was still hidden in mystery. He could smell the sea in the soft wind shaking the leaves around them, giving him a sense of urgency, even despair.

He tightened his arm around Zenoria's slim shoulders and thought of the night here, the last for some time in England.

He thrust the other thought from his mind: what every sailor, admiral or common seaman, had to consider each time his ship weighed anchor. It could be the last, forever.

A robin darting through the grass, revealed only by a swaying mass of daffodils, gave its lively, trilling call.

Keen said, 'It is almost time.' They paused at the old wall as if by some unspoken agreement. 'You will take care while I am away? I leave you in good hands, I know, but . . .'

She rested her head against his shoulder, and he drew her more closely to him. He said, 'I love you so much, Zenoria – and I am so afraid of failing you.'

In her eyes he saw the first faint daylight. 'How could you fail me, after all that you did for me? But for you . . .' She fell silent as he touched her mouth with his fingers.

'Don't think of then. Think of now. Think of *us*. I need your love so desperately . . . and I fear that I might drive you away. I am so . . . clumsy. I know so little. I find you one moment, and the next you are gone and a gulf yawns between us.'

She took his arm and turned him back along the winding path, her gown brushing against the stones, wet with dew.

'It has been difficult for me also, but not through lack of affection for you. Don't think of then, you said. But how can I not? It comes back, and I am in terror again.' She hesitated. 'I want to give myself, completely. When I see Sir Richard and his Catherine together I can hardly bear to watch them. Their love is something alive, beautiful . . .'

'You are lovely too, Zenoria.'

He laid his face against hers and felt tears on her cheek.

'I cannot bear to leave you like this.'

As if to mock his words, they heard horses being led unhurriedly from the stables. The carriage would be waiting.

He tightened his hold, caressing her hair. The light was growing; there was a bright smudge out there, like a careless brushstroke. The first view of the sea beyond Pendennis Point.

She whispered, 'I *want* to please you . . . like the girl you once had in the South Seas.'

Keen said, 'I never touched her, but I did love her. When she died I thought I could never . . . *would* never be able to love someone again.'

'I know. That is why I despair that I cannot give you my body . . . as you deserve.'

Keen heard Allday talking with Ferguson. So, if the rumour was true, he had found a woman to love, or one who had treated him with kindness after what he had done.

And I am losing mine.

She said, 'Please write to me, Val. I will never stop thinking of you . . . wondering where you are, what you are doing . . .'

'Yes. I will.' More movement, the tread on stone steps he knew so well; he could hear him speaking with Catherine. Waiting for himself, perhaps.

'I must go, Zenoria.'

'Cannot I come to the harbour and see you leave?' She sounded like a child again.

'A harbour is the loneliest place when you are being separated.' He kissed her, with passion and gentleness, on the mouth. '*I love you so.*'

Then he turned and walked out of the garden.

There was only Allday by the gate, looking at the land. Keen's own coxswain had gone ahead to the vessel with Ozzard and Yovell. Ferguson came out of the dark doorway and held out his hand. 'Good-bye, Captain. We shall take good care of your lady. Don't stay away too long.'

In his despair Keen thought even that sounded like a warning.

He climbed into the carriage and sat beside the flag-lieutenant, his coat sticking to the damp leather seats.

Catherine leaned against the window and whispered, 'Fare-well, old house! Be patient for us!' Her maid Sophie looked at her curiously: to her this was all a great adventure.

The carriage swayed as Allday clambered up beside Matthew, then, finally, the whip cracked, and the iron-shod wheels clattered across the cobbles.

Amongst the daffodils a young girl watched as the first sunlight touched the back of the carriage.

She wanted to cry, for her heart was breaking. But nothing came.

6

The Golden Plover

'There she lies!' Bolitho leaned forward and pointed at the vessel which was to carry them all the way to the Cape, his eyes agleam with professional interest.

Allday grunted. 'Barquentine.' He squinted as a shaft of watery sunlight played upon the gilt gingerbread around her poop and her name, also in gold across her raked counter. 'What's she called, Sir Richard? My eyes are playing up again.'

Bolitho glanced at him warmly. He knew that Allday could not read properly, but he could memorise the shape of a ship's name and never forget it. *We are both shamming.* 'She's the *Golden Plover*.' They grinned at one another like conspirators. 'At one time with the old Royal Norfolk Packet Company.'

Catherine watched the private exchange between them, and was surprised how such things could move her. And this time they were together. Sharing it; or as she had said to him this morning while they had watched the dawn, and Keen had been walking in the garden, *it will be Love in the guise of duty.*

It was strange for Bolitho to approach any vessel without some official reception at the entry port. There were several men aloft, and the barquentine's tan sails were flapping loosely, like a bird preparing for flight. He recognised Ozzard's small figure beside that of a great hulk of a man whom he guessed was Samuel Bezant, the vessel's master. Unlike most of *Golden Plover*'s company he had been in his command even before the vessel had come under Admiralty warrant, in those early days when the Terror and the daily slaughter at the guillotines had made the squares of France run with blood.

The masters of these packet-ships, like those of the famous Falmouth fleet, were truly professional sailors. From England to the Americas, Jamaica and the Caribbean, the Spanish Main, and now on to the Cape of Good Hope. Once in Admiralty service most of them had been fitted out with more cabin space for officials – officers and sometimes their wives – ordered to the far-flung corners of the King's growing empire.

Bolitho had been told that *Golden Plover* had begun her life as a barque, but had been cut down to her present, more manageable rig so that she could sail almost into the wind, but with fewer hands needed to trim and reset her sails. Only on the foremast, which still flew the old company pendant, was she square-rigged. On her main and mizzen she carried huge fore-and-aft sails which, for the most part, could be handled from the deck.

Keen twisted round just before the boat pulled past the vessel's stern, when he would lose sight of the jetty.

Catherine saw it too, the pain in his searching gaze, as if he still expected to see Zenoria there with the others: the idlers, the old sailors and the ones with the precious protection that kept them free of the King's ships.

She said quietly, 'You are everything to her, Val. All she needs is time.'

There was a frigate at anchor nearby, scarlet-coated marines watching suspiciously as the shore-boats crowded around her. Wares for the sailors. Knives, baccy, pipes; anything that might ease the harsh reality of discipline and danger.

She touched her breast but her heart was steady again. She had thought it might be Adam's *Anemone*. But it was not. She could understand well enough how easily they might be drawn to one another. Both from the West Country, both with bitter memories to plague them. She looked at Bolitho's strong profile and wanted to touch him. Their ages were closer too. But love, or more to the point, the danger of love, was something quite different.

She tightened the cord which drew the dark green hood over her hair. People had often remarked on her own age, that she was younger than Richard. She suddenly felt angry. *Well, let them, damn them*. At least he would be free of all that for a time.

The bowman shipped his oar and hooked on to the chains, while two seamen leaped lightly into the boat to attach tackles to the remaining boxes. The huge figure of the master did not move until Catherine had been assisted up the side, then he said in a thick voice, 'Welcome aboard *Golden Plover* – ' He doffed a battered hat from a mass of shaggy grey hair. 'Er – my lady!'

She saw Sophie watching with obvious excitement, quite delighted at Samuel Bezant's discomfort.

She smiled. 'She's a fine-looking ship.' Then, sharing the moment, she tugged the cord free and tossed the hood back over her shoulders. The men working by the mizzen mast turned to stare; another dropped a belaying pin which brought an instant threat from a boatswain's mate.

Bezant turned from her to Bolitho. 'Y'see, Sir Richard, I was only told the rest of my orders when your lieutenant came aboard.'

Bolitho said, 'So everything is now clear?'

The big man turned and frowned at his lovely passenger, her hair now released to the offshore wind.

'Just that most of my men have not been ashore for an eternity, Sir Richard, an' they're untried with the likes of a real lady. I'd not trust some of the knotheads further than I could pitch a kedge-anchor!'

She looked across at him, her eyes laughing. 'And what of you, Captain? How much can *you* be trusted?'

Bezant's rough features were brick-red from a liberal mixture of ocean gales and brandy.

If not, Bolitho thought, he would have been blushing.

The master nodded slowly. 'I fair requested that, m'lady. But I thought it right to warn you, their language an' the like.'

She walked to the unprotected wheel and ran her fingers along one of the spokes.

'We are in your hands, Captain Bezant. I am certain we shall get along famously.'

Bezant wiped his mouth with the back of one hand and said, 'If you are ready, Sir Richard? I'd like to up-anchor, for the tide in this port has a nasty way of showing displeasure.'

Bolitho smiled. 'I was born here. But I'd still not take the moods of Carrick Road for granted!'

He heard the man give a sigh of relief as his passengers were guided down the companion ladder, where, despite the lack of headroom, the cabin area was remarkably spacious and comfortable.

Ozzard said, 'I have the use of the pantry and lazaret, Sir Richard – what with all the pots and jars her ladyship brought down from London, I'll see you don't starve.' Even he seemed pleased to be leaving. Or was he still running away from something?

Catherine closed the slatted door of the cabin that had been made ready for them and looked around with sudden uncertainty.

Bolitho wondered if she was thinking of that other time at sea, when her husband Luis had been killed. The ship in which they had been taking passage had been attacked by Barbary pirates; Bolitho could still remember the white-hot anger when she had turned on him, cursing him for allowing it to happen. But her love had burned even more brightly when Fate had touched them.

She rested her hand on one of the swinging cots and smiled. When she faced him he saw the pulse beating in her throat, the sudden mischief in her dark eyes.

'I long to cross the ocean with you, dearest of men. But sleep in one of these coffins?' She laughed, and someone outside the door stopped to listen. 'On certain nights the deck will suffice!'

As he took her in his arms they heard the faint cry, '*Anchor's hove short!*'

The regular clink of a windlass, the stamp of bare feet as seamen rushed to braces and halliards, the sudden thump of the tiller-head as the helm was put over in readiness.

She whispered into his hair, 'The music of the sea. A ship coming alive . . . It means so much to you.' When she raised her head her eyes were shining with emotion. 'Now, for once I will share them.' Her mood changed again. 'Let us go on deck, Richard. A last look.' She paused, as though unwilling to say it. 'Just in case . . .'

'*Anchor's aweigh!*'

They staggered to the companionway, reaching out for

support as the lively barquentine broke free of the ground and leaned hard over like a frigate.

Bezant stood with his legs braced apart like trees, his eyes flitting from peak to compass, to the flapping jib until like the other canvas it filled out taut to the wind.

Catherine slipped her arm through Bolitho's and watched the great pile of Pendennis Castle begin to move abeam. The deck was already lifting to the lively water of the Channel.

Men from the foremast slid down the stays and came bustling aft to assist the others at the mizzen, where the great driver swung out over the dancing spray until it, too, was sheeted home.

There would be much gossip between decks when the watch was piped below. The officer who had thrown his reputation in society to the wind, for the love of this lady with the streaming hair, and the laugh on her mouth and in her eyes.

The ship changed tack again, and the sea boiled over the scuppers until the wheel brought her under command once more.

But as Bezant later remarked to his mate, 'For all them two cared, they could have been the only souls aboard!'

Richard Bolitho went on deck as the evening sun began to dip, and transform the sea from shark-blue to a shimmering rusty red. There was no sight of land, but the gulls still lingered hopefully, gliding around the hull or perching sometimes on the foremast yards.

Three days outward bound from Falmouth, and already the *Golden Plover* had displayed her speed, and the responding pride of her shaggy-haired master.

The two helmsmen stood, bare feet splayed on the deck, their eyes moving occasionally from compass to the driver's quivering peak. Neither glanced at Bolitho.

Maybe they were getting used to their passengers, he thought, or perhaps it was because like Keen and Jenour he had discarded his uniform coat, and was more recognisable as an ordinary man.

Three days, and already they were well past the hazards of Biscay, where just once the masthead lookout had called down to report a man-of-war's upper yards on the horizon. Samuel

Bezant had immediately altered course away from it, and confided to Bolitho that he cared not whether it was friend or foe. Either could bring the attention of another, and his orders were to stand away from involvement with the blockading squadron.

'Beggin' your pardon, Sir Richard, but any flagship will call on me to lie-to on some pretext or another.'

Of the enemy he had said almost scornfully, 'Many's the time my *Plover*'s outsailed even a frigate. She's broad in the beam, but so too is she deep-keeled, and can come about in most weather better than any other!'

Bezant was here now, in deep discussion with his mate, another wild-looking man by the name of Jeff Lincoln.

Bolitho crossed the deck to join them. 'You are making a fair speed.'

Bezant studied him carefully as if it might be taken as a complaint.

'Aye, Sir Richard, I'm well pleased. We should anchor at Gibraltar in two days.'

Like most masters he might have put into Madeira, even Lisbon, to replenish stores at more favourable prices. But it made good sense to keep away. With the French in occupation of Portugal it was possible they might have landed on some of the islands too. *Golden Plover* was well-stocked and had only a small company to supply rather than the mass of hands required for any King's ship; she could enjoy the luxury of long passages while keeping away from danger. There was always concern about fresh water, but Bezant had his own sources on lesser-known islands if for any reason the wind and weather turned against them.

The mere mention of Gibraltar seemed to squeeze Bolitho's heart like an icy hand. Where he had landed after losing *Hyperion*. How many, many memories linked him still to that old ship.

'I'll not be sorry to get under way again from the Rock, Sir Richard. It is in our best interest to keep well clear of the land – a thousand eyes watch the comings and goings of every vessel there. Sometimes I feel more like a pirate than a packet-master!'

'*Deck there!*'

They looked up at the masthead, where only the topsail was

still in bright sunshine. The lookout was pointing with one arm, like a bronze figure in a church.

'*Sail to the nor' east!*'

Bezant hardly seemed to need to raise his voice. 'You keep watching that 'un, Billy!' To Bolitho he added carelessly, 'Probably one o' *your* ships, Sir Richard. Either way, I shall lose him after dark.'

'What cargo do you carry?'

Bezant seemed to shy away. 'Well, seeing it's you, I suppose . . .' He looked at him with sudden determination, as if it was something which had been uppermost in his mind from the moment he had received his orders. 'It's another reason I don't need to draw attention to *Plover's* whereabouts.' He took a deep breath. 'It's gold. Pay for the army at Cape Town. Now, with such an important passenger aboard for good measure I feel the stuff is burning a hole right through the keel.'

He added with sudden bitterness, 'I don't know why they can't send a man-o'-war, a frigate or the like. Those fellows are used to looking for trouble. I'm paid to stay out of it.'

Bolitho thought of the growing pressure for action against the French in Portugal, Spain eventually as well, if Napoleon continued to mount pressure against his old ally.

He heard himself say, 'Because there are not enough such vessels.' He smiled, remembering his father. 'There never were.'

There was a light step at the companionway and Bolitho saw the waif-like figure of Sophie watching him, holding on to a handrail as if her life depended on it. Even though the Bay of Biscay had been kinder than usual, Sophie had taken it badly and had been sick for a whole day. Now she was her lively self again, her eyes, bright with curiosity, reflecting the dying sunlight. She must be finding all this very different from the Jewish tailor's shop in far-off Whitechapel.

'Supper's ready, Sir Richard. I was sent to fetch you, like . . .'

Catherine had been explaining to the girl how she should be careful where she went on board the *Golden Plover*.

Bolitho had heard her whisper in reply without any sort of

shyness, 'Oh, I knows about *men*, me lady. I'll watch me step right enough!'

The cabin looked welcoming, the deckhead lantern already lit and spiralling with each plunge of the stem. Keen was in quiet conversation with Catherine, and Jenour was apparently writing at a small, beautifully-carved desk. It could have a story to tell, he thought; it had probably been made by a ship's carpenter, like some of his own furniture at Falmouth.

He paused and glanced over Jenour's shoulder. But it was not an addition to yet another long letter to his parents; it was a sketch. Men washing down the foredeck, a gull with flapping wings perched on the bulwark screeching for food.

Jenour became aware of his shadow and looked up. He immediately blushed.

'Just a drawing to put in with the letter, Sir Richard.' He attempted to put it away but Bolitho picked it up and studied it with care. '*Just* a drawing, Stephen? I think it is quite excellent.'

He felt Catherine slip her hand under his arm as she moved across the gently swaying deck.

She said, 'I've already told him so – I have asked him to do a portrait of you and me.' Their eyes met and it was as before, as if the cabin were otherwise empty. 'Together.'

Bolitho smiled. Her eyes seemed to caress him. 'He is far better at it than being a flag-lieutenant!'

Ozzard waited for them to be seated, then joined Sophie in the pantry ready to serve them.

Catherine said, 'How every woman would envy me. Three handsome sea-officers, and nobody else to share them!' She looked at Bolitho and saw his change of expression. 'Tell me, Richard, what is wrong?'

Jenour forgot his embarrassment and his inner pleasure, and Keen was suddenly alert and all attention, as if he were himself in command of this vessel.

Bolitho said quietly, 'I believe we are being followed. The master says not, but I have a feeling about it.'

Keen remarked, 'I have rarely known your feelings to mislead you, sir.'

Catherine watched him from the opposite end of the table, wanting to be close to him, to share the sudden intrusion.

She asked, 'Why? Because of us?'

Bolitho glanced at the pantry hatch and said, 'We are carrying enough gold to pay the whole of the military at Cape Town.' He heard the clatter of plates and murmured, 'Tomorrow, Val, I shall want all your experience. Take a glass and go aloft. Tell me what you see.' He hesitated. 'My eye may try to deceive me.' He turned to Catherine and saw her dismay. 'I am all right, Catherine.' He looked away as Ozzard entered, the girl with serving dishes behind him. *I have to be.*

True to his word Samuel Bezant, master of the *Golden Plover*, dropped anchor beneath the Rock's towering protection just two days after sighting the strange vessel astern.

Bolitho sent Keen and Jenour ashore to offer his compliments to the port admiral but decided to remain in the comparative privacy of the poop. Catherine stood beside him staring up at the great wedge-shape of Gibraltar and said, 'I wish we could walk there together.' She gave a small sigh. 'But you are right to stay here. Especially if you still believe that sighting the other vessel was no accident.'

Keen had climbed aloft with his telescope and had reported seeing the topmasts and yards of a small, two-masted ship, very likely a brig. But a sea-mist had closed over the horizon and when it cleared the other craft, like a will-o'-the-wisp, had vanished; nor had she been sighted again.

Bolitho ran his hand down her spine and felt her stiffen. He said quietly, 'I cannot bear to leave you alone.'

She faced him, her lips slightly parted. 'What would they think if they came here and found us . . . well, *found* us?' She laughed and moved from his reach. 'But I love being here with you. Even at home you are still the King's officer. Here you are forced to stand aside and allow others to do the planning and sail the ship as they must . . . and there is time for us. I see you at peace; you reading your Shakespeare aloud to me in the evenings – you make it come alive. And you smoke your pipe, something you rarely do, even at Falmouth. It stirs me with need and desire at the same time.'

'Are they not the same?'

Her chin lifted and she looked at him straight in the eyes. 'I will show you the difference when . . .'

But a boat thudded alongside and shortly afterwards Bezant came aft to report on his visit ashore. He looked troubled, even angry.

'The port admiral would take no refusals and threatened to make his displeasure known to the Admiralty with the next mail-packet.'

He glanced uncomfortably at Catherine who said, 'You may speak in front of me, Captain. I am no stranger to bad news.'

Bezant shrugged. 'I am ordered to take twelve prisoners to Cape Town. This is no vessel for such miserable work.'

Bolitho asked, 'What kind of prisoners?'

Bezant was already rearranging things in his mind. 'Oh, just army deserters, Sir Richard, not true felons. They are said to have decided to hide aboard a transport when it left Cape Town. They decided to run, rather than remain out there.'

Bolitho barely remembered the port admiral but knew from his reputation that sending these soldiers back to their regiment would be his idea of justice. It was not his province to imprison them until another ship called, which could better accommodate them.

Catherine asked quietly, 'What will happen?'

Bezant sighed. 'They'll be hanged if they're lucky, m'lady. I once witnessed the army's idea of field punishment.' He looked at Bolitho and added, 'Like a flogging round the fleet, Sir Richard. Few survive it.'

Bolitho walked to the open stern windows and winced as sunlight reflected from the open sea lanced into his injured eye.

'What is it, Sir Richard?' Bezant stared from one to the other.

'It is *nothing*.' Bolitho tried to soften his tone. 'But thank you.' He turned and saw the pain in her expression. She knew. She always knew.

Someone tapped at the door and Bolitho heard the mate, Lincoln, muttering to his captain.

Bezant sent him away and said harshly, 'Hell's teeth! Beggin' your pardon, m'lady, but I am beset by trouble!'

He calmed himself with considerable effort, and yet seemed strangely glad to be able to share his problems with Bolitho, despite his fame and his rank.

'I sent my second mate ashore to visit the garrison surgeon. He has been in pain since we quit Falmouth. I thought it was caused by too many visits to the taverns or the like. But it seems it may be very serious, something eating at his insides. Jeff Lincoln and me have sailed watch-an'-watch afore when he got sick, but not on long passages like this 'un.' He dropped his glance to the deck, as if he were seeing the cargo glittering with menace somewhere below.

'Jeff Lincoln has brought off a temporary mate until we can make other changes. His papers seem in order, and the port admiral's aide doesn't appear ready to discuss *that* either.' He suddenly gave a broad grin. 'But sailors don't expect things easy, do they, Sir Richard?'

He lumbered away, calling out instructions to his boatswain as he went.

'It won't affect us, will it, Richard?' She was still watching him for some sign of pain in his injured eye.

Sophie entered with a pile of clean shirts and announced excitedly, 'There's other land over yonder, me lady! I thought this was all the land over 'ere!'

Catherine put her arm round the girl's thin shoulders. 'That's Africa you can see, Sophie.' They watched her astonishment. 'You've come quite a long way.'

But the girl could only stare and whisper, '*Africa*.'

Bolitho said, 'Go and ask Tojohns to take you where you can see it with a glass.' As the door closed he said, 'I'll not be sorry to get away from this place.' He almost shuddered. 'An unlucky landfall.'

The door opened again but it was Allday. 'You wanted me, Sir Richard?'

Their eyes met. How did he know? Bolitho said, 'I want to issue some pistols. A brace each. Do it when the hands are turned-to for weighing anchor.'

Allday glanced at Catherine's figure by the open stern windows. He said casually, 'Already done, an' me an' Tojohns have got a piece each.' He grinned. 'No sense in trusting Mr Yovell with one – he's likely to kill himself!'

Catherine said, 'I have my own little toy in the cabin.' Her voice was suddenly husky. 'I nearly used it once.' Bolitho looked at her, remembering the drunken army officer who had made a play for her in the Vauxhall Pleasure Gardens. Bolitho had called him out, but the soldier's friend had dragged him away, offering frantic apologies as he went. Afterwards Catherine had opened her reticule and had shown him the tiny pistol inside. Barely enough to do more than wound a man. But certainly it would have laid low the drunken soldier if things had gone against her man.

Once during that last night she had said aloud, 'If anyone tries to hurt you ever again, they will have me to reckon with. Your pain is mine, just as my love is always yours.'

And now she was here with him, and danger was once more closing in. He heard the plaintive tune of a fiddle, and the steady grate and clatter of the windlass. Men bustled about overhead, and in the *Golden Plover*'s shadow he could already see her sails being loosened. Ready to make the passage south along the African coast, skirting Tenerife where Spanish men-of-war might be resting until they knew what their feared ally might intend.

A longboat pulled beneath the stern and turned hastily towards the inner harbour. He saw discarded leg-irons in the sternsheets, and some marines, talking and laughing now that they had got rid of the admiral's unwanted prisoners.

As an example to others. It made Bolitho think of Herrick's court-martial. Where was he now? Had he already left for the West Indies, without even a word? Bolitho often thought of Captain Gossage's incredible change of evidence and attitude. His was the evidence which could have damned Herrick. But he was also the most important witness, almost the only one, who as flag-captain on that terrible day would have known the true state of affairs. But why? The question was still ringing in his mind when *Golden Plover*'s windlass finally hauled anchor, and her bowsprit swung around to point at the open strait with the great ocean shining beyond.

When most of the vessel was in darkness and the middle watch had taken over the deck, they made love as she had promised him. They took and received one another with deliberate slowness, as if each knew there might be no other time when they could forget the need for vigilance.

7

Conscience

The two riders came to a halt by a low wall and once again faced the sea which reached away from the foot of the cliffs. They could have been brother and sister. They might have been lovers. The sun blazed down on them from a cloudless sky and the air was filled with the sound of insects, and the ever-present gulls on the ledges far below them.

Adam Bolitho climbed down from his horse and said, 'It's not safe to ride any further.' He held up his hands and slipped them around her small waist to assist her to dismount.

A girl with misty brown eyes, her hair loose in the warm inshore wind, her companion without any sort of uniform, wearing only a shirt and seagoing white breeches tucked into his boots.

'Here, Zenoria, take my hand.' He felt hers in his grasp and tightened his grip without realising it. Together they scrambled and slithered down the wind-ruffled grass until they reached a long flat rock, from which they could look directly down to a small cove. The sound of the sea seemed to embrace them as it hissed through the scattered fragments of fallen cliff to sigh against the small crescent of sand.

They sat on the warm stone side by side. He said, 'It is *good* to be back.'

'Can you tell me what happened? You did not leave me much time to get ready!' She held her hair from her face and studied him: the young man who resembled his uncle so much it was uncanny.

Adam pulled a long strand of grass through his teeth. It

tasted of salt. 'We were chasing a schooner off Lundy Island. The weather was brisk.' He smiled at some memory, so that he looked like a young boy again. 'Maybe I was too eager. Anyway we sprung the foretopmast and I decided to come to Falmouth for repair. It is better than languishing for weeks in some Royal dockyard, in line behind all the senior captains and the admiral's favourites!'

She looked at his dark profile, the Bolitho hair and cheekbones. As the spring had given way to summer she had hoped he might call on her, as he had twice before. They rode and walked; they talked, but rarely about one another.

'May I ask you something?'

He rolled on his hip, his face propped in his hand. 'You can ask me *anything*.'

'How old are you, Adam?'

He looked serious. 'Twenty-eight.' He could not keep up the pretence. 'As of today!'

'Oh, Adam, why did you not say?' She leaned over and kissed his cheek very lightly. 'For your birthday.' She put her head on one side. 'You don't *look* very much like a captain.'

He reached out and took her hand in his. 'And you don't look very much like someone who's married.'

He released her as she stood up and walked nearer to the edge.

'If I have offended you, I can only beg forgiveness.'

She turned, her back to the sea. 'You do not offend me, Adam, you of all people. But I am married as you say – it is as well to be reminded.'

She sat down again, and wrapped her arms around her legs and her long riding skirt.

'Tell me about your father. He was a sailor too?'

He nodded, his eyes very distant. 'Sometimes I think I am very like him, as he must have been. Too easily hurt, too quick to consider consequences. My father was a gambler . . . much of the estate was sold to pay his debts. He fought on the other side during the American Revolution, but he did not die as everyone thought. He lived long enough to learn he had a son, and to save my life. One day I shall tell you the whole story, Zenoria. But not now . . . not today. My heart is too full.'

He stared out to sea and asked abruptly, 'Are you truly

happy with Captain Keen? This in return for asking *me* a question, eh?'

She said gravely, 'He has done everything for me. He loves me so much it frightens me. Perhaps I am different from other women . . . at times I begin to believe that is so. And I am quietly going mad because of it. I have tried so hard to understand . . .' She broke off as he took her hand again, very gently this time, and covered it with his like someone holding an injured bird.

'He is older than you, Zenoria. His life has always been the navy, as mine will be, if I live long enough.' He watched her hand in his, so brown in the sunlight, and was not aware of the sudden anguish in her dark eyes. 'But he will return, and if I am right, he will hoist his own flag as an admiral.' He squeezed her fingers and smiled sadly. 'It will be another change for you. The admiral's lady. And there is no captain who deserves it more. I learned so much from him, but . . .'

She watched him steadily. 'But – I have come between you both?'

'I will not lie, not to you, Zenoria. I cannot bear to see you together.'

She took her hand away very carefully. 'You had better stop, Adam. You know how much I enjoy your company. Anything more is a delusion.' She watched her words bring more emotions to his face. 'It has to be. If anyone discovered . . .'

He said, 'I have told nobody. I may be a fool, but I am an honourable fool.'

He stood up and helped her to her feet. 'Now you will dread the next time *Anemone* drops her anchor in Carrick Road.'

For a long moment they stood facing each other, their fingertips still touching.

'Just promise me something, Zenoria.'

'If I can.'

He held her hands more tightly and said, 'If you need me, for any reason at all, please tell me. When I am able I shall come to you, and God help any man who ever speaks ill of you!'

As they mounted the grassy slope and climbed through the old wall, so that the sounds of the sea amongst the rocks below became muffled and then lost, she saw his sword hanging from his saddle.

'You must never fight on my behalf, Adam. If anything happened to you because of me, I don't know what I would do.'

'Thank you. For saying that and so much more.'

She twisted round in his arms when he made to lift her to the stirrup. 'There can be no more!' Her eyes widened with sudden alarm as he tightened his hold around her. 'Please Adam, don't hurt me!'

He looked into her face, understanding, and suddenly full of pity. For them both.

'I would never hurt you.' He put his mouth to hers. 'For my birthday, if for no other reason.'

He felt her lips part, the sudden beat of her heart against his body, and the pain of his need for this strange girl was unbearable. Then he released her very carefully, expecting her to strike him.

Instead she said quietly, 'You must not do that again.' When she lifted her head her eyes were wet with tears. 'I shall never forget.'

She allowed him to raise her to the stirrup and watched as he walked back to the wall, still overcome with disbelief at what she had just permitted.

He stooped and picked several sprays of wild roses from where they tumbled over the wall, and wrapped them carefully in a clean handkerchief before bringing them to her stirrup.

'I am not proud to admit it, Zenoria. But I would take you from any man, if I could.' He handed her the roses and studied her as she lowered her face to them, her hair blowing in the wind like a dark banner.

She did not look at him. She knew she could not, dared not. And when she tried to find security from the foul memories of what she had once endured, there was nothing. For the first time in her life she had felt herself respond to a man's embrace, and she was stunned by what might have happened if he had persisted.

They rode on to the old coaching track in silence. Once he reached between them to take her hand, but nothing was said. Perhaps there were no words. When a small carriage approached they reined in to let it pass, but the coachman pulled the horses to a halt and a woman looked out of the window. A gaunt hostile face, whom Adam recognised as his uncle's sister.

'Well, well, Adam, I didn't know you were back again.' She stared coldly at the girl in the rough riding skirt and loose white blouse. 'Do I know this lady?'

Adam said calmly, 'Mrs Keen. We have been taking the air.' He was angry: with her for her arrogance; with himself for troubling to explain anything to her. Never once had she treated him as a nephew. A bastard in the family? It could not be accepted.

The cold eyes moved over Zenoria's body, missing nothing. The flushed cheeks, the grass on the skirt and riding boots. 'I thought Captain Keen was away.'

Adam calmed his horse with one hand. Then he asked evenly, 'And what of your son, Miles? I understand he is no longer serving the King.' He saw the shot go home and added, 'You can send him to *my* ship if you wish, Ma'am. I am not my uncle – I'd soon teach him some manners!'

The carriage jerked forward in a cloud of sand and dust and Adam said, 'I cannot believe she is of the same blood, damn her eyes!'

Later, as Zenoria stood in the garden, in the same place from which she had watched her husband depart some seven weeks ago, she could feel her heart beating wildly. If only Catherine were here. If only she could tear her mind from the thoughts which still pursued her.

She heard his step on the path and turned to watch him, now changed again into his uniform and even his unruly hair tidied, his gold-laced hat jammed beneath one arm.

She said, 'The Captain once more!'

He seemed about to come towards her, but checked himself. 'May I call again before we sail?' There was anxiety in his eyes. 'Please do not deny me that.'

She raised her hand, as if she were waving to someone a long way off.

'It is *your* home, Adam. I am the intruder.'

He glanced at the house like a guilty youth. Then he touched his breast. 'You intrude only here, in my heart.' He turned and walked from the garden.

Ferguson, who had seen them from an upstairs window, let out a deep sigh. The nagging thought still persisted. They looked so right with each other.

Admiral the Lord Godschale shook the small bell on his table and tugged impatiently at his neckcloth.

'God damn it, it is so hot in this place I wonder I do not fade away!'

Sir Paul Sillitoe sipped a tall glass of hock and wondered how they managed to keep it so cool here in the Admiralty.

The door swung noiselessly inwards and one of the admiral's clerks peered at them.

'Open these windows, Chivers!' He poured some more wine and said, 'Better to have the stench of horse dung and be deafened by all the traffic than sweat like a pig!'

Sillitoe gave a small smile. 'As we were *saying*, my lord . . .'

'Ah yes. The readiness of the fleet. With the extra vessels taken from the Danes, and the return of others from Cape Town, we shall be as prepared as anyone can expect. The yards are working as hard as they can – there is hardly a decent oak left in the whole of Kent apparently!'

Sillitoe nodded, his hooded eyes revealing nothing. In his mind he saw some great chart: the responsibilities entrusted into his care by the government. His Majesty the King was becoming so irrational these days that Sillitoe seemed to be the only adviser he would listen to.

Where was the *Golden Plover* now, he wondered? How long before Bolitho and his mistress were back in England? He often thought of his visit to her. The nearness of her, her beautiful throat and high cheekbones. A glance that could burn you.

'There is another matter, my lord.' He saw Godschale's instant guard. 'I am given to understand that Rear-Admiral Herrick is still without employment. He was to go to the West Indies, I believe?'

Sillitoe was a man who made even the admiral feel insecure. A cold fish, he thought; one without pity, who stood quite alone.

Godschale muttered, 'He is coming here today.' He glanced at the clock. 'Soon, in fact.'

Sillitoe smiled. 'I know.'

It was also infuriating how he seemed to know everything that happened within the barricades of admiralty.

'He asked for an interview.' He stared at Sillitoe's impassive features. 'Do you wish to be here when he comes?'

Sillitoe shrugged. 'I do not care very much either way. However, His Majesty's ministers have stressed the vital importance of complete confidence in the fleet. An admiral who loses in a fight is soon forgotten. But continued interference by that admiral might be seen as irrational. Some might term it – dangerous.'

Godschale mopped his florid face. 'God damn it, Sir Paul, I still don't understand what happened at the court-martial. If you ask me, somebody made a fine mess of things. We must be strong and *seen* to be strong at all times. That was why I selected Sir James Hamett-Parker as President. No nonsense about that one, what?'

Sillitoe looked at the clock, too. 'It might have been better to send Herrick to Cape Town instead of Sir Richard Bolitho,' and, briefly, he showed a rare excitement. 'By God, he'll be in his element when we invade the Peninsula.'

Godschale was still pondering on Herrick. 'Send *him* to Cape Town? God, he'd probably give it back to the Dutch!'

The door opened and another clerk said in a hushed tone, 'Rear-Admiral Thomas Herrick has arrived, m'lord.'

Godschale snorted. 'About time. Send him along from the waiting-room.'

He walked heavily to the window and looked across the busy road to where a dainty, unmarked carriage was waiting beneath the trees, the horses nodding in the dusty sunshine.

Sillitoe remarked, 'I thought you always made them kick their heels a while before allowing them to see you.'

The admiral said over his shoulder, 'I have other business to attend to.'

Sillitoe's hawkish features were quite empty of expression. He knew about the 'other business'; he had already seen her waiting in the unmarked carriage. Doubtless some officer's wife, looking for excitement without scandal. As a bonus, her absent husband might find himself in some better appointment. Sillitoe was surprised that Godschale's dull wife had not heard about his affairs. Everyone else seemed to know.

Herrick entered the room, and glared at Sillitoe with obvious surprise. 'I beg your pardon. I did not realise I was too soon.'

Sillitoe smiled. 'Pray forgive me. Unless you have any objection . . .?'

Herrick, realising there was no choice, said abruptly, 'In that case,' and stood in silence, waiting.

Godschale led on smoothly, 'Please be seated. Some hock perhaps?'

'No thank you, m'lord. I am here to discover satisfaction on the matter of my next appointment.'

Godschale sat down opposite him. He saw the strain, the deep shadows under Herrick's eyes, the bitterness he had already displayed at the court-martial.

'Sometimes it takes longer than usual. Even for flag-officers, the powers in the land!' But Herrick showed no reaction and Godschale's own patience was fast running out. But more than anything, he thought, matters must remain within his grip and control. That was how he had risen to his lofty position, and how he intended to hold on to it.

Herrick leaned forward, his eyes flashing angrily. 'If it is because of the court-martial, then I demand . . .'

'*Demand*, Admiral Herrick?' Sillitoe's incisive voice cut the sultry air like a rapier. 'You had a fair trial, in spite of a lack of reliable witnesses, and your own misguided insistence upon refusing any offer of defence, and circumstances, I believe, were very much against you. Yet still you were found not guilty? I hardly think you are in a position to demand anything!'

Herrick was on his feet. 'I do not have to put up with your comments, *sir*!'

Godschale interrupted, 'I am afraid you do. Even I bow to his authority,' hating the admission which he knew to be true.

Herrick said, 'Then I shall take my leave, my lord.' He turned and added, 'I have my pride.'

Sillitoe said calmly, 'Do sit down. We are not enemies – yet. And please do not mistake conceit for pride, for that is what

101

you have.' He inclined his head with approval as Herrick sat down. 'That is better. I was at the court-martial. I heard the evidence, and I saw what you were trying to do. To have yourself condemned, to absolve yourself of the tragedy – for that was what it was.'

Godschale closed the windows: someone might hear Sillitoe's words. He returned angrily to the table. The little carriage had gone.

'I was prepared for whatever verdict they might present.'

Sillitoe stared at him pitilessly. 'You hold the rank of rear-admiral.'

'I earned it many times, sir!'

'Not without the backing of your captain, who became your admiral, eh?'

'Some.' Herrick was watching like a terrier facing a bull.

'A great deal, as I see it. But you are still only a rear-admiral. You do not have any private means of your own?'

Herrick relaxed a little. This was familiar ground. 'That is true. I have never had things given to me, no family tradition to support *me*.'

Gosdchale said unhappily, 'I think what Sir Paul is trying to say . . .' He fell silent as Sillitoe's eyes flashed towards him.

'Hear me, *if* you please. Article Seventeen clearly states that if found guilty, you would not only have faced the very real peril of execution but more to the point, you would have been, in addition, responsible for reparation to all the ship-owners, merchants and others involved with the convoy. On a rear-admiral's pay – ' His voice was suddenly laced with contempt. 'What sum would you have been able to afford? Twenty ships, I believe? Fully laden with supplies of war, and the men to wage it? How much could you offer to placate all those who would condemn you?' When Herrick said nothing he added, 'Perhaps enough to pay for the horses that died that day.' He got up lightly and crossed to Herrick's seated figure. 'To hang you would have been a stupid gesture of revenge, useless and without value. But the total bill for that whole convoy would have been laid here, at the doors of admiralty.'

Godschale exclaimed thickly, 'My God! I had not considered that!'

Sillitoe eyed him. The glance said, No, obviously not.

Then he waited for Herrick's attention and said in his silky voice, 'So you see, sir, you *had* to be found not guilty. It was . . . more convenient.'

Herrick's hands opened and closed as if he were grappling with something physical.

'But the court would not do that!'

'You turned upon Sir Richard Bolitho, the one man who could have saved your neck. If you had allowed him . . .'

Herrick stared at him, his face pale with disbelief. '*I never needed his help!*'

The door opened and Godschale shouted, 'What the bloody hell do you want? Can't you see we're busy?'

The grim-faced secretary was unmoved by his master's rage. He said, 'This has just been received by telegraph from Portsmouth, my lord. I think you should see it.'

Godschale read through the note, and said after a silence, 'Of all the damnable things to happen.' He handed it to Sillitoe. 'See for yourself.'

Sillitoe felt their scrutiny, Herrick staring without comprehension. Then he looked at the admiral, who gave a despairing nod. He passed the note to Herrick.

Sillitoe said coldly, 'Well, you have nothing more to fear. You will have no more help from that quarter.' And he strode out of the room as if escaping from some contagion.

When Herrick finally put the note on the table he realised that he was alone. Quite alone.

Belinda, Lady Bolitho, paused at the entrance of the elegant square, her parasol raised to protect her complexion from the afternoon sun.

She said, 'Summer again, Lucinda. It seems no time at all since the last.'

Her confidante, Lady Lucinda Manners, gave a quiet laugh. 'Time flies away when one enjoys oneself.'

They walked on, their light gowns floating in the warm breeze.

'Yes, we shall take tea presently. I am quite exhausted by all the shopping.'

They both laughed so that two grooms turned to watch them, and touched their hats as they passed.

Her friend said, 'I am so glad that your Elizabeth is fully recovered. Was her father distressed by her injury?'

Belinda shot her a quick glance. Her best friend, yes; but she knew her other side as well. The wife of an elderly financier, Lady Lucinda was one of the first to spread a rumour or some lively titbit of scandal.

'He paid the fees. It is all I ask.'

Lady Lucinda smiled at her. 'He seems to take care of most things for you.'

'Well, I cannot be expected to pay for everything. Elizabeth's education, her music and dancing lessons, they all mount up.'

'It is such a pity. He is still the talk of London, and *she* flaunts their relationship like some common trollop!' She gave her a sideways glance. 'Would you take him back, if . . .?'

Belinda thought of her confrontation with Catherine in that quiet house in Kent, when Dulcie Herrick had been on the threshold of death. She still shivered when she recalled it. She herself might have contracted the fever. Just to think of such a terrible possibility made all else seem unimportant . . . That thrice-cursed woman, so proud despite her lecherous behaviour. Scornful even when Belinda had lost her own self-control and shouted at her, 'I hope you die!' She had never forgotten Catherine's emotionless response. *Even then, he would not come back to you*.

'Take him back? *I* will choose that moment. I shall not make bargains with a whore.'

Lady Lucinda walked on, partly satisfied. Now she had gleaned the truth. Belinda *would* take him back to her bed no matter what the price. She considered Bolitho when she had last seen him. No wonder the Lady Somervell had dared scandal for him: given a chance, who would not?

'What is he doing now? Do you hear from him?'

Belinda was tiring of her friend's curiosity. 'When he writes to me I burn his letters, without opening them.' But, for once, the lie gave her no satisfaction.

A figure emerged from one of the mews, pushing another on what appeared to be a small trolley. Both wore various oddments of old clothing, but it was obvious that they had once been sailors.

Lady Lucinda put a handkerchief to her face and exclaimed, 'These beggars are everywhere! Why is something not *done* about them?'

Belinda looked at the man on the trolley. He had no legs and was completely blind, his head moving from side to side as his trolley came to a halt. His companion had only one arm, and a scar so deep on the side of his head that it was a marvel he was still alive.

The legless man asked timidly, 'Who is it, John?'

Belinda, who had nursed her previous husband until his death, was shocked nevertheless. Even the man's name. John, like Richard's faithful coxswain, his 'oak', as he called him.

'Two fine ladies, Jamie.' He put his foot on the trolley to prevent it from rolling away and pulled out a cup from his tattered coat.

'A penny, ma'am? Just a penny, eh?'

'Damn their insolence!' Lady Lucinda took her arm. 'Come away. They are not fit to be seen in this place!'

They walked on. The man replaced his cup and patted his friend on the shoulder. He murmured, 'God damn *them*, Jamie.'

The blind man peered round as if to comfort him. 'Never mind, John, we'll get lucky soon, you'll see!'

On the fashionable side of the square Belinda stopped again, suddenly uncertain.

'What is it?'

'I don't know.' She looked back, but the two crippled sailors had vanished; perhaps they had never been there. She shivered. 'He used to tell me about his men. But when you see them, like those two . . .' She turned again. 'I wish now I'd given them something.'

Lady Lucinda laughed and pinched her arm. 'You *are* peculiar sometimes.' Then she gestured at a carriage outside Belinda's house. 'You have visitors. Another reception, and me with nothing new to wear!'

They laughed and Belinda tried to dismiss the man with the outthrust cup from her mind. He had had a tattoo on the back of his hand. Crossed flags and an anchor; it had been quite clear even through the grime.

The door opened before they had even mounted the steps and one of the maids stared at them with relief.

'There be a gentleman here to see you, m'lady!'

Lady Lucinda tittered. 'I told you!'

Belinda silenced her with a quick shake of her head. 'What gentleman? Make sense, girl!'

Someone came from the drawing-room at the sound of her voice and Belinda's heart almost stopped; the stranger wore the uniform of a post-captain, and his face was stern, as if he had been waiting for some time.

'I am sent by Lord Godschale, my lady. I thought it too important to wait for an appointment.'

Belinda walked a few paces to the great staircase and back again. 'If you believe so, Captain.'

He cleared his throat. 'I have to tell you, my lady, that I am the bearer of sad news. The packet *Golden Plover* in which your husband Sir Richard Bolitho was taking passage to Cape Town is reported missing.'

Lady Lucinda gasped, 'Oh, my God. I pray that he is safe?'

The captain shook his head. 'I regret, the vessel was lost with all hands.'

Belinda walked to the stairs and sank down on to them.

'Lord Godschale wishes to offer his sympathy and the condolence of every King's sailor in the fleet.'

Belinda could barely see through the mist in her eyes. She tried to accept it, to imagine it as it must have been, but instead she could only think of the two men she had just turned away. *A penny, ma'am? Just a penny!*

Her friend snapped at the maid, 'Fetch the doctor for her ladyship!'

Belinda stood up very slowly. 'No doctor.' Suddenly she knew; and the shock was overwhelming.

'Was Lady Somervell with him, Captain?'

The man bit his lip. 'I believe so, my lady.'

She saw Catherine in the darkness of Herrick's house, the contempt like fire in her eyes.

Even then, he would not come back to you.

At the end, they had still been together.

8

Breakers

Bolitho sat on the bench below the *Golden Plover*'s stern windows and stared out at the small, bubbling wake. One day passed very like the one before it, and he felt continually restless at being no part of the vessel's routine. It was noon, and on deck the heat would be scorching like the wind across an empty desert. At least down here there was some pretence of movement, the hull creaking occasionally to the lift and fall of the stem, the air stirring through the cabin space to help ease the discomfort.

At the opposite end of the bench young Sophie sat with one shoulder bared while Catherine massaged it gently with ointment she had brought with her from London. The girl's skin was almost red-raw where the sun had done its work during her strolls on deck.

Catherine had told her severely, 'This is *not* Commercial Street, my girl, so try not to lay yourself open to the possibility of being burned alive.'

The girl had given her cheeky grin. 'I clean forgot, me lady!'

Jenour was in his cabin, either sketching or adding to the endless letter to his parents. Keen was probably on deck; brooding about Zenoria, wondering if he were taking the right course of action.

Bolitho had had several conversations with Samuel Bezant, *Golden Plover*'s master. The man came originally from Lowestoft, and had begun life at sea at the age of nine, naturally enough in that port, aboard a fishing lugger. Now that he understood he could speak with Bolitho without fear of instant rebuke or anger he had explained that most of *Golden Plover*'s troubles had been caused by the navy. To begin with, he had welcomed the offer of an admiralty warrant. But as he had explained, 'What use is "protection" if their lordships or some senior officer can take experienced seamen whenever they choose?' Bolitho knew it was useless to try and explain to any master what it was like for the captain of a man-of-war. If the pressgangs were lucky he might get a few good hands; he might even poach some prime seamen from an incoming merchant ship if her master was so mean that he had paid off his company even before the ship had reached her destination. To do so left those unfortunate sailors open to impressment, if the officer in charge of the party was fast enough. But mostly the new hands were either farm workers, 'hawbucks' as most seamen contemptuously called them, or those who might otherwise have faced the public hangman.

Bezant had said on one occasion when Bolitho had joined him to watch the vivid sunset off the Canary Islands, as they had crossed the thirtieth parallel, 'There's only the bosun left from the original afterguard, Sir Richard. Now the second mate's on the Rock I'm expected to run this vessel like a King's ship with men who have no feel for the sea!'

Bolitho asked, 'What about your mate, Mr Lincoln? He seems capable enough.'

Bezant had grinned. 'He's a good seaman. But even he's only been in the *Plover* for six months!'

Perhaps by the time the sturdy barquentine had reached Good Hope Bezant would have led or bullied his mixed collection of sailors into one team, as much a part of the vessel he so obviously loved as the canvas and cordage that drove her.

Bolitho saw a splash as some unknown fish fell back into the sea again, probably trying to escape from hidden predators.

Since leaving Gibraltar there had certainly been a run of misfortunes. A topman had fallen from aloft during a heavy squall and his body had smashed onto the lee bulwark, killing him instantly. He had been buried at sea the following day. Bolitho had never known the man, but as a sailor himself he had felt the same sense of loss as Bezant had rumbled slowly through his well-thumbed prayer book. *We commit his body to the deep . . .*

There had only been one sighting of the strange ship's topmasts, the day after they had weighed anchor in the Rock's shadow. After that they had seen nothing; and only on rare occasions, usually just after dawn, had they seen the hint of land. A group of islands, like low clouds on the horizon, and another time a solitary islet like a broken tooth, which Bezant had described as an evil place where no man could survive and would in any case go mad with loneliness. Pirates had been known to maroon their prisoners there. Bezant had remarked, 'It would have been kinder to cut their throats!'

And all the while there remained the great presence of the African coastline. Invisible out of necessity; and yet each one of them was very aware of it.

Catherine glanced across the girl's reddened shoulder and saw his expression. Separate incidents stood out clearly as she gently massaged the ointment into Sophie's skin, and she wondered if he were sharing them.

The seaman who had fallen from an upper yard during the squall. And that other time when they had been sitting here, everyone unwilling to make the first move to turn in for the night, to be tormented again by the fierce, humid air between decks.

It had been very quiet and quite late, during the middle watch, Jenour had recalled.

They had all heard the sound of dragging feet on the poop overhead and then, it seemed an age later, the frantic cry of 'man overboard!' The master's door had banged open and Bezant had been heard bawling out orders. *Back the fore-tops'l! Stand by to come about! Man the quarter-boat!* Catherine had accompanied Bolitho on deck, astonished by the eerie quality which a full moon had given to the taut canvas and quivering shrouds. The sea, too, had been like molten silver, unending and unreal.

Needless to say, the boat had returned empty-handed. The crew had been more frightened of losing their ship in that strange, glacial glow than of leaving someone to drown alone.

The mate, Lincoln, had been on watch. He explained to the master that he had been told one of the military prisoners was having some kind of fit, to the despair and anxiety of his companions.

Lincoln had described the scene, how out of pity for the prisoner and the need to quieten the others he had had the man brought on deck, thinking it would calm him. What had happened next was not clear. Without even a cry, the prisoner had broken from his escort and hurled himself over the bulwark. He had still been wearing manacles on his wrists, although this had not been reported until after the quarter-boat had been sent on its fruitless search.

Catherine watched Bolitho's hand resting on his thigh. The hand that knew her so intimately, that could tease her to the height of passion until neither could wait.

Then there had been the incident of the flogging, a rare occurrence, she had guessed, aboard the *Golden Plover*. A seaman had been found drunk on watch, and had set about Britton, the boatswain, who had discovered him sprawled in the forecastle when he should have been at his station.

She had seen Keen's face, like a mask as the sound of the lash had penetrated this sealed cabin. Imagining Zenoria as she must have been, enduring the bestiality of the transport's captain and the excitement of many of the prisoners who had swarmed to watch her punishment, the whip laid across her naked back.

She said, 'There you are, my girl.' She smiled as Sophie modestly refastened her clothing. 'Now be off with you and help Ozzard prepare some food.'

Alone with Bolitho Catherine said, 'I love to watch you.'

'Are you bored, Kate?'

'Being with you? Never.'

Bolitho pointed abeam. 'In a few days, if the wind is kind, we shall pass the Cape Verde Islands to starboard, and the coast of Senegal over yonder.' He smiled. 'I doubt if we shall see either!'

'You have memories of these parts, Richard?'

He looked at the blue water astern. 'A few. I was a midshipman at the time in the *Gorgon*, an old seventy-four like *Hyperion*.'

'What age were you?'

She saw the sudden pain in his grey eyes. 'Oh, about sixteen, I think.'

'You were with your friend then?'

He faced her. 'Aye. Martyn Dancer.' He tried to shake it off. 'We were chasing slavers even then. I expect that damnable fortress is still there to this day. Different flag, but the same foul trade.'

The door opened slightly and Ozzard peered in at them. He saw Catherine and was about to withdraw when Bolitho asked, 'What is it? Please speak freely.'

Ozzard tiptoed into the cabin and carefully shut the screen door behind him.

Catherine placed her hands on the sill of the stern window and stared out at the empty ocean. 'I shall not listen, Ozzard.'

Ozzard looked at her body, framed against the sparkling water. Her long dark hair was piled on her head, held in place by a large Spanish comb, 'brailed up' as Allday had called it. He watched her partly-bared shoulder, the fine arch of her neck. It was like being bewitched. Constantly reminded and tortured by that other hideous memory.

He said abruptly, 'I've been in the after hold, Sir Richard. I was getting some of that hock her ladyship brought from London. It stays cool there.'

Bolitho said, 'We shall look forward to it.' He felt the little man's desperation: it was something almost visible. 'And what happened?'

'I heard voices. I found a vent and listened. It was those prisoners. One said, "With that gutless fool out of the way, we can stand together, eh, lads?"' He was reliving his discovery, his face screwed up as if afraid of missing something. 'Then the other man said, "You'll not be sorry. I'll see to that!"'

Catherine did not turn from the ocean but asked gently, 'Who was it? You know, don't you?'

Ozzard nodded wretchedly. 'It was the mate, Mr Lincoln, Sir Richard.'

'Go and find Captain Keen, if you please.' He held out one hand. '*Walk*, Ozzard. We do not want to rouse suspicion, eh?'

As the door closed she moved across the deck and sat by him. 'Did you know, Richard?'

'No. But I did notice that all the incidents happened during either Lincoln's watch or Tasker's.' He was the new mate who had come aboard at Gibraltar.

She felt his hands tighten around her body, pressing the damp skin beneath her gown. She said, 'Have no fear for me, Richard. We have been in peril before.'

Bolitho looked over her shoulder, his mind racing from one possibility to the next. Whichever way you considered it, at best it was mutiny, at worst piracy. Neither crime would permit the survival of witnesses. And there was Catherine.

She said very calmly, 'It is because of me that you are here and not in some King's ship with all the power to do your bidding. Tell me what to expect, but never think of defeat for my sake. I am by your side.' She held the flashing ring to the sunlight. 'Remember what this means? Then so be it.'

When Keen entered he saw nothing untoward until Bolitho said, 'We must talk, Val. I believe there will be an attempt to seize this vessel and then make a rendezvous with our "shadow", which I am convinced is still somewhere close by.'

Keen glanced at Catherine, trying to put her possible fate out of his mind.

'I am ready, sir.' Whatever lay ahead he was surprised to discover that he was unmoved by it.

The following day passed without incident until late in the afternoon. Another hard, cloudless sky, with the sea and the vivid horizon too bright to look at. Bolitho stood with Keen abaft the wheel and watched the slow-moving activity of the watch on deck.

Bezant had taken sun-sights with his sextant and now seemed satisfied with his vessel's progress. The warm north-westerly wind filled every sail, and was strong enough to throw white pellets of spray high over the bowsprit.

'Will you tell him, sir?'

Bolitho glanced toward Catherine and her maid sitting on a makeshift seat beneath a canvas canopy. Sophie knew nothing of their suspicions, and it was better so. And what of Bezant? He had seemed genuinely surprised to discover the status of his passengers when Jenour had gone ahead to inform him at Falmouth. Usually he carried minor officials, garrison officers and sometimes their wives. The vice-admiral and his lady could hardly be classed as ordinary.

'Tell him?' He watched the fish leaping astern. 'When you tell your best friend a secret, Val, it is no longer a secret. And Bezant, capable though he must be, is no friend.'

Keen said evenly, 'Ozzard might have made a mistake. Or perhaps the mate was genuinely trying to calm the prisoners after what had happened.'

Bolitho smiled and saw Catherine look away. 'But *you* do not think so, eh?'

Keen tried not to stare as a seaman paused near them. Every move seemed suspicious. Who was friend or possible enemy?

Bolitho saw Jenour appear from the companionway, his sketching book in his hand.

He crossed the slanting deck and joined them.

'What did you discover, Stephen?'

Jenour shaded his eyes as if to search for some new subject for his collection.

'This vessel was originally pierced for some four-pounders. There is a gunport directly beneath the mizzen chains. Allday found it. He says he can force it open if need be. It's only sealed with tar.'

Keen frowned. 'I do not see the point.'

Bolitho turned aside. They should separate soon. They must not appear to be forewarned conspirators.

'There is a swivel-gun mounted on the starboard bulwark, Val. It is always loaded. Not uncommon in small merchantmen sailing alone. It *could* be trained inboard as well as out.'

Jenour made a few scratches in his book. 'Allday says it would need someone thinner than himself to get through.' He gave an uncertain smile. 'It seems I am exactly the right size!'

More pictures flashed through Bolitho's mind. In his frigate *Phalarope*, where there had once been a mutiny, he could recall a small midshipman named John Neale; Bolitho and some others had covered his naked body with grease to force him through a vent to raise the alarm. John Neale's face changed in the next picture. A young frigate captain, as Adam was now, but dying of his wounds when he and Bolitho had been taken prisoner in France. *We Happy Few*. It seemed to strike back and mock him.

Bolitho said abruptly, 'It may prove to be smoke without fire this time. By tomorrow . . .' With the others he peered up as the masthead lookout yelled, 'Deck there! Sail to th' north!'

Bezant strode over to join them. 'That damned rascal is back with us again!'

'What are your usual duties, Captain?'

He saw Bezant's mind grappling with this new complication. 'Duties, Sir Richard?' He rubbed his chin noisily. 'Gibraltar, then sometimes to Malta with stores and despatches for the fleet there. In better times we used to enter the Baltic, get work from Swedish ports – anything that paid.'

'Could it be that this strange ship waited off Gibraltar to make certain you were not continuing to Malta?'

Bezant stared at him without comprehension. 'For what purpose? I can outsail that bugger once we're clear of Cape Blanco. There's the reef, y'see.'

Bolitho nodded, his eyes slitted against the glare, the injured one already sore and pricking, 'Yes, Captain, the reef. It runs a hundred miles out from Cape Blanco and has torn the guts out of many a fine ship.'

Bezant answered stiffly, 'I am well aware of it, Sir Richard. I intend to change tack and run for the shore once we have weathered the reef.'

Bolitho glanced past him at Keen's intent features. As Bezant stamped resentfully away to examine his chart, he said gently, 'I can tell him nothing.' He heard Catherine laugh, the sound churning through him like pain. 'We must take no chances, Val. There would be none of us left to tell the tale.' He gazed at Catherine so that their eyes seemed to lock across the sun-bleached planking. 'My guess is that Lincoln, and that new mate we took aboard at the Rock – what is his name?'

Keen smiled despite the tension. The admiral asking his flag-captain for information again.

'Tasker, sir.'

'Well, I believe he was already known by *Mister* Lincoln.'

Keen ran his fingers through his fair hair. 'They have probably never carried so much coin and gold before, and they may never be ordered to do so again.' He made up his mind.

114

'It will be tomorrow then. For if Lincoln intends to turn thief and worse, he will need the support of that damned brig to wind'rd of us.'

Jenour wandered away with his book. Like the rest of them, he was unarmed, in his shirt and breeches alone. Any sign of a weapon would cause instant bloodshed.

'Perhaps the people will remain loyal to their master?'

Bolitho clapped his arm so that several faces turned to watched their outwardly casual exchange.

'With the promise of a share of the spoils, Val? Greed is the master here!'

As the sun began to dip over the western horizon the wind became stronger, and reefs were set in the forecourse and topsail. The sea's face broke into long advancing ranks of white horses but as the sun continued to go down, they, too, were painted like molten metal, like the cargo *Golden Plover* carried in her hold.

In the cabin they tried to do everything as usual. Any sign that something was wrong would be like a spark in a gunner's store.

In a dark corner Catherine was pushing some things into two bags, watched with alarm by Sophie.

Catherine had told her quietly, 'There may be trouble, Sophie, but you will be safe. So stay with me until it is over.'

Keen sat at the table playing cards with Yovell. It could not be an easy game. But anyone on watch could see them through the cabin skylight.

Bolitho found Allday breathing heavily in the spare cabin, which was being used for sea-chests and unwanted belongings.

'Here, Sir Richard!' He hauled on a line and Bolitho felt the salt air sweep into the musty space as the disused gunport opened a few inches. He could see moonlight on the tumbling water, hear the creak and clatter of rigging, an occasional call from the helmsman.

A ship already doomed. Bolitho felt a surge of sudden anger. Keen was right. It was tomorrow or not at all. Even Bezant would quickly recognise any further attempts to slow the *Golden Plover*'s progress, and after that it would be too late.

Allday's breathing sounded very loud and unsteady. He said, 'Old Tojohns is castin' a weather eye on the companion ladder, Sir Richard.' He signed and added wistfully, 'I wonder what Jonas Polin's little widow is called? In the heat of things I clean forgot to ask.' He shook his head, 'I am gettin' old, an' that's no error!'

Bolitho reached out in the darkness and seized his massive arm. He could find no words, but each understood the other.

There had been no unusual sound, and he never knew what had roused him to a state of instant readiness. One second he had been dozing in a chair beside Catherine's swinging cot and the next he was wide awake, his ears groping for some clue to the reason.

He moved softly to the door and stared aft through the open screen. The first light of dawn was showing through the stern windows, the blurred horizon like an unending silk thread.

He saw Keen, who had been keeping watch with Tojohns, on his feet; and although his features were lost in shadow Bolitho could sense the presence of danger like some evil spirit right here amongst them.

A pale shape moved from a corner and almost collided with him. He seized her quickly, one hand across her mouth as he said in a sharp whisper, 'Rouse your mistress, Sophie, but not a word!'

Keen took a few paces towards him, keeping well clear of the skylight's pale rectangle. 'What is it, sir?'

'Not sure.' It was hot and clammy in the cabin but the shirt against his spine felt as if it had been drawn across ice.

It was as if the ship had already been abandoned. At some time during the night watches that same evil presence had removed every other living soul, so that the vessel was sailing on with only a phantom to guide her.

The loose flap of canvas and the occasional crack of halliards certainly gave the impression that little heed was being paid to the trim and handling of *Golden Plover*'s progress.

Bolitho felt her come into the cabin, her perfume touching his face as she brushed against him.

She was fully dressed and had replaced the Spanish comb in her hair. He could see it glinting slightly as the light strengthened through the skylight overhead.

Bolitho took her arm as the deck rolled sluggishly in the

swell. He had faced the risk of death and the dread of a surgeon's knife too often not to recognise the lurking fear that attended it. Two men-of-war approaching one another on a converging tack, the sea otherwise empty. Or other vessels scattered in disarray like yeomen on the field of battle, who pause in the bloody business of war to watch their lords and masters kill each other in single combat.

The waiting: *always the waiting*. That was the worst part. Like now. The madness would follow, if only to keep that same mortal fear at bay.

He heard Allday's breathing outside the screen door, where he and Keen's coxswain Tojohns would be watching the companion ladder, waiting perhaps for the stab of a pistol shot, or the stealthy approach of men with blades.

When it came it was both startling and terrible. It was unreal, out of place in this morning watch off the coast of Africa.

There was a sudden crash of glass, and a great, unearthly yell which broke instantly into a torrent of wild and uncontrollable laughter.

Keen exclaimed, 'They've broached the rum!'

A door flung open and they heard Bezant's powerful voice raised in a furious bellow, so loud he could have been here in the cabin.

'You bloody scum! What in hell's name are you doing?'

Somebody else laughed, high-pitched, the cry of one who had already gone beyond reason.

Something heavy, a belaying pin perhaps, clattered across the deck, and Bezant roared, 'Get back, you whore's bastard!' He must have fired a pistol, and as the echo of the shot rebounded from the bulkhead Bolitho heard the laughter change to a terrible scream.

Bezant again, as if with relief. 'Ah, here you are, Jeff!' Then in astonishment, 'In God's name, think what you're doing!' There was another shot, seemingly from high up, and a body crashed across the deck above like a heavy log.

'Ready?' Bolitho took her wrist. 'Don't provoke anyone.' His eyes flashed in the dimness. 'One wrong move . . .' He did not finish it. Someone drove a musket-butt through the skylight and yelled down, 'Come on deck! No trouble, y'hear, or we'll cut you down!'

Bolitho saw Jenour slithering into the unused cabin where Ozzard was already waiting to cover the gunport with some of the stored cabin goods and chests.

Wild thoughts ran through his mind. Suppose Jenour could not get through it? And even if he did, what were his chances?

He saw Allday and Tojohns at the foot of the ladder, the shadows of other figures who were waiting on deck to confront them.

He took Catherine's arm and turned her towards him. 'Remember, Kate, *I love thee.*'

Keen passed them. 'I shall go first, sir.' He sounded completely calm. Like a man facing a firing squad when all hope is gone, and even fear can find no cause to gloat. 'Then we shall know. If I fall, I pray to God that He will protect you both.'

Then he walked to the foot of the ladder and took the handrails without hesitation. He paused just once by the small polished coaming, which was folded back when not in use, but which, in rough weather, was supposed to prevent incoming seas from cascading down the ladder to the deck below. Not even Bolitho saw the deft movement as he touched the butt of the pistol he had lodged there during the night.

On deck, even though it was only dawn, the sight that awaited Keen was as sickening as it was predictable. Bezant the master lying on his side gripping his thigh as blood poured on to the pale planking around him. A corpse sprawled wide-eyed in the starboard scuppers, with a gaping hole in his throat where Bezant's pistol had found its mark. Small groups of men, some armed and threatening the others, the rest staring around as if still expecting to be rudely awakened from a nightmare.

Up in the weather shrouds a man was casually reloading his musket. He must have marked Bezant down the moment he had burst on deck. The mate, Jeff Lincoln, faced Keen, his beefy hands on his hips; there was blood on one sleeve but it was not his own.

'Well, Captain?' He watched him for any hint of danger. 'Are you alone?'

Keen saw the wavering muskets, and more professional

118

handling by men who were obviously the released soldiers. All except one. He sat against the mainmast trunk, crooning to himself and taking long swallows of rum from a stone jug.

Keen said, 'My companions are coming up, Mister Lincoln. If you lay a finger . . .'

Lincoln shook his head. 'You give no orders here, *sir*. I understand you have lately taken a young wife?' He saw Keen flinch. 'So let us not make her a widow so soon, eh?'

There was a lot of laughter, a wild sound: men committed without realising yet what they had done.

Keen regarded them. 'You could still relent. Any court would show mercy under the circumstances.' He did not look at the big, beetle-browed mate. He wanted to strike out at him. Kill him before he himself was hacked down. He continued, 'You know the navy's ways, Mr Lincoln.' He saw the new mate Tasker staring at him, his eyes shifting quickly between them, and continued relentlessly, 'Mutiny is a bad thing, but to seize people as important as my vice-admiral and his lady . . .'

Tasker said hoarsely, 'We didn't know they were going to be aboard!'

Lincoln swung on him and snarled, 'Shut your face, man! Can't you see what this bloody aristocrat is trying to do?' To Keen he said, 'I command here.' He glared at the wounded master. 'If you want to save him, and yourself, lend that old bull a hand!'

Keen knelt down beside the groaning master and tied his neckcloth tightly above the wound. The ball was lodged there, small and deep, and from a musket, so that it had probably deflected against bone.

All these things passed through his mind, but his eyes were on the hatch measuring the distance, one last strike at the enemy if all else failed.

He saw the boatswain, Luke Britton, being supported by two of his men, blood running from his forehead where he had been savagely attacked. At least he had stayed loyal, as were the men around him. Frightened maybe, because mutiny was as much feared as yellow jack. But more so, perhaps, of what would happen to them when they were caught.

The released prisoners were the most dangerous. Men who

knew harsh discipline were usually the first to run wild if that same control was broken. They had nothing to lose but their lives. They had all known that when they enlisted, or had been coaxed into taking the King's shilling in exchange for a brief, drunken taste of freedom.

Lincoln's shadow passed over them. "Ere, fetch a cask!' To Keen he added, 'Get this bugger to sit up beside the wheel. I can keep an eye on him there.'

An unknown seaman shambled aft and shouted, 'He gave me the cat, the bastard! Give him to me, I'll lay his back in ribbons!'

Lincoln faced him with cold contempt. 'Can you navigate these waters, you oaf? You *asked* for that punishment – if the master hadn't ordered it, damn your eyes, I'd have laid into you meself!' The sailor staggered back as if he had been punched.

Everyone fell silent as Catherine and Bolitho came on deck, the maid clutching her mistress's hand while she stared fixedly at the deck. Catherine turned slowly and looked at the watching figures. '*Rabble.*'

Lincoln glared. 'Enough o' that!' He saw Bolitho's old sword at his hip and said, 'I'll have that, if you please.' Something in Bolitho's grey stare must have warned him that his plan might go astray before it had really begun, and he relented. Instead his fist shot out and he seized Sophie's wrist and dragged her to his side where she began to shake like a puppet.

Catherine said, 'Are you so brave?' She gently released herself from Bolitho's restraining grip and stepped towards him. 'If you need a surety, then take a lady, not a child.'

Several of the onlookers laughed, and a soldier yelled, 'An' I'm the next after *you*, matey!'

Catherine forced herself to show no emotion; nor did she look at Bolitho. The least sign, the smallest action and he would lose his self-control. She said, 'Go to Mr Yovell and the others, Sophie. I will remain with this *gentleman*.'

Bolitho stood beside Keen, his mind held in a vice. He said to the groaning Bezant, 'They will kill us – you know that, don't you?'

'I – I don't understand.' He seemed more shocked than angry now that it had happened. 'I've always been a fair man.'

'It's over.' He tightened his hold around Bezant's bulky shoulders and stared hard through the spokes of the wheel. 'You are the only one who can prevent it.' He felt Keen tense suddenly as Lincoln touched one of Catherine's earrings, his thick fingers playing on the edge of her gown and against her skin. Any second now and all reason would go. Not even a mutiny, but brutality and murder at its worst.

He heard her say in reply to something Lincoln had asked or implied, 'I value my life more than precious things.'

The man called Tasker said urgently, 'Tell 'em what to do! They're 'alf-stupid with drink already, God damn them!' He turned on Catherine and said quietly, 'I shall give you a time to remember, my bloody ladyship! I was in a slaver afore this, an' I've learned a trick or two on them long passages with our black ivory!'

Lincoln pushed him aside, angry or jealous at his intrusion, it was hard to tell. All Bolitho could think of was her lovely body in their hands, her despair and agony acting only as encouragement to men such as these.

Bezant took a grip on himself. 'You don't know what you're asking of me. You of all men should know!'

Bolitho stepped away from him and murmured, 'Remember what I said.'

Lincoln stood on a hatch cover, his legs braced against the deck's uneven roll. To one of the soldiers he said, 'Watch our master at the wheel. If I order you to shoot him, then do it. I'll not risk an ounce of gold for a few moments of drunken lechery.' His eyes moved quickly to the woman who stood just below him. He would tame her. She might fight all she could, but he would do it. A creature like her, the kind of woman he had never seen or known in his whole life.

He took a grip on himself. 'Begin hoisting the boxes from the hold.' He pointed at the boatswain with the bleeding wound on his head. 'Take charge of rigging tackles and see to it that each box is secured and guarded.' Again the casual signal to the soldier. 'If he disobeys, kill him!'

Bolitho looked at Allday. 'Bear a hand with the tackles, John.' He spoke easily, seeing the instant anxiety in his eyes. 'It will give you something to do.'

John. He had called him by name. Allday felt it touch him

like a cold hand. In minutes, they could be dead. Or perhaps nothing would happen until rum and the thought of two women in their midst finally broke down the last barricade of Lincoln's control.

Tasker walked to the scuppers and bent over the corpse. After removing a money-pouch from the dead man's belt he gestured with his thumb. 'Over with him!' He did not even turn as the corpse hit the water alongside and drifted rapidly towards the stern. He was still imagining that proud, arrogant woman, just as he had seen the screaming black slave girls when he had turned his men on to them.

Below his feet, Jenour put his weapons on to the deck and peered out through the open gunport. It was all moving too fast; the sea so bright, and so early.

He gave Ozzard a quick nod. The little man was obviously terrified. It seemed suddenly important that he should not leave him without a word, some crumb of support.

'I'll do a sketch of you when this is over, eh?' He touched his shoulder as he had seen Bolitho do so often; the contact he always seemed to need, when people who did not know or understand him thought he wanted for nothing.

Ozzard did not seem to hear. 'Take care, Mr Jenour, sir. We're all very fond of you.'

Jenour stared at him and then began to worm his shoulders through the port. It was not going to be easy. He had never imagined it would be. He looked down and saw the hull's copper sheathing gleam in the frothing water below him, then up to the mizzen chains, and a glimpse of the blocks and tarred cordage beneath the quivering ratlines. The gun was very near there, but as yet out of sight.

He cringed against the warm timbers as a corpse heaved over the bulwark just by the shrouds struck the water beneath him. One flapping hand casually brushed his arm as it dropped past him, and he waited with sick horror for the sound of a shot, or the agonising thrust from one of the boarding pikes he had seen stacked around the mizzen trunk.

He stared down as something glided into the cresting water cut back by the barquentine's raked stem. For only a few seconds he saw the black, empty eyes watching him before the shark turned deftly and plunged after the drifting corpse.

Jenour gritted his teeth and pulled himself to the chains and then swung himself round and up on to the mizzen channel. He waited for an eternity before he dared to raise his head. The bulwark was only feet away – at any moment a curious face might look down and see him. Perhaps, although he had heard no sound, all of his companions had been butchered. He thought of the letter which was still unfinished, the sketches his family in Southampton would never see. He felt his eyes smarting; his body was shaking, so that he had to force himself to look directly down again into clear water. There were two sharks now. He gave a quick sob. They would not have long to wait. He whispered, 'God bless you!' He did not know to whom.

On deck, the first of the heavily-barred boxes was swayed up into the full view of the expectant mutineers. They gave a wild cheer, and more rum was already being broached from the other hold.

Catherine saw some of the men watching her and looked away, her eyes meeting with Bolitho's as if to some unspoken word.

His eyes moved, just once, and she turned her head very slightly. She felt her heart pounding, and put her hand to her breast. She had seen what Bolitho had intended: Jenour's grimy, bloodied fingers feeling up for the lower ratlines, while directly beneath the mounted swivelgun two of the armed seamen were resting in the shade. At any second Jenour might make some sound and bring them down on him.

Lincoln swallowed a mug of rum and gasped noisily, his reddened eyes on the hand against her breast.

'That should be my place, *my lady!*'

She turned aside and reached up to adjust her piled hair.

She felt his breath, stinking of rum, smelt the dirt and sweat of his body as he gripped her waist and stared wildly at the shadow between her breasts.

It was all she could do to look at him as she felt his hands moving on her body.

Then she said, 'I must loosen my hair!'

If she thought of Bolitho now, all would be lost.

Deftly she pulled the long comb from her hair and even as it tumbled over her shoulders, she raised the comb and drove it into Lincoln's eye.

He fell backwards, screaming, the decorated comb protruding from his eye like an obscene growth.

Someone dropped a musket and it exploded, so that men who had been yelling and running for weapons froze in their tracks and watched with sick disbelief while Lincoln rolled on his back, his heavy seaboots drumming on the deck while his blood encircled his agony.

Tasker, the new mate who had once been a slaver, dragged out his pistol and shouted, 'Leave him! Take the others below and shackle them, 'til we can deal with 'em properly!'

He looked at the tall, dark-haired woman who, despite the levelled weapons, had walked to Bolitho's side.

Tasker laughed. 'That pig-sticker of a sword won't help you now, Admiral!'

Bolitho gripped his sword, but felt only her arm against his side. He was even surprised at the unemotional tone of his voice, when just an instant ago he had been about to throw himself to her defence.

He said, 'Help is here *now*.' He saw Tasker's astonishment as he slipped the old sword back into its scabbard, then watched it change to stunned understanding as the swivel-gun swung inboard and was depressed on to the bulk of the mutineers.

Allday had torn a cutlass from one of the sailors guarding the loyal hands and now ran aft, bending almost double in case Jenour should jerk the lanyard and rake the deck into a bloody shambles with a full charge of canister.

Bolitho shouted, 'Throw down your arms! In the King's name – or I swear to God I will order my lieutenant to fire!'

Keen stood up from the companionway and cocked his hidden pistol. Tojohns had also produced a pair from another hiding place.

Keen found time to notice Bolitho's voice, the intensity of his stare, recalling the moment when he had ordered them to continue pouring broadsides into the enemy that had destroyed *Hyperion* in another sea.

If they do not strike they will die! He was still not sure whether Bolitho would have continued to fire if the French flags had not come down.

He had that same expression now.

The men on deck stared at one another, some probably already planning how they would defend their actions by pleading that they had intended to overthrow the mutineers. A few of the loyal men wondering, perhaps, how their circumstances might have indeed changed had they thrown in their lot with the others. Gold to keep them free of danger and want, the rigours of the common seaman.

There was one man in the ship who had not been consulted or threatened either way, nor even considered when the others had been fanned into an uprising.

He was a seaman from Bristol by the name of William Owen, who had been aloft in the crosstrees, the first masthead lookout at the start of this new and terrible day.

Throughout the fighting on deck, he had witnessed the astounding sight of his messmates turning upon one another after the master had been shot down and the military prisoners released; then, it seemed, in the twinkling of an eye, the roles had been reversed. He had seen the admiral's lady, her bearing defiant even from this high perch, and had sensed the seething cauldron of mutiny as more and more rum had flung reason to one side. Now, his hands shaking badly, he twisted round and peered across the quarter for the other ship's topsails. He rubbed his eyes as relief flooded through him. He was safe, and the other vessel was stern-on as she went about on an opposite tack.

Safe. He had taken part in nothing. He had been doing the job he knew best, for Owen was the most experienced lookout in the *Golden Plover*'s company.

He shaded his eyes again and stared until they watered. He knew all the signs but had never before witnessed it, and he had been at sea for fifteen years.

Stretching away beyond the bows, it made the sea change colour without breaking the surface. Like fast-moving smoke, or steam from a kettle, as if the sea were boiling in its depths . . .

He leaned over and peered down at the deck, his voice carrying above all else. The cruelty and the greed were forgotten.

'*Deck there! Breakers ahead!*'

9

Abandon

Bolitho seized Catherine's arm and said, 'That was a brave deed, Kate! But for you Stephen would have been seen, and everything lost with him!'

She stared at him, her eyes very wide, as if she too were trying to grapple with the speed of their changing circumstances; the crushing blow from the masthead lookout. *Breakers ahead*.

She said, 'I would *kill* for you.' She stared across at the place where Lincoln had fallen, his face mercifully hidden as his blood continued to run down the deck and into the scuppers.

Bolitho peered up at the masthead lookout. 'Fetch that man down!' There was so much he needed to know and do, and yet he could not leave her. He could feel the pretence through her arm, the taut muscles hardening as she fought to retain control. She said suddenly, 'Do as you must. I will be all right . . . no matter what.'

Bolitho spoke to Keen. 'Muster the hands. I want the vessel lightened as much as possible.' He pointed at the two boats on their small tier; each was filled to the thwarts with water to prevent their seams opening in the sun's glare. 'Empty them, and have them lowered immediately. They can be towed with the quarter-boat.' He saw Jenour wrapping a rag around one hand where he had torn it on the corroded metal of the chains in his frantic climb from the gunport. 'Stephen! All guns over the side! Either way, we'll not be needing them now.' He saw

Jenour's eyes move to the swivel, his swivel, and added, 'That one too.'

A man slithered down a stay and stood awkwardly before him.

'I'm the lookout, sir.' He knuckled his forehead. 'That brig 'as put about – she'll be waitin' for us when we weather the reef.'

Bolitho said, 'Owen, isn't it?'

The seaman stared at him. 'Well . . . aye, Sir Richard, that be m'name!'

'Go with the other loyal men. There is much to do, and few to do it.'

Allday called, 'The master wants a word, Sir Richard!'

Bolitho stooped by the wounded man. 'What went wrong?'

'I intended to cut it as fine as prudent, Sir Richard.' Bezant's eyes rolled in pain as he stared at the swaying compass. 'But the wind's backed a piece . . . unusual hereabouts.'

He looked like death, Bolitho thought desperately. His normally reddened features were ashen, his breathing slow and uneven. And despite all that had happened in so short a time, he had managed to notice the shift of wind; it was rising too, flinging spray over the men who were already draining out the two boats.

Bezant was saying, 'There be one way through the reef. I done it afore in the old *Plover*, a year or so back.' The memory gave him sudden strength and he shouted at the prisoners and mutineers alike who were standing under guard, as shocked, it seemed, as anyone by what had happened. 'That was afore you murderin' scum were aboard! By God, I'll be there to watch you dance on air, you cowardly bastards!'

He saw Catherine and gasped, 'Beggin' yer pardon, m'lady!'

Catherine was looking at the dark blood on her gown and shuddered.

'Save your strength, Captain.' But her eyes told Bolitho how near she had been to collapse.

Bolitho saw Allday stand back from one of the hoisting tackles and gasp with pain while he massaged his chest. *Not him too* . . .

He called, 'Take over the helm, Allday.' He saw the protest. 'No arguments this time, old friend!'

127

Bezant dragged a telescope from the rack, and while two men held him steady he levelled it towards the distant cloud of drifting spray.

'Steer sou'-east-by-south. Close to the wind as she'll hold.'

Bolitho said, 'We must shorten sail.' He tried not to hurry the wounded man, but time was too valuable to waste. 'What say you?'

Bezant gasped and nodded gratefully as Ozzard tilted a mug of brandy against his mouth.

Then he said thickly, 'Jib an' fore tops'l, driver too. With this wind, I'm not sure of anythin'!'

Bolitho saw Keen watching him, his fair hair rippling in the freshening wind. 'You heard that, Val?'

'Leave it to me.' He turned to seek out the boatswain. 'The guns are gone – boats as well.' He glanced meaningly at the first crates of gold, which had been hoisted on deck by the jubilant mutineers.

Bolitho said, 'That too.' He heard yells of protest from Tasker and shouted back at him, '*It all goes*, or we'll end up on the reef!' He gestured with the pistol he had been holding since Jenour's appearance by the swivel-gun. 'One word out of you, and I'll have you run up to the fore-yard, *here* and *now*!'

He turned away, sickened by what had happened, by the knowledge that he would shoot the man down himself without waiting for any hangman's halter.

He said harshly, 'Put an armed man in the hold with them. Then start hoisting the gold on deck.' He touched Keen's arm. 'If we can ride this out, Val, we can still shake off that brig and run for the mainland.'

Carrying less canvas, the *Golden Plover*'s pace slowed considerably. But the motion was more violent, and men fell cursing as water boiled over the gunwale, or flooded amongst them to dislodge their hold.

He saw Catherine by the companionway speaking urgently to her maid and Ozzard. He called, 'Keep away from the bulkheads – there may be some men in hiding. No risks, Kate!'

Their eyes met again; for mere seconds it was as if nobody else were near. Then she was gone.

Keen came aft, pushing his fingers through his dripping hair. 'All secured, sir. But she'll not come closer to the wind. If it dropped – well, that might be different.'

There was a piercing scream, which stopped almost instantly as if shut off by an iron door.

Then there were more shouts from the hold and one of the mutineers appeared on the coaming, his eyes wild with fear as he clawed his way in to the sunlight.

He shouted, 'I'm not waitin' to go down with the ship! I'll take me chances with . . .'

He got no further but fell back down the ladder, the sunlight glinting briefly on the knife that had been flung from below, and which protruded between his shoulders.

Bolitho walked to the hold and saw Britton, the boatswain, levelling a musket in case someone tried to rush the ladder.

Bolitho called, 'Don't be fools!' Even in the brisk wind he could smell the heady aroma of rum. They were mad with it. Men without hope who still saw the crated gold as a chance of heaven.

Tasker shouted, 'Don't try to bluff us! That bloody Bezant knows this reef well. He'd not run his precious ship aground to get revenge!'

Bolitho said nothing. It was becoming more futile by the minute, and when he glanced aft he saw Allday, who was clinging to the spokes with another man, give a quick shake of the head. *Golden Plover* was not responding; the pressure of wind in her scanty canvas and the fierce undertow near anything like the Hundred Mile Reef were too much for her.

The hatch across the hold was slammed shut, and he thought he heard wild laughter as they wedged it from below. It would be the richest coffin of all time, he thought. There was nothing else to jettison that would, or could, make a difference.

He said, 'Put that man Owen in the chains and start sounding, Val.'

He covered his right eye with his hand and stared up at the whipping masthead pendant. He almost cried out aloud. His other eye had misted over completely, and felt raw and painful with salt.

In the pitching cabin Catherine stared round at the chaos of scattered chairs and fallen books. She recognised some of

Bolitho's Shakespeare and wanted to gather them up. Through the stern windows she saw the endless array of surging white horses, felt the rudder thudding violently as if to tear itself away. She clenched her fists and closed her eyes tightly against the fear. Now she was *needed*, needed more than ever before.

Then she looked at Sophie, who was cowering by the screen door, her naked terror barely under control.

She said, 'Help Ozzard carry those bags to the companionway.' She waited for her words to sink in. '*No* . . . wait a minute.' She groped in one of the bags and pulled out a clean pair of white breeches and one of Bolitho's shirts, which Ozzard had been pressing yesterday. Was it only yesterday?

She said, 'Go on deck now.'

Sophie gasped in a small voice, 'Are we going to die, me lady?'

Catherine smiled, even though her mouth and lips were as dry as dust.

'We are going to be ready, my girl.' She saw her nod as she replied with an attempt at courage, 'I wish we was at 'ome, me lady!'

Catherine took several deep breaths and turned away, so that Sophie should not see her despair.

Then, very deliberately she unfastened her gown and stepped out of it, letting it fall with her petticoats until she was quite naked, standing in the watery glare like some goddess in a pagan ceremony. She pulled on the white breeches and Bolitho's shirt and tied her hair back from her face with a piece of dark red ribbon, and gathered up the petticoats, folding them under her arm; she knew enough about wounds to recognise that Bezant was in serious trouble and would need bandages. As she kicked off her thin shoes one fell on to the gown where Lincoln's blood still shone as if it were alive. It was only then that she felt the knot of vomit in her throat and knew she could contain it no longer.

She found little Ozzard crouching on the companion ladder, with a satchel hung over his shoulder. He knew. He had been with the others in *Hyperion* when she had finally gone down . . . who would know better than he?

'Thank you for waiting for me.' She saw him glance at her bare legs and feet and somehow sensed that he had been watching her, had seen her naked against the stern windows. It did not seem to matter now.

She gripped the handrail and paused as someone called from the fore-chains, '*No bottom*, sir!' The leadsman's voice, carried on the wind, made her skin chill. Like a spirit from hell.

'What does it mean?'

Ozzard came out of his thoughts. 'Means we're in plenty of water, m'lady.' He shook his head. 'Early days yet.'

Bolitho turned as she climbed on to the wet planking. She waited for the deck to fall again and let it carry her to his side.

'I took these from your bag, Richard. This is no place for gowns and pretty tea-cups!'

Keen watched, and shook his head as Bolitho held her for a few moments. Then he heard her laugh and thought Bolitho used the word *entrancing*. He saw Jenour staring too, so absorbed that he was probably wishing he had his sketch book.

Bezant groaned, 'Not long now. If only I had the *feel* of her!'

Allday put his weight on the spokes and felt the vessel fighting wind and sea and him all at the same time. He stared hard at the leaping line of breakers, the occasional gaps in between. He heard drunken laughter from the sealed hold and envied them the rum. *Just one mug before she strikes*. He gritted his teeth and thought of the woman he had rescued on the road. *And strike she will.*

He glanced at Bolitho and his lady and felt the old despair closing in. *Always the pain.* Ships gone, old faces wiped away. He had always trained himself to accept it when it eventually found him. But not like this. For nothing . . .

Keen walked past, his shoes skidding on the streaming deck.

Allday heard him say to Bolitho, 'I've told the bosun what to expect, sir. He will take the cutter and follow us. We will have the smaller boat. Once clear of the reef, things might be easier.'

Bolitho kept his voice low. 'So you think there's no hope of finding this passage?'

Keen stared back at his level grey eyes, and did not even flinch as the lookout yelled, 'By th' mark *seventeen*!'

'Do *you*, sir? It's shoaling already. Without the gold to weigh us down . . .' He shrugged. It did not need any words.

Bolitho jerked his head towards the hold. They were still shouting and laughing like lunatics. But surely Tasker or one of the ringleaders would know and understand?

'*By th' mark ten!*' God, they were as close as that. He looked at the boatswain and his companions. Staring about, not knowing what to do. Their own master barely able to pass his instructions to Allday, another blinded and probably dead, while the third had locked himself below with the gold. At any second they might panic and rush to the boats.

He shouted, '*Mr Britton!* If we abandon you must stay near to the jolly-boat. Once away from the reef we can make sail and work clear.' He smiled across at Catherine in her breeches and frilled shirt. 'Now that we have an extra sailor amongst us, we should be in safe hands!'

For a few seconds nobody moved or spoke, and Bolitho thought he had failed. Then Britton, his head wound seemingly cleansed by the drenching spray, yelled, 'Our Dick'll do it, lads! *Huzza!*'

The lookout William Owen, who was also an excellent leadsman, swung the line round and round, up and over his shoulder before allowing the heavy fourteen-pound lead to fly ahead of the bows.

Afterwards, he was certain that he had seen the reef rising to meet them even as the lead struck at just over keel-depth, and he yelled, '*By th' mark three!*' But it was all in seconds. The towering wall of spray lifting and bursting over the bowsprit in the cruel sunshine, then the first awful shuddering crash as they struck. Owen fought his way out of his leadsman's apron and flung himself down even as a great shadow plunged past and hurled splinters and flapping canvas in all directions: the *Golden Plover*'s foretopmast, with clattering blocks and rigging, thundering over the side. Someone was crying out but Owen knew it was his own voice he heard, as he ducked and dodged another great mass of falling rigging.

He stared wildly aft and saw that they had managed to free the flapping driver, which had added to their thrust into the reef. But the great swell lifted the hull easily and allowed it to fall again with a second sickening crash.

Owen ran towards the only sign of order and discipline, where men clung to broken cordage and bowed down under the great sweeping onslaught of water over the side, and stared dazedly at the tall figure all in white by the wheel before his reeling mind told him it was the admiral's lady. He saw Bolitho too, one arm pointing at the hold where another seaman was banging on the hatch with a pistol butt.

Bolitho looked at Bezant who was being half-carried to the side, to which the boats had been warped in readiness.

He said, 'You tried. We all did. It was not enough.' He had to make this wounded, stricken man understand. Accept it. The deck felt steadier except for the violent surge of undertow. But at any moment she might slide off. There would be no hope for any of them. He rubbed his injured eye and did not hear her call out, in the din of wind and waves, for him to stop.

He watched them lower Bezant over the side and then joined Catherine by the motionless wheel. The ship was already breaking up, and he could hear the sea booming into the foreward hold, smashing down anything that barred its way.

Allday shouted, 'Here come the rats!'

Some of the mutineers and the released soldiers were pulling themselves on deck, staring around with disbelief or madness. Tojohns pointed his pistols and roared, 'You bastards can take the quarter-boat!'

Keen said, 'Abandon, sir?' He spoke quietly, his voice almost drowned.

Bolitho gripped Catherine's arm and dragged her to the side. The boatswain's cutter had already cast off, the oars thrashing in confusion until some sort of order and timing came into play.

The jolly-boat, a small eighteen-foot cutter, was rising and dipping wildly directly below the bulwark. Bezant had been lashed in the sternsheets, and Jenour was already loosening the oars. Such a small boat, he thought, against such a mighty sea.

She clutched him, hard. *'Don't leave me.'*

He held her face against his as he lifted her over the side and down to Allday and Yovell. 'Never!'

Then he turned and looked at the rum-crazed fools who were dragging great bags of gold across the deck. They did not even appear to see him. He swung himself over the side and instantly felt the jolly-boat veer away, with a clatter of looms as each man tried to find his rowlock in the confusion.

Allday croaked, 'Mainmast's a-comin' down, Sir Richard!'

It was difficult to see what happened through the leaping, blinding spray, but they all heard the crash of splintering planking as the main topmast sliced down and across the quarter-boat.

The lookout, Owen, dug his feet into the wooden stretchers and lay back on his oar with all his strength. He was glad that the women were in the sternsheets and did not see what was happening. The swell eased very slightly so that the spray parted across the passage old Bezant had been heading for. The *Golden Plover* was now quite mastless and leaning over on her side; the boat which had been smashed by falling spars had vanished, but the frothing water told its own story. Instead of gold from the high sun, it was bright red, and the sea was churning with great, flashing bodies as the sharks tore into the attack.

Bolitho saw Allday grimace as he heaved on his oar, and called, 'Lay aft, Allday. We need a good cox'n today!'

He looked at their stricken faces. All sailors hated leaving their ship. The sea was the constant enemy, and their future was unknown.

Bolitho clambered over to take Allday's oar and called out, 'You know what they say, lads? Only one thing more useless in a boat than a harpsichord, and that's an admiral!'

Nobody laughed, but he saw her watching him while she stooped to bale water from beneath the gratings.

Jenour pulled at his oar, the unaccustomed motion tearing at his cut fingers. *They were still together*, more than he had dared to hope. He felt his beautiful sword rubbing his hip. All that he had with him. Even his sketches had been in his sea-chest.

Someone gasped, 'There she goes, lads!'

Bezant began to struggle. 'Help me up, damn you! *Must see!*'

Allday laid his arm on the tiller bar but reached out with the other to calm the man. 'Easy, matey. You can't help her now.'

With a roar and in a great welter of spray, the *Golden Plover* slid from the reef and vanished.

The jolly-boat seemed to slide through the turbulent water and then settle again, her oars rising and falling to carry her away.

Bolitho tried to gauge the sun's position but his eye was too painful.

Two things were uppermost in his aching mind.

They were through the reef and into calmer water. And they were quite alone.

The big grey house below Pendennis Castle seemed cool and refreshing after the heat of late afternoon. The girl loosened the ribbons of her wide straw hat and allowed it to fall on her shoulders, to lie across her long, sun-warmed hair.

How quiet the house was. She guessed that Ferguson and his wife and the servants were probably having a meal before evening church; in the meantime she had enjoyed the peace of her walk along the cliffs and down the steep track to the little curving beach where she liked to look for shells. Ferguson had warned her about the cliff path and she had listened dutifully to his advice, all the while thinking of Zennor, where she had been born. After those cliffs this walk had been easy.

Because it was Sunday she had barely seen anyone except a coastguard who had been peering out across the shimmering bay through his long brass-bound telescope. He was friendly enough, but Zenoria felt they were all watching her whenever she went into town. Curiosity perhaps, or was it the usual suspicion cherished by the Cornish for 'strangers', even those from a different part of the same county?

This house, too. She crossed to a small table, the wood of which was so dark with age and polishing it could have been ebony. She watched her hand as she placed it on the great family Bible, and saw the wedding ring with something like surprise. Would she never get used to it? Might things never change, so that she would never be able to give freely of the love Valentine needed from her?

She opened the massive brass locks and raised the cover. Like the house, so much history. It was somehow awesome – frightening, she thought.

They were all there, written in by hands unknown. A family's record, like a roll of honour. She gave a small shiver. It was as if the same portraits that matched these names were watching her, resenting her intrusion.

Captain Julius Bolitho who had died a young man of thirty-six. She felt the strange apprehension again. Right here in Falmouth during the Civil War, trying to lift the Roundhead blockade. She had seen the castle this afternoon, hunched on the headland. It was still a place of menace.

Bolitho's great great grandfather, Captain Daniel, who had fallen fighting the French in Bantry Bay. Captain David, killed fighting pirates in 1724, and Denziel, the only one until Sir Richard to gain flag rank. She smiled at the way she had come to absorb and understand the terms and the traditions of the navy.

And Bolitho's father, Captain James, who had lost an arm in India. She had studied his portrait closely, seen the family likeness found once more in Bolitho. Her mind seemed to hesitate, like guilt. In Adam too.

And now a separate entry in Sir Richard's own sweeping hand, on the occasion when Adam's name had been changed to Bolitho, asserting his right to all that he would one day inherit. On the same page Bolitho had also written, 'To the memory of my brother Hugh, Adam's father, once lieutenant in His Britannic Majesty's Navy, who died on 7th May 1795. The Call of Duty was the Path to Glory.'

Zenoria closed the Bible with great care, as if to keep its memories undisturbed.

And what of the women? Waiting for their men to return, wondering every time, perhaps, if this parting was the last one?

Zenoria thought of her husband and tried to discover her innermost feelings. She had been unable to give him what he truly deserved. She was not even certain that she loved him. Adam had made it clear that he thought she had married Keen out of gratitude for what he had done to save her person and restore her good name. Was that all it had been, then – gratitude? Did Valentine really understand what it had been like for her; why she was incapable of any sexual response after what had happened to her? When he had entered her she had wanted more than anything to please him.

Instead she had felt pain, terror, revulsion; and had expected him to lose patience, to thrust her away in disgust, to behave with brutality. But he had done nothing: he had accepted it, and blamed himself. *Perhaps when he came back* . . . How many times had that gone through her mind? It was torture, so that as the weeks had dragged past she had almost come to dread their reunion.

If Catherine had been here, it might have been different. She would have been compassionate; she might have had wisdom to offer. Zenoria turned and stared around the big room. *I must keep faith with him.* She imagined she could hear the words rebounding from the cool stone.

There was a sound of horses in the stable yard. Matthew perhaps, getting a carriage to take Ferguson and his wife down to church. She stiffened. No, not horses, just the one, and from the clamour of its stamping hooves it was difficult to calm and must have been ridden hard. A visitor then.

Then she heard Ferguson's voice, hushed, hesitant, so that she could not grasp the sense of his words. Someone came around from the courtyard, and disappeared towards the front of the house; there was no mistaking the gold lace and cocked hat, the jingle of the sword Adam always wore.

She touched her breast and felt herself flush. But he was supposed to be at Plymouth now . . . She glanced at herself in the mirror and was dismayed to see the sudden pleasure in her eyes.

The outer doors opened and closed and she turned to face him as he came in.

'You surprise me again, Captain Adam, *sir*!' He ignored her teasing humour. She felt her body chill in spite of the warmth. 'What is it, Adam? Are you in trouble?'

He did not speak but threw his hat on to a chair; she saw the dust on his boots, the leather stains on his breeches, evidence of the haste of his journey.

He placed his hands on her shoulders and gazed at her for what seemed like an age.

Then he said quietly, 'I am the bearer of bad news, Zenoria. Try to be strong, as I have tried to be since I was told of it.'

She did not resist as he pulled her gently against him. Later she was to remember the exact moment, and knew it had not been out of tenderness but the need to hide from her face while he told her.

'It is reported that the barquentine *Golden Plover*, while on passage to Cape Town, struck a reef off the west coast of Africa.'

She could hear the hard, fast beating of his heart against her cheek. He continued to speak in the same empty voice. 'A small Portuguese trader was stopped by one of our ships. It told them the news.' He paused, counting the seconds as a good gunner will measure the fall of shot. 'There were none saved.'

Only then did he release her and walk blindly to one of the portraits. Probably without knowing what he was doing his fingers touched the old family sword in the painting. Now it would never be his.

'Is it certain, Adam?'

He turned lightly, as he always did. 'My uncle is the best seaman I have ever known. The fairest of men, loved by all who tried to know him. But . . . she was not *his* ship, you see?'

She tried, but she did not understand. All she knew was that her husband, who had given her everything, was now only another memory. Like all those who haunted this house, and were named in their roll of honour.

Adam said, 'I have asked Ferguson to tell the servants. I did not . . . feel capable. By this time tomorrow, all Falmouth will know.' He thought suddenly of Belinda. 'As all London knows now.'

He seemed to reconsider her question. 'There is always hope. But it may be unwise to dream too much.' He faced her again, but seemed distant, unreachable.

'I have called for a fresh horse. I must ride to the squire's house without delay. I would not want Aunt Nancy to hear it on the wind like common gossip.' For the first time he showed his emotion. 'God, she *worshipped* him.'

Zenoria watched his distress with pain. 'Adam – what must I do?'

'*Do?*' He wiped his face with the back of his hand. 'You must remain here. He would have wished it.' He hesitated, realising what he had said, and what he had omitted. 'So would your husband. I am sorry . . . I will ask Mrs Ferguson to keep you company.'

A horse was being led into the yard, but there were no voices.

'Please come back, Adam. Neither of us must be alone.'

He looked at her steadily. 'I liked your husband very much. I also envied him to an unhealthy degree.' He came to her again and kissed her forehead very gently. 'I still do.'

Then he was gone and she caught sight of Bolitho's one-armed steward standing out in the dusty sunshine, staring at the empty road.

She was suddenly alone, and the pain of bereavement was unbearable.

She cried out, 'Are you all satisfied now, damn you? There he rides, the last of the Bolithos!' She stared about her, blinded by hot, unexpected tears. '*Is that what you wanted?*'

But there was only silence.

She did not know what time it was or how long she had managed to sleep; it was as if someone had spoken her name. She slipped out of bed and moved to the window. The night was warm, and a bright half-moon spilled a glittering silver cloak down from the horizon until it was lost beneath the headland.

She leaned further from the window so that her robe slipped from one shoulder, but she did not notice it, nor think of the livid scar which was revealed there. A mark of endurance, but to her it was a mark of shame, of sick humiliation.

She could smell the land, the sheep and cattle, and thought of the ideas Catherine had shared with her, plans which would have brought life back to the estate.

Then she heard it; not words but something else, a soul in pain. She glanced round in the darkness. She had not heard Adam return, and had imagined him to be passing the night at Roxby's house.

The next moment she was on the big landing, her bare feet soundless on the rugs, her candle lighting up each stern face on the wall: ships burning, men dying, and Bolitho's own words in the Bible as every portrait slid away into the shadows.

Adam was sitting at the table, his face buried in his arms, sobbing as if his heart were breaking. His hat and sword and the coat with its gleaming lace were flung across a chair, and there was a smell of brandy in the air.

He looked up sharply and saw her with the outstretched candle. 'I – I did not mean to wake you!'

Zenoria had never seen a man cry before, and certainly not from such depths.

She whispered, 'Had I known I would have come earlier.' She saw his hand hesitate over the brandy and added, 'Take some. I think I might quite like a little myself.'

He wiped his face roughly and brought another goblet, and watched her as she placed the candle on the table and curled up on the rug in front of the black, empty grate. As he passed he lightly touched her hair as he might a child's. He stood looking at the Bolitho crest and fingered the carving, as others had done before him.

'What happened?' Zenoria felt the brandy searing her throat. She had only tasted it once before, more as a dare than for any other reason.

'The squire was very kind to me.' He shook his head, as if still dazed by what had happened. 'Poor Aunt Nancy. She kept asking me how it must have been.' He gave a great sigh. 'What could I tell her? It is a sailor's lot. Death can lie on every hand.' He thought suddenly of Allday and his quaint comments. 'An' that's no error,' as his old friend would have said. Thank God they had been together, even to the end.

He said abruptly, 'I am no company, dear Zenoria. I had better leave.'

She leaned over to replace the goblet and heard him exclaim, 'What is *that*? Did they do this to you?'

She covered her bared shoulder as he dropped on his knees behind her; he carefully moved her hair to one side and felt her tremble as light played on the top of the scar.

'I would kill any man who laid a finger on you.'

She tried not to flinch as he lowered his head and kissed the scar. Her heart was beating so hard she thought it would alarm the whole house. But she felt no fear; where there had been disgust, there was only an awareness which seemed to consume her completely. She could not even resist as he kissed her shoulder once again, and touched her neck with his lips. She felt him pulling at the cord around her shoulders, and only then did she attempt to fight it.

'Please, Adam! *You must not!*'

But the robe fell about her waist and she felt his hands caressing her as he kissed the terrible scar that ran from her right shoulder to her left hip.

With tender strength he laid her down and gazed at her body, pale as marble in the filtered moonlight, and his hands gave persuasion to what they both now realised was unstoppable, as it had been inevitable.

She closed her eyes as he held and imprisoned her wrists above her head, and heard him whisper her name again and again.

She waited for the pain, but she returned his kiss even as he entered her and they were joined.

Later he carried her upstairs to her room and sat near her, watching her until the sun began to drive away the shadows.

Only then did he finish his brandy and leave the room.

The candle had long been gutted when the first sunlight touched the big room and lingered on the family Bible, with its memories of dead heroes and the women who had loved them.

They were all ghosts, now.

10

Poor Jack

To anyone unused to the sea's ways its sudden change of mood, which had followed the jolly-boat's precarious passage through Hundred Mile Reef, was impossible to believe. The squall had departed and had not returned, and the vastness of this great ocean stretched away on every bearing, unbroken, and in the noon sunshine, like blinding glass.

Bolitho climbed forward into the bows where a small canvas awning had been rigged to provide the barest of privacy for the two women. Catherine was waiting for him there, her borrowed shirt dark with sweat, her forehead showing signs of sunburn as she watched him over the slumped shoulders of the resting oarsmen.

She took his hand and guided him down to the bottom boards so that he could rest his back against the curved side.

'Let me see.' She held his face in her hands and gently prised open his left eyelid. Then she said, 'I'm going to put a bandage over it, Richard.' She kept her voice very low so that nobody else could hear. 'You must rest it.' She looked aft where Allday sat at the tiller, as if he had never moved. She had to give herself time, so that she would reveal no despair to Richard. Three days since the *Golden Plover* had slid from the reef. Hours of work on the oars, and rigging the solitary mast and sail to stand away from the reef's fierce undertow, and set some sort of course for the mainland. For all they had seen or done they might have remained stationary. She tried to picture how this small, eighteen-foot craft would appear to an onlooker, had there been one, while it rode sluggishly to a canvas sea-anchor and the men rested. Probably like a crumpled leaf on an immense, motionless lake. But here, in the boat's over-crowded interior, it was something very different. Apart from the seaman named Owen, who had been the masthead lookout at the time of the mutiny, there were two other hands from the doomed *Golden Plover*: Elias Tucker, a frightened youth who came originally from Portsmouth, and Bill Cuppage, a hard man in every sense, with a harsh northern accent. Including the wounded Bezant, who hovered between delirium and bouts of agonised groaning, there were thirteen souls in all.

She raised a length of dressing cut from a petticoat and tied it carefully across his forehead to cover his salt-reddened eye.

Bolitho touched it and exclaimed, '*Water!* You've used fresh water, Kate!'

She pulled his hand away. 'Rest a little. You cannot do everything.'

He lay back while she slipped her arm beneath his head. Her words had reminded him of Admiral Godschale. What might he be doing now, with *Golden Plover* probably reported missing? He sighed as she raised some canvas to shade him from the relentless sun. Three days, with no end in sight. And if they reached land, what then? It might be hostile, for this was slave territory where any white sailors would be seen as enemies.

He opened his sound eye and stared along the boat. They were divided into two watches, pulling on the oars after dusk, and waiting to reset the sail at the touch of even the smallest breeze. He saw Allday looking at him, still brooding perhaps about being ordered to take the tiller at all times because of his old wound. Ozzard too, stooping down over a satchel checking the stores that remained: a small man who seemed to have gathered unsuspected strength in his new role of purser. Bolitho's secretary, the round-shouldered Yovell, was resting across the loom of an oar, his hands bandaged like Jenour's from the hard, back-breaking work at something he had never trained for. His coat was split down the seams to show the extent of his efforts.

Tojohns, without whose strength at the oars it was unlikely they would have made more than a few miles; and Keen, who was crouched beside Owen, his eyes moving around the boat as if to measure their chances of survival. Bolitho raised his head very slightly and felt her stiffen against him. She knew what he was looking for.

Bolitho saw it: the shadow, their constant companion since the wreck. Usually no more than that, but just occasionally it would show its sharp dorsal fin as it glided to the surface, dispelling any hope that it had tired of the hunt.

He heard her ask, 'What do you think happened to the other boat?'

It was hard even to think. 'The bosun might have decided against following us through the reef. His was the larger boat, and carried far more people. He may have decided to remain on the other side, and then head for land.' In his heart he knew that the big cutter might have suffered the same fate as the mutineers, and had either capsized in the breakers, or foundered on the reef. The sharks would have left no one to tell the tale.

He said, 'There would have been precious little to eat and drink but for your preparations. Cheese and ship's biscuits, rum and brandy – many have survived on far less.' He tried to focus his eye on the two barricoes which were lashed on the bottom boards between the thwarts. Fresh water, but shared among thirteen, how long would it last?

Catherine smoothed the hair from his face and said, 'We will reach help. I know it.' She lifted the locket from his open shirt and looked down at it. 'I was younger then . . .'

Bolitho twisted round. 'There is none more beautiful than you *now*, Kate!'

There was such anguish in his voice that for a few moments she saw the youth he had once been. Unsure, vulnerable, but caring even then.

Bezant gave a great groan and cried out, 'In the name o' God, *help me*!' And then in almost the next breath he shouted, 'Another turn on the weather forebrace, Mister Lincoln – lively, I say!'

The seaman named Cuppage swore savagely and retorted, 'Why don't you die, you bastard!'

Bolitho stared at the sea. Endless. Pitiless. Cuppage was only voicing what most of the others thought.

Catherine said, 'Why, hello, Val – have you come a-visiting?'

Bolitho bit his lip. He had not even seen Keen groping his way over the thwarts and between slumped, exhausted bodies. *I am no better than Cuppage.*

Keen tried to smile. 'Allday says he can smell a breeze.' He shielded his eyes against the blinding glare of reflected sunshine. 'But I can see no evidence of it.' He glanced at the others. 'I fear Bezant's wound has gone against him, sir. Ozzard told me he noticed it when he took him some water.'

'The wound has become mortified, Val?' There was little need to ask. Both he and Keen had known it happen often enough. Crude surgery, indifferent medical skills – it was said that more men died of their treatment than from the enemy's iron.

Catherine watched them, astonished that she could still feel such pride at being here with him. Her clothing was soiled and clung to her skin from spray and perspiration, and left little to imagination. Even the wrap of canvas they had rigged to hide her bodily functions provided only the illusion of privacy.

But she could escape even that when she watched and listened to the two she knew best in this world. The man she loved more and beyond life itself, and his friend, who had seemingly gained extra strength from what he believed he had lost and left forever in England.

She knew what they were discussing but nobody else would even guess. And she was seeing it for herself, even if she never lived to describe it. The other man, the hero of whom they sang and gossiped in the taverns and ale-houses, the man who inspired courage as well as love by his own qualities of leadership, which he would be the first to doubt. He believed that many men envied him because of her. It would never occur to him that it might be the other way round.

She heard him say, 'It must be soon then?'

Keen nodded slowly, as if the motion was painful. 'We shall need the light. And if Allday is right about the wind . . .' He looked aft towards Bezant, now lost in merciful oblivion. 'I think he knows, sir.'

Catherine said, 'I will help.'

Bolitho gripped her and shook his head. 'No, Kate, I will

145

speak with Allday.' He glanced with sudden emotion at his
flag-captain. 'He once cut a splinter out of Val the size of a
baby's leg when the ship's surgeon was too much in the arms
of Bacchus to care.'

She looked from one to the other. It was no longer just their
private world. She was part of it now.

Bolitho released his hold and whispered, 'Think of the
house, Kate. Of that small beach where we loved each other
until the tide drove us away.' He saw her eyes clearing. 'It is
all there, just as we left it. Can we allow it to desert us?' Then
he was gone, touching a shoulder here, or murmuring a quiet
word there, as he lurched his way aft.

Catherine wiped her face with a shirtsleeve and watched
him. Filthy and dishevelled; but even a total stranger would
know him for what he was.

Bolitho reached the sternsheets and said, 'Are you certain
about the wind, old friend?'

Allday squinted up at him, his mouth too parched to respond
immediately.

'Aye, Sir Richard. It's shifted a piece too. More westerly,
I'd say.'

Bolitho crouched beside him staring at the sea, containing
his feelings for this big, invincible man. If only they had a
compass, or a sextant . . . But they had nothing, only the sun
by day, the stars by night. Even their progress through the
water was no more than a guess.

He murmured, 'So be it.' He looked across and saw Jenour
studying them.

'Take the tiller, Stephen. Hold her steady.' Then he waited
for the others to rouse themselves. It was painful to watch.
Those who had been asleep crept from the refuge of their
dreams only to see all hope fade as they accepted the reality.
Others stared around as if they still expected to hear the squeal
of the boatswain's call, the stamp of feet on *Golden Plover*'s
deck.

Bolitho thought suddenly of England, but not the one he
had just described to Catherine. He wondered what they
would be thinking and saying. The spiteful would hide their
cruel glee as they had over brave Nelson, and there would be
others already competing to replace him.

But on the waterfronts, and in the fields of the West Country there would be many more who would remember. Poor Adam, he would soon learn to extend his hand to those, as well as recognising the unworthy.

He began, 'Mister Bezant is suffering badly.' He saw Yovell swallow hard and guessed he had realised that the intruding, vile smell was gangrene. 'I need one volunteer. Captain Keen and my cox'n know what to do.' He looked round as Ozzard appeared as if by magic at his elbow. 'Are you certain?'

Ozzard met his gaze calmly. 'I cannot pull an oar, nor can I reef or steer.' He gave a small shrug. 'This I understand.'

Bolitho glanced at Allday's grim features above the little man's back, and guessed that he more than any knew something about Ozzard which he would share with no one.

Keen said quietly to Owen and Tojohns, 'Run out your oars – pull or back water to hold her as steady as you can.' He glanced at the small medical kit Catherine had found in the cabin and tried not to shudder; he had never forgotten Allday's strength and gentleness that day aboard the frigate *Undine*. Keen had been a seventeen-year-old midshipman then, and the great splinter had lanced up into his groin. Ignoring the drunken surgeon, Allday had stripped him naked and had cut the splinter out with his own knife. Mercifully he had fainted after that. The terrible scar was still there. And so was he, because of Allday's courage and care.

He felt a sudden stab of despair. Zenoria had never seen or caressed the ugly, bunched scar. Now, she never would.

Bolitho understood his expression. '*Together*, Val. Always remember that.' He saw Sophie huddled in the bows, her face hidden in Catherine's breast.

Ozzard asked, 'Ready, Sir Richard?'

They forced open the master's jaws, and Ozzard poured a large measure of brandy into his mouth before putting a leather strap between his teeth.

Allday took the knife and looked along the bright blade as he might check the edge of a boarding cutlass before an engagement. It had to be swiftly done: knife, then saw. He would likely die anyway, at least before the rest of them. What would happen when only the last one was still alive? A boat full of scarecrows . . . He dashed the sweat from his eyes and thought of the master's mate named Jonas Polin, and his trim little widow with the inn at Fallowfield. When the news reached her, what would she think? Might she not even remember him?

He said harshly, 'Hold him!' He pointed the knife, his stomach rebelling against the foul stench.

As the knife came down Bezant opened his eyes and stared at the blade. His choking scream seemed to hang over the boat, rendering them all helpless, under a curse.

Once again it was the man called Owen who broke the spell. 'Here comes the wind, lads!' His voice almost broke. 'Oh, thank God, the wind!'

Allday was right after all, just as he had known about Bezant. The master died with an obscenity on his lips even as dusk closed in, when the oars were cutting across the lively whitecaps and the wet sail drummed to the wind.

In between baling and comforting the distraught Sophie, Catherine saw and heard it all. Her man's voice raised above the din of wind and canvas as he spoke a few words from a prayer he must have used many times. She covered the girl's ears as the body went over the side, for even in the depths there could be no peace for the Golden Plover's master. The shark denied him even that.

Captain Valentine Keen looked up at the flapping sail and swung the tiller sharply. To see the canvas momentarily out of control came as a shock, for he knew he must have slipped into a doze. And worse, nobody in this overcrowded boat had noticed it.

The ocean was moving in a deep swell, but the wind was not strong enough to break it into crests. The sun was almost on the horizon; soon it would be cooler, and the nightly business of using oars and sail combined to carry them to the east would begin.

He glanced at the others, some curled up on the bottom-boards, others resting on the oars, which were propped in their rowlocks across the boat.

Lady Catherine was sitting in the sternsheets, her shoulders covered with some canvas while Bolitho leaned against her as if asleep.

Ozzard was on his knees, examining his rations and checking the water in the remaining barricoe. It could not last much longer. One more day, then the despair would sap any remaining resistance like some creeping fever.

Over a week now since the barquentine had thundered across the reef. It felt ten times that long. The meagre rations had finally gone except for a bag of biscuits. Brandy for the sick, rum for when the water ran out. Tomorrow; the next day?

Catherine stirred and gave a quiet sob. Bolitho was instantly roused, his arm cradling her body away from the lurch and pitch of the sun-blistered hull.

Keen tried not to think back over the years, twenty to be exact, to when they had served together in the Great South Sea. Bolitho had been his young captain in the frigate *Tempest*, and he a junior lieutenant. There had been another escape in an open boat. Bolitho would be remembering it now, how the woman he had loved had died in his arms.

A larger longboat, but the same hopelessness and danger. Allday had been there too, had called on the others to restrain Bolitho when he had wrapped her body in a length of chain and lowered her gently over the side.

How could Bolitho ever forget, especially now that he had found the love which had always been denied him?

Allday was down on the boards, lolling against the side, his shaggy, greying hair rippling in the breeze.

Keen felt his eyes prick with emotion at the memory of two nights ago. They had all been close to collapse when a freak rain squall had come out of the dusk and advanced on the boat like a curtain, tearing the sea into a mass of spray and bubbles. They had come to life, clutching at buckets and pieces of canvas, even mugs in readiness to catch a little of the fresh rainwater.

Then, as if a giant's hand were deflecting the rain, it had seemed to veer away within half a cable of the boat.

The young sailor named Tucker from Portsmouth had broken completely, sobbing out his heart until fatigue wore him down into silence.

It had been then that Catherine had said, 'Now, John Allday! I've heard you singing about the gardens at Falmouth – you have a fair voice indeed!' She had looked at Yovell, suddenly pleading, desperate for support. 'You will vouch for that, Mr Yovell?'

And so it had been. As the first stars had appeared and they had tried to gauge the course to steer, Allday had sat by the tiller and had sung a song much beloved by sailors, and written by the mariner's friend, Charles Dibdin, who, it was said, had composed the song *How Hyperion Cleared The Way* to commemorate her last valiant fight.

It was claimed by even the hardest man who served at sea and braved all its dangers and cruelties, that no matter what might happen there was always an angel at the masthead to care for his safety.

'Clear the wreck, stow the yards, and bounce everything tight,
And under reefed foresail we'll scud:
Avast! nor don't think me a milksop so soft
To be taken for trifles aback,
For they say there's a Providence sits up aloft,
To keep watch for the life of Poor Jack.'

Exhausted, blistered and tortured by thirst, they had listened, and it seemed that for just a few minutes their perils had been held at bay.

There had been tears, too, and Keen had seen Jenour with his head in his hands, the girl Sophie staring at Allday as if he were some kind of wizard.

Bolitho cleared his throat. 'How is it, Val?'

Keen glanced at the stars. 'Due east as far as I can tell, although I've no idea how far we've drifted.'

'No matter.' Bolitho cupped her shoulder in his hand and felt its smoothness through the stained shirt. The skin was hot, burning. He brushed some of her hair from her eyes and saw that she was watching him; caring and fearing for him, her spirits beginning to desert even her.

'How long, dearest of men?'

He pressed his cheek against her hair. 'A day. Maybe two.' He kept his voice low, but the others probably knew as well as anyone.

The seaman Tucker gave a wild laugh, cut short by the sore dryness of his throat.

Bolitho gestured to the oars. 'Time to begin, watch by watch!'

Keen exclaimed, 'What is the matter with Tucker?'

Owen said heavily, 'He took some water, sir.' He gestured towards the sea as it lifted almost to the gunwale before sliding down again.

Allday muttered, 'That's him done for.' He said it without emotion one way or the other. 'Bloody fool.'

Tucker pushed his oar away and tried to reach the side before Jenour and Cuppage seized him and dragged him to the foot of the small mast. Cuppage pulled out some codline and tied the babbling man's wrists behind him. 'Shut your trap, you stupid bugger!'

Bolitho clambered into Tucker's place and thrust the oar out over the water. It seemed to weigh twice as much as before. He shut his ears to Tucker's cracked, rambling voice. The beginning of the end.

Catherine sat with Keen while Ozzard poured some water one cup at a time, across the barricoe's leather lip.

Keen raised it to her mouth. 'Hold it there as long as you can. A sip at a time.'

She shivered, and almost dropped the cup as Tucker screamed, '*Water! Give me water, you poxy bitch!*'

In the deep shadows there was the sound of a fist on bone, and Tucker fell silent.

Catherine whispered, 'There was no need. I have heard far worse.'

Keen tried to smile. It had not been merely out of regard for her feelings that Allday had laid him low. One more outbreak from Tucker, and it might consume the boat in fighting madness.

Keen felt the pistol in his belt and tried to remember who else was armed.

She saw his hand on the pistol and said softly, 'You've done this before, Val . . . I guessed as much.' She turned away as something fell heavily in the sea astern. The shark or its victim, it was too dark to tell.

She said, 'He must not see me suffer.' She tried to control

151

her voice, but her body was shaking too badly. 'He has given enough because of me.'

'*Give way all!*'

The oars rose and fell once more while the water was passed carefully from hand to hand.

Then they changed around yet again, and Bolitho slumped down beside her in the sternsheets.

'How is your eye?'

Bolitho forced a smile. 'Better than I thought possible.' He had sensed rather than seen her despair when she had been speaking with Keen.

'You lie.' She leaned against him and felt him stiffen. 'Stop worrying about me, Richard . . . *I* am the cause of all this. You should have left me in that prison. You might never have known . . .'

Great white shapes flapped out of the darkness and circled the jolly-boat before continuing on their way.

He said, 'Tonight, those birds will nest in Africa.'

She pushed her wet hair away as spray drifted over the gunwale.

'I would like to be in some secret place, Richard. Our beach perhaps . . . To run naked in the sea, to love on the sand.' She began to cry very quietly, the sound muffled by his shoulder. 'Just to *live* with you.'

She had fallen into a deep sleep when the young seaman named Tucker choked and died. The oarsmen rested on their looms like souls beyond care or caring. Only Yovell crossed himself in the darkness as the body went over the side and drifted away.

Bolitho held her shoulder, ready to shield her from the frenzy of a shark's attack. But there was nothing. The shark had patience enough for all of them.

When the first hint of dawn opened up the sea around them, Catherine saw that Tucker was missing. It was too draining even to think what it must have been like for him in his dying moments of madness. It was over now. A release.

She saw Ozzard sounding the barricoe, his quick shake of the head to Bolitho beside him.

'Half a cup, then?' Bolitho was almost pleading.

Ozzard shrugged. 'Less.'

Sophie stepped carefully across the outflung legs and the sprawled bodies of the ones off watch.

Catherine held out her arms. 'What is it, Sophie? Come here to me.'

The girl gripped her hand and hesitated. 'Is that *land*? Over there?' She seemed afraid that she might be going mad like Tucker.

Keen stood up from his oar and shaded his eyes.

'Oh, dear God! *Land it is!*'

Allday peered up at the boat's masthead and tried to grin. 'See? He keeps watch for the life of Poor Jack!'

As the light strengthened it became more and more obvious that the land Sophie had sighted was little more than an island. But just the nearness of it seemed to put new life into the jolly-boat, and when the oars were manned and the sail reset, Bolitho could see no disappointment in their sunburned faces.

Keen said between strokes on his oar, 'Do you know it, sir?'

Bolitho turned and saw Catherine watching him. 'Yes, I do.' He should have felt pleased, proud even that he had brought them this far. At least they were not merely heading into an empty horizon and going mad in the process.

Jenour panted, 'Does it have a name, Sir Richard?'

She was still watching him. Reading him like a book. Knowing the desperation, the sudden despair this place had rekindled from some old memory. Like the other midshipman, his friend, of whom he rarely spoke even to her: these recollections were equally painful.

It was a barren place, an island to be avoided, with a treacherous, rocky coastline. This was slave territory, and in earlier times the haunt of pirates. But the latter had now gone further south, to the richer pickings on the sea-routes to and around the Cape of Good Hope.

'I forget what it is called.' Even that she would know was a lie. This small, hostile island was known by local traders as the Island of the Living Dead. Nothing grew there, nothing survived. He said suddenly, 'Twenty miles beyond this place is a rich, wooded island. Fresh streams, fish too.'

Yovell asked politely, 'This place cannot help us then?'

He sounded so lost that Bolitho answered, 'There may be rock pools with rainwater. Shellfish.' He saw the strength draining out of them like sand from a glass. He insisted, 'What say, all of you? One more try? We can gather shellfish and mix them with the last of the biscuits.'

Yovell seemed satisfied. 'We've nothing else to do, have we, sir? Not for the present, in any case.'

Owen grinned and wiped his cracked lips. 'Well said, sir! Twenty miles after what we've been through? I could swim there, but for the sharks, that is!'

Catherine watched them returning to life, instead of the spectres they had almost become. But how long could he persuade them?

By noon the boat had entered a small cove, where the rocks slid beneath the keel in water so clear it could barely be seen.

Bolitho stood and shaded his eyes as they glided above their own shadow.

'Ready with the grapnel! Stephen, Owen, over the side now! Back water, the rest of you!'

With the flag-lieutenant and the keen-eyed lookout floundering and slipping on the bottom while they guided the stem clear of any jagged rocks, the jolly-boat finally came to rest.

Bolitho watched them lurching and falling on the shelving beach as they left the boat and tried to run up the slope. A ship was one thing, but having been penned up in a small open boat made them stagger like drunken men.

Catherine stared with surprise as Allday handed her a pair of leather sandals he had cut and fashioned from Ozzard's satchel.

She said huskily, 'You are a dear man, John.'

Allday was embarrassed, the danger this place might hold momentarily forgotten.

'Well, m'lady, as Mr Yovell rightly said, I had nothing else to do.'

Bolitho walked with her through the shallows and waited while she tied on her sandals. It was just as well. The beach was as hot as a stove.

'See to it, Val. Take your cox'n and climb that hill. Might even be able to see the other island in this light . . . it would give them heart.'

Keen said gravely, 'I believe you have done that, sir, to all of us.'

Allday was about to leave the beached boat when Ozzard tugged at his sleeve. 'Look, John!'

It was a small pouch, hidden carefully behind the empty barricoe. It was tightly tied and very heavy.

Allday felt it. 'It's gold, matey.'

'But whose?'

'Whoever put it there is one of the mutineers, an' that's no error.'

They stuffed the pouch back into its hiding place. Allday said, 'Leave it to me.'

Ozzard said, 'I'll keep watch over the last of our supplies.' He added meaningly, 'Especially the *rum*.'

Keen started up the hillside, the highest point on this barren place, but in truth little more than a sun-scorched hump.

As they passed some scattered rocks Tojohns grunted, 'Jesus, look at that!'

It was a skeleton, lying where the man had fallen, shipwrecked, marooned or murdered. They would never know.

They were almost at the top, and Keen tried not to think of water, even the sound of it in a glass.

They reached the summit, and Keen dropped to his knees and said sharply, '*Down*, man!'

The other island was visible as Bolitho had prophesied, like a pale green mist below the horizon.

But all Keen could see was the anchored vessel directly below him, the brig he had observed from *Golden Plover*'s masthead. The slaver which had come to collect the gold now scattered across the Hundred Mile Reef.

'I'll go and warn our people. You stay here, Tojohns. If you see a boat heading ashore, come at once.'

He scrabbled down the dry hill, his mind stunned by this new discovery. Even this lifeless place had been a symbol of their success. Now it was only a trap.

Bolitho listened to him without comment, his eyes on Sophie and Ozzard as they collected some of the shellfish Jenour's party had discovered in a rock pool.

They all stood round, waiting for Ozzard's judgment as he dipped his cup into the bucket Owen had filled with water from a small hillside gully. Then he said solemnly, 'Rainwater. I'll put it in the cask.'

Yovell flung his arms around the young maid and beamed. 'Like wine, eh, my dear!'

Bolitho called, 'Listen to me, all of you. The slaver that was after us is anchored yonder.' He saw them coming to terms with it. 'And we cannot survive here.' He thought of the skeleton Keen had described. There were probably others. 'So at dusk we will leave.' He let each word sink in. 'We *must* reach that island. There's a fair breeze . . . we might not even need the oars.'

Allday watched their reactions, especially those of the two remaining hands from the *Golden Plover*. Not Owen, surely. He had proved his loyalty more than once. What about the tough Tynesider, Cuppage? But his expression had not changed at the mention of the slaver. It might have been the salt-water-crazed Tucker, who had taken his secret with him. Or even the old master, Bezant: some pitiful compensation for losing his ship to men he had once trusted.

Allday fingered the old dirk in his belt. *Whoever it is, I'll see him to hell!*

Where trees had once stood and now lay like whitened bones in the sand, Catherine took Bolitho in her arms and held him, free only for a moment from curious eyes.

They stood looking at one another in complete silence. Then she said quietly, 'Once I doubted. Now I know we shall reach safety.'

On the hillside the sandblown skeleton could have been listening, sharing the hope to which he had, once, also clung.

11

A Day to Remember

'Easy all!' Bolitho peered up at the stars and saw Allday's shadow move while he pushed the tiller-bar to windward. The oars rose dripping from the water and stayed motionless above it. It was strange to feel the boat still moving ahead, the tilt of the hull as the wind filled the sail, dark against the great panorama of stars.

It had gone better than Bolitho had dared to hope. They had refloated the boat before dusk and had pulled steadily, close inshore almost within an oar's length of some of the rocks, until they had headed out to sea. The anchored brig had been hidden out of sight on the other side of the island, and even when the jolly-boat had spread her sail in the darkening shadows, they had seen no lights, no movement at all.

Perhaps the brig's master had given up hope of discovering if anyone had survived the wreck, and was now intent only on gathering another human cargo, transferred perhaps from another slaver.

Ozzard whispered, 'Last of the water, sir.'

Bolitho thought of the rainwater Jenour's party had discovered. They had all but filled one barricoe, and after consuming a foul-tasting meal of shellfish and a mash of ship's biscuits they had each taken a mug of water. In ordinary times nobody would have touched it, but as Yovell had remarked, it seemed like wine.

Keen climbed up beside him and said, 'We shall see the island clearly at first light. Two more miles, maybe less with

157

this wind.' He was calculating aloud. 'At least we can survive there until we find help.'

On the bottom boards Catherine stirred and took the cup from Ozzard, while in the bows they could hear Sophie retching. She was their only casualty from eating the raw shellfish. A fire had been out of the question with the brig so near.

Tojohns wiped his mouth with his hand. 'I can hear surf, sir!'

Bolitho breathed out slowly and felt Catherine reach for him in the darkness.

He said, 'That's it, Val. The outer spur. Once daylight comes we can follow it until we find a passage. All we have to do after that is make for the beach. There might even be a merchantman there, with a watering party ashore. It is a favourite place, and the streams are somewhat better than Stephen's gully!'

Surprisingly, someone laughed this time, and Sophie managed to control her retching to listen.

Bolitho gripped Catherine's hand. 'Try to rest, Kate. You've done enough for ten able-bodied seamen.'

She said quietly, 'It's hard to accept that there is land out there.'

Bolitho smiled. 'Old hands will be able to smell it soon.'

He made her comfortable and then climbed over to the nearest thwart to relieve Tojohns at his oar.

Allday said harshly, 'Stand by! Give way all!'

He thought he already had the scent of the island, and marvelled at the way Bolitho and Keen had managed to get them this far. But they were not safe yet. He grimaced in the darkness. After coming all this way it would be the devil's work if they hit one of the smaller outflung reefs.

But once on the island he knew they could manage to keep going. After that other fearful place, the others all knew they could survive until Lady Luck took over. *Lady Luck* . . . He thought of Herrick, and wondered if he would ever make it up with Bolitho. After what Lady Catherine had done for Herrick's wife, and what she had given to all of them in this damned boat, he didn't much care either way. A sailor's woman; and even in her soiled breeches and shirt, her hair brailed up and clinging with salt, she was still a sight to make any man stare.

Catherine lay with one arm covering her face as men moved about the boat, retrimming the sail so that the bottom boards tilted even further. She was not asleep although she knew they all believed so, and in these moments of privacy she allowed herself reflection and despair. And thoughts . . . whether any of them would ever be the same, how long it might be before she saw Falmouth again. The leaves would have gone from the trees, and the petals from the roses she found so beautiful. She had clung to the memory in the hours and days in this pitching boat to prevent herself from breaking down and allowing her hopelessness to infect the others. *Just let us reach there*, she whispered, *I will do the rest.* But when, when . . .

There was another pause for it was hard work, and the time spent at the oars became shorter for each man.

She looked over her arm and saw Allday at the tiller, one elbow propped on the gunwale as if he was part of the boat. Bronzed faces, some with badly sunburned skins: men usually so clean and disciplined were now bearded with stubble, their hair as matted as her own.

She turned her head so that she could see Bolitho, his injured eye closed as he lay back on his loom, taking the stroke from the seaman Owen.

'Here comes the dawn.'

'And there's part of the reef!' That was Jenour, unable as usual to hide his emotion.

Some strange gulls flew low overhead, their wings very white while the boat still lay in shadow. Allday murmured approvingly to Ozzard, 'One o' those in th' pot'll do me!'

The seaman named Bill Cuppage plucked his filthy shirt from his body, and stared with astonishment as something caught the dawn's first light and held it like a mirror. Jenour saw his expression and swung with a gasp. 'Ship, sir!'

Bolitho squinted across the quarter and felt his jaw tighten with disbelief and disappointment.

He called sharply, 'Easy, all! Take in the sail!'

With neither oars nor canvas to steady it, the jolly-boat slid down into the swell and broached-to in steep, sickening rolls.

Keen said hoarsely, 'Brig, sir. All sails set.'

Catherine had one hand across her mouth as she watched the distant masts with their pale, bellying sails. As yet, no vessel showed herself above the receding shadows.

'Might it be another, Val?'

Keen tore his eyes from the pyramid of sails and looked at her. 'I fear not.'

Allday muttered, 'Might not see us. We're low in the water.'

Ozzard climbed forward and handed a mug of brandy to Sophie.

'Here, drink this, miss. Give you strength.'

She stared at him over the rim, 'What shall we do?'

Ozzard did not answer but turned aft to watch as the brig's two masts began to turn, the sails in momentary confusion while she changed tack until she was bows-on towards them.

Bolitho said, 'Make sail again! Man your oars! The brig won't risk passing through the reef at this stage.'

There was a dull bang, and seconds later a ball splashed down astern of the slow-moving jolly-boat.

Tojohns lay back on his oar and said between his teeth, 'That bugger don't need to!'

Catherine climbed on to a thwart and added her own strength to Yovell's oar, her bare feet pressing hard on a stretcher.

There was another bang, and this time the ball ricocheted across the water like an enraged dolphin before hurling up a tall, thin waterspout. Cuppage was a big man, but he moved like lightning. Tossing his oar away, he vaulted into the bows and gripped Sophie with his arm around her neck, his other hand producing a cocked pistol, which he pressed against her face.

'Let her go!' Bolitho saw the girl staring aft at him, her eyes wide with terror. 'What use is this, man?'

'*Use?*' Cuppage flinched as another ball ripped across the water. 'I'll tell you what! Yon brig's master will want a word with you, or he'll kill us all! It'd only take one ball!' He began to work his way along the boat, dragging the half-strangled girl with him.

Owen called, 'I thought you was one of them, you bastard! I never saw you with the bosun's party!'

Cuppage ignored him, his teeth bared with exertion. 'One move, an' she gets 'er 'ead blown off!'

Bolitho looked at him without emotion. He was beaten. Whether the slaver's master accepted Cuppage's story no longer mattered.

Aboard the brig they must have realised what was happening. She was shortening sail, tacking once more to remain well clear of the reef.

Allday said, 'Changing sides again, matey?' He sounded very calm. 'Well, don't forget your little bag.'

Cuppage swung round and saw Ozzard holding the bag over the side.

Allday continued, 'No gold, no hope – not for *you*, matey. They won't believe your yarn and they'll kill you with the rest of us!'

Cuppage yelled, 'Give me that, you little scum!'

'Catch, then!' Ozzard flung it towards him and Cuppage gave a scream of fury as the bag flew past his outstretched hand and splashed into the sea.

Allday stopped in front of Catherine and spat out, 'Don't look.'

The knife flashed in the sunlight and Cuppage lolled against the gunwale, while Tojohns and Owen pulled the girl to safety.

Allday moved with surprising speed and reached Cuppage even as he fell gasping across the gunwale, and as he tugged his old knife from his back he exclaimed savagely, 'Go and look for it, you bastard!'

Cuppage drifted away, his arms moving feebly until he vanished.

Keen said dully, 'That was well done, Allday.' He stared at the brig, which was shortening sail yet again as she ran down on the drifting jolly-boat.

Allday looked at Bolitho and the woman beside him. 'Too late. God damn that bloody mutineer. But for him . . .'

Bolitho glanced towards the lush, green island. So near, yet a million miles away.

But all he could hear was her voice. *Don't leave me.*

He had failed.

Rarely had the Falmouth parish church of King Charles the Martyr seen so mixed and solemn a gathering. While the great organ played in the background the pews soon filled with people from all walks of life, from the governor of Pendennis Castle to lowly farm workers, their boots grubby and scraped from the fields on this early harvest. Many stood on the cobbles outside the church, watching out of curiosity, or to capture some private memory of the man whose life and service were to be honoured here today. Not some stranger, or mysterious hero of whom they had read or been told about, but one of their own sons.

The Rector was very aware of the importance of the occasion. There would of course be a grander memorial service in London with all the pomp of traditional ceremony. But this was Sir Richard's home, where his ancestors had come and gone, leaving only their historic records in stone along these same walls.

The whole county had been shocked by the news of Sir Richard Bolitho's death and of the manner in which he had died. But there had always been hope, and the speculation which this man's charisma had long encouraged. To fall in battle was one thing; to be lost at sea in some kind of accident was difficult for most of these people to accept.

The Rector glanced at the fine marble bust of old Captain Julius Bolitho, who had fallen in 1664. The engraving seemed to fit the whole of this remarkable family, he thought.

> *The spirits of your fathers*
> *Shall start from every wave;*
> *For the deck it was their field of fame,*
> *And ocean was their grave.*

Today's service seemed to have killed the last of their simple faith, and many of the ships in Carrick Road had half-masted their ensigns.

He saw Squire Lewis Roxby guiding his wife Nancy to the family pew. Roxby looked grim, watching over her with a tenderness he rarely showed either as a magistrate or as one of the wealthiest men in the county. This was another side to the King of Cornwall.

Captain Keen's lovely young widow was seated between her husband's sisters, who had come all the way from Hampshire.

One of them would be thinking of her own husband, who had been killed at sea a year or so earlier.

There was a very distraught couple who had taken the coach from Southampton to be here. They were Lieutenant Stephen Jenour's parents.

In another pew with members of the household and farm staff, Bryan Ferguson gripped his wife's hand and stared fixedly at the high altar. He discovered that his wife had the true strength today, and was determined to get him through it as the faces crowded into his mind.

All the memories, the comings and goings from the old grey house. He had been a major part of it, and as steward of the estate he was very conscious of Bolitho's trust in him. He wiped his eyes as he freed his only hand from her grip. Poor old John Allday. No more yarns, no more wets when he was home from sea.

He glanced across the aisle and recognised Lady Belinda with another woman, her oval face and autumn hair making the only colour against her sombre black. A few people bobbed to her – sympathy or respect, who could tell? Squire Roxby was receiving all of them in his great house afterwards. *Afterwards*. Even that made Ferguson bite his lip to steady himself.

Bolitho's older sister was here too, severe and grey, while her son Miles, formerly a midshipman aboard Bolitho's flagship *Black Prince* after having been dismissed from the Honourable East India Company's service under some sort of cloud, was now gazing around as if he expected everyone to be admiring him. He had even been required to leave the King's service, or as Keen had put it, face a court-martial instead. Was he calculating how he might benefit from his uncle's death?

And there were uniforms a-plenty. The port admiral from Plymouth, some officers of the Coastguard, even a few dragoons from the garrison at Truro.

Overhead the bell began to toll; it sounded faraway from within the body of the church. But on the hillsides and in the harbour men and women would be listening to its finality.

Others arrived: Young Matthew the head coachman, Tom the revenue officer, even Vanzell the one-legged sailor who had once served Bolitho, and been instrumental in freeing Lady Catherine from that stinking jail to the north of London. It was rumoured that Lady Catherine's husband had planned to have her falsely imprisoned and deported with the connivance of Bolitho's wife. What was she thinking now as she whispered to her elegant companion? Pride in her late husband? Or more incensed by the victory death had granted her rival?

Whenever she turned from her friend to stare around the church Ferguson had the impression that it was with contempt, and no kind of regret for the life she had left in this ancient seaport.

And in months, maybe sooner, the legalities would have to be settled. Squire Roxby had never made any secret of his readiness to take over the Bolitho estate and add it to his own. That would certainly preserve it for his wife and their two children, if nothing else. Belinda would want a settlement to compensate for the lavish life and fashionable house she enjoyed in London. Ferguson felt his wife gripping his hand again as the straight-backed, solitary figure of Captain Adam Bolitho strode up the aisle to take his place in his family pew.

Ferguson believed him the one man who would save the estate and the livelihood of all those who depended on it. Even that reminded him of Allday again. His pride at living there when he was not at sea. *Like being one of the family*, he had so often proclaimed.

He watched Captain Adam shaking hands with the Rector. It was about to begin. A day they would all have cause to remember, and for such diverse reasons. He saw Keen's young wife lean out towards Adam. He was to be posted next month, and had been so looking forward to seeing his uncle with the coveted second epaulette on his shoulder, when Bolitho had returned from his mission.

Ferguson had been troubled by Adam's frequent visits to the house. But for his vehement insistence that Bolitho was still alive and somehow, even by a miracle, would return home, Ferguson might have suspected some unexpected liaison between him and Zenoria Keen.

The bell had stopped and a great silence had fallen over the church; the glittering colours of the tall windows were very bright in the noon sunlight.

The Rector climbed into the old pulpit and surveyed the crowded pews. Not many young faces, he thought sadly. And with the war already reaching into Portugal and perhaps Spain, many more sons would leave home, never to return.

At the very back of the church, seated on two cushions so that she could see over the shoulders of those in front of her, the widow of Jonas Polin, one-time master's mate in the *Hyperion*, was aware of the people all around her in this grand place, but could think only of the big, shambling man who had rescued her that day on the road. Now the admiral's coxswain would never call on her at the Stag's Head at Fallowfield. She had told herself not to be so stupid. But as the days had dragged past after the news had broken over the county, she had felt the loss even more. Like being cheated. She closed her eyes tightly as the Rector began, 'We are all very aware of why we are come here today . . .'

Ferguson stared blindly around him. And what of Catherine Somervell? Did nobody grieve for her? He saw her on the cliff walk, her face brown in the sun, her hair on the wind from the sea like a dark banner. He thought of what Allday and the others had told him, how she had risked her life to help Herrick's dying wife. A thousand things; most of all what she had done for her Richard, as she called him. *Dearest of men.* Unlike so many, they had been together when death had marked them down. He half-listened to the drone of the Rector's voice, let it wash over him as he relived so many precious moments.

One man sat in an almost empty pew, shielded from the great mass of people by a pillar, his hooded eyes inscrutable while he paid his respects in his private fashion. Dressed all in grey, Sir Paul Sillitoe had arrived uninvited and unannounced, his beautiful carriage bringing many curious stares when he had reached the church.

Ferguson need not have worried on Catherine's behalf. Sillitoe had driven all the way from London and, although he had greatly respected Bolitho, he was more shocked by his grief at the loss of Bolitho's mistress, for reasons he could not define, even to himself.

The Rector was saying, 'We must never lose sight of the great service this fine local family has offered . . .' He broke off, aware from long experience that he no longer held the attention of the congregation.

There was a distant noise, and shouting, like a tavern turning out, and Roxby was glaring round, flushed and angry as he hissed, 'These *oafs*! What are they thinking of?'

Everyone fell silent as Adam Bolitho stood up suddenly, and without even a customary bow to the altar strode quickly back down the aisle. He glanced at nobody, and as he passed Ferguson thought he looked as if he had no control over what he was doing. 'In a trance,' he would later hear it described.

Adam reached the great, weathered doors and dragged them wide open so that the din flooded into the church, where everyone now was standing, their backs to the Rector marooned in his pulpit.

The square was crammed, and a recently arrived mail coach was completely surrounded by a cheering, laughing mob. In the centre of it all two grinning sea-officers on horseback, their mounts lathered in sweat from a hard ride, were being hailed like heroes.

Adam stood quite still as he recognised one of them as his own first lieutenant. He was trying to make himself heard above the noise, but Adam could not understand him.

A man he had never seen before ran up the church steps and seized his hands.

'They'm alive, Cap'n Adam, sir! Your officer's brought word from Plymouth!'

The lieutenant managed to fight his way through, his hat knocked awry.

'All safe, sir! A bloody miracle, if you'll pardon my saying so!'

Adam led him back into the church. He saw Zenoria with Keen's sisters standing in the aisle, framed against the high altar. He asked quietly, 'All my uncle's party? Safe?'

He saw his lieutenant nod excitedly. 'I *knew* my uncle could do it. The fairest of men . . . I shall tell the Rector myself. Wait for me, please. You must come to the house.'

The lieutenant said to his companion, 'Took it well, I thought, Aubrey?'

166

'He had more faith than I did.'

Adam reached the others and held out his hands. 'They are all safe.' He saw Zenoria sobbing in the arms of one of Keen's sisters, and beyond her Belinda, now strangely out of place in her sombre black.

At the rear of the church Sir Paul Sillitoe picked up his hat and then turned as he saw the woman who had been just behind him. She was crying now, but not with grief.

He asked kindly, 'Someone very dear to you, is he?'

She curtsied and wiped her eyes. 'Just a man, sir.'

Sillitoe thought of Adam's expression when he had re-entered the church, of the sudden ache in his own heart when the news had broken over them like a great, unstoppable wave.

He smiled at her. 'We are all just men, my dear. It is better not to forget that sometimes.'

He walked out into the jostling, noisy square and heard the peal of bells following him.

He thought of their first encounter at one of Godschale's ridiculous receptions. Like no other woman he had ever met. But at this moment in Falmouth his own words to her were uppermost in his mind. She had protested that Bolitho was being ordered back to immediate duty after all he had suffered, and suggested angrily that some other flag-officer be sent instead. Sillitoe seemed to hear himself, in memory. *Fine leaders – they have the confidence of the whole fleet. But Sir Richard Bolitho holds their hearts*.

He looked round for his carriage, at these simple, ordinary people who were a far cry from those he knew and directed.

Aloud he said, 'As *you*, my dear Catherine, hold mine.'

His Britannic Majesty's brig *Larne* of fourteen guns rolled untidily in a steep offshore swell, sailing so close to the wind that to any landman her yards would appear to be braced almost fore-and-aft. The island lay enticingly abeam, its greenness shimmering in heat-haze, the nearest beaches pure white in the sunshine. But like an evil barrier between the island and the sturdy brig lay the protective reef, showing itself every so often in violent spurts of broken spray.

Right aft in *Larne*'s stern cabin her captain lay sprawled on the bench seat beneath the open windows, so that the quarter-wind stirred the stale air and gave his naked body a suggestion of refreshment. Commander James Tyacke was staring up at the dancing reflections that played across the low deckhead. The cabin was like a miniature of the stern cabin in a frigate, but to Tyacke it still seemed spacious. He had previously commanded the armed schooner *Miranda* and had taken part in the recapture of Cape Town, and it had been then that he had first served alongside Richard Bolitho. Tyacke had never held much respect for senior officers, but Bolitho had changed many of his views. When *Miranda* had been sunk by a French frigate and her crew left to die, Tyacke, who had already lost so much, had felt that he had nothing more to live for.

That was something else Bolitho had done to give him back his dignity and his pride: he had asked him to command the *Larne*.

Ordered to the newly formed anti-slavery patrols, Tyacke imagined that he had at last found the best life still had to offer him. Independent, free of the fleet's apron strings and the whims of any admiral who chose to accost him, the role had suited him very well.

Larne was well-found and manned by some excellent seamen. And as for the wardroom, if you could rate it as such, Tyacke had three lieutenants and a sailing master and rarest of all, a fully-qualified doctor who had accepted the poor rewards of service as a ship's surgeon in order to enhance his knowledge of tropical diseases. Dealing with slaves and slavers alike, he was getting plenty of experience.

Larne even boasted five masters' mates, although there were only two aboard at present, the others having been sent away as prize-masters in some of Tyacke's captures.

And then, without any sort of warning, the news had hit him like a mailed fist. They had met with a courier schooner and Tyacke had learned of Bolitho's loss at sea.

He knew them all: Valentine Keen, Allday, who had tried to help him, and of course Catherine Somervell. Tyacke had last spoken to her at Keen's wedding at the start of the year. He had never forgotten her, or the way she had conversed with him so directly, and looked at him without flinching. Tyacke stood up abruptly and walked to the mirror above his sea-chest. He was thirty-one years old, tall and well built, and his left profile was strong, with the grave good looks which might catch any woman's glance. But the other side . . . he touched it and felt only disgust. The Arab slavers called him *the devil with half a face*. Only the eye lived in it. A miracle, everyone told him. It could have been so much worse. But could it? Half his face burned away and he had no idea how it had happened. His world had exploded at the Nile, while all those about him had been killed. *It could have been worse . . .*

But Bolitho had somehow put him together again. A vice-admiral, one of England's heroes even if he had outraged many of his contemporaries, who had taken passage in Tyacke's tiny *Miranda* and never once complained at the discomfort, Bolitho had got to know him as a man, not as a victim, and had taken the trouble to care.

He turned away and walked aft to the open windows again. Ten days ago, while they had been searching for a well-known slaver who was said to be in the area, the lookouts had sighted a drifting longboat, the cutter from the *Golden Plover*. Andrew Livett, *Larne*'s surgeon, had earned his keep that day. The survivors had been almost finished, mostly because the cutter's water supply had been inadequate, and they had been in too much of a hurry abandoning the wreck to replenish it.

Tyacke had sat, face in shadow, in this cabin and listened to the senior survivor, Luke Britton the boatswain, describing the mutiny, the sudden change of fortune while Bolitho had turned the tables on the men who had betrayed their master.

He had told of the jolly-boat entering the reef itself, while his own cutter, loaded as it was with some twenty hands, had been carried away to the other side. Tyacke had pictured it as the man blurted out each item of tragedy: the mutineers' boat being smashed by falling spars, the sharks gorging on the floundering, screaming sailors.

All plans to capture the slaver, the notorious *Raven*, had gone. Instead, Tyacke had laid a new course in a giant triangle to search along the reef and look for signs of life on the small, scattered islands, or perhaps even smoke signals, which might indicate that some of the party had survived. There had been nothing, and Tyacke had been forced to admit what his first lieutenant, a Channel Islander named Paul Ozanne, had believed from the beginning. A fruitless search; and with two women on board, what hope could there be?

And now *Larne* was herself dangerously short of water and the fruit which any King's ship needed to prevent scurvy in these sweltering waters.

He half-listened to the chant of his two leadsmen in the chains, watching out for the reefs while their best lookouts manned both mastheads for an hour at a time, before the glare rendered them useless.

What more can I do?

His people would not let him down; he knew that now. At first he had found this new command and her different company hard to know, but eventually he had won them over, just as he had done in his beloved *Miranda*. However, if anyone else discovered that he had abandoned his hunt for the *Raven*, they might be less understanding.

There was a tap at the screen door and Gallaway, one of the master's mates, peered in at him.

'What is it?' He tried to keep the despair and grief out of his voice.

'The Master sends 'is respects, sir. It will be time to wear ship in about 'alf an hour.' He showed no surprise at seeing his captain naked, nor did he drop his eyes when Tyacke looked directly at him. *Not any more*.

So it was over. When *Larne* came about he would have to take her to Freetown to receive new orders, to replenish stores and water supply. All the rest was a memory: one he would never lose, like the wound on his face.

'I'll come up.' Tyacke pulled on a shirt and breeches and glanced at the cupboard where the thirteen-year-old cabin boy kept his rum and brandy. He rejected the idea. His men had to manage; so would he. Even that reminded him of Bolitho. Leadership by example, by a trust which he had insisted went both ways.

On deck it was scorching, and his shoes stuck to the tarred deck-seams. But the wind, as hot as if it blew across a desert, was strong enough. A glance at the compass, a critical examination of the yards and flapping canvas as his ship heeled over to the close-hauled sails, then he looked along the deck. Both watches were assembling in readiness to change tack. A few raw youngsters but mostly seamen, glad to get away from the harsh discipline of the fleet, or some tyrannical captain. He smiled sadly. And no midshipmen, none. There was no room on anti-slavery work for untrained, would-be admirals.

The first lieutenant was watching him, his face troubled. He knew about Tyacke and the vice-admiral. A powerful relationship, although Tyacke could rarely be drawn to speak of it. But *Larne* could not stand away from the land for much longer; they were on halved rations as it was. In the same breath, Ozanne knew that if his captain required it he and the others would drive the brig to eternity. Ozanne himself was no stranger to risk, or to dedication: he had once been the master of a lugger running out of St Peter Port in Guernsey, but French men-of-war and privateers had made trade impossible for such small craft, and he had gone into the navy, becoming a master's mate, and eventually a lieutenant.

Tyacke did not notice his scrutiny. He was shading his eyes to study the nearest island. *Nothing*. He tried not to think of the sharks *Golden Plover*'s boatswain had described. Better that than to be taken by natives or Arab slavers, especially the two women. He wondered who the other one was – surely not Keen's young wife?

He said, 'Change the lookouts, Paul. I'd anchor inshore despite the danger and send a watering party over. But it would take more time.'

Ozanne pondered on it. What did the captain mean, 'more time'? Did he still intend to carry on with the search? Some of the men would soon be getting worried, he thought. They had seen the state of the survivors from the cutter. One had already died, and another had gone since they had been snatched from the sea.

They were quite alone, and with three prize crews taking their captures back to Freetown they were short-handed. He trusted his men, but he never trusted what the sea might make them do.

Tyacke waited for the new lookouts to climb aloft and then said, 'Both watches, if you please, Paul. We'll come about and steer sou'-east-by-south.'

Ozanne stood his ground. He was older than Tyacke, and

would never go any higher in the navy. But this suited him; and he found he wanted to comfort Tyacke in some way.

'You done your best, sir. It's God's will – I believe that.'

'Aye, mebbe.' He was thinking of the girl he had been hoping to marry. He persistently told himself that no one could blame her for rejecting him when he went home with his terrible scars. But it still hurt him deeply, more than he could rightly understand. Was that God's will, too? What would all these sunburned seamen think of him if they knew he still had her portrait in his sea-chest, and the gown he had once bought for her in Lisbon?

He was suddenly angry with himself. *'Stand by on deck!'*

Pitcairn the sailing master joined the first lieutenant by the wheel.

'Takin' it badly, is he?'

'He's . . . lost something. I'm not certain what.'

'Off tacks and sheets! Stand by! Man the braces, lively there!'

Men crouched and stooped over braces and halliards were suddenly changed into living statues as the distant crash of gunfire echoed across the reefs.

'Belay that order!' Tyacke snatched a telescope from the rack. 'Get the t'gallants on her!'

'Hands aloft!' A master's mate had to push one man bodily to the shrouds.

Tyacke studied the sweeping green arm of the island as it began to dip down towards the eye-searing water.

Another shot. He gritted his teeth. It might be anything. *Come on, old lady, you can fly when it takes you thus!*

'Deck there! Sail on the lee bow! Brig, she is!'

Tyacke shouted impatiently, 'What other vessel?'

The man, even at that height, sounded puzzled. 'None, sir!'

'They've sighted us, sir.'

Tyacke gripped his hands behind him until the pain steadied him.

'Clear away larboard battery! Stand fast all other hands!'

Men stumbled from their various stations and ran to the seven guns of the larboard battery.

Then, as the land fell completely away, Tyacke saw the

other brig. He said almost in a whisper, 'She's the bloody *Raven*, by God.'

Ozanne rubbed his hands. 'We'll dish that bugger up afore he knows it!' He turned away and did not see Tyacke's expression. 'Run up the Colours! Mr Robyns, a shot across her snout, and the next into 'er belly if she fails to heave-to!'

The forward gun lurched inboard and seconds later a ball splashed down some fifty feet beyond the *Raven*'s bowsprit.

But Tyacke had shifted his glass, the slaver almost forgotten as he saw the low shape of the jolly-boat.

'*Raven*'s shortening sail, sir!'

Tyacke moved the glass with elaborate care on to the pitching boat and flapping sail.

'*It's them*. It can't be, but it is.' He turned to the lieutenant, his eyes shining. 'God's will, after all!'

Ozanne shook his head. 'I've been at sea too long. I just can't take it in.'

Tyacke tried to drag his mind from the picture in his powerful telescope.

'Heave-to and send a boarding party across to the *Raven*.' He heard the boat already being hoisted over the side, the clatter of weapons as the armed men clambered after it. 'And Mr Robyns – don't let them know how short-handed we are. Tell that bloody slaver that if he tries to rid himself of evidence, I'll not wait till Freetown to see him dance!'

Lieutenant Ozanne remarked, 'So that is the famous Bolitho.'

Tyacke watched the oars coming to life, the jolly-boat labouring round towards the drifting *Larne*.

Ozanne observed, 'Not many of them, sir.' He glanced at Tyacke's face, the tension and intensity in his uninjured profile. What *was* it, he wondered. Instinct? Somehow he knew it was more; much more. He shaded his eyes. 'Who's the young officer beside him, sir?'

Tyacke turned toward him, and his hideous face split into a great grin of relief. 'My God, Paul, you *have* been at sea too long!' He handed him the glass. 'Take a look – even you might recognise a woman after all this time!' He touched his arm. 'The admiral's lady . . . and ours is the honour.'

173

Someone called, 'They've run up our flag over the *Raven*, sir!' But Tyacke did not even hear. 'Man the side, Paul. This is a day to remember.'

12

Welcome . . .

Lewis Roxby, 'the King of Cornwall', chose his moment with some care and then rose to his feet. It had been a magnificent dinner even by Roxby's expansive standards – his kitchen was said to produce the finest food in the whole county, and this would be talked about for months. It was not a large gathering by any means – twenty people in all – but it was an affair to be proud of, he thought. The best silver was on display, and all the candles had been changed throughout the meal: no smoke or untidy guttering here.

It was an event nobody had considered even remotely possible when they had all been gathered in the church at Falmouth. Now that was past, like a return from the dead.

Roxby looked along the table and saw Bolitho sitting beside Nancy, and wondered what it had all been like, truly like. Adam was halfway down the table, his face impassive, almost withdrawn as he toyed with a glass of madeira. He seemed different, perhaps because of the second gleaming epaulette on his shoulder, the coveted post-rank which had been granted even as Bolitho and Lady Catherine had returned home to a tumultuous welcome. The square, the coaching road, even the lane that led up to the Bolitho house had been packed with cheering people.

Roxby saw Lieutenant Stephen Jenour speaking quietly to his parents. The Jenours were very much in awe of the other guests, but the excellent meal and an endless procession of wines had done much to put them at their ease.

Bolitho's sister Felicity was also here, as was her son Miles who, Roxby noted, had splashed his shirt with red wine, like the victim of a duel.

A fellow magistrate and local landowner whose fortune was second only to Roxby's, Sir James Hallyburton and his lady, the port admiral from Plymouth, and a few other people who were useful business acquaintances rather than friends, completed the assembly.

Roxby cleared his throat. 'Ladies and gentlemen, friends all – we are here to welcome home a man who is very special to us for many different reasons.' He saw Bolitho staring along the table, not at him, but at the woman who sat at his right hand. When Bolitho had brought her into the drawing-room where Roxby had begun the reception, with its tall glass doors still open to the gardens despite the nearness of autumn, there had been many gasps of surprise. In a dark green gown, her hair piled above her ears to reveal Bolitho's gift of earrings, she was not as they had expected to see her after such an ordeal. Her neck and shoulders were bare, darkened so much by the scorching sun that she could have been from the South Americas, and her beauty seemed somehow more exotic, more defiantly unconventional. Roxby glanced down at her now, and saw the one revealing burn on her shoulder, as if she had been branded. She met his eyes, and he said quietly, 'And we welcome *you*, Lady Catherine, and thank God for your safety. I thought this private gathering of friends would suit you far better than something grand, after all the travelling you have been forced to do since you reached Portsmouth, and then came west to us!'

She bowed her head, so that her high cheekbones caught the light from the candles, and her voice was composed as she answered, 'Your kindness means so much to us.'

Then she allowed her mind to drift as Roxby continued with his well-prepared speech.

It was still almost impossible to believe it was over, behind them. Separate incidents stood out more than others. Some she could not bear to think about. Perhaps most of all she recalled her shocked disbelief when the brig *Larne* had been sighted tacking around a necklace of reefs.

And poor Tyacke trying to welcome her, his seamen cheering as they had been pulled up from the jolly-boat; the boat that had been their salvation and prison, where men had died, and others had clung to their simple faith that Bolitho would somehow get them to safety, even when everything suggested otherwise.

Then, with exhaustion sweeping over her, she had felt her resistance give way because of Tyacke's unexpected gift: a gown, badly creased from months, perhaps years, of being crammed into a chest, which she now knew he had carried with him ever since the girl he had wanted for his own had rejected him.

He had muttered awkwardly, 'You're a mite taller than she was, m'lady, but – '

She had gripped him in her arms and whispered, 'It will suit *very well*, James Tyacke. I shall wear it with pride.' And so it had been; the Portuguese gown he had bought for another woman had covered her bruised and burned body all the way to Freetown, where they had found a homeward-bound frigate about to weigh anchor.

More memories. Bolitho. Her man shaking hands with the *Larne's* officers, and then speaking alone with her commander, *the devil with half a face*. Then more cheers from the frigate's company, and weeks later, entering Portsmouth at the head of a blustery south-westerly. The ramparts of the old port's battery had been shining like silver in a sudden rain-squall even as they ran down on their anchorage. Afterwards the coaches, through more cheering crowds to London where Bolitho had seen Admiral Godschale, the news preceding them on the telegraph's line of towers all the way from Portsmouth.

They had paused at the small house on the river in Chelsea, where she had at last changed out of Tyacke's gown into her own clothing. When Sophie had picked up the discarded gown and asked, 'What about this, me lady?' she had answered, 'Take good care of it. One day I shall return it, and remind him of his kindness.' Sophie had watched her without understanding. 'Apart from Richard, he is the only man who has ever made me cry.'

She glanced now along the table and saw him watching her. She touched the ring on her finger, the rubies and diamonds flashing in the chandeliers' glittering light: a message to him from her. In response she saw him put his hand on his shirt where against his skin the locket was still in place, as it had been throughout those endless days and nights in the open boat.

She had accompanied him to the Admiralty, but only when he had insisted. 'We are *one*, Kate. I am heartily sick of pretence!'

Godschale had appeared genuinely pleased to see her, and he had certainly noticed the ring, with which she considered Richard had married her in the little church at Zennor. Then while Bolitho had gone to discuss other matters, she had walked through the corridors of Admiralty to the carriage waiting for her by the steps.

She realised now that Richard's other sister Felicity was watching her with hostile eyes. An enemy, and she would always be so.

Catherine thought instead of Richard, speaking to the men in the jolly-boat, hiding his disappointment when they had sighted land only to discover it was that cruel, deserted island. She remembered his face, feature by feature, when he had rallied them together with the promise of another island, water, and survival. No, she would never forget.

She looked at Adam's thoughtful profile and wondered if he had seen Zenoria, who had left with Keen's sisters to be reunited with her husband in Hampshire.

It was strange how everyone seemed to have changed . . . even the house, where they had been received with wild excitement by Ferguson and the others, and not without a few tears, either. Richard, in contrast, was able to accept it; he was used to being away at sea for far longer periods. But his reunion with Adam had been very moving, and only when she herself had embraced Adam had she seen the quiet desperation in his eyes. *Vulnerable*. Like Tyacke, who had lost something he would never regain. She looked away as Adam turned towards her. It might be safer not to dwell upon it.

Roxby unintentionally put paid to all that.

He beamed along the table, his forehead shining from exhilaration and good port.

'My one regret is that Captain Valentine Keen and his lovely young bride are not with us tonight. I'll lay odds there were some wet eyes when they came face to face, for it seemed everything was set against them.' Catherine saw Adam's fingers bunch into a tight fist as Roxby continued, 'But a sailor has to have someone waiting for him when he returns from serving his King.' He glanced fondly at his own two children, James and Helen. The latter had recently married a prosperous young lawyer; no risk of separation there, he thought. 'So I am hoping that our gallant Captain Keen will soon know the joy – ' he winked towards his wife ' – and the *challenge* of raising a family!'

That brought some laughter and banging on the table. Catherine knew Richard was watching her still. She was probably wrong, imagining it; and Richard must never know.

Roxby became solemn. 'I bid you all stand and raise a glass to Falmouth's greatest son, and to the Lady Catherine, whose beauty is matched only by her courage!'

They drank the toast and then made themselves comfortable again while the servants began to set plates of fruit compote at every place.

Bolitho sighed. He had never had much of an appetite since he had been a midshipman. He smiled at the memory. Even ship's rats fed on biscuit crumbs had sometimes been the young gentlemen's lot . . . He looked at Catherine, wanting to be near her, touch her: this separation and interminable hilarity reminded him of the night they had met again at English Harbour, when her treacherous husband had given a dinner such as this for him. It had been torture; and he had seen all the dangers, and had disregarded them.

He plucked at his waistcoat. He had returned home much thinner after their ordeal in the jolly-boat, but Lewis Roxby's massive feast of fish, fowl, venison and a procession of other dishes was taking care of that.

He thought over the extraordinary things Godschale had told him. He had asked what had happened to Captain Hector Gossage, Herrick's flag-captain in the ill-fated convoy.

Godschale had been pouring some wine, and had paused to wag a finger at him.

'Rear-Admiral Gossage, *if* you please. He will also have a special pension when he is finally finished with the navy . . . at present he's in charge of a mission seeking out timber for ship building. God knows there are few enough forests left in England suitable for the purpose.' He had shaken his head. 'In truth, it makes little sense.'

Bolitho recalled the private discussion he had observed between the judge advocate and Sir Paul Sillitoe during Herrick's court-martial. *Am I so naïve that I cannot recognise a bribe?* They had persuaded Gossage to give evidence clearing Herrick's name, to say nothing of absolving the Admiralty of debts it would otherwise have had to pay.

Other news. When *Golden Plover* had been reported lost, Godschale had hastily sent a replacement to the Cape of Good Hope. Yet another face: Rear-Admiral the Right Honourable Viscount Ingestre, who had been one of the three senior officers of the court-martial.

Godschale had been in a jovial mood. 'God's teeth, Sir Richard, it does my heart good to see you and that lovely creature who came with you. Only think, man, if you had arrived a month or so later you could have attended a splendid memorial service in your own honour, here in London!'

So *Golden Plover*'s loss had changed everything. Keen would not now be a commodore, and any role in the Portuguese campaign was out of the question. He had told Catherine most of it, while the carriage rolled along the embankment and into the peace of Chelsea. When it suited their lordships, he would hoist his flag again over *Black Prince*, which was still lying at Portsmouth. His flagship's latest caprice seemed scarcely credible – could a ship so new, without memories, possess a will of her own as his old *Hyperion* had once done? She had left her moorings at the completion of her repairs, with a new captain in command and an admiral yet to be selected, and had immediately collided with an old two-decker being used as a stores hulk. The two-decker had heeled over and sunk with her side still above water, and *Black Prince* had returned to her dock for further repairs. Her new captain was now faced with a court-martial. Fate. It had to be.

Godschale studied him grimly. 'It'll be the Caribbean again if you accept, Sir Richard. I'd not blame you if you rejected it, after all you've endured.'

Bolitho knew the admiral well enough to understand that he really meant the opposite.

Catherine had listened to him in silence, her eyes moving over the passing scene, the river and the traders, the stray dogs and the soldiers with their women by the tavern.

'I'll not argue, my love. I know what you are. I have seen and shared that other life as few could ever do.' She had faced him with sudden pride. 'I love thee so . . .'

He looked up from something Nancy was murmuring to him and heard his sister Felicity say, 'To be alone in a boat with all those men, Lady Catherine. It must surely have presented certain . . . difficulties?'

Catherine looked at her, her eyes flashing. 'We did not serve tea every day, Mrs Vincent, and the privacy we can take for granted here was scarce. But we had other things to distract us.'

'It is the opinion of some that you possess great beauty, Lady Catherine. I would have thought . . .'

Roxby began to intervene as everyone else fell silent, but Catherine reached out and touched his arm. She said, 'I think everyone here knows what you would have thought, Mrs Vincent.' She saw Miles Vincent hide a snigger. 'But out of respect for our hosts, and because of the love I bear the bravest, kindest man I have ever known, I will curb my tongue. But I must say, if it occurs again I shall be *less* than agreeable.'

Felicity rose and a footman ran to hold her chair.

'I have a headache. Miles, give me your hand – '

Nancy said hotly, 'She fills me with shame and disgust!'

But Bolitho was looking at the woman who had just declared her love for him, openly, without question, without shame.

Roxby said loudly into the silence, 'I think some more port, eh?' He shook his head at his wife and sighed noisily with relief. 'That was good of you, Lady Catherine. I did not want her to spoil this little affair for you.'

She laid her gloved hand on his. 'Spoil it?' She threw back her head and gave her bubbling laugh. 'When you have shared an ocean with blood-crazed sharks, even that embittered woman seems none too bad!'

Much later, as young Matthew drove the carriage along the narrow lanes and the fields gleamed in bright moonlight,

Catherine opened both windows to it, so that her bare shoulders shone like silver.

'I never dreamed I would see this again, nor smell the richness of the land.'

'I am sorry about my sister – '

She swung round and put her fingers on his mouth. 'Think only of what we did together. Even when we are separated, for so must we be, I will be with you as never before. Your ship and your men are a part of me too.' Then she asked tenderly, 'How is your eye now?'

Bolitho glanced out at the moon. The misty circle was still around it. 'It is much better.'

She leaned against him so that he could smell her perfume, her body.

'I am not convinced. But I shall write to that doctor again.' She hugged him, and gasped as he bent over and kissed her bare shoulder.

'But first, *love me*. It has been so long. Too long . . .'

Matthew, half dozing on his box, because the horses knew this road like their own stable, jerked awake as he heard their voices, their laughter and then the intimate silence. It was good to have them back, he thought. Complete again.

Allday had told him how she had stood beside Sir Richard and had faced the mutineers fearlessly, until they had won the day.

Matthew grinned, and knew that had it been lighter he might have been seen to be blushing.

With a woman like that, Sir Richard could conquer the whole world.

Bodmin, the county town of Cornwall, was filled with inns and post-houses, as well as cheap lodgings for the passengers of the many coaches that spread their routes eastward to Exeter and as far afield as London, north to Barnstaple and to the great ports of the West Country like Falmouth and Penzance. It was a plain old town, set on the fringes of the forbidding moor, which had long been the haunt of footpads and highwaymen, some of whom could be seen rotting in chains at the roadside as a warning to others.

The parlour of the Royal George was low-ceilinged and

pleasant, little different from most other coaching inns where travellers could take a tankard of ale or something stronger to wash down the excellent cheese and cold cuts of meat while the horses were changed for the next leg of the journey to Plymouth.

Captain Adam Bolitho declined to offer his hat and cloak to an inn servant but found a high-backed seat away from the fire, retaining his outer clothing as a kind of protection against local curiosity. In any case he was not particularly warm, despite the body heat of the other passengers and, now, a blazing log fire. He had left Falmouth early, on the first available coach, his collar turned up and the clasp of his boatcloak fastened to conceal his rank. His fellow passengers had been civilians, merchants mostly, and those who had managed to remain awake during the journey had been discussing the new possibilities they saw in trade with Portugal and later with Spain, as the war expanded. One of them had noticed Adam's hat, which he had kept more or less discreetly beneath his cloak.

'A commander, eh, sir? One so young, too!'

Adam had said shortly, 'Post-captain.' He did not intend to be rude, nor to give offence, but those sort of people made him sick. To them, war was profit and loss in business, not broken bones and the roar of cannon fire.

The man had persisted, 'When will it be over? Can *nobody* destroy this Bonaparte?'

Adam had replied, 'We do our best, sir. I suggest that if more gold were put into sound shipbuilding, and less into the bellies of City merchants, it would be over much sooner.' The man had not troubled him again.

That particular passenger was not here in the cosy parlour, and Adam guessed, thankfully, that Bodmin was the end of his journey.

One of the maids gave him a quick curtsy. 'Something for the cap'n?' She was young and saucy, and no stranger to the attention of lecherous passengers, he thought.

'Do you have brandy, my girl?'

She giggled. 'Nay, zur – but to you, yes.' She hurried away and soon returned with a large goblet and some fresh cheese.

'From the farm, zur.' She watched him curiously. 'Be you in command of a King's ship, zur?'

He glanced at her, the brandy hot on his tongue. 'Aye. *Anemone*, frigate.' The brandy was excellent, no doubt run ashore by members of the Trade.

She said with a smile, 'Tes an honour to serve *you*, zur.'

Adam nodded. And why not? He did not need to be in Plymouth as early as he had said. His first lieutenant would be enjoying his temporary command in his absence. The next coach would do. She recognised the uncertainty on his grave features and said, 'Well, now, if you be a-passing of this way again . . .' She took his goblet to refill it. 'My name be Sarah.'

She placed the goblet beside him and hurried away as the red-faced landlord bellowed out some demands from waiting passengers. It did not take long to change horses, and for the guard and coachman to down a few pints of cider or ale. Time was money.

Adam sank back against the tall chair and let the din of voices wash over him. The dinner; Lady Catherine's sharp exchange with *Aunt* Felicity, who would never acknowledge him as her nephew. His uncle . . . His thoughts stopped there. It had been like finding a brother, after fearing him to be dead.

He was glad to be returning to Plymouth for orders: despatches for the Channel Fleet, patrols in the Bay of Biscay or around Brest to assess the enemy's strength or intentions. Anything to keep him busy, his mind too full to allow any thought of Zenoria. In the same instant he knew he could not forget her, any more than he could stop himself remembering their lovemaking, her lithe body naked in his arms, her mouth like fire upon his. He had known several women, but none like Zenoria. Her fear had gone, and she had returned his passion as if it were all new and unspoiled, despite what she had endured.

He glanced at the goblet. Empty, and yet he had barely noticed it. When he looked again it was refilled. Perhaps he could sleep for the rest of the journey, and pray that the torment did not return.

Now she was with her husband, offering herself out of duty, out of guilt, but not out of love. It made him sick with jealousy even to think of them together. Keen touching her, brushing away her shyness, and possessing her as was his right.

He could not hate Valentine Keen. He had, in fact, always liked him, and knew that Keen felt as deeply towards his uncle as Adam himself did. Brave, fair, a decent man whom any woman would be proud to love. *But not Zenoria.* Adam sipped the brandy more carefully. He must be doubly careful in everything he did and said. If he were not, Valentine Keen would become a rival, an enemy.

I have no right. It is not merely a matter of honour, it is also the name of my family.

Horses clattered in the yard, and more voices announced the arrival of another coach; it would be the one that had left Falmouth this morning too, but which had travelled by way of Truro and outlying villages. The landlord's face split into a fixed grin. 'Mornin', gentlemen! What'll it be?' The girl named Sarah was there too, running her eye over the incoming faces.

Adam ignored them. What if he and Zenoria were brought together again? And if he persisted in avoiding her, would that not make it even more obvious? How would she behave? Submit, or tell her husband what had happened? That was unlikely. Better so, for all their sakes.

He would go outside and let the air clear his head until the coach was ready to proceed. He reached for his hat and then his hand poised, motionless, as he heard someone mention the name 'Bolitho'.

Two men were standing by the fire, one a farmer by the look of his clothing – sturdy boots and heavy riding gloves. The other was plump and well-dressed, probably a merchant on his way to Exeter.

The latter was saying, 'Such a commotion while I was staying in Falmouth – I was glad not to miss it. All the town turned out when Sir Richard Bolitho came back. I never knew that any man could inspire such affection.'

'I was there too. Often go for the market sales. Better 'n some, as good as most.' He tilted his tankard and then said, 'The Bolitho family's famous thereabouts – or notorious, should I say?'

'Are they, by God? I've read something of their exploits in the *Gazette*, but nothing . . .'

185

His companion laughed. 'Rules for some, but not for t'others, that's what *I* say!' Their coach must have stopped at other inns longer than the Royal George. His voice was loud and slurred.

He continued, as if addressing the whole room. 'Sleeping with another man's wife, an' talk of rape an' worse. Well, you know what they say about rape, my friend – there's usually two sides to it!'

Adam could feel the blood pounding in his brain, the man's voice probing his mind like a hot knife. Who was he talking about? Catherine? Zenoria? Or was he even hinting about Adam's own father, and his mother who had lived like a whore to raise the son Hugh Bolitho had not known about until it was too late?

He stood up and heard the girl ask, 'Be you a-goin', zur?'

'Directly – er, Sarah.' She was staring at him, unsure what was happening. He added, 'A tankard, if you please. A large one.' She brought it, mystified, as Adam moved out of the shadows and to a hatch which opened on to the inn kitchen. A face peered out at him. '*Zur?*'

'Fill this with the filthiest scummy liquid you have.' He pointed at a large tub where a young girl was rinsing out the bedroom chamber pots. 'That will do quite nicely.'

The man still gaped at him. 'Oi don't understand 'ee, zur . . .' He hesitated, and then something in Adam's face made him hurry away to the tub. Adam took the tankard and carried it towards the fire.

The landlord, polishing a jug, called out, 'Plymouth Flier be ready to board, gentlemen!'

But nobody moved as Adam said, 'I gather you were speaking of the Bolitho family in Falmouth.' His voice was very quiet and yet, in the silent parlour, it was like a clap of thunder.

'And what if I was?' The man swung on him. 'Oh, I see you're a gallant *naval* gentleman – I would expect the likes of you to disagree!'

Adam said, 'Sir Richard Bolitho is a fine officer – a gentleman in the truest sense, which obviously you would never understand.'

He saw the bluster begin to fail.

'Now, just a minute – I've had enough of this!'

The landlord called, 'I'll have no trouble here, gentlemen!'

Adam did not drop his gaze from the other man. 'No, landlord, not here. I am offering a drink to this loud-mouthed oaf.'

It took him off guard. '*Drink?*'

Adam said gently, 'Yes. It is piss, like the foulness of your mouth!' He flung it into his face and tossed the tankard to one side. While the other man spluttered and choked he threw back his cloak and said, 'May I introduce myself? Bolitho. Captain Adam Bolitho.'

The man stared at him wildly. 'I'll break your back, damn your bloody arrogance!'

'How much more must I insult you?' Adam struck him hard in the mouth, and said, 'Swords or pistols, sir? The choice is here and now, before the next coach.'

The landlord said urgently, 'You take it back, Seth. The young cap'n 'ere d'have a reputation.'

The man seemed to shrink. 'I didn't know. It was just *talk*, y'see!'

'It nearly cost you your wretched life.' He glanced at the sweating landlord. 'I beg your pardon for all this. I will make it worth your while.' There were gasps and a sudden, hurried grating of chairs as he produced a pistol and examined it, giving himself time. He knew he would have killed him. It was always there – lies about his family, several attempts to tarnish their honour, while the liars hid themselves in secret cowardice.

The man was practically in tears. '*Please*, Captain – I'd had too much to drink!'

Adam ignored him and turned towards a solitary brass candlestick where the flame was always kept burning for the tapers of customers wishing to light their pipes.

The crash of the shot brought shouts of alarm and screams from the kitchen. The flame had gone, but the candle was still intact. Before thrusting the pistol beneath his coat he asked quietly, 'Who told you these things?'

A coach guard stood in the doorway, a blunderbuss in his hands, but even he fell back when he saw the gleaming epaulettes of a naval captain.

The man hung his head. 'Some young blade, sir. I should've guessed he were a liar. But he said he was connected with the family.'

Adam knew instantly. 'Named Miles Vincent? Yes?'

The man nodded unhappily. 'In the market, it were.'

'Well. We shall just have to see, won't we?' He walked from the silent parlour and paused only to put some coins in the landlord's fist. 'Forgive me.'

The landlord counted it at a glance: it was a large amount. The ball had smashed into the wood panelling. He smiled. He would leave it there, and perhaps put a little plate above it to tell its story for the benefit of customers.

The girl was waiting beside the coach, while passengers bustled past averting their faces, in case they too provoked some violence.

Adam took out a gold coin and said, 'Live your life, Sarah. And don't sell yourself cheap.' He slipped the coin between her breasts. 'For a place that sells no brandy, you certainly know how to fire a man's spirits!'

The coach was long out of sight and its horn almost lost in distance as it approached the narrow bridge and the road for Liskeard before anyone spoke in the inn parlour, where the pistol smoke hung near the low ceiling like some evil spirit.

The man protested, 'How was *I* to know?' But nobody would look at him.

Then the landlord said, 'By God, Seth, it was nearly your last hour!'

The girl Sarah plucked the coin from her bodice and gazed at it intently, remembering the touch of his fingers, the easy way he had addressed her. She had never been spoken to like that before. She would never forget. She carefully replaced the coin, and when she stared down the empty road her eyes were filled with tears.

'God keep you safe, young cap'n!'

The landlord ambled from the inn door and put his arm around her shoulders. 'I knows, my dear. There's not many d' think much o' they hereabouts, and what they risk every time they do leave harbour.' He gave her a squeeze. 'I'd not care to fall afoul o' that fiery young master!'

Aboard the Plymouth Flier Adam stared out of the dusty

window at the passing countryside. Whenever he glanced at his travelling companions they were all either asleep or pretending to be. But sleep was denied him, and in the window's reflection he seemed to see her face. The girl with the long, beautiful hair: the girl with moonlit eyes, as his uncle had once called her.

He had been a fool back there at the Royal George. Post-captain or not, he would have been ruined if he had killed the other man in a duel. It would have meant disgrace for his uncle yet again. Was it always to be so?

. . . Miles Vincent. Yes, it would be. Perhaps his mother had put him up to it. Adam doubted it: the motive was too obvious. Hate, envy, revenge . . . his fingers tightened around his sword and he saw a flicker of apprehension cross the face of the man opposite him.

He thought suddenly of his father. He had heard from an old sailing-master who had known Hugh that he had been violent and quick-tempered, ready to call any one out if the mood took him: the memory of him still hung over the old house at Falmouth like a storm-cloud. *I will not make the mistake of following in his wake*.

Watery sunlight played across the sea for the first time in this journey.

He thought of his *Anemone*, daughter of the wind. She would be his only love.

Bryan Ferguson sat at the kitchen table of his cottage and surveyed his friend, who was standing by the window. He wanted to smile, but knew it was far too important a moment for amusement.

Allday plucked at his best jacket, the one with the gilt buttons, which Bolitho had given him to mark him as his personal coxswain. Nankeen breeches and buckled shoes: he was every inch the landsman's idea of the Jack Tar. But he seemed troubled, his deeply-sunburned features creased with uncertainty.

'Lucky I didn't lose this on that damned *Golden Plover*.' He tried to grin. 'Must have known there was something wrong with that little pot o' paint!'

Ferguson said, 'Look, John, just go and see the lady. If you don't, others will. She'll be a rare catch if she get the Stag on its feet again.'

Allday said heavily, 'An' what have I got to offer? Who wants a sailor? I reckon she'd have had a bellyful o' that after losing her man in *Hyperion*.'

Ferguson said nothing. It would either blow over, or this time it would be in earnest. Either way, it was so good to have Allday back again. He marvelled at the fact that Grace had never lost faith; she had earnestly believed that they would be saved.

Allday was still talking himself out of it.

'I've no money, just a bit put by, nothing for the likes of her . . .'

Ozzard came through the door. 'You'd better make up your mind, *matey*. Young Matthew's brought the cart round to drive you to Fallowfield.'

Allday peered at the looking glass on the kitchen wall and groaned. 'I don't know. I'll make a fool of myself.'

Ferguson made up his mind. 'I'll tell you something, John. When you and Sir Richard were said to be lost, I went over to the Stag.'

Allday exclaimed, 'You didn't *say* nothing, for God's sake?'

'No. Just had a stoup of ale.' He prolonged it. 'Very good it was too, for a small inn.'

Allday glared at him. 'Well, *did you*?'

Ferguson shook his head. 'But I did see her. Done wonders for the place.'

Allday waited, knowing there was something else.

Ferguson said quietly, 'I'll tell you another thing. She came all the way into town just to be at the memorial service.' He grinned, the relief still evident on his face. 'The one you missed!'

Allday picked up his hat. 'I'll go then.'

Ferguson punched his massive arm. 'Hell, John, you sound as if you're facing a broadside!'

Ozzard said, 'Her ladyship is coming.'

Ferguson hurried to the door. 'She'll want to see the books. 'Tis a fair tonic to have her here again.'

Ozzard waited for him to bustle away and then, secretively,

laid a leather bag on the table. 'Your half. Sounds as if it might come in useful.'

Allday opened the string and stared with disbelief at the glittering gold inside.

Ozzard said scornfully, 'You didn't think I'd throw good gold to the sharks, did you? I sometimes wonder about you, I do indeed.' He relented. 'Lead pellets made just as much of a splash, or so I thought at the time.'

Allday looked at him gravely. 'Anything I can ever do for you – but you knows that, don't you, Tom?'

Ferguson came back, puzzled. 'Lady Catherine wasn't there.'

Ozzard shrugged his narrow shoulders. 'Probably changed her mind. Women do, you know.'

Allday walked out into the pale sunlight and climbed into the little cart, the one used for collecting wine or fresh fish from the harbour. Young Matthew, too, took particular notice of Allday's smart appearance, but like Ferguson he decided not to risk making any sort of joke.

When they reached the little inn, with the Helford River showing itself beyond the trees, Matthew said, 'I'll be back for you later.' He looked at him fondly, remembering what they had once seen and done together, the 'other life' Lady Catherine had once wanted to learn about, which she had now so bravely shared.

'I've never seen you like this afore, John.'

Allday climbed down. 'Hope you never do again.' He strode towards the inn and heard the cart clatter away before he could change his mind.

It was cool inside the door, a smell of freshness, the simple furniture scrubbed and decorated with wild flowers. There was a lively fire in the grate, and he guessed it would be getting cold earlier in the evenings so close to the river and the sea.

He tilted his head like an old dog as he caught the aroma of newly baked bread and something cooking in a pot.

At that moment she came through a low door and stopped dead when she saw him. With one hand she tried to wipe a smudge of flour from her cheek, while with the other she swept a loose lock of hair from her eyes.

'Oh, Mister Allday! I thought it was the man with the eggs! Seeing me like this – I must look an awful sight!'

He crossed the room carefully as if he were treading on something delicate. Then he put down his parcel on a serving table. 'I brought you a present, Mrs Polin. I hope you like it.'

She unwrapped it slowly, and all the while he was able to watch her. *An awful sight*. She was the dearest woman he had ever laid eyes on.

Without looking up she said shyly, 'My name's Unis.' Then with a gasp of surprise she lifted out the model ship on which Allday had been working before leaving for the Cape of Good Hope.

He said nothing; but somehow she knew it was the old *Hyperion*.

'Is it really for me?' She stared at him, her eyes shining.

Then she reached out and took one big hand in both of hers.

'*Thank you*, John Allday.' Then she smiled at him. 'Welcome home.'

13

. . . and Farewell

James Sedgemore, the *Black Prince*'s first lieutenant, paused in his endless pacing of the quarterdeck to take a telescope from the midshipman-of-the-watch. His face was reddened by the lively south-easterly wind, and he was very aware of the activity around him as the ship prepared to get under way. Lying to her anchor off Spithead, she was already responding, her masts and rigging shivering, while above the decks tiny figures swarmed like monkeys amongst the black tracery of shrouds and stays, halliards and ratlines.

Sedgemore trained the glass on the sally port and saw *Black Prince*'s long green barge standing off the stairs, the oars pulling and backing to hold her clear of any damage in the choppy water. Tojohns, the captain's coxswain, was in charge, and would make sure that everything was all right.

The whole ship was alive with rumour and speculation after some of the tales Tojohns had brought aboard with him. The shipwreck, a mutiny, man-eating sharks, and through it all, the admiral's lady suffering and enduring with the rest of them.

A man gave a yelp of pain as a boatswain's mate swung at him with his rope starter. It would be good to get the people out to some sea-room, Sedgemore thought. The officers for the most part were as green as the bulk of the hands, half of whom had never set foot in a King's ship before. They would soon learn, he thought grimly. He was not going to lose his chances of further promotion because of their ignorance or stupidity. He glanced at this same deck, where his predecessor had been cut in halves by a French ball. That was often how promotion came, and you never questioned it, in case the chance never offered itself again.

He thought too of his captain, so changed in manner from the time he had left the ship for some vague appointment in Cape Town: his temporary replacement had been swiftly removed after the ship's unfortunate collision. That had been lucky for Sedgemore too. He himself had been ordered ashore with despatches for the port admiral, and was quite blameless.

It was good to have Captain Keen back. The other man had been so distant he had been impossible to know. Keen on the other hand had returned cheerful and confident, and apparently not even troubled too much by the large proportion of landmen and scum from the jails.

There had been one awkward moment however, when *Black Prince* had left her moorings and sailed through the narrow entrance of Portsmouth Harbour to anchor here off Spithead. The wind had been unusually strong, and Sedgemore had felt the hair rising on his neck as he watched the shallows beneath Portsmouth Point and its cluster of houses seemingly just a few yards clear. He had turned towards his captain, and had seen him smiling as men scampered to the braces, and extra hands had flung themselves on the great double-wheel. Looking back, Keen had shown a new, youthful recklessness, which had not been there when they had waited for Rear-Admiral Herrick's court-martial to begin.

Surviving the perils of an open boat, or returning to a young wife – it was probably a bit of both.

More men ran to loosen belaying-pins in readiness to free the halliards, so that nothing would stick in the heavy drift of spray when the anchor broke free.

Sedgemore smiled to himself. Yes, it would be good to go. Not Portugal but the West Indies, it appeared. Where he would be out of reach of his creditors until his fortune improved. Sedgemore was ambitious to a point of devotion. A command of his own, then post-rank; it was like a mapped-out road of his own fate. But his weakness was gambling, and a spell safely in the Indies would keep him out of trouble . . . until the next time. And Sir Richard Bolitho would soon be aboard again. Surely with his experience and leadership, there would be even better chances for advancement.

He saw Jenour appear momentarily on deck with Yovell before they vanished beneath the poop. Jenour, previously such a lively young officer, full of experiences with which he had sometimes entertained the wardroom, of all those who had come back from almost certain death, seemed subdued and unwilling to talk. However, Sedgemore knew nothing would remain a secret from anyone after a few weeks at sea.

The fourth lieutenant, Robert Whyham, who was officer-of-the-watch, said, 'Barge is shoving off, sir!'

'I'll tell the captain. Pipe the guard to the side.' He liked Whyham, who was the only lieutenant from the original wardroom, and had been promoted from sixth place in the past few months. He also envied him without really knowing the reason, except that Whyham had served under Captain Keen in a previous flagship, the French prize *Argonaute*. There had been glory in her great fight too. Sedgemore rarely allowed his mind to dwell on the harsher side of things.

He hesitated, a last look round: nothing adrift which he might be blamed for. 'And tell that midshipman to go forrard and make certain the admiral's flag is already bent-on and ready to break on the last order of the salute.'

Whyham touched his dripping hat. 'Aye, sir.'

At least the reception would go smoothly; both of the Royal Marine officers were from the original detachment which now made up an eighth part of *Black Prince*'s eight hundred officers and men.

Lieutenant Sedgemore straightened the lapels on his coat and removed his hat as he reached the rigid marine sentry outside the captain's screen door.

One day, I shall have something like this. For a terrible moment he imagined he had spoken aloud, but when he glanced at the sentry's eyes he was thankful to see they were suitably blank.

He rapped on the door with his knuckles. 'Captain, sir?'

The *Black Prince*'s captain stood directly below the skylight of his day cabin and looked through the spray-dappled glass. The sky was grey, the clouds fast-moving in the occasional gusts against the ship's high tumblehome, which made itself felt in the very bowels of the hull. He glanced at Jenour, who was half-heartedly examining some papers Yovell had left for Keen's signature. It was hard to see him in that open boat with his torn hands hauling on an oar; the blood in the bottom after Allday had amputated the *Golden Plover*'s master's infected leg. Hard to picture himself either, for that matter.

He knew what was troubling Jenour, and said, 'It had to happen eventually. You have been Sir Richard's flag-lieutenant longer than anyone. He likes you, and this is his way of rewarding you, as is only proper.'

Jenour came out of his dark thoughts. Bolitho had told him himself that after they had reached the West Indies, and at the first opportunity, he would appoint him in command of some suitable vessel. It was customary, and in his heart Jenour had known it was inevitable. But he did not want to leave the vice-admiral. He had become a part of this precious body, *we happy few* as poor Oliver Browne had once called it. There were *very* few of them left now, but that had never deterred him.

Keen took his silence for a persisting doubt and said, 'Responsibility is not yours to toss away. It is a privilege, not a right, as I and others like me soon discovered. Once you were less certain.' He smiled. 'Less mature, if you like. But your experience has grown with you, and it is needed more than ever. Look at this ship, Stephen. Boys and old men, volunteers and rascals. It is the way of things. Sir Richard is ordered to the Indies to command a squadron of fourteen sail of the line.' He gestured across the litter of papers. 'So what have their lordships offered him? Six instead of fourteen, one frigate instead of the promised three. It never changes. Which is why your skills, like it or not, are sorely needed. Take the vice-admiral's nephew, for instance. He too was once his flag-lieutenant – now he is posted, and commands a fine frigate.'

Jenour could not compare himself with Adam Bolitho. He was so like his uncle, but had a touch of fire which came from elsewhere, probably his dead father.

Jenour sighed. 'It was good of you to listen, sir.'

Keen watched him leave and began the routine of preparing himself for sea. Once the anchor was up and catted, he would not leave the quarterdeck until his ship was safely clear of the narrows and with the Needles well abeam. Then south-west into open waters, where his untried hands could find their skills, or lack of them, as the great ship bore down towards the Western Approaches.

Feet were moving everywhere, with the occasional shout, muffled by distance and the stoutness of the timbers, to tell of the activity and the tension of getting a man-of-war under sail. There would be other thoughts, too, apart from fear of heights above the swaying hull, or fighting out along the yards to learn the mysteries and terrors of making and reefing sails in half a gale. Thoughts of leaving home, perhaps never to return. Men snatched from the streets and lanes by press-gangs who had no time for heart or pity. That was a peculiar aspect of the character of seamen. For the most part those already in the King's service, even the pressed men, saw no reason why others should not share their own fate.

He crossed to the larboard side and peered through the streaming glass of the quarter gallery. Blurred, like a painting left out in the rain: the dull grey of fortifications, and the cheerful red roofs beyond. He recalled bringing this ship through the narrow harbour entrance, how Julyan the sailing-master had exclaimed, 'God, I thought we was going to take the veranda off the old Quebec Inn for a moment or two!'

Have I changed so much? Has she done that for me too?

After all, what had he really expected? He loved her; why had he been surprised that she could at last find it within herself to return it? Perhaps it was merely gratitude . . .

But it had been none of these things. For a long, long time she had stood pressed in his arms, sobbing quietly, murmuring into his chest.

Even then, he had doubted it.

They had sat by the fire in the rooms set aside for them in the great house in Hampshire. For all they knew, it might have been empty but for themselves. Then she had taken his hand and had led him to that adjoining room, where another fire made the shadows dance around them like rejoicing spectres. She had faced him, paces away, her eyes shining in the flames' reflections, then very deliberately had let her gown fall to the floor. She had come to him, and together they had fallen on to the great bed. He had been in a daze as she had drawn his lips to her thrusting breasts, held his mouth to each nipple until he was roused to madness. But it was not to be so soon. She had stretched herself naked on the bed, so that her curving scar had been laid bare in the flickering firelight: he had never been permitted to see it so unashamedly revealed. She had looked at him over her bare shoulder and had whispered, 'Take me as you will. I have the courage now.' Her voice had broken as he had gripped her body with both hands, 'And the love you were denied.'

It had been like that until Keen had received his orders for Portsmouth: passion, exploration, discovery. The parting had been difficult, and left an ache in his heart he had never before experienced.

There was a tap at the outer door and he said, 'Enter!' No wonder he had risked even this ship in a moment of remembered ecstasy.

Sedgemore glanced around the cabin, where important members of the court-martial had taken refreshment during the various adjournments.

'Sir Richard Bolitho's barge has just left the sally port, sir.'

'Very well.' Keen looked at his watch. Another departure, but this time with hope, the knowledge that she would be waiting for him. He knew now why he had been so unmoved by the events in the jolly-boat. Because he had not cared if he had lived or died, and had nothing to lose.

'Fast current running, sir.'

Keen nodded, his thoughts lingering on those nights and sometimes, the days. She had introduced him to a desire and torment he had never known, to pleasures he had never imagined.

He said abruptly, 'Yes. Put all spare hands on the capstan bars today. I want to break out the anchor as soon as possible.'

'I've already done that, sir.'

Keen smiled. *You would.* Given time, Sedgemore would become a good first lieutenant; he had already shown that. It was just as well, with all the raw hands at their disposal.

Sedgemore, he noted, was well turned-out to greet his admiral. His uniform coat had not been thrown together by some dockside Jew, but spoke of a good costly tailor. His sword, too, was expensive, its blade embossed and patterned in blue steel. It certainly did not come out of a lieutenant's pay, and Keen knew that Sedgemore's father was a humble saddler.

Keen brought his mind back to the ship's business. 'I see we have more than a fair share of squeakers amongst our young gentlemen.'

'Aye, sir. Two of the midshipmen are but twelve years old.'

Keen picked up his sword. 'Well, watch them, Mr Sedgemore.'

'As if they were my own sons, sir!'

Keen eyed him calmly. 'It was not what I meant. At that tender age they are often the cruellest bullies in the ship. I'll not have the people harassed more than need be.'

He strode past him and glanced at the sentry. 'How's the wife, Tully?'

The marine brought his heels smartly together. 'We're expecting a third bairn, thank you, sir!' He was still beaming as Keen and his first lieutenant came into the watery grey daylight beyond the poop.

Sedgemore shook his head. He was learning a lot about his captain today. Had he been more perceptive he might have guessed where Keen had first gained his own experience.

Keen watched the green-painted barge, turning now to pass astern of a motionless yawl. Without the aid of a telescope he could see Bolitho hunched in his boatcloak at the stern-sheets, Allday beside him, and his own coxswain at the tiller. Remembering, yes. Perhaps him most of all. The lovely woman beside him, her body revealed by the soaking spray as she had taken her place in the crowded boat. The mutineers who had died, one at Allday's hand, the other, if he had indeed been one of the mutineers, under the merciless agony of drinking seawater. There had been news of one other mutineer who had been taking refuge in the boatswain's big cutter. He had been hanged at Freetown within hours of being marched ashore. Justice was always harder and faster the more sea miles you were from high authority.

Lady Catherine would have been here in Portsmouth, whatever Bolitho had said. She would be over yonder now, watching the lively barge, clinging to his image as she would soon have to hold on to his memory.

Keen smiled briefly to the senior Royal Marines officer,

Major Bourchier, as he completed inspecting the guard of honour.

'Sorry to leave, Major?'

Bourchier puffed out his cheeks, which were almost the colour of his scarlet coat.

'No, sir, I'm ready for a spot of soldierin', what?'

Little imagination, but in truth a good soldier, Keen thought. The only time he had seen him show any emotion had been aboard Herrick's *Benbow* after the battle. The marines, the whole afterguard had been scattered like toy soldiers, their mingled blood marking them down for what they were. Perhaps he had seen himself there. What they all thought, at one time or another.

'Stand by aft! Royal Marines, *ready!*'

It seemed bitterly cold on Portsmouth Point, with a wet, blustery wind making the green barge shine like glass as its crew fought to hold station on the stairs.

Bolitho glanced past the weathered opening of the sally port, through which he and so many others had gone before. This time it was so different. He put his arm around her shoulders, hating the moment of parting. He saw Allday on the stairs watching the boat, a sergeant of marines nearby keeping an eye on a squad of his men. Their duty was to see that Bolitho's remaining minutes in England were undisturbed by curious onlookers. Not that there were many of those. This must surely be a foretaste of the winter, and the October gales.

Catherine brushed some wet hair from her face and gazed at him searchingly.

'You will take care, dearest of men?'

He held her. 'You know I will. I have everything to live for – now.' He had begged her not to wait, but to go straight on to Falmouth. But he had known it would not happen.

She said, 'When we were in that boat . . .' She hesitated, wanting to be anywhere but on this windswept street. 'I knew I could face death with you beside me. Without you . . .' Again he heard the difficult pause. 'You see, I am not so brave.'

On their way here, with Matthew guiding the carriage through the deep ruts, which would become a bog as soon as winter closed in, he had told her about his squadron: six sail of the line instead of fourteen, one frigate instead of three. Even with the addition of *Black Prince*, arguably one of the most powerful ships in the world, it was not much of a force for finally stamping out French power and possessions in the Caribbean. And all because Bonaparte had wanted to take Portugal and put his own son on the throne of Spain. The action had divided their forces yet again, so that the Danish ships seized to complement the fleet were still not enough.

He said, 'I shall miss you with all my heart.' She said nothing and he knew she was finding it equally hard. *Release her shoulders, step out on to the stairs and into the barge. It will be over.*

He recalled how she had shown immediate dismay when he had told her that his solitary frigate was to be the old *Tybalt*, a ship he knew very well, with a captain who would be worth his weight in gold when sniffing out the enemy's strength in the Indies.

'Not Adam, then?' Was she so concerned for his safety that she wanted all those dearest around him?

He asked, 'What shall you do?'

She was watching him intensely, desperately. 'I shall help Ferguson – and maybe Zenoria will ask my advice in seeking a house of her own in Cornwall. I know that Valentine's family still awes her . . .' Bolitho was not surprised. Lavish houses in London and in Hampshire, one brother a wealthy lawyer and the other who described himself simply as a 'farmer': he owned even more land than Roxby.

She turned in his arms and studied him again. 'I have sent a few things over to the ship. To keep you well nourished – to remind you of me sometimes.'

He kissed her hair. It was wet from spray and perhaps drizzle. But it could have been tears.

'Take care of your eye.'

It was all she said. There might once have been hope, the surgeon had said yet again. Something might still come about. But he had left little doubt in their minds that it was now only a matter of time.

Bolitho heard the horses stamping on the cobbles, eager to go, as if they knew they were returning this time to their own warm stables in Falmouth.

He said, 'I have arranged for some out-riders for the journey, Kate.'

She pulled off her glove and laid her hand on his cheek.

'Have you forgotten your tiger so soon? Have no fears for me, Richard. Just remember the house, waiting for you . . . D'you remember telling me to do that after the *Golden Plover* was lost, and our chances of survival were so small?'

He looked past her. 'I will never forget.' There was silence, then she said, 'If only we could have had more time.'

'What all sailors lament, my love.'

'And it will be your birthday in three days. I . . . so wanted to be with you.'

So she felt it too, he thought. Age; time; always the passing of time. It seemed so very precious now.

He walked her to the shelter of the wall. In his mind's eye he could see his flagship already there in the Western Ocean. A great ship, sailing alone, but a mere speck on that vast expanse of hostile sea.

'I shall raise a glass to thee, Kate.'

Allday did not turn but called, 'I think it's time, Sir Richard. The tide's on the turn an' Tojohns is hard put to hold the barge steady.'

'Very well. Signal him alongside.' Then he turned away from the sea and held her tightly against his spray-spotted boatcloak.

'I love thee so, Kate. My heart is splintered in the pain I feel at parting from you.'

They kissed for a long while, holding on to the moment and all the memories which had triumphed over danger, even death.

When she looked at him again there were real tears in her dark eyes.

'I cannot bear the thought of you being at English Harbour again without me. Where you came, and our love was freed for all time.'

Bolitho had already thought of that, but had hoped she had been spared the reminder.

He heard the oars being tossed and saw her eyes turn towards Allday who was standing beside the pitching barge, in which a youthful lieutenant was sitting, staring about him as if he had never been in charge of a boat before.

She called, 'This is not the first time, Allday. But take care of him for me!'

Allday tried to smile. 'We both got a lot to come back for, m'lady – leastways, I think I have!'

He watched them kiss, knowing what this parting was costing the man he served and loved beyond all others; then he climbed down into the barge and glared at the gaping lieutenant. 'It's customary for the officer to be ashore when the vice-admiral comes down, *sir!*' He saw Tojohns give a quick grin as the lieutenant jumped on to the pier and all but lost his cocked hat to the wind.

Allday said between his teeth, 'Bloody hopeless, that's what!'

Bolitho saw none of it. 'Go now. Do not wait. You will catch cold up here.'

She released him very slowly, so that their fingertips were just touching when their arms were outstretched.

He said, 'I have the locket.'

She answered as she always did. 'I will take it off for you when we lie together again, my dearest man.'

Then, with the old sword swaying against his hip, Bolitho went down the stairs and touched his hat to the lieutenant and coxswain.

'I am ready.' He sat beside Allday, his boatcloak turned up over his ears, his hat beneath it on his lap.

'*Bear off! Give way all!*'

The oars rose and fell, and with the tiller hard over the smart barge turned quickly away from the slime-covered, treacherous stairs.

In his aching mind the oars seemed to beat a steady rhythm, up, down, up, down, rising and falling like wings as each pull carried him further away from the shore.

Back to the life he had come to expect since he had gone to sea at the age of twelve. *It will be your birthday in three days.* He could still hear her voice on the wind. Later on, in the seclusion of his cabin, he would remember every hour of their time together. Their walks, the happiness of silence and understanding, the sudden and demanding love and hunger for one another which had left them breathless, and sometimes shy.

He shifted round to watch the land drifting away, the anchored black and buff hulls of several men-of-war swaying heavily to their cables. *My world.* But try as he might, he could not accept that there was nothing else. Perhaps in the privations of the *Golden Plover*'s jolly-boat there had been something to learn, even for him. The suffering which had brought a strange comradeship beyond rank and title, the loyalty which had kept Catherine and her maid safe in spite of the very real danger all around them.

Don't leave me.

The master, Samuel Bezant, cursing those who had betrayed him; Tasker the mate, who had been a part of the plot. He wondered if she ever allowed her mind to return to her Spanish comb, and how she had used it on the traitor Jeff Lincoln. She must have been planning what she must do to save Jenour from being discovered even as Lincoln had been pawing at her body. And Tyacke, his horribly scarred face so full of pleasure and pride that it should be his own ship which had finally found and saved them.

He glanced around, imagining her voice across the frothing choppy water, almost expecting to see her. But the walls were nearly out of sight in the spray that hung like mist on a low shore.

Don't leave me.

He stared ahead and saw each bargeman trying to avoid his gaze. Most of them at least would know him; but what of the others, and the small squadron assembling out there in the tropical heat and the fierce revolving storms that could tear the sticks out of any ship? *They would have to learn.* Like all those who had been left behind as a part of the price of admiralty.

Keen would be relieved to be sailing without any other consorts or responsibilities. It would give him time to train his people, to work them at sail and gun until they were a match for any ship which had been in commission far longer. It had been like seeing the old devil-may-care Keen again; it must have been a wonderful reunion for him with his girl with the moonlit eyes. The sailor and his mermaid.

He felt Allday stir. 'There she is, Sir Richard.' He displayed neither enthusiasm nor regret. She was his ship. This was his lot.

Bolitho shaded his eyes and saw Allday give him a quick, worried glance. *Black Prince* seemed to tower above the nearest seventy-four. There were tiny figures working on the yards and in the topmasts' rigging; others moved along the gangways or waited in groups, no doubt being given more instructions by their lieutenants and warrant officers.

A ship to be proud of, but one without memory or tradition.

To settle his troubled thoughts Bolitho said quietly, 'I am glad you have found your lady. I hope that all is well for the future.'

It was pointless to remind Allday that he was free to quit the sea whenever he chose. He had earned it as much as many, and more than most. And now with the recurring pains in his chest from the Spanish sword thrust, he ought to be given a chance to enjoy something of his life. But it was no use. He had tried before. Allday only got angry, or hurt, which was much worse in so big a man in every other way.

Allday replied, 'She's a fine little craft, Sir Richard. Can't imagine what she ever saw in poor Jonas Polin!' He chuckled, 'God rest his soul!' Neither saw the curious stares from some of the bargemen. A coxswain chatting with his flag-officer was not an everyday sight in the King's navy. Allday added, 'We has an understanding, so to speak. I must keep my place, but she'll entertain no other.' He frowned. 'Well, summat like that.' He glanced at Bolitho uncertainly. In a few moments there would be too much to do, too many faces for his admiral to recognise and acknowledge. Not many of the former, he thought.

He said, 'If anything was to happen, Sir Richard.' He spoke so quietly that his voice was almost drowned by the creak of oars and the surge of tide.

Bolitho laid his hand on the big man's sleeve. 'Speak no more of it, old friend. It is the same for us both.' He tried to smile. 'The good die young, so there's an end to it, eh?'

When he looked again Bolitho saw the jib-boom sweeping past as Tojohns steered the barge as close around the bows as he dared. The fierce-eyed figurehead loomed overhead:

Edward, Prince of Wales and son of Edward III, in chain mail and black armour with a splash of colour, the fleur de lys and English lions on the surcoat. Menacing enough to strike at the heart of any enemy, as it had on that terrible morning when they had shattered the French ship that had reduced Herrick's *Benbow* to a broken hulk.

Bolitho had the usual tense dryness in his throat as he saw the side-party waiting by the entry port, the blue and white of officers, the scarlet of the marines.

It often amused him when he thought of it at other times. Who would ever guess that he too might be nervous and unsure? It did not amuse him now.

'*Bowman!*'

Bolitho took out his hat and wedged it on to his head. Remembering her face, when he had rid himself of his queue in favour of the more modern haircut which Allday, who had the longest pigtail he had ever seen, had referred to as 'a custom of the younger wardroom bloods!' But Kate had not chided him for it, nor laughed at his apprehension at being older than she.

Allday hissed, 'Ready to come about, Sir Richard?' The ship stood high above them, the barge dipping and pitching as if to cast off the bowman's attempt to hold on to the chains.

Their eyes met. 'Ready, it is.' Bolitho moved the sword clear of his leg and reached out for the hand-ropes. It would only need one wrong step. And then, all at once or so it seemed, he was through the entry port and on to the comparative shelter of the gundeck.

The squeal of calls, the slap and bang of bayonetted muskets and the flash of the marine officer's sword: it never failed to overwhelm him. And here was Keen hurrying to greet him, his youthful features all smiles.

'Welcome aboard, Sir Richard!'

They gripped hands and Bolitho said with a wry smile, 'I am sorry you didn't get your broad pendant, Val. Fate was against it this time.'

Keen grinned. 'It is unimportant, Sir Richard. Like poor Stephen Jenour, I am not eager for that moment!'

Bolitho nodded to the assembled officers, seeing their expressions of curiosity, of hope perhaps. They depended on him for the future; to them, he *was* their future, for better or worse.

'I shall go aft directly, Val. I know you are all eagerness to weigh anchor.' He broke off and stared at a group of men who were being mustered by one of the lieutenants. 'That man, Val – '

'Aye, sir. New hands. But the one you're looking at is the self-same William Owen, *Golden Plover*'s lookout on that unfortunate day.'

Bolitho said, 'Put him ashore. He has a protection. And after what he did – '

But for his respect Keen would have laughed. 'He volunteered, sir. "Thought we should keep together", were his words.' He watched Bolitho's unmasked surprise. *You don't understand, do you? Not even now. Perhaps you never will.*

He led the way aft, knowing that Bolitho was probably recalling the court-martial, that bitter memory.

Inside the great cabin Ozzard and Jenour were waiting. Bolitho looked around. Her wine cabinet and cooler was already in position. It had been removed from the ship when he had been reported killed.

Ozzard said apologetically, 'We've not got everything stowed yet, Sir Richard, but I've fresh coffee ready.' He glanced around, proud of what he had managed to achieve in so short a time. Bolitho noticed that he showed no regrets about leaving. After the shipwreck he could have been forgiven for remaining on hard, dry land.

There was an open chest on the black and white checkered deck, and inside he saw some neatly parcelled books. They were new, bound in fine green leather and beautifully tooled in gilt so delicate it might have been finished with a gold pen.

'What are these?'

Ozzard wound his hands into his apron. 'From her ladyship, Sir Richard. Came out in the guard-boat.'

Keen saw his face and said quickly, 'Come with me, Stephen.' To Ozzard he added, 'You may bring Sir Richard some coffee.'

The doors closed and Bolitho heard the sentry put down his musket.

He got down on his knees and studied the collection: all the plays he had lost when *Golden Plover* had gone down. He took out one volume which lay apart from the rest. Shakespeare's collected sonnets, the printing of which was very clear, obviously chosen with great care to ensure that he could read them easily.

He felt his heart lurch as he saw a ribbon marker closed between the pages: swiftly he opened the book and held it where it would catch the best light on this grey day.

It was her own message, to comfort him when the thought of ageing and separation sought to depress him.

> *It is the star to every wandering barque,*
> *Whose worth's unknown, altho' his height be taken.*

Then he seemed to find her reassurance.

> *Love's not time's fool, though rosy lips and cheeks*
> *Within his bending sickle's compass come;*
> *Love alters not with his brief hours and weeks . . .*

He got up, oblivious to the shouted commands from the deck, the squeal of tackles, the shiver of the capstan through every timber.

He went to the stern windows and hoisted one open, his face and chest instantly drenched in rain and spray.

Just once, he called her name, and across the tumbling water he heard her cry.

Don't leave me.

14

Bad Blood

Ozzard waited for the deck to sway upright again before refilling his vice-admiral's cup with fresh coffee.

It was the afternoon of the sixth day since leaving Spithead, and it seemed as if every contested mile of their passage so far had been dogged by foul weather and the inevitable stream of accidents. Captain Keen had been forced to up-anchor with the ship's complement still fifty short, and with so many unskilled landmen aboard it was no wonder there had been injuries, and worse.

One man had vanished during a shrieking gale in the middle of the night, his cries unheard as he was swept over the side by a great white-bearded wave. Others had suffered cracked bones and torn hands, so that Coutts, the surgeon, had pleaded personally with Keen to reduce sail and ride out each storm under reefed canvas.

But day by day, bad weather or not, the drills continued, one mast racing the other to make or shorten sail, the rigging of safety nets over the upper gundeck to become used to doing it even in pitch darkness if required, so that the crews of the thirty-eight twelve-pounders would not be crushed by falling spars and rigging should they be called to action.

Deck by deck, from the massive carronades in the bows to the middle and lower gundeck where the main armament of powerful thirty-two pounders, or 'long nines' as they were nicknamed, the men lived behind sealed ports as great seas boiled along the weather side, and flung solid sheets of water high up over the nettings.

Keen had shown his faith in his warrant officers and those specialists who were the backbone of any ship, and had been quick to display his confidence in them over matters of discipline. With a company so mixed, and with many completely inexperienced, tempers frayed and fists flew on several occasions. It led inevitably to the harsh and degrading spectacle of punishment, the lash laying a man's back in cruel stripes while the rain spread the blood around the gratings, and the marine drummer boys beat out the time between each stroke.

Bolitho, more than any other, knew how Keen hated the use of flogging. But discipline had to be upheld, especially in a ship sailing alone, and each day standing deeper and deeper into the Atlantic.

Keen was equally unbending with his lieutenants and midshipmen. The former he would take aside and speak to in his quiet, contained fashion. If the officer was foolish enough to ignore his advice, the second interview was of a very different nature. James Cross, the sixth lieutenant who had accompanied the barge to ferry Bolitho from Portsmouth Point, was a case in point. He seemed eager enough, but at most duties he had displayed an incompetence which made even the most hardened petty officer groan.

Allday had been heard to comment, 'He'll be the death of someone afore long. Should've been strangled at birth!'

The midshipmen, for the most part, came from established naval families. To sail in the flagship under an officer so renowned, or notorious as some insisted, was a chance of advancement and promotion which could not be overlooked. It was strange that after so many years, victories and setbacks, bloody battles and the demanding rigours of blockade duty, there were many who still believed that the war would soon be over, especially now that English soldiers stood on enemy soil. For young officers hoping for a rewarding life in the King's service, it might be a last chance of making a name for themselves before their lordships cut the fleet to the bone, and cast their sailors, from poop to forecastle, on the beach: such was a nation's gratitude.

Ozzard opened the screen door and Keen stepped into the cabin, his cheeks glowing from the sharp northerly wind.

'Coffee, Val?'

Keen sat down, but his head was still tilted as if he was listening to the activity on the upper deck.

Then he took the coffee and sipped it gratefully. Bolitho watched him, thinking of Joseph Browne's old shop in St James's, to which Catherine had taken him during their visits to London, and where she must have arranged for all the fine coffee, cheeses and wine to be sent to the ship. Close by had been another shop, Lock's the hatters. Bolitho had been reluctant for her to indulge in what he had believed extravagance when she had wanted to buy him a new gold-laced hat, to replace the one he had tossed to Julyan the sailing master when they had sailed to meet the great *San Mateo*. She had insisted, reminding him, 'Your hero purchased his hats here. Did he, I wonder, deprive his Emma of the pleasure of paying?'

Bolitho smiled at the memory. So many things found and enjoyed in that other London, which he had never known until she had shown him.

Keen said absently, 'The master says we have logged some eight hundred and sixty miles, give or take. If the wind eases I'll get more canvas on her. I am heartily sick of this!'

Bolitho looked at the salt-caked stern windows. *Six days*. It already felt a month or more. He had not kept his promise to raise a glass to Catherine on the night of his birthday. There had been a great gale, the one when they had lost a man outboard, and he had been on deck rather than endure the torment of listening and wondering. As the old heron-like surgeon, Sir Piers Blachford, had remarked, 'In your heart you are still a captain, and you find it hard to delegate that task to others.'

Keen remarked, 'I wonder what Zenoria is doing. To have thought her husband lost, and to recover him only to lose him again is sour medicine. I would gladly spare her it.'

Bolitho glanced at the books, one of which was lying open, as he had left it. Such good company. It was as though he read to her in the late watches of the night, and not merely to himself. When he closed his eyes he could see her so clearly, the candlelight playing around her throat and high cheekbones; could imagine the silk of her skin beneath his hands, her eager response. What would he feel when the ship anchored at English Harbour? She would be thinking about it, remembering the inevitability of it. Fate.

The sentry tapped his musket on the deck and shouted, 'First lieutenant, *sir!*'

Keen grimaced. 'Why do they bellow so much, I wonder? You would think we were in an open field.'

Ozzard opened the door, and Lieutenant Sedgemore stepped swiftly inside.

'I do beg your pardon, Sir Richard.'

Bolitho listened to gun trucks squealing somewhere. The middle gundeck most likely, the seamen gasping and slipping as they ran out the twenty-four pounders, each action made more dangerous by the tilting obstinacy of the damp planking.

But Keen knew what he wanted, and would take no second-best.

Bolitho said, 'If it is the ship's business that cannot wait, my quarters are yours, Mr Sedgemore.'

The lieutenant looked at him uneasily, as if expecting another motive, or some new sarcasm.

'Er – thank you, Sir Richard.'

Bolitho hid a smile. *I have obviously passed the test.*

To Keen the first lieutenant explained, 'The masthead reported a sail to the nor'-east during the morning watch, sir.'

Keen waited. 'I know. I bid the midshipman insert the sighting in the log.'

Another flicker of surprise, as if Sedgemore had not expected his captain to concern himself with the ordinary deck-log.

Bolitho commented as he glanced around the spacious cabin, 'This is no *Hyperion*, Val. I could hear almost every-thing from my quarters then!' They smiled briefly at one another, sharing the memory.

Sedgemore said, 'She has just been sighted again, sir. Same bearing.'

Keen rubbed his chin. 'Not much choice in this wind.' He looked at Bolitho. 'Not another case of *Golden Plover*, surely, sir?'

Bolitho said, 'If the stranger is an enemy he will keep his distance, and we are surely too slow to run him down. As for

212

secrecy, I expect half of England knows what we are about, and our eventual landfall.'

Keen was thinking aloud, 'Mr Julyan predicts a clear sky this afternoon – like Allday, I think he has an ear in the Almighty's court. I'll have our new "volunteer" go aloft, with a glass if need be. Some eyes cannot be trusted.' He hesitated, suddenly uncertain. 'I am a fool, Sir Richard. I meant no comparison.'

Bolitho touched his arm impetuously. 'You are no fool, and you speak good sense.'

Keen said, 'Secure the gun crews, Mr Sedgemore. We will exercise repel-boarders drill at six bells.'

Sedgemore backed out, his eyes everywhere until the door was shut.

'How is he progressing, Val?'

Keen watched him anxiously as he touched his left eye with his fingertips. He guessed that Bolitho did it unconsciously: the irritation was never far away. Like a threat.

'He is not yet *quite* ready to assume my command, sir, but it does no harm to allow him that belief!'

They laughed, the threat once more held at bay.

That same afternoon the northerly wind eased slightly, and the sea's face showed some colour as the scudding clouds began to scatter. But when the sun eventually revealed itself it held no warmth, and the salt-hardened sails shone in the glare but gave off no tell-tale steam.

Bolitho went on deck and stood with Jenour by the quarter-deck rail, keeping out of the way as both watches of the hands were turned-to for making more sail as Keen had hoped. Keen was on the opposite side, looking aloft as the first topmen dashed quickly up the quivering ratlines – the captain, his own world revolving around him. Bolitho felt the old touch of envy, and wondered what Zenoria would say if she could see her husband now. His eyes squinting against the hard sunlight, wings of fair hair flapping from beneath his plain, seagoing hat, he was in command and controlling a dozen things at once.

The senior midshipman, a haughty youth named Houston, was beckoning to the seaman William Owen. Due for lieutenant's examination at the first opportunity, Houston was very aware of Bolitho's nearness.

He called importantly, 'Wait!'

Allday was below the poop with Tojohns and said scornfully, 'Look at him, cocking his chest like a half-pay admiral! He'll be a proper little terror when he gets made up!'

Tojohns grinned. 'If someone don't stamp on him first!'

Keen looked round and smiled. 'Ah, Owen! How are you finding life in a somewhat larger craft than your last, eh?'

Owen chuckled, the midshipman forgotten. 'It'll suit, sir. I just wish her ladyship was here to give some advice to the cook!'

Bolitho approved. Keen had shown the arrogant 'young gentleman' that Owen was a man, not a dog.

Keen glanced across. 'Shall he go aloft, Sir Richard? I'll not make more sail until he has looked for our companion.'

Bolitho called, 'Take the signal midshipman's glass, Owen. You may scorn such things, but I think it will aid you.'

Another memory. In an elegant London shop selling navigational instruments, he had seen Catherine examine a telescope, and heard the establishment's rotund owner explaining that it was the very latest and best of its kind. He had been very conscious of her inner battle while she touched the gleaming glass; then she had shaken her head, and Bolitho thought he knew why. She had been remembering Herrick, and the beautiful telescope which had been Dulcie's last present to him. She wanted no part of it, nor any sort of comparison.

'*Deck there!*'

Bolitho shook himself. Owen had reached the main crosstrees while he had been day-dreaming.

'Sail to the nor'-east, sir!'

Bolitho looked at the cruising white crests. The wind was still easing; he had no difficulty in hearing Owen's cry. Yesterday, even this morning, it would have been lost in the violence of wind and sea.

Bolitho said, 'Fetch him down, Captain Keen. You are eager to make her lift her skirts, I'll wager!'

Owen arrived on deck even as the great maincourse and foresail boomed and thundered in noisy disarray until the yards were hauled round to trap the wind, and make each sail harden like a steel breastplate.

'Well, Owen, what is she?'

Men who were not actually working at halliards and braces, or fighting their way out on the great yards to free more canvas, loitered nearby to listen.

Owen replied, 'Frigate, Sir Richard. Not big – twenty-eight guns or thereabouts.' He returned the long telescope to Midshipman Houston.

'Thank you, sir.'

Houston almost snatched it, with such bad grace that Keen remarked, 'Mr Sedgemore, I think a word during the last dogwatch would be useful.'

The first lieutenant paused in the tumult of chasing men to their proper stations, in one case stopping to thrust a loose line into a man's grasp, and stared at him. His eyes flashed dangerously as they settled on the midshipman and he said sharply, '*See me*, Mr Houston, sir!'

Owen continued in the same unruffled tone, 'She wears no colours, Sir Richard, but I'd say she's a Dutchman. I've been close enough to some of them, too close sometimes.'

Jenour said, 'Another enemy, then.' He sounded surprised. 'I expected a Frog, Sir Richard.'

Bolitho kept his features impassive. Once Jenour would never have considered voicing his own opinion; he had always been so trusting, willing to leave judgment and assessment to those who were better experienced. He was ready now, mature enough to offer what he had learned to others. Bolitho knew he would miss him greatly.

'Sou'-west-by-west, sir! Full an' bye!' Julyan the sailing-master was beaming at his mates and rubbing his beefy hands together. Once again, he had been proved right.

Keen shouted, 'Secure and belay, Mr Sedgemore!' Loud enough for all those around him he added, 'That was *well* done. Two minutes shorter this time!'

True or not, Bolitho saw some of the breathless seamen looking at each other and giving reluctant grins. It was a beginning.

He said, 'Perhaps this fellow is under French orders. We have seen too much of that.' But he was thinking of the depleted squadron awaiting him in the Caribbean. They lacked frigates, and the French would know it. This was no Brittany coastline, or the cat-and-mouse encounters in the North Sea. Here there were countless islands, which would have to be patrolled and searched in case an enemy squadron was in hiding amongst them, and these waters abounded with craft of all kinds: Dutchmen and Spaniards, vessels from the South Americas, all ready to pass their intelligence to the French at Martinique and Guadeloupe. There were also the Americans, who had not forgotten their own fight for independence; they had to be handled with great care. They resented being stopped or examined as possible blockade-runners, and several serious complaints had been presented to the government in London by that young but ambitious nation.

Bolitho smiled as he recalled Lord Godschale's warning. 'We need tact as well as initiative, and someone who is known to these people.' Bolitho was not quite certain what he had implied by *known*, but he had never considered himself particularly tactful.

He said, 'Thank you, Owen. I shall need you again presently.'

Keen watched the man knuckle his forehead and stride away to rejoin his division.

He said, 'A valuable hand, that one, sir – I'll rate him up to petty officer shortly. He makes many of our landmen look like bumpkins!'

The wind got up again as darkness closed in around the ship, but the motion was less violent and the hands were able to consume hot food, and an extra ration of rum to make the long day seem less miserable.

Outside the wardroom which stretched across *Black Prince*'s massive beam, and was situated directly beneath the admiral's quarters, Lieutenant James Sedgemore sat more comfortably on a locker with a goblet of madeira in one hand as he completed his onslaught on the senior midshipman. The latter stood like a ramrod, moving only to the ponderous lift and fall of the great hull, and all the men, weapons and supplies crammed into it. He gestured to the open screen doors, where, in the wardroom, Houston could see the officers he observed every watch in their very different guises. Drinking, writing letters, playing cards, while they waited for the last meal of the day. A few of the lieutenants who were feared for their sense of order and discipline sat or lolled in their chairs while a mess-boy bustled amongst them with a jug of wine. The surgeon, usually so grave-faced, was roaring with laughter at something the Royal Marines major had told him. The purser, Julyan the sailing master: the very company Houston wanted to join, if not here then in another ship. He felt much as Sedgemore about his own future, but at present Sedgemore was in no mood for sympathy. 'I'll not have you throwing your weight about in my ship, simply because a man dare not answer back – do you understand?'

Houston bit his lip. He had wanted the captain to notice him, but he had certainly never intended to bring all this down on his head.

'And do not try to get your own back, Mr Houston, or you will think that the horned god of hell has fallen on your miserable shoulders! On our last commission, after Copenhagen – something which even you will have heard about from the older hands – there was one such midshipman, who was a little tyrant. He loved to see the people suffer, as if they didn't have enough to deal with. They feared him, despite his lowly rank, because he was Sir Richard's nephew.' He gave a fierce grin. 'Sir Richard packed him off the ship, an' Captain Keen offered him a court-martial unless he agreed to resign. So what chance d'you imagine *you* would have?'

'I – I'm sorry, sir. Really . . .'

Sedgemore clapped him on the shoulder as he had seen Bolitho do on occasions. 'You are *not*, Mr Houston, but by God you will be, if it happens again. You will become known as the oldest midshipman in the fleet! Now be off with you. It ends here.'

The surgeon strolled past. 'Busy, Mr Sedgemore?'

The first lieutenant grinned. 'We all go through it.'

The surgeon made for the companion ladder. 'Not *I*, sir.'

On the quarterdeck Houston, still smouldering, reported to the officer-of-the-watch for the extra duties Sedgemore had given him. The lieutenant was Thomas Joyce. He was the third most senior, and had seen close action even at the tender age of eleven in his first ship.

It was bitterly cold, with spray and rain falling from the straining canvas and rigging like arctic rain.

Joyce snapped, 'Masthead, Mr Houston. A good lookout, if you please.'

Houston saw one of the helmsmen give a grin as his face showed briefly in the compass light. 'But – but there will be nothing in sight, sir!'

'Then it will be easy for you, won't it? Now up you go, or I'll have the bosun liven your dancing for you!'

Lieutenant Joyce was not an unduly hard man. He sighed and glanced at the tilting compass, then forgot the luckless youth high above the windswept deck.

We all go through it.

Down one deck further aft Allday sat in Ozzard's pantry and watched the little man slicing cheese for the cabin.

Ozzard asked testily, 'What did you want to go and do a stupid thing like that for, John? I always thought you were a bit cracked!'

Allday smiled. What did he really care about it? He had told him that he had left his share of the gold with Unis Polin at the Stag's Head. Just in case.

Ozzard continued, his knife flashing as a mark of his anger. 'She could walk off with the lot! You see, I know you, John Allday – know you of old. A pretty face, a neat ankle, and you're all aback! Anyway, you could have put it in the strongbox at the house.'

Allday filled his pipe carefully. 'What's the matter with you, Tom? Don't you like women or summat?'

Ozzard swung round, his eyes flaming. It only made him look more brittle. 'Don't you ever say that to me again!'

They both realised that the door was open, and a young seaman who had been cleaning around the great cabin stood staring at them, his eyes shifting nervously from one to the other.

Allday roared, 'Well? What do *you* want?'

'Th' – the vice-admiral needs you, Cox'n!'

Ozzard added sharply, 'Be off with you!' The youth fled.

Ozzard laid down the knife and looked at his hand as if expecting to see it shaking.

He said hesitantly, 'Sorry, John. Not your fault.' He would not look up.

Allday replied, 'Tell me if you like. One day. It'll go no further.' He shut the door behind him and walked beneath the massive beams towards the marine sentry outside the great cabin.

Whatever it was, it was tearing Ozzard apart. Had been, since . . .? But he could not remember.

In his pantry Ozzard sat down and rested his head in his hands. In the *Golden Plover*'s last moments when he had been by the companion ladder, he had seen her framed against the stern windows. He had wanted to turn away, to hide in the shadows. But he had not. He had watched her stripping off her bloodstained clothing until she had been standing completely naked with the sea's great panorama tumbling beyond her. There had been so much salt on the glass the windows had acted as a broad mirror, so that no part of her lovely body had been denied him.

But he had not seen Catherine until she had pulled on her borrowed breeches and shirt. He had seen only his young wife, as she must have looked when her lover had visited her.

He wrung his hands in despair. Why had none of his friends or neighbours told him? He could have stopped it, made her love him again as he had always believed she had. *Why?* The word hung in the air like a serpent.

The way she had looked at him on that hideous day in Wapping. Surprise, contempt even, then terror when she had seen the axe in his hand.

He said brokenly, 'But *I loved you!* Can't you see?'

But there was no one to answer him.

Lewis Roxby dismounted heavily and patted his horse as it was led away to the stables. The air was bitterly cold, and mist hovered above the nearest hillside like smoke. He noticed that someone had been breaking the ice on the horse troughs, a sure sign of a hard winter. He saw his groom watching him, his breath steaming.

Roxby said, 'Nothing moving on the estate, Tom. Can't even get the men working repairing the walls. Slate's frozen solid.'

The groom nodded. 'One o' the cook's possets will set you up, sir.'

Roxby blew his nose noisily and heard the sound echo around the yard like a rebuke. 'Something a mite stronger for me, Tom!'

He thought of the two thieves he had sent to the gallows a few days back. Why did they never learn? England was at war; people had little enough of their own without some oaf stealing from them. One of the thieves had burst into tears, but when Roxby had ignored it he had poured curses on him until a dragoon had dragged him away to the cells. Ordinary folk had to be protected. Some said that hanging a man never stopped crime. But it certainly stopped the criminal in question.

'Hello, who's this then?'

Roxby came out of his thoughts and turned to look at the great gates as a lively pony and trap clattered across the cobbles.

It was Bryan Ferguson, Bolitho's steward. A rare visitor here indeed. Roxby felt vaguely irritated; the vision of that warming glass of brandy was already receding.

Ferguson swung himself down. Few people realised he had but one arm until he faced them.

'I beg your pardon, Squire, for coming like this unannounced.'

Roxby sensed something. 'Bad news? Not Sir Richard?'

'No, sir.' He glanced awkwardly at the groom. 'I got a bit worried, you see.'

The glance was not lost on Roxby. 'Well, you'd better come inside, man. No sense in freezing out here.'

Ferguson followed him into the great house, seeing the paintings that adorned the walls, the thick rugs, the flickering fires through every open door. A very grand house with property to match, he thought. Very fitting for the King of Cornwall.

He was very nervous again, and he tried to reassure himself that he was doing the right thing. The only thing. There was nobody else to turn to. Lady Catherine had ridden to the other side of the estate to visit an injured farm worker and his family; she must not know of this latest trouble. He glanced around at the elegant furniture, the immense painting of

Roxby's father, the old squire, who in his day had fathered quite a few children around the county. At least Roxby stayed faithful to his wife, and was more interesting in chasing game than women.

Roxby reached the fire and held out his hands. 'Private, is it?'

Ferguson said unhappily, 'I didn't know who else to see, sir. I couldn't even discuss it with Grace, my wife – she'd probably not believe me anyway. She thinks nothing but good of most people.'

Roxby nodded sagely. So it was serious. Ferguson had a lot of pride, in his work and in the family he served. It had cost him a lot to come here like this.

He said magnanimously, 'Glass of madeira, perhaps?'

Ferguson stared as the squire offered him a chair by the fire. 'With respect, sir, I'd relish a tot of rum.'

Roxby tugged a silk bell-cord and smiled. 'I'd all but forgotten you were a sailor too, at one time.'

Ferguson did not look at the footman who entered and went like a shadow. He stared into the flames. 'Twenty-five years ago, sir. I came back home after I lost a wing at the Saintes.'

Roxby handed him a large glass of rum. Even the smell made his head swim. 'Don't know how you can swallow that stuff!' He eyed him over his own goblet of brandy. The latest batch. It was sometimes better not to know where it came from, especially if you were a magistrate.

'Now tell me what this is about. If it's advice you want – 'He felt rather flattered that Ferguson had come to confide in him.

'There's been talk, sir, gossip if you like. But it's dangerous, more so if it reaches the wrong ears. Someone has been spreading stories about Lady Catherine, and about Sir Richard's family. Filthy talk, damned lies!'

Roxby waited patiently. The rum was working.

Ferguson added, 'I heard it from a corn chandler. He saw an argument between Captain Adam and some farmer in Bodmin. Captain Adam called him out, but the other man backed down.'

Roxby had heard a few things about the youthful Adam Bolitho. He said, 'Sensible. I'd likely have done the same!'

'And then – ' he hesitated, 'I heard someone saying things

about her ladyship – entertaining men in the house, that kind of thing.'

Roxby eyed him bleakly. 'Is it true?'

Ferguson was on his feet without realising it. 'It's a bloody lie, sir.'

'*Easy* – I had to know. I admire her greatly. Her courage has been an example to us all, and the love she bears my brother-in-law, well – it speaks for itself.'

Like a fine English ballad, he had thought privately, but he was incapable of voicing such a sentiment, particularly to another man.

Ferguson had slumped down again, and was staring at his empty glass. He had failed. It was all going wrong. He had only made things worse by losing his self-control.

Roxby remarked, 'The point, really, is that you know who's behind all this. Am I right?'

Ferguson looked at him in despair. *When I tell him, he will shut his ears to me.* An outsider was different. One of the family, no matter how indirectly, was another matter.

Roxby said, 'I shall find out anyway, you know. I'd prefer to hear it from you. Now.'

Ferguson met his grim stare. 'It was Miles Vincent, sir. I swear it.' He was not certain how Roxby would react. Polite disbelief, or open anger in order to protect Vincent's mother, his wife's sister.

He was astonished when Roxby held his breath until his face reddened even more, and then exploded, 'Hell's teeth, I knew that little maggot was involved!'

Ferguson swallowed hard. 'You *knew*, sir?'

'Had to hear it from someone I could trust.' He was working himself into a rage. 'By God, after all the family has tried to do for that ungrateful baggage and her son!' He controlled himself with a real effort. 'Say nothing. It is our affair, and must go no further.'

'You have my word, sir.'

Roxby eyed him thoughtfully. 'Should Sir Richard ever decide to leave Falmouth, I will always have a good appointment for you in my service.'

Ferguson found he could smile, albeit shakily. 'I think it may be a long wait, sir.'

'Well spoken.' He gestured to the other door. 'M'wife's coming. I heard the carriage. Go now. *I* shall attend to this unseemly matter.'

As Ferguson reached the door he heard Roxby call after him, 'Never question it. You did the right thing by coming to me.'

A few moments later Nancy entered the room, muffled to her eyes, her skin glowing from the cold.

'Whose is that nice little pony and trap, Lewis?'

'Bryan Ferguson's, my dear. Estate business, nothing to trouble your pretty head about.' He pulled the bell-cord again and when the footman appeared he said calmly, 'Find Beere, and send him to me.' He was Roxby's head keeper, a dour, private man who lived alone in a small cottage on the edge of the estate.

As the door closed Nancy said, 'What do you want him for? Such an odious man. He makes my skin creep.'

'My thoughts entirely, m'dear.' He poured another measure of brandy and thought of Ferguson's quiet desperation. 'Still, he has his uses.'

It was pitch dark when Ferguson's smart little trap reached the Stag's Head at Fallowfield. After the coast road, and the knife-edged wind off the bay, the parlour offered a welcome so warm that he could barely wait to throw off his heavy coat.

The place was empty but for an old man dozing by the fire, with a tankard on a stool beside him. At his feet a black and white sheepdog lay quite motionless. Only the dog's eyes moved as they followed Ferguson across the flagged floor. Then they closed.

She came in from the kitchen and gave him a friendly smile. Allday was right; she *was* a trim little craft, and more in command since Ferguson had last seen her, when he had briefly introduced himself.

'Quiet tonight, Mr Ferguson. Something hot, or something strong?'

He smiled. He could not get Roxby out of his thoughts. How would he deal with it? Vincent's mother lived in one of his houses; Roxby might add fuel to the fire by dragging her into it. Rumour had it that she was friendly with Bolitho's wife; that might also ensure that the scandal would not die so quickly. Allday had told him about the son, and his short career as a midshipman. A real little tyrant, and cruel too.

She said, 'You're miles away.'

He tried to relax. He had wanted to get out, hide from the estate and the familiar faces who relied on him. He had met Lady Catherine after her visit to the injured worker, and during a general conversation she had mentioned Captain Adam. Just for an instant he had imagined she had heard about the incident in Bodmin. But how could she?

Instead, Catherine had asked if Adam had visited the house frequently during their absence. He had told her the truth, and why not? He was seeing too many devils when there were none.

He said, 'Some of your pie, and a tankard of ale, if you please.'

He watched her bustling about and wondered if Allday would ever settle down. Then he saw the carved ship model in the adjoining room: Allday's *Hyperion*. Then it must be serious. It made him strangely glad.

She put the tankard down on his table. 'Aye, 'tis quiet, right enough.' She shifted uneasily. 'Did hear there's some sort of meeting going on.'

Ferguson nodded. Probably a cock-fight, something he hated. But many enjoyed it, and large bets changed hands in the course of an evening's sport.

Ferguson turned and looked at the dog. It was no longer asleep but staring fixedly at the door, its teeth bared in a small, menacing growl.

Unis Polin said, 'Foxes, maybe.'

But Ferguson was on his feet, his heart suddenly pounding like a hammer.

'What is it?'

Ferguson clutched the table as if to prevent himself falling. It was all there, coming back: the moment when he had heard the feet. Except that it was no longer a brutal memory. It was now.

The old man reached down and touched his dog's fur, quietening him.

He croaked, 'There be a King's ship in Carrick Road.'

The feet drew closer, marching and dragging.

Ferguson stared around as if he were trapped.

'My God, it's the press.'

He wanted to run. Get away. Go back to Grace and the life he had come to value and enjoy.

The door banged open and a tall sea-officer loomed out of the darkness, his body shrouded in a long boatcloak glittering with drops of sleet or snow.

He saw the woman by the table and removed his hat with a flourish. For one so young, in his mid-twenties at a guess, his hair was streaked with grey.

'I beg pardon at this intrusion, ma'am.' His eyes moved quickly around the parlour, missing nothing. The comely woman, the one-armed man, the dog by the fire which was still glaring at him, and finally the old farmer. *Nothing.*

Unis Polin said, 'There's nobody here, sir.'

Ferguson sat down again. 'She's right.' He hesitated. 'What ship?'

The other gave a bitter laugh. 'She's the *Ipswich*, thirty-eight.' He threw back his cloak, to reveal an empty sleeve pinned to his lieutenant's coat. 'It seems we've both been in the wars. But there's no ship for me, my friend – just this stinking work, hunting men who will not serve their King!'

To the woman he added more calmly, 'There is a place near here called Rose Barn, I believe?'

The old man leaned forward. 'Tes 'bout a mile further on this road.'

The lieutenant replaced his hat and as he opened the door Ferguson saw lanterns shining on uniforms and weapons. Over his shoulder he said, 'It would be unwise to raise a warning.' He gave a tired smile. 'But of course you know not what we are about, eh?'

The door closed, and all at once the silence was around them, like something physical.

Ferguson watched as she removed the pie from the table and replaced it with a piece that was piping-hot.

He said, 'The press-gang must be heading for the fight you mentioned.'

The old farmer cackled. 'They'll get naught there, me dear. Men with protection, and soldiers from the garrison.'

Ferguson stared at him, his spine like ice. *So this was Roxby's way*. He would know all the officers of the dreaded press, and the times and locations of cock-fights and other sport. He suddenly felt quite sick. They might catch a few, despite what the old farmer had said, just as they had taken him and Allday when the *Phalarope* had put a press-gang ashore. One thing was quite certain in his mind. Miles Vincent would be one of them.

'I must leave. I – I'm sorry about the pie . . .'

She watched him anxiously. 'Another time then. I want you to tell me all about John Allday.'

The mention of the big man's name seemed to strengthen him. He sat down again at the table and picked up a fork. He would stay, after all.

He glanced at the dog, but it was fast asleep. Outside the door there was only stillness.

He thought with sudden anger, *And why not? We protect our own and those we love. Or we go down with the ship.*

What else could he have done?

By morning it was snowing, and when Lewis Roxby walked into his stable yard he saw his head keeper, Beere, pause just long enough to give him a nod before he was swallowed up in a gust of swirling snow.

The frigate *Ipswich* had sailed before dawn, as was the navy's way, and it was a long time before anyone realised that Miles Vincent's bed had not been slept in.

15

From the Dead

Lieutenant Stephen Jenour handed his hat to Ozzard and then strode aft to the broad day-cabin where Bolitho was seated at a small table. The *Black Prince* was in the process of changing tack yet again, and as the sun moved slowly across the stern windows Jenour felt its heat through the smeared glass like an opening oven door.

Bolitho glanced up from his letter to Catherine. He had forgotten how many pages he had written so far, but it never seemed difficult to confide in her even when the distance between them mounted with each turn of the glass.

Jenour said, 'Captain Keen's respects, Sir Richard, and he wishes to inform you that Antigua is in sight to the south-west'rd.'

Bolitho laid down his pen. Seven weeks to cross an ocean and find their way to the Caribbean's Leeward Islands. It was ironic that his old *Hyperion* had done the same passage in a month, and at exactly this time of year. Keen must be both relieved to have made the landfall and disappointed at the time taken, and the many shortcomings which had presented themselves in the ship's company.

Perhaps the deceptive calm of bright sunshine and warmth on their hard-worked bodies might make amends. The Atlantic had been at its worst, at least in Bolitho's experience, producing great surging gales, while men half-frozen on the yards fisted and fought icy canvas until their hands were torn and raw. The high winds had been perverse too, and the ship had been driven a hundred miles off-course when the wind direction had veered so suddenly that even Julyan the master had been astonished.

Gun-drill had been out of the question for the latter part of their passage. It was all Keen could do to get his men fed and rested before the Western Ocean again released its ferocity.

It said much for Keen's example and that of his more seasoned hands that they had not lost a spar or another man overboard.

'I'll go up, Stephen.' He glanced at his unfinished letter, seeing Falmouth as it would be now. Much like the Atlantic: gales, rain and perhaps snow.

Catherine would be thinking of the ship, wondering where she was, if she had arrived safely. When she might be called to action. So many questions which only time could answer.

Jenour looked around the great cabin, a place he had come to know so well. During the passage from England he had been able to put the prospect of leaving Bolitho to one side. The gales, the deafening roar of the sea thundering over the hull and upper deck to make every footstep a separate hazard, and the gaunt faces of the people while they were chased and bullied from one task to the next, kept such thoughts at bay. Now it was different. Out there beyond the tapering jib-boom was English Harbour: order and authority, where each day might offer him the challenge of promotion. He thought of the first lieutenant, Sedgemore, some of the others too; they would give their blood for such an opportunity. A small command, with the blessing of a famous flag-officer – who could wish for more? He had heard Bolitho refer to it as *the most coveted gift*.

Jenour thought also of his parents at Roxby's dinner, when Bolitho had made it his business to have them feel at home with such illustrious people.

He saw him touching his eyelid as he did more and more frequently nowadays. That secret too had been entrusted to him. It was safe until Bolitho required it otherwise. But who else would be able to understand him and his ways when he himself was promoted out of this ship?

He had even shared in the conspiracy of Bolitho's reunion with Lady Catherine, that too in Antigua.

'Why so thoughtful, Stephen?'

228

Jenour faced him and replied quietly, 'I think you know, Sir Richard.'

Bolitho touched his eye again. He had noticed that Jenour rarely flushed when his private thoughts were revealed, not since the *Golden Plover*'s jolly-boat. A man then. But one who could still feel distress and show compassion for others.

Bolitho walked to the stern gallery and looked out at the undulating water, bank upon bank of it, as if worn out by all the anger it had expended to prevent their journey from being a fast one.

He said, 'It has to be. That does not mean I do not care. It is the opposite, and I think *you* know that!'

They went on deck where Keen and some of his officers were studying the approaching island sprawled out on either bow, misty green, the hump of Monk's Hill all but lost in haze.

Bolitho appreciated that even that was suspect. From flat calm to a raging storm, every captain worth his salt knew better than to trust these waters at this time of year.

Keen crossed the deck to join him, his shoes sticking to the tarred seams as he did so.

'Barely making way, sir.' They both looked up at the great spread of canvas, flapping in the hot breeze but hardly filling enough to move the ship. Buckets of salt water were being hauled up to men on the upper yards so that it could be poured on the sails to harden them, to make use of even a cupful of wind. The watch on deck was flaking down lines and securing halliards again after the last change of tack, their movements slow in the hot sunshine and lacking the brisk response to commands any captain would expect.

Bolitho took a telescope from the rack by the poop and trained it through the mesh of rigging until he found the nearest spur of land. He had had the crazed Captain Haven on that last visit. One so filled with suspicion and jealousy over his young wife that he had tried to kill the first lieutenant, whom he had believed responsible for his wife's pregnancy. He had been proved wrong, but he had been held for attempted murder nonetheless.

An island of so many memories. He had been here in his first command, the little *Sparrow*, and again in his frigate

Phalarope. He saw Allday watching him from the larboard gangway and their quick exchange of glances was like part of an enduring link. The battle of the Saintes; his previous coxswain Stockdale falling dead while trying to protect his back from enemy marksmen. Bryan Ferguson losing an arm, and Allday eventually taking over as his coxswain. Yes, there was plenty to remember here.

Keen said, 'We shall be anchored by this afternoon, sir.' He frowned as the masthead pendant flicked out, the life draining from it. 'I could lower the boats and take her in tow.' He was considering the dwindling possibilities.

Bolitho said, 'I'd stay your hand with the boats, Val. Another hour more will make little difference now.' He glanced at the nearest seamen. 'They look like old men!'

Keen smiled. 'They will have to learn. If we are called to battle . . .' He shrugged. 'But the sight of land is sometimes a tonic, sir.' He excused himself and went to join the sailing-master by the chart table.

Bolitho raised the glass again. Still too far away to discern any prominent landmarks, and certainly none of the houses beyond the dockyard. He could see her now as if it were today. Dazzled by the lights at the reception, he had almost fallen at her feet. But she had discovered his injury, inevitably, and had insisted that he seek advice and treatment from the best surgeons in London.

He touched his eyelid again, and felt the painful prick which seemed to come from right inside his eye. And yet sometimes he could see perfectly. At others he had felt utter despair, as Nelson must have done after his own eye had been wounded.

And this was the time when every experienced officer was needed, as he had explained both to Keen and Jenour. But for the failure of his mission to Cape Town and the resulting delay caused by the loss of the *Golden Plover*, where might they have been now? Keen a commodore and ready for the next step to flag rank. And but for *Black Prince*'s unfortunate collision at the completion of her refit, she might well be with the major part of the fleet supporting the army in Portugal or beyond. It was fate. This was where they were destined to be. But would it prove as useful as Godschale and his superiors seemed to think?

One thing stood out above all else. Bonaparte intended to divide his enemy's forces at all cost. His failure to seize the Danish fleet had made him even more determined. Small groups of ships had been reported slipping through the English blockade, and many had headed for the Caribbean, perhaps to attack Jamaica or other islands under the English flag. That would certainly force their lordships to withdraw more urgently needed ships from blockade and military convoy duties.

It was possible that the sighting of the vessel described by the volunteer William Owen as 'Dutch-built' was no more than another coincidence. Bolitho thought privately that it was more than that. One modest frigate sailing alone was more likely to be taking despatches to some senior officer. Reinforcements, in the shape of *Black Prince*, were on their way, but no sign of any other frigates. They would have gone for the stranger like terriers had there been any. And then there was the matter of Thomas Herrick, the man he had always believed his best friend. It was strange that Godschale had made a point of not mentioning him at their last meeting; nor had the admiral displayed any interest at what Bolitho might expect when they next met. For unless some other vessel had sailed ahead of *Black Prince*, Herrick would still believe him to be dead after the *Golden Plover*'s reported loss.

He shaded his eyes against the glare and watched the distant island, which appeared to have drawn no nearer.

So many ifs and maybes. Suppose the plan to land on and capture the French islands of Martinique and Guadaloupe misfired? Without overwhelming superiority at sea the scheme would certainly fail. To draw the main enemy force together and engage it in battle was their only sane approach. He kept his face impassive, knowing that Jenour was watching him. Seven sail of the line and one frigate was hardly an overwhelming squadron.

He heard the first lieutenant call, 'Permission to carry out punishment, sir? Able Seaman Wiltshire, two dozen lashes.'

Keen sounded suddenly dispirited. 'Very well, Mr Sedgemore.' He looked up at the limply flapping sails and added bitterly, 'It seems we have nothing better to do!'

Bolitho turned towards the companionway. He had seen the

expressions on the faces of some of the new hands. Resentful, hostile.

Hardly the faces of men who would rally and fight to the death if so ordered, not by a long stretch of the imagination.

He said, 'I'm going aft, Val. Keep me informed.'

Keen stood beside Jenour as the ritual of rigging a grating on the larboard side was supervised by the boatswain and his mates.

Jenour said with concern, 'Sir Richard seems depressed, sir.'

Keen tore his eyes from the boatswain who was examining his red baize bag, in which he kept the cat-o'-nine-tails.

'He frets for his lady, Stephen. And yet the sailor in him craves the solution to his problem of command here.' He glanced at the vice-admiral's flag barely moving at the foremast truck. 'Sometimes I wonder . . .' He looked round as Sedgemore called, 'Pipe the hands, sir?'

Keen acknowledged him curtly, but not before noting the first lieutenant's complete indifference. As one who hungered for promotion, and had already shown his ability under fire, it was surprising he had not become aware of the need to care for the people he might soon have to lead in battle.

The calls shrilled and twittered from deck to deck. 'All hands! All hands lay aft to witness punishment!'

As he walked aft to his quarters Bolitho understood the unpleasantness and necessity as if he were Keen. Holding his ship together, administering punishment with the same equality and fairness as he would reward and promote a promising seaman. He found Yovell waiting with a sheaf of papers requiring his signature but said wearily, 'Later, my friend. I am at low ebb, and am poor company at the moment.'

As the portly secretary left the cabin, Allday entered.

'What about *me*, Sir Richard?'

Bolitho smiled. 'Damn your impertinence! But yes – take a seat and join me in a wet.'

Allday grinned, partly reassured. It would all come right in the end. But this time it would take a bit longer.

'That would suit me well, Sir Richard.'

The first crack of the lash penetrated the cabin.

Allday pondered. A beautiful woman, his own flag at the fore, a title from the King. The lash cracked down again. But some things never changed. Ozzard padded into view with his tray: a tall glass of hock and a tankard of rum, as usual.

When Bolitho leaned over to take the glass Ozzard saw the locket hanging around his neck. He had studied it several times when the vice-admiral had been having a wash or a shave. Her lovely shoulders and the suggestion of her breasts, just as he had seen her that day in the barquentine's cabin. He heard the lash crack down again, but felt only contempt. The man being punished had asked for it, had drawn a knife on a messmate. In a month he would be boasting about the scars left by the cat across his back.

My wounds will never heal.

Towards the close of the afternoon watch, with the reddest sun most of them had ever seen dipping over the island, *Black Prince* glided slowly towards the anchorage.

Keen watched as Bolitho took a glass and trained it on the shore and the other ships resting at anchor, their spars and rigging already glowing like copper in the failing light. He was relieved to see that Bolitho appeared outwardly restored, with no hint of anxiety in the face he had come to know so well.

Bolitho studied the nearest men-of-war, all seventy-fours, and none of them strangers to him. They were part of his squadron, but likely expecting another to command them. *Back from the dead.*

He said, 'I shall pay my respects to Lord Sutcliffe, Val, as soon as we are anchored.' He turned, surprised as the first crash of a gun-salute echoed and rebounded across the quiet harbour.

'They have fired first, Sir Richard! That will not please Admiral the Lord Sutcliffe.'

Keen dropped his hand and the first gun of *Black Prince's* upper battery fired out in reply, the pale smoke hanging low on the water like something solid.

'Take in the courses! Extra topmen aloft, Mr Sedgemore!' Keen strode to the compass and watched the sudden bustle of activity which had entirely replaced the torpor during their slow approach.

Bolitho recognised the seventy-four drawing nearer: the old *Glorious*, which like most of the others had been with him at Copenhagen, when he had received the news of Herrick's convoy and its obvious danger. Her captain, John Crowfoot, was no older than Keen, but he was so grey and stooped that he looked more like a country parson than a highly experienced naval officer.

The guardboat was already here, her flag hanging limp but still bright enough for Keen to mark down their proposed anchorage, where the flagship would have sufficient room to swing around her cable without fear of fouling any of the other vessels moored there.

The last shot echoed away across the water, thirteen guns in all. Keen was quick to order the gunner to cease firing and commented, 'It would seem that Lord Sutcliffe is not here, sir. The salute was to you, as the senior officer.'

Bolitho waited, outwardly calm, but unable to control the old excitement at any landfall.

'Stand by to come about! Ready aft!' The merest pause, then, '*Helm a-lee!*' Very slowly and heavily *Black Prince* came into the remaining breath of wind, her topsails already vanishing as the order was shouted along the upper deck, '*Let go!*'

The anchor fell with a mighty splash into the clear, coppery water, spray bursting over the beakhead like hail.

Keen called, 'Awnings and winds'ls, Mr Sedgemore! All eyes are on us, it seems!'

At least it might ease the heat and discomfort between decks. He had learned that early in life as Bolitho's very junior lieutenant.

Bolitho handed the telescope to a minute midshipman. 'Take it, Mr Thornborough, and inform your lieutenant if you sight something that might be of interest.' He saw the boy's eyes widen at the casual confidence, as if God had just descended to speak to him. He was one of the twelve-year-olds, but it was never too soon to learn that the men who wore the bright epaulettes were human, too.

'Listen!' Keen swung round, his teeth very white in his tanned face. 'The old *Glorious* has manned her yards!' He could not conceal his emotion as the great wave of cheering broke from the nearest seventy-four. Men were standing in her shrouds and on her yards; the gangways too were lined with waving and cheering sailors and marines. 'The news preceded us after all, Sir Richard! They *know* you are among them – listen to them!'

Bolitho glanced at some of the seamen below the quarter-deck, who were staring from the anchored *Glorious* and her consorts to the man whose flag flew at the foremast. A man they knew by rumour and reputation, but nothing more.

Bolitho walked to the nettings and then waved his new hat back and forth above his head, to the obvious delight of the *Glorious*'s company.

Keen watched in silence, sharing the gesture. How could he ever doubt the men he had known and led, or his own ability to inspire them? One of the other ships had taken up the onslaught of cheering. Keen saw Bolitho's profile and was satisfied. He understood now anyway. Until the next time.

Sedgemore came aft and touched his hat. 'Ship secured, sir!'

Keen said, 'Prepare the sheet-anchor, if you please.' He saw no comprehension there and added sharply, 'Remember, Mr Sedgemore, we lie on a lee-shore, and we are in a season of storms.'

Midshipman Thornborough, his young face enraptured by all the noise of their reception, called, 'Barge approaching, Mr Daubeny!'

Bolitho replaced his hat and stood aside as the marines stamped to the entry port for their first visitor. It would soon be dark; sunset came here like a curtain. But when the shore lights were brighter he might be able to recognise that same house where he had dined beside her, their hands almost brushing one another on the table while she had exchanged polite smiles with her husband, Viscount Somervell, at the opposite end.

The side-party was in position, boatswain's mates moistening their silver calls on their tongues while the Royal Marines gripped their bayonetted muskets in readiness.

Keen lowered his glass and said quietly, 'It's Rear-Admiral Herrick, Sir Richard.' He was suddenly drained of the excitement he had felt at their arrival. 'I will be honest, sir. It will cost me dear to make him welcome.'

Bolitho stared at the approaching barge, the oars like bare bones in the deepening shadows.

'Never fear, Val, it is doubtless costing him a great deal more.'

The barge vanished from view and then, after what seemed like an eternity, Herrick's head and shoulders appeared in the entry port. While the guard presented arms and the calls paid their tribute, he doffed his hat, and stood motionless as if he and Bolitho were quite alone.

In those seconds Bolitho saw that Herrick's hair appeared to have gone completely grey, and that he held his body stiffly, as if his wound still troubled him.

Bolitho stepped forward and reached out with both hands. 'You are welcome here, Thomas.'

Herrick grasped his hands and stared at him, his blue eyes catching the last of the sunshine.

'So it *was* true . . . you are alive.' Then he lowered his head and said, loudly enough for Keen and Jenour to hear, 'Forgive me.'

As Jenour began to follow the two flag-officers aft, Keen thrust out his arm. 'Not this time, Stephen. Later perhaps.' He hesitated. 'I have just seen something I thought had died. But it's still there . . . like a bright flame.' The words seemed to be printed on his mind. *Forgive me*.

Jenour did not completely understand, and he had never been intimately acquainted with Herrick. If anything he had felt only jealousy when his name had been mentioned, because of his relationship with Bolitho, and the experiences they had shared. But like Keen, he knew he had witnessed a rare moment, and wondered how he might describe it in his next letter.

Allday was standing in the poop's shadow when Bolitho led the way to the companion ladder; around him the ship was settling down for the dog-watches and their first night at anchor. He could smell the land, and felt the same restlessness he always knew on these occasions.

But all he thought about was Herrick, and how hard it was to believe that he was the same man. Just for those few seconds when they had passed him, it had all come back: Bolitho as the young captain and Herrick the first lieutenant who had believed so passionately in his sailors' rights.

Allday shook himself and watched the first squad of marines

splitting up into sentry pickets at the ship's vantage points. Poop and forecastle, and the gangways which joined them to one another, where additional heavy shot would be kept handy if some native trader or bumboat came too close during the night watches. One ball dropped through a boat's hull would soon discourage the others. The sentries were to prevent those tempted by the island from deserting. But even the fear of a flogging or worse would not put some off, he thought.

He rubbed his chest as the wound came alive again. Like the sea itself, it was always a reminder.

Always the pain.

Thomas Herrick stood by the stern windows and stared across the water towards the lights of the port.

Ozzard waited with a tray, his eyes opaque as he watched the visitor, preparing for the worst or the best, as fortune dictated.

'A drink, Thomas? We are presently well stocked, so you can have what you will.' Bolitho saw the indecision.

Herrick sat down carefully, his body still held at a stiff angle.

'I would relish some ginger beer. I've almost forgotten what it's like.'

Bolitho waited for Ozzard to bustle away and then tossed his heavy coat on to the stern bench seat.

'How long have you known, Thomas?'

Herrick's eyes moved slowly around the great cabin, remembering other visits perhaps, or the days when his own flag flew above his *Benbow*.

'Two days – a fast packet from England. I could scarcely believe it, and even when your ship was reported offshore I thought some fool might have made a mistake.' He lowered his head and rested it on his hand. 'When I think of all we went through . . .' His voice almost broke. 'I still believe it all part of a nightmare.'

Bolitho walked to his chair and rested one hand on his shoulder, as much to steady Herrick as to conceal his own sudden emotion from the returned Ozzard.

Herrick made another effort, and held the fine goblet critically to the lanterns. 'Ginger beer.' He watched the clear bubbles. 'No wonder they call these the Islands of Death.

They try to pretend this is a part of England, and if they don't drink themselves into early graves, then they fall to a list of fevers that are more than a match for most of our surgeons.' He drank deeply and did not protest when Ozzard refilled the goblet.

Bolitho sat down and took a glass of the hock Catherine had had sent aboard. Ozzard had a knack of keeping such wines cool in the spacious bilges, but it was still something of a miracle how he managed – the hock tasted as if it had been lying in some icy Highland stream.

'And Lord Sutcliffe?' He spoke with care, and could feel Herrick's uncertainty and discomfort like a part of himself.

Herrick gave a shrug. 'Fever. He has been moved up to St John's – the air is better, they say, but I fear for his life. He placed me in command here until the new squadron was formed . . . then I was to be at the disposal of its flag-officer.' The blue eyes lifted and fixed on Bolitho, regarding him steadily for the first time since he had stepped aboard. '*You*, in fact, Sir Richard.'

Bolitho said, 'Richard. I'd prefer it.'

It was hard to come to grips with this new, remote Herrick, difficult to see him in either of his past guises: the earnest lieutenant, or the defiant rear-admiral who had been within a hair's breadth of death at his own court-martial. There was something of each still remaining, but nothing of both as a single person.

Herrick gazed through the cabin's dimness again as from somewhere in the ship they heard the far-off calls and the thud of bare feet as watchkeepers rushed to right a wrong above or below deck.

Herrick said, 'I never thought I would miss all this after what happened. I've had a bellyful of transports – vessels under warrant with masters I personally would not trust to scrub out the heads!'

'And you have had all this to carry on your shoulders, as well as your other work here?'

Herrick did not seem to have heard. 'Your eye, Richard. Is it still as bad?'

'You've told nobody, Thomas?'

Herrick shook his head, the gesture so familiar that it turned a knife in Bolitho's heart.

'It was 'twixt friends – I've said nothing. Nor would I.' He hesitated, turning over another thought which had troubled him since *Black Prince*'s arrival. 'The *Golden Plover*.' He faltered. 'I saw Keen and Jenour just now. Was – your – lady saved? Forgive me – I must ask.'

'Yes.' One wrong word or mistimed memory might break this contact forever. 'In truth, Thomas, I think that but for her we would all have been lost.' He forced a smile. 'After *Golden Plover* I take your point about transports under warrant!'

Herrick was on his feet, moving beneath the lanterns to throw his shadow across the tethered guns and leather-covered furniture like some restless dancer.

'I've done what I can. Without authority I have commandeered twenty schooners and cutters from here and from St Kitts. Without further authority I have swept the dockyard and barracks of lieutenants and ancient mariners, and packed them off on patrols which we cannot otherwise sustain.'

It was like watching someone coming back to life. Bolitho said quietly, 'You have *my* authority, Thomas.'

Herrick, reassured, reeled off all the things he had introduced to give early warning of enemy men-of-war, blockade runners or any suspicious vessel, be it slaver or genuine neutral trader.

'I've told them to stand no nonsense. If any master defies our flag he will not move freely in these waters again!' He smiled, and again his whole being changed. 'You will remember, Richard, I was in a merchantman myself between wars. I know a few of their tricks!'

'Is our frigate in harbour?'

'I sent her to Port Royal with some additional soldiers on board – another slave revolt. It was best to act with all haste.'

'So we have the squadron, seven sail of the line. And your flotilla of smaller "eyes".'

Herrick frowned. 'Six, for the present anyway. The seventy-four *Matchless* is in dock. She was caught in a storm two weeks back and lost her foremast. It's a marvel she didn't drive ashore.'

He sounded suddenly angry, and Bolitho asked. 'Captain Mackbeath, is it not?'

'No, he was replaced after Copenhagen.' His eyes clouded over. Remembering *Benbow* again, all those who had died that day. 'She has a new captain now, more's the pity – the Lord Rathcullen, who seems unable to take advice about anything. But you know what they say about Irishmen, peers or otherwise.'

Bolitho smiled. 'About we Cornishmen too, on occasions!'

Herrick's eyes crinkled, and he gave a brief laugh. 'Aye, damme, I asked for that!'

'Will you sup with me tonight, Thomas?' He saw Herrick's immediate caution. 'I mean with me alone. I would take it as a favour . . . the land can bide awhile. We are sailors again.'

Herrick shifted in his chair. 'I had it all prepared . . .' He seemed, again, embarrassed and ill at ease.

'It is done. I cannot say what it means to me. We have each had our own reefs to cross, but others will look to us, and care little enough for *our* troubles.'

Herrick said after a silence, and rather uncertainly, 'I shall tell you my ideas if I may. When I return to my residence . . .' He smiled at some recollection. 'The yard-master's house in fact – frugal and without pretence – I shall work on the plan I was going to present to our new flag-officer.'

Bolitho asked quietly, 'Do you ever sleep, Thomas?'

'Enough.'

'Did you receive any other news from the packet?'

Herrick took several seconds to drag himself back to the present.

'We are promised another frigate. She's the *Ipswich*, thirty-eight. Captain Pym.'

'I don't know the ship, I'm afraid.'

Herrick's eyes were distant once more. 'No. She's from my part of the world, the Nore.' He changed tack suddenly. 'You heard about Gossage, I suppose.' His mouth tightened. '*Rear-Admiral* Gossage, indeed. I wonder how many pieces of silver that rated?'

He was driving himself hard in his unexpected and temporary command, giving himself no time to brood on what had gone before, or on the loss of his ship, for *Benbow* was a hulk, and would never leave the dockyard again. What a way to end, after all they had done together.

'Easy, Thomas. Put it behind you.'

Herrick eyed him curiously, as much as if to ask, 'Could you?'

Bolitho persisted, 'Life still has much to offer.'

'Maybe.' He sat stolidly, with the empty goblet clasped in his square hands like a talisman. 'In truth, I am grateful to be of some use again. When I heard the news about you . . .' He shook his head. 'I thought it was another chance. Lady Luck.' He looked at him, suddenly desperate. 'But it's not been easy.'

'Who knows what we might achieve this time?'

Herrick sounded bitter. 'They are fools out here. They don't understand, nor do they know what to expect. Pink-cheeked soldiers more used to the bogs of Ireland than this godforsaken place, and senior officers who've scarcely heard a shot fired!'

Bolitho said quietly, ' "He never set a squadron in the field, Nor the division of a battle knows, More than a spinster." '

Herrick stared at him. 'Our Nel?'

Bolitho smiled as he saw his friend emerging. 'No, Shakespeare. But it could easily have been.'

In the pantry Allday nudged Ozzard. 'More like it, eh?' But he had been thinking of the little inn in Cornwall, and came awkwardly to the point. 'Will you pen a letter for me, Tom?'

Ozzard said darkly, '*Be warned*, that's all I ask.' He saw Allday's expression and sighed. 'Course I will. Anything for a bit o' peace!'

The big three-decker lay to her cable, her open gunports reflected in the calm anchorage like lines of eyes. The sentries paced their sections, and from one of the messdecks came the plaintive notes of a fiddle. The officer-of-the-watch paused in his discussion with a master's mate as the captain appeared by the abandoned double wheel, where men had fought wind and sea only a week ago as they strove to reach calmer waters.

Keen turned away from the shadowy watchkeepers and walked, deep in thought, to the poop ladder.

His ship and all her company, prime sailors, felons, cowards and honest men who would soon depend on him again, from his ambitious first lieutenant to the squeaking midshipmen, from surgeon to purser's clerk, they were his to command. An honour; but that he could take for granted. He watched the guardboat pulling slowly between the moored ships, a riding-light gleaming momentarily on a naked bayonet. He tried to imagine Sir Richard Bolitho and his old friend warily coming together in the great cabin. It would be difficult for both of them. The one who had found all he had ever wanted in his woman; the other who had lost everything, and nearly his life as well.

Seabirds flashed past the lights from the wardroom windows and he thought of that night in the open boat.

Tonight they will nest in Africa.

What price survival then?

He summoned her face, and the memory of unexpected love, which had left them both dazed with disbelief. For the first time in his life, there was someone waiting for him.

He recalled her last embrace, the warmth of her body against his.

'Captain, sir?' The lieutenant hovered on the top of the poop ladder.

'What is it?'

'Mr Julyan's respects, sir, and he thinks the wind is getting up from the west'rd.'

'Very well, Mr Daubeny. Inform the first lieutenant and pipe the larboard watch.'

As the lieutenant hurried down the ladder Keen pushed all else to the back of his mind.

As he had heard Bolitho say on occasions, 'That was then. This is now.'

He was the captain again.

16

Power of Command

Lady Catherine Somervell stood by one of the tall windows in the library and looked across the garden. The snow was heavier now, and the wheel-tracks of Lewis Roxby's smart phaeton had almost vanished in just half an hour. Kneeling on a rug before a crackling fire, Nancy was finishing her story of Miles Vincent's disappearance, and how it was later discovered that he had been taken by the press-gang and put aboard a man-of-war in Carrick Road.

Catherine watched the persistent snow and thought of *Black Prince* as she had last seen her standing out to sea, taking her heart with her.

She had spoken to some of the old sailors who worked on the estate, men who had served Richard in the past, before they had been cut down in battle; she was even jealous of them when they spoke of days she had never, could never share. One of them calculated that given the time of year and the inexperience of her company, *Black Prince* should have reached the Indies by now. A world away. Her man, doing things he had been ordered to do, hiding his own worries so that his men would see only confidence.

She turned away from the snow and asked guiltily, 'I'm sorry, Nancy – what did you say?'

'I shouldn't burden you with it, but she *is* my sister, one of the family . . . and despite her shortcomings I feel responsible for her, especially with her husband dead.' She looked up as though uncertain. 'I was wondering, dear Catherine, if you could tell Richard about it when next you write. Lewis is doing all he can, of course, as it was obviously a mistake.'

Catherine studied her thoughtfully. What Richard's mother must have been like. Fair, with clear fresh skin. She had a pretty mouth, perhaps all that remained of the young girl who had been in love with Richard's friend.

Nancy took her silence for disagreement. 'I know Miles does not make a favourable impression, but . . .'

Catherine walked to the fire and sat on the edge of a stool, feeling the heat on her face, imagining him here with her, now.

She said, 'When I first met him, I found him glib, with a higher opinion of himself than I would have thought healthy. What I have heard of him since has not improved that image.'

She saw Nancy's dismay and smiled. 'But I will tell Richard in my next letter. I write every few days, in the hope they will reach him in some sort of order.' Inwardly she believed that the young Miles Vincent had probably got what he deserved. He had apparently been at a cock-fight somewhere out towards the Helford River, and the press-gang had burst in on it. They had only found three men who did not possess a legal protection – one of them had been Vincent. She thought of his arrogance, the way he had stared at her during Roxby's dinner, with the smirk of a conceited child. She thought of Allday and others like Ferguson and the estate workers, seized by the hated press without pity or consideration. The navy needed men, and always would as long as the war dragged on. So men would be taken from the farms and the taverns, from the arms of their loved ones, to rub shoulders with those who had escaped the gallows for the sea at the assizes.

Nancy was saying, 'Lewis has already written to his friend, the port admiral at Plymouth . . . but it might take so long.'

Catherine adjusted her gown and Nancy exclaimed, 'My dear – I can still see that place where the sun burned you!'

'I hope I never lose it. It will always remind me.'

'Will you come for Christmas, Catherine? I would be so unhappy to think of you alone here. Please say you will. I would never forgive myself otherwise.'

Catherine reached out and pressed her arm. 'Sweet Nancy,

you are all responsibilities today! I shall think about it . . .'
She turned as her maid entered the room. 'What is it, Sophie?'

'A letter, me lady. The boy just brought it.'

Nancy watched her as she took the letter and saw her eyes
mist over as she quickly scanned the handwriting.

'I shall leave, Catherine. It is no moment to share . . .'

Catherine opened the letter and shook her head. 'No, no –
it is from Adam.' The handwriting was unfamiliar, and yet
similar. It was a short impetuous letter, and somehow typical
of him: she could see his grave dark features as he had written
it, from Portsmouth it appeared, no doubt with his *Anemone*
coming to life all around him as she completed storing and
made ready for sea.

He wrote, 'You have been much in my mind of late, and I
would that I had been free to speak with you as we have done
in the past. There is no one else with whom I can share my
thoughts. And when I see what you have done for my beloved
uncle I am all gratitude and love for you.' The rest of the letter
was almost formal, as if he were composing a report for his
admiral. But he ended like the young man who had grown up
in war. 'Please remember me to my friends at Falmouth, and
to Captain Keen's wife should you see her. With affectionate
regard, Adam.' She folded it as if it were something precious.

Nancy said, 'What is it?'

'It seems that the French are out. The foul weather was their
friend, not ours . . . Adam is ordered to the West Indies with
all haste.'

'How do they know with such certainty that the French are
heading there?'

'They know.' She stood up and walked back to the window.
Two grooms were reharnessing a fine pair of horses to the
phaeton, and as the snow drifted down on them they flicked
their ears with obvious displeasure.

Nancy came up beside her and put her arm around her
waist. Afterwards Catherine thought it could have been the
act of a sister.

'So they will all be together again?'

Catherine said, 'I knew in my heart it would happen. We
both believe in fate. How else could we have lost each other
and then come together again? It was fate.' She turned her

head and smiled at her. 'You must be glad that your man has his feet on dry land.'

Nancy looked at her very directly. Her eyes, Catherine thought, were the colour of lavender, opened to the sun, and they did not blink as she said quietly, 'I once thought to become a sailor's wife.' Then she threw her arms around her. 'I am so selfish – '

'That you are not.' She followed her into the adjoining room and picked up the old cloak she sometimes wore when riding; Richard had once taken it to sea with him, in that other world.

Ferguson, muffled against the weather, was talking with the grooms and helped Nancy into the carriage, noting the tears and the brightness of her eyes as he did so.

As the horses thudded across the packed snow Catherine said, 'Do you wish to see me?'

Ferguson followed her through the doors. 'I wondered if there was anything I could do, my lady?'

'Take a glass of something with me.' He looked uneasily at his filthy boots but she waved him down. 'Be seated. I need to talk.'

He watched her as she took two glasses from a cabinet, her hair shining like glass in the firelight. He still could not picture her in a boat with only some ragged survivors for company.

He stiffened as she said over her shoulder, 'You heard about young Miles Vincent, I daresay.'

Did she know of his visit to Roxby? Was that what the squire's wife had been here about?

'Yes, I did hear something. I didn't want to trouble you.' He took the glass gratefully. 'He was put aboard the *Ipswich*, according to one of the coastguards. She was off to the Caribbean soon afterwards, it seems. But never fear, m'lady, I am sure her captain will deal fairly with the matter.' He hoped it sounded convincing.

Catherine barely heard him. 'The West Indies, you say? It seems everyone is going there, except us. I heard from Captain Adam, you see – he is probably out there off the Lizard at this very moment.'

For the first time Ferguson realised he was drinking brandy. He tried to smile. 'Well, here's to Sir Richard, m'lady, and all our brave fellows!'

She let the cognac run across her tongue like fire.

The French are out. How many times had they heard that? She looked up the staircase where the candlelight flickered on the stern faces of those who had gone from here before, to meet that same challenge. *The French are out.*

'Oh, dear God, that I was with him now!'

It was, as Ferguson later said to his wife, a cry torn from her heart.

'*Land ho!*'

Captain Adam Bolitho pressed his hands on the chart and stared at the neat calculations that marked their progress. Beyond the tiny chart-room he knew there would be excitement as the call came from the masthead. Beside him Josiah Partridge, *Anemone*'s bluff sailing-master, watched his young captain's face, noting the pride he obviously felt for his command and at the fast passage they had almost completed. In mid-Atlantic they had met with fierce winds, but the frigate seemed to have a charmed life, and once into the sun they had lost no time in sending down the heavy-duty canvas and replacing it with the lighter sails that seemed to make *Anemone* fly.

Adam said, 'You've done well, Mr Partridge! I never thought we'd do it. Four thousand miles in seventeen days – what say you about *that*?'

Old Partridge, as he was called behind his back, beamed at him. Adam Bolitho could be very demanding, perhaps because of his illustrious uncle, but he never spared himself like some. Day and night he had been on deck, more often than not with both watches turned-to while the wind had screamed around them, matched only by the insane chorus of straining rigging and banging canvas.

Then into the friendly north-east trade winds, with the final run across the Western Atlantic where the sunshine had greeted them like heroes. It had been wild and often dangerous, but *Anemone*'s company had come to trust their youthful captain. Only a fool would try to deceive him.

Adam tapped his brass dividers on a small group of islands to the south of Anguilla. French, Spanish and Dutch, often visited by ships sailing alone, but rarely fought over. Those nations, like the English, had far more important islands to protect in order to keep their sea-lanes open, their trade prospering.

'What about this one, Mr Partridge? It is as close to the passage we must take as makes no difference.'

The sailing-master bent over the table, his purple nose barely inches away; Adam could smell the rum but would overlook it. Partridge was the best sailing-master he had ever known. He had served in the navy in two wars, and in between had made his way around the world in everything from a collier brig to a convict ship. If there was to be foul weather he would inevitably inform his captain even before the glass gave any hint of change. Uncharted shallows, reefs which were larger than previous navigators had estimated, it was all part of his sailor's lore. He rarely hesitated, and he did not disappoint Adam now.

'That 'un, zur? That be Bird Island. It's got some fancy dago name, but to me it's always been Bird Island.' His round Devonian accent sounded homely here, and reminded Adam of Yovell.

'Lay off a course. I shall inform the first lieutenant. Lord Sutcliffe will not be expecting us anyway, and I doubt if his lordship would think we could make such a speedy passage even if he were!'

Partridge watched him leave and sighed. What it was to be young. And Captain Bolitho certainly looked that, his black hair all anyhow, a none-too-clean shirt open to the waist – more like someone playing the part of a pirate than a skilled frigate captain.

On the quarterdeck, Adam paused to stare up at the great pyramid of sails, so fresh and bright after the dull skies and patched canvas of the Western Ocean.

Many of the men on deck probably thought they were carrying secret despatches of the greatest importance to the Commander-in-Chief, that he should drive his ship so hard. At one time the great mainyard had been bending like a bow under the wind's powerful thrust, so that even Old Partridge had expected to lose a spar if not the entire mast.

In the whole ship, nobody knew the devil that drove him. Whenever he had snatched time to sleep or bolt down some food, the torment had returned. It was never far away, even now. In his sleep it was worse. Her naked body writhing and slipping from his grip, her eyes angry and accusing as she had pulled away. The dreams left him gasping in his wildly swinging cot, and once, the marine sentry at the screen door had burst in to his assistance.

He strode up the tilting deck and stared across the glistening water, like ten million mirrors, he thought. The gulls were already quitting their islands to investigate the frigate.

Perhaps it was because he had known, *really* known that somehow his uncle would survive; not only that, but would save anyone who had depended on him. Maybe she believed that he had been as disappointed to learn that her husband lived, as he was overjoyed to hear the news of his uncle's safety.

And knowing all these things he had taken her, had loved her and compelled her to love him until they had both been exhausted. Now she might see that act as a betrayal, his plea of love nothing but a cruel lie to seize the advantage when she was most vulnerable.

He clenched his fingers into a tight fist. *I do love you, Zenoria. I never wanted to dishonour you by forcing myself upon you . . .*

He turned sharply as Peter Sargeant, his first lieutenant, who had ridden all the way from Plymouth to the church in Falmouth to bring him the news of the rescue, came up to join him.

'Bird Island, sir?'

A close-run thing. He could feel the shirt clinging to his skin, and not merely because of the sun.

'Yes. A whim perhaps. But vessels call there for water sometimes . . . Lord Sutcliffe can wait a while longer, and we might get him some news.' He smiled. 'And there is always the possibility of a prize or two.' He glanced up at the streaming masthead pendant. 'We will alter course directly, and steer south-west-by-west. We should be up to the islands before noon with this wind under our coat-tails!'

They grinned at each other. Young men, with the world and the ocean theirs for the asking.

'*Deck there!*' They stared up at the bright, washed-out sky. 'Sail on th' starboard bow!'

Several telescopes were seized and trained, and then Lieutenant Sargeant said, 'Big schooner, sir.'

Adam levelled his telescope and waited for *Anemone* to lift her beakhead over a long glassy roller.

'A Guinea-man, I'll wager.' He snapped the glass shut, his mind already busy with compass and distance. 'Full of slaves too, maybe. This new slavery act will come in useful!'

Sargeant cupped his hands. 'Both watches, Mr Bond! Stand by on the quarterdeck!'

The sailing-master watched the far-off sliver of sail, clearly etched now against an overlapping backdrop of small islands.

'We'll lose that 'un, zur, if us lets 'em slip amongst they dunghills!'

Adam showed his teeth. 'I admire your turn of phrase, Mr Partridge. And *no*, we shall not lose him.' He turned aside. 'Get the royals on her! Then send the gunner aft to me!'

Even though the other vessel had also made more sail, and had changed tack slightly away from her pursuer, she was no match for *Anemone*. Within an hour she could be clearly seen by everyone on deck who had the time to look. In two hours she was within range of *Anemone*'s bow-chasers. The gunner laid one of them himself, one hard thumb raised and moved this way or that to direct the crew to use their handspikes and adjust the long nine-pounder until he was satisfied.

Adam called, 'As you will, Mr Ayres! Close as you dare!'

Several of the seamen who were near enough to hear grinned at one another. Adam saw the exchanges and was moved. They had become a better ship's company than he had dared to hope for. Few were volunteers, and many had been transferred from other ships when *Anemone* had first commissioned without even being allowed to go ashore and visit their homes. And yet, over the months, they had become a self-dependent unit of the fleet. A new ship and her first captain, just as *Anemone* was Adam's first frigate. He had always dreamed and hoped for this, to follow in the footsteps of his uncle. He asked a lot of himself, and expected the support of his officers and men. Somehow, the magic had worked.

Just before they had left Spithead to beat down-Channel in a rising gale, they had discovered twelve seamen from a merchant vessel pulling ashore, probably without permission, for a night in the taverns. Adam had sent his third lieutenant and a party ashore and pressed those unfortunate revellers before they had realised what had happened. It had not been strictly legal but, he argued, they should have remained on board until officially paid-off by their captain. Twelve trained hands were a real find, instead of the usual dockside scum and jailbait most captains had to train and contend with. He could see one of them now, not only reconciled to his situation but actually showing a young landman how to use a marlin spike on some cordage. It was the way of sailors.

A bow-chaser roared out, the pale smoke fanning away through the staysail and jib.

There were several shouts of approval as the ball slammed down hard alongside the other vessel, flinging a tall waterspout high over the deck.

Adam took a speaking-trumpet, '*Close*, I said, Mr Ayres! I think you must have parted his hair!'

'He's heaving-to, sir!'

'Very well. Run down on him and send a party across. And no nonsense.'

Old Partridge lowered a glass and remarked, '*Looks* like a slaver, zur.' He sounded doubtful.

'Spit it out, man. I'm no mind-reader.'

'Too many ships-o'-war hereabouts, zur. Most Guinea-men give these parts a wide berth. From my experience they runs further to the west'rd to that damned hole Haiti or down to the Main where the Dons always find use for more slaves.' He was quite unperturbed by his young captain's manner; he knew many would have considered it beneath their dignity even to consult a lowly warrant officer.

Adam watched the other vessel floundering about in a cross-wind, her sails in disarray.

'That makes good sense, Mr Partridge. Well said.'

Partridge rubbed his chin to conceal a grin. Despite all his fire and impatience you could not help but like Captain Adam Bolitho.

'*Ready*, sir!'

'Go yourself, Mr Sargeant.' He gave him a searching look. 'No risks.'

Moments later the cutter pulled away from the frigate's swaying shadow, the boarding-party crowded amongst the oarsmen and a swivel-gun mounted above the stem.

Adam watched *Anemone*'s sails filling and banging as she was caught in a powerful undertow from the island.

He glanced at the masthead pendant. 'Back the main tops'l, Mr Martin!'

The second lieutenant dragged his eyes from the cutter as it bounced and pitched over the blue water towards the schooner.

To the sailing-master Adam said, 'Plenty of sea-room, eh?'

'Aye, plenty, zur. An' no bottom neither.' He pointed vaguely at the land. 'Shallows there though.'

Adam took a glass and relaxed slightly. It was always a risk so close to land. Too much depth to anchor, not enough time to weigh if things went wrong. He trained it on the schooner. A few figures on deck but little sign of excitement. If she was a slaver, her master obviously had nothing to hide. But there might be evidence of his trade, or at least enough to question him. They had stopped and searched so many vessels, and had rarely come away empty-handed. Intelligence, the casual mention of some enemy shipping movements. He smiled. Best of all, they might take the ship herself as a prize. He knew he had been lucky; so did his men.

During the last overhaul Adam had arranged to have all the ship's stern carvings and beakhead, the 'gingerbread' as it was nicknamed, painted with real gilt, and not merely dockyard yellow paint: a mark of success for a captain who was skilful enough to gain himself and his company the allotted share of prize-money.

Someone said, 'Almost there!' Lieutenant Sargeant could be seen standing in the sternsheets, a speaking-trumpet to his mouth as he shouted to the men on the schooner's deck. A good officer who had become a friend, or as close to one as Adam could ever accept.

He glanced along the deck. *Anemone* was a ship any young officer would kill for. Twenty-eight eighteen-pounders and ten nine-pounders, two of which were chasers. He turned away, and saw Partridge watching him from beside the compass box.

'What is it, zur?'

Adam plucked at his shirt, suddenly cold in spite of the glaring heat. Like fever.

'I'm not sure.'

Partridge rubbed his chin. He had never heard the captain reveal such uncertainty before. Right or wrong, he was always ready with an answer.

The second lieutenant called, 'The cutter's turning to go alongside, sir!'

Adam said sharply, 'Recall the boat, Mr Martin! *Now!*' To the startled Partridge he added, 'Prepare to get under way!'

The sailing-master stared at him. 'But – but we can rake that bugger, zur!'

Men were already dropping from the shrouds and gangways from where they had been enjoying the spectacle across the water.

The cutter had seen the recall signal, and Lieutenant Sargeant probably felt much the same as Old Partridge. *Too much sun.*

'He's standing away, sir!'

There were some ironic cheers from the gundeck, to cover a sense of disappointment. The cutter was almost bows-on now, the oars moving quickly. Sargeant probably thought the lookouts had sighted another vessel further out to sea, which appeared more promising.

'Deck there! Smoke on th' 'eadland!'

Adam hurried to the opposite side and trained his glass on the misty green slope.

He heard a man say, 'A camp o' some kind, I reckon.'

Adam shouted, 'Hands aloft, Mr Martin! Loose tops'ls! Pipe the hands to the braces!'

Partridge glanced at the shore as the topmen dashed to the shrouds and scampered up the ratlines. To his helmsmen he growled, 'Be ready, my lads! We'll be all aback else!' He had been at sea a long time, and was the oldest man in the ship. He knew that what some simpleton had mistaken for a camp fire was the smoke of an oven, an oven which had just been flung open when the cutter had begun to come about and return to *Anemone*.

'*Break out the main-course!*'

There were cries of alarm and surprise as a gun banged out, and seconds later a ball slapped through the foretopsail even as it was released to the wind. Adam tried to swallow but his mouth was too dry. Where the ball had punched its hole through the sail was a blackened circle, the mark of heated shot. If it ploughed into the hull the whole ship could become a pyre in minutes. With tarred rigging, sun-dried canvas and a hull filled with powder, paint, spirits and cordage, fire was the dread of every sailor, more than any storm. The worst enemy.

Discipline reasserted itself as men charged to the gangways with water buckets and even sponges from the guns.

Another shot, and the ball skimmed across the sea's face like something alive.

Adam shouted, 'Bring her about! Weather the headland if need be, but I'll not lose Peter Sargeant!'

Under command again, her forecourse and topsails filling to the hot wind, *Anemone* showed her copper as she heeled over in the bright sunshine.

The men in the cutter seemed to realise what their captain was doing, and when the boat crashed and ground against the frigate's side, they flung themselves on to the lines and rope ladders the boatswain had made ready for them. One man slipped and fell, and by the time his head broke surface *Anemone* had already left him astern.

Adam grasped the nettings until the tarred ropework cut his skin.

I nearly lost her. It kept repeating itself in his aching mind. *I nearly lost her*.

'Ready about, sir!'

Lieutenant Sargeant hurried aft and turned to stare at the abandoned cutter and the drowning seaman, who was still thrashing helplessly in the water.

'What happened, sir?'

Adam looked at him but barely saw him. 'Bait, Peter. That's what they were.' He turned and looked towards the land as another shot echoed across the placid water. Another few minutes and his ship, his precious *Anemone*, would have been either hit by some of those white-hot balls or forced into the shallows like a stranded whale. He felt the anger surge through him. He could scarcely believe he could feel like this. Like madness.

'Clear the larboard battery, Mr Martin! Load and run out, double-shotted, if you please!' He ignored the startled expressions, the relief of some of the cutter's crew obvious as they grinned and shook hands with their comrades.

Sargeant said, 'Course to steer, sir?' He must have known, and even beneath his sunburn his face looked pale.

'I want to pass her at half-a-cable!'

Gun-captains were racing each other as the larboard battery of long eighteen-pounders were loaded, their wads tamped home, before they were run squealing to the open ports.

Adam raised his glass as each gun-captain faced aft. He saw the earlier disinterest aboard the schooner already giving way to panic as the frigate changed tack and bore down on her, her broadside catching the sun like a line of black teeth.

'The hull, Mr Sargeant, not her rigging this time.'

Adam watched intently. A group of men were trying to hoist out a boat, and now there were uniforms clambering on deck from hatchways and holds. French soldiers, some armed, others in obvious terror as they ran about the drifting schooner like blind things.

'Go forrard, Peter.' Adam did not look at him. 'If need be, lay each gun yourself. I want every ball to strike true.'

Sargeant ran along the gangway, pausing only to call down to each gun-captain.

A midshipman exclaimed, 'Some of them are jumping overboard!' Nobody answered; they were either staring at the schooner or at their own captain.

Sargeant drew his sword and stared aft as if still expecting the order to stand-down, then he shouted, 'On the uproll, gun by gun, *fire!*'

The crews were very experienced, and knew their drill by heart. Down along the frigate's tilting side each gun belched orange fire and hurled itself inboard on its tackles. At one hundred yards' range they could not miss. Holes appeared in the schooner's hull and a ricochet burst through the side and brought down a mass of writhing rigging and blocks.

At the fourth gun the sea seemed to split apart in one terrible explosion. Men covered their ears, and others ducked down as splinters and whole lengths of timber and snapped spars cascaded over the sea, changing the clear water into a mass of splashes and pieces of charred wood. When the smoke finally drifted clear there was no piece of the schooner afloat.

Adam closed the glass with a snap. 'Put it in the log, Mr Martin. Vessel carried soldiers, powder and shot. There were no survivors.' He handed the glass to the signals midshipman and said tonelessly, 'What did you expect, Mr Dunwoody? War can be a bloody business.'

Sargeant came aft and touched his hat. 'I didn't realise, sir. Nor did I know why you recalled my boat.'

'Well, remember in future.' He laid his hand on the lieutenant's shoulder. It was shaking so badly he needed to. 'I should have known – realised what was happening. It will not happen again.'

He watched the seamen throwing themselves back on the braces until their half-naked bodies were angled to the deck. Beyond them he could see the darting shapes of gulls as they overcame their fear of the explosion and circled above the grisly flotsam in search of food.

'*I nearly lost her!*' Only when he looked at his friend's tense features did he realise he had said it aloud.

He shrugged heavily. 'So let us go and inform Lord Sutcliffe that he has the French army camping on his back doorstep.'

Four days after *Black Prince* had dropped anchor Bolitho was lying back in a chair, while Allday shaved him with his usual panache. It was early morning: a good time for a shave, to sip some of Catherine's fine coffee, and to think. The stern windows and quarter galleries were open to the breeze and he could hear men moving about, washing down decks, preparing the flagship for another day. Visitors and visits: it had been endless, and Bolitho knew he had done little to spare either Jenour or Yovell in his search for information.

He had received every captain, even Herrick's new enemy, Captain the Lord Rathcullen of the *Matchless*, a languid, disdainful man, but one with a fiery reputation. That and the ancient family title would be enough to enrage Herrick at any time.

But he was amazed by the change in his old friend since that last terrible day of his court-martial. Herrick drove himself without respite, and his inspections of ships and docking resources had left several officials and sea-officers cringing from his anger if there were any faults discovered.

It was like being in a sealed room, despite the lush surroundings and the brilliant colours of sea and sky. Until the frigate *Tybalt* returned from Jamaica or the other reinforcement from England, the *Ipswich*, arrived, he was without frigates. The other squadrons were scattered, some in Jamaica or St Kitts, others as far away as Bermuda. Every ship under a foreign flag was suspect; without fresh intelligence he knew nothing of greater affairs in Europe. A Spanish or Dutch flag might now be an ally, a Portuguese perhaps hostile. All of his captains, great or lowly, were governed by the old law of admiralty: if you were right, others took the credit. If you were wrong, you carried the blame.

Yovell let out a sigh. 'I shall have these orders copied and ready for signature before noon, Sir Richard.'

Bolitho glanced at his red, perspiring face. 'Sooner, Mr Yovell. I would appreciate it.'

Jenour finished his coffee and sat pensively gazing across the great cabin. One of the best moments of the day, he thought. This, he shared with no one. Soon the procession would begin: the squadron's captains, traders wanting favours or escorts for their vessels until they were out in open water, senior officials from the dockyard or the victualling yards. They usually wanted to discuss money, and how much Sir Richard might be persuaded to authorise.

Ozzard opened the door. 'The Captain, sir.'

Keen came into the cabin. 'I apologise for disturbing you, sir.' He glanced at the razor in Allday's hand which was suddenly motionless. How a man with fists so large could shave so precisely was beyond understanding. Like his ship models, he thought, not a spar or a block out of scale. Perfect . . . It sparked off another memory: Allday flinging his knife at the man in the jolly-boat while he dragged poor Sophie aft to the sternsheets.

'What is it, Val?'

'Rear-Admiral Herrick's boat has just left the jetty, sir.'

Bolitho noted the hostility, and was saddened by it. This was one rift which would never heal, particularly as it had been a court of enquiry under Herrick which had questioned Keen's right to remove Zenoria from the transport ship. It had nearly happened to Catherine, so Bolitho did not blame Keen for so bitter a resentment.

'He is up and abroad early, Val.' He waited, knowing there was more.

'The master's mate-of-the-watch reported that the admiral's flag has been rehoisted above the battery, sir.'

'Lord Sutcliffe?' He could hear Allday's painful breathing. After what Herrick had told him he had not expected Sutcliffe to return to duty.

'Inform the squadron, Val. I'd not wish the admiral to imagine he is being snubbed.'

By the time Herrick reached the flagship Bolitho had changed into a fresh shirt and some new stockings which Catherine had bought for him. They greeted one another informally in the great cabin, where Herrick wasted no time in explaining.

'Came down from St John's overnight, it appears.' He waved Ozzard's coffee aside. 'He insists on seeing you.' The blue eyes hardened. 'It seems that *I* may not be considered competent enough to control matters here!'

'Easy, Thomas. Perhaps I should speak with the senior surgeon?' He glanced round for Jenour. 'The barge, if you please, Stephen.' It gave him time to consider this limited news. It was true that Lord Sutcliffe was still in overall command. He could not be unseated because a subordinate did not agree with his strategy.

Herrick stood, feet apart, staring at the open stern windows.

'Look out for squalls, that's what *I* say!'

Bolitho heard the faint squeal of tackles as his barge was hoisted up and outboard of the ship's side. Perhaps Sutcliffe had some private information he wanted to offer? Or did he know something of the enemy's movements? That seemed unlikely. If the French did have ships of any consequence in the Caribbean they must have been well concealed.

Herrick added wearily, 'I am to accompany you.'

Bolitho saw Jenour signalling through the other door.

He said, 'That at least is good news, Thomas.'

Herrick picked up his hat and followed him. As he did so, his coat brushed against the wine cooler which Catherine had had made, with its beautiful carved inlay on the top: the Bolitho coat of arms in three kinds of wood.

He hesitated, then laid one hand on the top. 'I had forgotten.' He did not explain.

With the shrill of calls lingering in their ears, they remained silent as the barge pulled smartly from the flagship's tall shadow and into the first real heat of the day.

Every captain in the squadron would know that Bolitho was going ashore for some official reason; he could see the sunlight flashing on several trained telescopes. The *Sunderland* and the *Glorious*, the old *Tenacious* which had been launched when Bolitho had first entered the navy at the age of twelve. He smiled grimly. *And we are both still here.*

Allday moved the tiller-bar very slightly and watched the land pivot round, obedient to his hand at the helm. He tensed as the sunshine reflected on fixed bayonets and a squad of marines which was moving up a slope towards the big house with the white-painted walls. The guard to receive Sir Richard Bolitho, but it was not that. Allday glanced at Bolitho's squared shoulders, his hair so dark against his companion's greyness. Bolitho had not noticed. Not yet anyway. Lord Sutcliffe could not have chosen a worse place for his stay at English Harbour.

Allday could remember it like yesterday. Where Sir Richard had found his lady again after the years had forced them apart. Where he himself had waited out the night on another occasion, smoking his pipe and enjoying his rum under the stars, knowing that all the while Sir Richard had been with her. *With her*, in the fullest sense of the word. Another man's wife. A lot of water had gone through the mill since then, but the scandal was greater than ever.

He saw Bolitho reach up to his eye, and Jenour's quick, worried glance.

Always the pain.

It seemed as if they could never leave him alone. Their lives were in his hands, and not some poxy admirals who seemed to have done nothing.

He barked, '*Bows!* Toss your oars!'

He narrowed his eyes to watch the small reception party on the jetty. Bolitho had sensed the edge in his tone and turned slightly to look up at him.

'I know, old friend. I know. There is no defence against memory.'

The barge came alongside the jetty so expertly that you could have cracked an egg between the piles and her hull.

Bolitho stepped down from the boat and paused just long enough to look up at the house. *I am here, Kate. And you are with me.*

Once Bolitho had realised where he was to meet the admiral-commanding he had prepared himself as if for a confrontation with a person from his past. The trouble was that it was exactly as he had remembered it, with the same wide, paved terrace that overlooked the anchorage, from which Catherine had watched *Hyperion* standing into harbour, and where she had heard his name mentioned as the man whose flag flew above the old ship.

A few black gardeners loitered around the luxuriant shrubbery, but Bolitho had already formed an impression that the house, like the squad of Royal Marines, was to discourage visitors and not the reverse.

Herrick had introduced him briefly to the senior surgeon, a sad-eyed little man named Ruel. Now as they approached the house Ruel was walking beside him, slowly, Bolitho noticed, as if he were reluctant to visit his charge again.

Bolitho asked quietly, 'How is the admiral? I understood he was too ill to return here.'

Ruel glanced around at the others: Jenour and Herrick, two of the admiral's staff and a captain of marines.

He answered cautiously, 'He is dying, Sir Richard. I am surprised he has survived so long.' He saw Bolitho's questioning gaze and added, 'I have been a surgeon in the islands for ten years. I have become accustomed to Death's various guises.'

'Fever then.' He heard Herrick speaking to Jenour and

wondered if he was thinking of his wife Dulcie, who had died so cruelly of typhus in Kent. And if he realised at long last that Catherine might easily have died too by refusing to abandon her in her last hours on earth.

'I think you should know, Sir Richard.' Ruel was finding it hard to be confidential in the bright sunshine with people around him discussing England, the war and the weather as if nothing at all were unusual.

'Tell me. I am no innocent, and no stranger to death, either.'

He saw the surgeon raise one hand to his lips. 'It is not fever, Sir Richard. Lord Sutcliffe is diseased, beyond medical aid. Spiritual too, I would imagine.'

'I see.' Bolitho looked up at the elegant house, the best in English Harbour. Where they had found one another, where they had loved so fiercely, ignoring the challenge to honour and reputation, and the harm their liaison might provoke.

He said shortly, 'Syphilis.' He saw the quick nod. 'I had heard something of the admiral's reputation, but I had no idea . . .' He broke off. What was the point of involving the surgeon? Common seamen became diseased from their rare contacts with women of the town; senior officers were never discussed in the same breath.

The surgeon hesitated. 'I fear you may get little sense from his lordship. His mind is failing, and he has iritis, and cannot bear the pain of daylight.' He shrugged ruefully. 'I am sorry, Sir Richard. I know of your care for the ordinary sailor, and the assistance you gave to Sir Piers Blachford, under whom I had the honour to prepare myself for this sickening profession.'

Blachford. He never seemed to be far away. Bolitho said, 'I thank you for your frankness, Doctor Ruel. Your calling is not so sickening as you proclaim – I am all the more confident now that I have met you.' He nodded to the others. 'I shall go in now. Stephen, come with me.'

Herrick sounded surprised. 'What about me?'

Bolitho said calmly, 'Trust me.'

Two marines opened the doors and they stepped into the great hallway. Like yesterday. Like now. The smiling, insincere faces, the women in their daring gowns and jewels, the sudden brightness of the light. Then stumbling on an unseen step. Catherine stepping away from the others to assist him. A contact which, after so long, had seemed to burn like a fuse.

Although it was morning and the harbour outside gleaming with sunlit reflections and deep colours, it was like that night again.

A nervous black servant bowed to them and gestured to the nearest doorway.

Bolitho murmured, 'The admiral cannot see very well – any kind of light sears his eyes. Do you understand?'

Jenour gravely commented, 'He does not have long, Sir Richard. It is tertiary syphilis at the most virulent stage.'

Despite his anxiety, Bolitho found time to be surprised at the young lieutenant's understanding. But then his father was an apothecary, and his uncle a doctor of some repute in Southampton. They had probably hated Jenour's throwing away a possible career in medicine for the risks and uncertainty of naval service.

He said, 'Help me, Stephen.' He did not need to explain further.

As the door was opened he found himself in complete darkness. But as he strained his eyes he saw a sliver of hard sunlight between two curtains and knew he was in the room where she had discovered his injury, and he had been unable to distinguish the colour of a ribbon in her hair. *Yesterday*.

'Be seated, Sir Richard.' The voice came out of nowhere, surprisingly strong, petulant even, like someone who had been kept waiting.

Bolitho gasped, and instantly felt Jenour's hand at his elbow. He had collided with a low stool or table, and the realisation of his helplessness made him suddenly despairing and angry.

'I am sorry to greet you in this fashion.' The tone said otherwise.

Bolitho found a chair and sat on it carefully. In that one sliver of light he could see the man's outline against the wall, and worse, his eyes, like white stones in the solitary beam.

'And *I* am sorry that you are thus indisposed, my lord.'

There was silence, and Bolitho became aware of the sour stench in the room, the odour of soiled linen.

'I am, of course, aware of your reputation and your family history. I am honoured that you should be sent here to replace me.'

'I did not know, my lord. Nobody in England has heard of your . . .'

'*Misfortune?* Was that how you were about to describe it?'

'I meant no disrespect, my lord.'

'No, no, of course, *you* would not. I command here. My orders stand until . . .' He broke off in a fit of coughing and retching.

Bolitho waited and then said, 'The French will surely know of our intentions to attack and, if possible, seize Martinique. Without it they would be unable to operate in the Caribbean. My orders are to seek out the enemy before he can use his ships to attack and weaken our assault. We need all our strength.' He paused. It was hopeless. Like talking to a shadow. But Sutcliffe was right about one thing. He did hold overall command, diseased, mad or otherwise. He continued, 'May I suggest that when *Tybalt* returns from Jamaica you send a fast schooner there and request the admiral to give you further support?'

Sutcliffe cleared his throat noisily. 'Rear-Admiral Herrick authorised the impressment of those schooners, but then he is a man well acquainted with insubordination. I have every intention of informing their lordships of any further acts of disloyalty. Do I make myself clear?'

Bolitho answered quietly, 'It sounds like a threat, my lord.'

'No. A *promise*, certainly!'

Jenour shuffled his feet and instantly the disembodied eyes shifted towards him. 'Who is that? You brought a witness?'

'My flag-lieutenant.'

'I see.' He laughed gently, a chilling sound in such a stifling room. 'I knew Viscount Somervell, of course, when he was His Majesty's Inspector General in the Indies and I was in the Barbados. A man of honour, I thought . . . but you will doubtless disagree, Sir Richard.'

Bolitho touched his eye, his mind reeling. The man was mad. But not so mad that he had lost the use of spite.

'You are correct, my lord. I do disagree.' He was committed

now. 'I know him to have been a knave, a liar and a man who enjoyed killing for the sake of it!'

He heard the admiral vomit into a basin and clenched his fists in disgust. God, were these the wages of sin the old rector at Falmouth had threatened them with, when they had all been frightened children? The legacy of doom?

When Sutcliffe spoke again he sounded quite calm, dangerously so.

'I have heard your reports of some so-called Dutch frigate, your passionate belief that the enemy intends to divide our forces. Here, you will obey *me*. Carry out your patrols and exercise your people; that would make good sense. But try to discredit me and I will see you damned to hell!'

'Very probably, my lord.' He stood up and waited for Jenour to guide his arm.

'I have not dismissed you yet, *sir*.'

Bolitho turned wearily. It was so pointless, so futile. With the greater part of the fleet held in readiness to repel an attack on Jamaica, the way was wide open for French counter-action. *And all I have is six ships*.

Jamaica was nearly thirteen hundred miles to the west. Even with favourable winds it would take ships far too long to regain their command of the Leeward Islands.

He said, 'I believe that the enemy intend to attack our bases here, my lord.'

'Here? Antigua? St Kitts perhaps? Where else do you imagine them?' He gave a shrill laugh which ended in another bout of retching. This time it did not stop.

Bolitho found the door open, Jenour's face filled with concern as the half-light of the hallway greeted them.

The surgeon was waiting for him, standing apart from the others as if he had guessed what had happened.

'How long, Doctor?' He heard Sutcliffe ringing his bell, saw the obvious reluctance of the servants to answer it. 'Can you tell me that?'

The doctor shrugged. 'Out here, men and women die every day, quietly and without complaint. It is God's will, they say. I have grown accustomed to it, though I can never accept it.' He considered the question. 'Impossible to say, Sir Richard.

264

He might die tomorrow; he could survive a month, even longer, by which time he will not know his own name.'

'Then we are done for.' He felt the fury rising again. There were thousands of men depending on their superiors. Did nobody care? The admiral was going to die, eaten alive by his disease. But to the outside world, if it believed the lie, he was a man worn out by his devotion to duty.

The surgeon stood by one of the shaded windows, and pointed at the bright silver line of the horizon.

'Yonder lies the enemy, Sir Richard. He is not there for no purpose.' He studied Bolitho's grave features. 'For *you*, God's will is not enough, is it?'

For a long moment Bolitho stood with Jenour on the sunbaked jetty while the barge was manoeuvred alongside the stairs. In the violent light the same officers who had been sent to greet him hovered discreetly and at a distance. Perhaps they were glad to see him leave after disturbing their secluded world, thinking perhaps that routine would save them. Sutcliffe would die, and after a fitting ceremonial funeral, another admiral would arrive. Life would go on.

'Well, Stephen, what do you think of this?'

Jenour stared out to sea. 'I believe that Lord Sutcliffe is fully aware of his authority, Sir Richard.'

Bolitho waited. 'I need to know, Stephen. To rest on one's own views can be like an unbaited trap.'

Jenour bit his lip. 'None of the officers here would dare to defy him. Right or wrong, Lord Sutcliffe commands their destinies. To speak otherwise would be seen as treason, or at best, mutiny.' His open face was filled with anxiety. 'Nobody will support you, Sir Richard.' He faltered. 'Except the squadron and your captains, who will expect you to act on their behalf.'

Bolitho said bitterly, 'Yes, and ask them to die for me.' He turned aside as the barge hooked on. 'What of Rear-Admiral Herrick? Come on, speak out, man – as my friend now!'

'He will do nothing. He risked all for his own satisfaction at his court-martial.' He watched the pain in Bolitho's eyes. 'He will never do so again.'

Allday stepped on to the jetty and removed his hat, immediately taking in Bolitho's expression and the flag-lieutenant's unusual intensity.

Bolitho climbed down after Jenour and settled in the stern-sheets.

It was the second time in the day that Jenour had surprised him. Once again, he knew he was right.

17

Ships Passing

Bolitho went on deck, the taste of coffee lingering on his tongue. Keen was about to exercise the upper gundeck's twelve-pounders and he saw the casual glances as he walked to the quarterdeck rail. They had become used to seeing their vice-admiral dressed so informally in only shirt and breeches, and Bolitho was pleased that Keen had impressed it on all his officers to do likewise. If it did not make them seem more approachable, it might at least show them as human beings.

Keen smiled. 'Sail in sight, sir. Hull-up to wind'rd.' He tried to make it interesting, a piece of news to break the day-to-day monotony.

Black Prince was steering due south, some two hundred and fifty miles from Antigua. Abeam, the lookouts could just manage to distinguish the island of St Lucia, the silent volcano of Soufrière a prominent landmark that had saved many seafarers over the years.

Astern of the flagship the two seventy-fours *Valkyrie* and *Relentless* kept their snail's pace, their reflections barely moving on a dark blue sea which appeared solid enough to walk on, like crude glass. The remaining ships Bolitho had placed under Crowfoot's command, and sent to patrol the Guadeloupe Passage to the north.

This was frustration at its worst. The ships were too slow, and on several occasions they had sighted unidentified vessels, which had soon headed away rather than face the prospect of being stopped and searched by the powerful men-of-war. They had to have smaller ships in support. Godschale, a frigate captain himself in that other war, should have moved heaven and earth to get them.

Who was the newcomer? Obviously not an enemy. He would have been off like a fox at the sight of hounds if he was.

Sedgemore was shouting to Lieutenant Whyham, 'Keep them at it, sir! I want these twelve-pounders cleared for action in ten minutes, less if they have the will for it!'

Bolitho glanced at the gun crews. Bare backs less rawly burned, and more the colour of leather. He had not timed the upper batteries, but he knew by his own standards as a captain that they were a long way from Sedgemore's target.

'Deck there! She's a frigate!'

Bolitho saw Keen watching him. What was it this time, Sutcliffe's death or news of home? Or the war had ended, and they had been the last to know.

'Heave-to, Captain Keen. Let him run down on us.' He looked again at the gun crews. 'I would suggest you continue the drills, Mr Sedgemore. It has been known for ships to carry on fighting even when adrift.'

'Aloft with a glass, Mr Houston!' Keen turned away to escape Sedgemore's sudden deflation. 'Mr Julyan, stand by to wear ship, if you please!'

While the big three-decker floundered round into the wind and her two consorts endeavoured to remain on station, their pyramids of sails almost lifeless, the upper deck's twenty-eight guns went through the frantic routine of clearing for action.

'Deck, sir! She's made her number!' The midshipman's voice was shrill when calling from such a height and Bolitho guessed that he hated the fact. 'She's the *Tybalt*, thirty-six, Captain Esse!'

Bolitho tried to contain his sudden hope. The last of his squadron, and a frigate. It was like an answered prayer.

He lifted a glass from the rack and trained it on the approaching ship. Where was Adam now, he wondered? And where had the time gone? It was now mid-January 1809. A new year, without anything to show for it. He thought of England, the bitter wind off the Atlantic seeping around the old house and gardens. What of Catherine? Could she really be happy in that kind of life, alone amongst people who for the most part would always remain strangers? Or might she become bored, impatient, and turn to other distractions?

In two hours *Tybalt* was almost in gunshot range and Bolitho said, 'Captain repair on board as soon as is convenient, Val.'

He frowned when one of the gun crews fell about in confusion as the twelve-pounder, released from its breeching-rope, ran momentarily out of control.

Sedgemore yelled, 'God damn your eyes, Blake, your people are all cripples today!'

Bolitho touched the locket beneath his damp shirt and smiled. What was he thinking of? They were lovers. Nothing could break that.

He waited until the frigate was hove-to and had lowered her gig and then went below to his cabin. *Let there be news this time*.

Captain William Esse was tall and thin with a pleasant smile and an old-fashioned manner, which seemed at odds with his twenty-five years. He laid a canvas bag on the cabin table and seated himself with great care, as if afraid his long legs might become entangled.

'What news, Captain Esse? I must know without delay.'

Esse smiled and took a glass from Ozzard. 'Jamaica was hot, Sir Richard, and the slave-revolt little more than a skirmish. The extra soldiers were not needed at all.' He shrugged. 'So we brought them back to Antigua.'

'What of Lord Sutcliffe?'

Esse gave him a blank stare. 'He is still alive, Sir Richard, although I was not asked to see him.' He saw Bolitho's expression and added hastily, 'A fast packet visited English Harbour. There are letters for you from England.'

Bolitho touched the heavy pouch. Letters from Catherine, one at least. It was like a hunger, a longing. All the rest was disappointment. There was no news of the enemy. Perhaps the threat was only in his mind. Or maybe the journey in the open boat had blunted his reckoning in some way?

Over three months since he had left Spithead. It felt like eternity. And Sutcliffe was still defying death. He wondered how Herrick was managing to stay out of trouble.

Esse exclaimed, 'But I almost forgot, Sir Richard! As we weighed anchor, *Anemone* entered harbour. I was not able to speak much with Captain Bolitho, but I gather he was bringing despatches for Lord Sutcliffe. He shouted across to me that it was something important. But I did not catch the gist of it.'

'How strange. My nephew was in my mind just now as I watched *Tybalt* running down on us. But why here? It must be serious.' The unanswered questions hung in the cabin's still air. Despatches for the admiral. But the Admiralty would be in ignorance about Sutcliffe's condition.

He persisted, 'Can you remember nothing further of this conversation?'

Esse frowned so that his pale eyes disappeared. 'I took little notice, Sir Richard, as it did not concern the squadron.'

'What did he say?'

'The French. He said something about enemy ships . . . I assumed he meant in home waters.'

'My God.' Bolitho saw Ozzard peering through his hatch. 'Fetch the captain and my flag-lieutenant!'

To the bemused Esse he said, 'I shall give you written orders. You must return to English Harbour with all haste. You will see Rear-Admiral Herrick and make certain that copies of my despatches are sent immediately to St Kitts and to London.' He turned away so that Esse should not see his despair. London? It could as well be the moon for all the good it would do now.

Keen and Jenour entered. Bolitho said tersely, 'Adam has come from England. Despatches from the Admiralty, no doubt – they'd never release a frigate otherwise.'

Keen said gently, 'But we don't know for certain, sir.'

'My responsibility, Val.' He tried to smile but it eluded him. It had been reported over the months that the French were secretly reinforcing their squadrons in the Caribbean. Now they were ready. In a matter of weeks a combined naval and military force would attack Martinique. And with some of the English supporting squadrons tied down in Jamaica . . . He felt a cold touch on his spine. It would be Herrick's massacred convoy all over again.

He said quietly, 'Make *quite sure* that Rear-Admiral Herrick understands. Every available ship and garrison must stand-to. For once the enemy has scattered our invasion force, they will surely turn upon Antigua.'

Esse nodded, his face very calm. 'I shall do my best.'

'Leave me now. I have matters to dictate.'

Alone with Keen and Jenour, while the ship pitched on a low swell and the upper deck echoed to the squeak and thud of Sedgemore's mock battle, Bolitho said, 'You think me mad?'

'Far from that, sir.' Keen paused. 'But it must be said: it is all surmise.'

'Possibly. But we know from the past week that there is no enemy movement down here. So the ships must be elsewhere, correct?'

'If they *are* coming this way, sir.'

Bolitho strode about the cabin. There was no news. So why should he care, with a mad superior who would see any initiative, even by him, as gross insubordination? It would be a bitter twist of fate if Herrick were a witness at *his* court-martial!

Aloud he said harshly, 'But I *do* care. It is what we are here for!'

To Keen he said more evenly, 'Bring the ship about, Val, and signal the others to keep station on us. We will pass through the St Lucia Channel tonight. A longer haul, but it will give us more favourable winds. With luck we shall meet with Captain Crowfoot's ships and then we can beat up to wind'rd. *Tybalt* will have rejoined us by then. If not . . .' He did not need to say more.

Keen said, 'I'm ready, sir.'

Bolitho smiled at him. 'To the final battle, the gates of hell if need be, eh, Val?'

Keen did not smile in return. 'Yes,' he said. 'Always.'

Rear-Admiral Thomas Herrick stood by an open window and mopped his face with his handkerchief. The noon heat made it hard to think, and the persistent attacks by mosquitoes and other insects were a constant irritation.

Seated at a table, Captain John Pearse, now his second-in-command because of the admiral's disgusting illness but normally captain of the busy dockyard, watched him guardedly. Pearse was content enough with his appointment even though he knew he would rise no higher in the navy. He had been a long time in the Indies and was used to the extremes of climate; also long enough to avoid the many fevers and diseases which weekly led to sea-burials or funerals in the small garrison cemeteries, with their pathetic regimental crests and the names of towns and villages in the mother-country Pearse could barely remember. He wondered what was so disturbing Herrick. Sutcliffe was dying; he must die, or he would drive his staff as mad as himself. The horror of his appalling condition – sores, black vomit and near-blindness – pervaded the whole building, and Herrick's temper was daily growing more fraught.

There had been one such display of unreasonable anger just now when a messenger had come to inform them that the frigate *Tybalt* had cleared the entrance and was now on passage to join Bolitho's squadron, and that yet another frigate had been reported standing inshore. 'She's the *Anemone*, sir, thirty-eight, commanded by . . .' He had got no further. Herrick had snarled, 'I *know* who commands her, man – Sir Richard's nephew! *Stop wasting my time!*'

Pearse said carefully, 'I think it would be prudent to recall *Tybalt*, sir. *Anemone* may have news which might need attention.'

Herrick saw the two frigates passing one another on a converging tack, the red coats moving on the battery to prepare a salute.

'I think not.' The two vessels were slowly drawing apart now. Why was Adam here? Surely there was no more news since *Black Prince* had arrived at English Harbour? He heard feet running by, servants going to assist the admiral no doubt. Diseased of body and diseased of mind. He were better dead.

Pearse fiddled with some papers and looked warily at Herrick. 'Perhaps the French have surrendered.' He regretted it immediately.

"Surrendered? Never in a million years, man! Damned barbarians, they'll fight to the last ditch.'

He winced as the first guns echoed around the harbour. He strode to the sill and watched the frigate gliding towards the guardboat. The breeze was fresher; it might clear the air. He saw the gunsmoke drifting close to the water and recalled his own service in frigates. *But never in command of one.*

It had been Adam who had brought the news to him of Dulcie's terrible death. Had it been anyone else he might have been able to contain it, at least for a while, from the curious. But Adam was a Bolitho, even if he held the family name only because of his uncle; he had been born a bastard, and his father had deserted the navy to join the American rebels . . . and yet that shame never tarnished *him*, or impeded his promotion.

It was all so unfair. Dulcie had given him everything: stability, pride, and above all, love. But a child had been denied them. He watched the flash of the final gun, the anchor throwing up spray as *Anemone* came to rest. Even Richard and his wife had been blessed with a daughter. How could he have turned his back on her? He thought suddenly of Catherine. She had stayed with Dulcie to the end, in very real danger to herself. *Why can I not come to terms with it?*

He said abruptly, 'Pass the word to the signal-station, Captain Pearse. I want to see *Anemone*'s captain before anyone else does.'

Captain Pearse nodded uneasily. It was unlikely that Lord Sutcliffe would know or care what was happening.

It was another hour before Adam Bolitho arrived, his hat crammed under one arm, his short hanger pressed against his thigh.

Herrick shook his hand. 'Do not keep me in suspense, Adam! This is most unexpected. How long have you been at sea?'

Adam glanced around. Although the officer-of-the-guard had shouted to him from his boat that Lord Sutcliffe was sick, he had somehow expected to find him here.

'Eighteen days, sir.' He smiled, the recklessness on his tanned face wiping away the shadows of command.

Herrick waved him to a chair and sat down opposite him, frowning.

'Why the urgency?'

'I have important despatches from the Admiralty, sir. It seems that the bad weather in the Atlantic allowed some French ships to avoid our blockading squadrons.' He waited, expecting some reaction he could recognise. 'I am ordered to acquaint Lord Sutcliffe with the despatches without delay.'

'Impossible. He is too ill. I cannot tell him anything.'

'But – ' Adam grappled with Herrick's blunt reply. 'It may be vital. It is said that the enemy ships are on passage *here*, though I believe that some, if not all, are already arrived. I clashed with a shore-mounted gun a day ago. Heated shot – I was nearly in irons until we worked clear. French soldiers too . . .'

'You had time to go after the enemy then? Looking for a prize, perhaps?'

Adam regarded him with surprise. 'Yes, there was a schooner, sir. She was carrying powder and soldiers and I dished her up as we left.'

'Very commendable.' Herrick looked at his hands in his lap. 'Your uncle is to the south'rd; he has divided his squadron. You see, we *had* no frigates until *Tybalt* returned from Port Royal. And now you.' He looked up, his blue eyes very bright. 'And I gather there is another on passage too. A veritable fleet indeed!'

Adam controlled his disappointment and a growing impatience with effort. 'What is it, sir? Is something wrong? Maybe I could help.'

'Wrong? Why should there be?' He was on his feet again and standing by the window without realising he had moved. 'Your family seems to think it holds the answer to all ills, wouldn't you say?'

Adam stood up slowly. 'May I speak plainly, sir?'

'I would expect nothing else.'

'I have known you since I was a midshipman. I have always thought of you as a friend, as well as an experienced sailor.'

'Has it changed?' Herrick squinted into the light, seeing the distant activity aboard this young man's ship.

'Later I seemed to become someone who came between you and your true friend.' He gestured toward the sea. 'Who is out there now, and in ignorance of these French reinforcements.' His voice was sharper, but he could not help it. 'I am no longer that midshipman, sir. I command one of His Majesty's finest frigates, and I believe I am successful at it.'

'There is no need to shout.' Herrick faced him. 'I am not empowered to open Lord Sutcliffe's despatches – even you must realise that. Your uncle commands the squadron, and our other vessels are gathered either at Jamaica or the Barbados. We have only local patrols, which sail out of here and St Kitts, but you must know that, surely.' His tone was impatient. 'I only wish *Rear-Admiral* Hector Gossage were here to share the rewards of his damned folly!'

Adam watched him uneasily. 'That would be difficult. I heard he had died within weeks of taking up his appointment.'

Herrick stared at him. 'My God! I did not know.'

Adam looked away. 'Then I shall make sail forthwith and seek out my uncle's squadron. He must be warned.' He hesitated, hating to plead. 'I beg you, sir, for his love if for nothing else, open the despatches!'

Herrick said coldly, 'There is a lot of the rebel in *you*, did you know that?'

'If you are referring to my late father, sir, remember what they say about casting the first stone.'

'Thank you for reminding me. You may return to your ship and prepare for sea. I will order the water-lighters alongside immediately.' He saw the cloud lift from the young captain's face and added harshly, '*No*, not for you to skip about the ocean in search of glory! I am ordering you to Port Royal. The admiral there can decide. He and General Beckwith are to lead the invasion of Martinique.'

Adam said with disbelief, 'But by then it will be too late!'

'Don't lecture me, my boy – this is war, not the pulpit.'

'I will await your pleasure, sir.' He was a stranger; there was nothing more to be said or done here. 'I can scarce credit what has happened, what has become of something which was so dear to my uncle.' He swung away. 'But no longer to me, *sir!*'

It was dusk by the time *Anemone* had again weighed anchor and was setting her topsails in a glowing copper sunset. Herrick watched from the window, and after some hesitation raised a goblet of cognac to his lips. The first he had taken since Gossage's astounding evidence on the last day of the court-martial.

Damn that young tiger for his impertinence. His arrogance. Herrick drained the brandy and almost choked on it. He would take no more risks, no matter how the critics might jabber about it later. They were safe. He would never be that now.

In any case, *Black Prince* was a big ship, far larger than his poor *Benbow* had been on that terrible day. She was capable of her own defence.

The door opened and Captain Pearse entered the silent room. He looked at the empty goblet and the unopened despatches, which lay by the strongbox.

Herrick said heavily, 'I said no interruptions! I want to think! And if it's about Captain Adam Bolitho, I'll trouble you not to interfere!'

The captain replied coldly, 'The surgeon has been to see me, sir. Lord Sutcliffe has just died.'

His eyes glowed in the candlelight as he watched Herrick take the news, gripping the sill with one hand. 'So *you* command here until relieved, sir.'

Herrick felt the blood pounding in his temples like insistent hammers. He had sent Adam away. It was too late now. By dawn, not even a schooner would find him.

Very deliberately he walked to the table, unfastened the canvas envelope and removed the enclosure with its bright Admiralty seal. He still could not bring himself to open it. The contents were likely already out of date and intended only for the man who now lay dead in his own filth. Distance and communications, time and strategy which could only be guess-work, left for the man who had to execute it. He had seen Bolitho in his young nephew's face. Never once had he hesitated, even when he was judged at fault. A charmed life. What had they called it? Charisma. Like Nelson, who had paid for it with his life.

The captain saw his hesitation. 'Nobody will blame you, sir.'

He stood like a witness as Herrick picked up a knife and slit open the seal. Earlier he had been afraid that Herrick was going to ask him to be his ally in overthrowing Sutcliffe's authority. He had wondered how he was going to refuse. Now it was no longer necessary.

Herrick looked up, as though trying to see him in the poor light.

'It states that five sail of the line were forced through the blockade. Rear-Admiral André Baratte – ' he could not bring himself to use the French title, 'escaped out of Brest in a

Dutch frigate, the *Triton*.' He paused, as if in silent agreement. 'So he was right about that too.'

Captain Pearse asked, 'You know the French admiral, sir?'

'Of him. His father was a great man, but went to the guillotine with all the rest during the Terror.' He did not conceal his disgust. 'But his son survived. He has distinguished himself in matters of deceit and secrecy.' He looked through Pearse without seeing him. 'What they call strategy, in high places.'

'What shall we do, sir?'

Herrick ignored him. 'Why didn't that poxed-up object over there die before Adam came? I could have done something then. Now it's too damned late.'

'Five sail of the line, sir. Plus those already here in the Caribbean . . . it makes this Baratte a formidable threat.'

Herrick took up his hat. 'Arrange the burial party for Lord Sutcliffe. And tell the major commanding the main battery that the next time he fires a salute, it will likely be at the French fleet!'

He left Pearse staring at the despatches, his mind in a daze. All so quick. At the stroke of a pen.

Aloud he exclaimed, 'But it was nobody's fault!' Only the buzzing insects answered.

Far out to sea, her topsails and upper yards painted silver by the moon, the frigate *Anemone* heeled over to a freshing north-easterly. Lieutenants Sargeant and Martin picked their way into the small chart-room where they found their captain poring over his charts.

The first lieutenant said, 'You wanted us, sir?'

Adam smiled and touched his arm. 'I treated you badly when I came aboard.'

Sargeant sounded relieved. 'I was slow to understand, sir. We felt – all of us who know – saddened by your news, your orders not to go in search of the flagship.'

'Thank you.' Adam picked up the brass dividers. 'Nelson once said that written orders are never any substitute for a captain's initiative.'

The two lieutenants watched him in silence, while the third and most junior paced the planks overhead, probably speculating as to what was happening.

Adam said quietly, 'There will be some risk, but not to you, if I am proven wrong.' He glanced around, seeing the whole of his ship as if she were laid out like a plan. 'But chances must be taken.'

Sargeant looked at the dividers and the scrawled calculations. 'You do not intend to sail for Port Royal, sir. You are going to hunt for Sir Richard's ships.' He said it so calmly, and yet, in its implication, it sounded like a thunderclap.

Lieutenant Martin exclaimed, 'You might lose everything, sir!'

'Yes. I have thought about it.' He studied the chart. 'Even my uncle could not help me. Not this time.' He looked up, his eyes very bright. 'Are you with me? I would not blame you if . . .'

Sargeant placed his hand over his on the chart and Martin laid his on top. Then he said, 'I'll tell Old Partridge. He never liked Jamaica anyway.'

They left him alone and for a long while Adam stood loosely in the chart-room, his body swaying with his ship.

He thought of his uncle, out there in the darkness with Keen. His lover's husband. A strange rendezvous.

He tossed down the dividers and smiled. 'So be it, then!' There would be no regrets.

Bolitho walked up the tilting deck until he could see the frigate *Anemone* riding hove-to under *Black Prince*'s lee, her sails and slender hull pale pink in the early morning light.

He turned and stared at his nephew, who was holding an empty coffee cup, his expression that of a young boy who had just been scolded by someone he loves or respects. In this case, both.

Bolitho said, 'I can scarcely believe it, Adam. You deliberately disobeyed orders to come and seek me out?' It had been dawn when the masthead lookout had reported *Anemone*'s top-gallants, and for an instant longer Bolitho had believed it was *Tybalt* returning already after taking his letters to Herrick. 'You know what this can mean. I knew you were a wild young devil, but I never thought . . .' He broke off, hating what he was doing to him. 'Enough of that. How did you find me and reach me before *Tybalt*?'

Adam put down his cup. 'I know your ways in these waters, sir.'

Bolitho walked down the deck and put his hands on his shoulders.

'I am damned pleased to see you nonetheless. If you leave at once, your despatches for Vice-Admiral Sir Alexander Cochrane will not be delayed more than a day. And you did not sight the other half of my squadron? That is strange.'

Adam stood up and looked for Ozzard. He was never far away. 'Tell them to call my gig alongside.' He turned to Bolitho. 'I could not simply sail away and leave you without news, Uncle. I tried to pass it to *Tybalt*, but it was all too quick.'

'It was warning enough, Adam. But your own news about the schooner, the shore-mounted gun – that is serious. I cannot think why Thomas Herrick would not go over Lord Sutcliffe's head. He was beyond reason when I saw him; Thomas would be fully justified. I simply do not understand.'

Adam bit his lip. 'I wish I could remain with you. But for you I would be nothing, but I'd risk it all if the same circumstances offered themselves again.'

Bolitho walked with him to the companion ladder. It was stranger still that Herrick had not opened the despatches before Adam had been sent away. French ships, but what kind and how many? And whose was the mind that controlled them?

The decks were crowded as both watches were mustered in readiness to get under way again. The other two seventy-fours were falling off downwind, their captains doubtless fretting to know what had happened.

Keen was watching his men. The sail-drill had certainly improved, but there was a long way to go yet. He nodded cordially to Adam and remarked, 'You are all surprises!' He had purposefully left them alone together in the great cabin. So much to say in so short a time. And like every sailor, each would know it could be for the last time.

Adam said, 'I have given a sketch of the island to the flag-lieutenant.' He sighed. 'Though I doubt if the French will linger there. They will know I carried the news to Antigua.'

He added with sudden bitterness, 'For all the damned good it did!'

Bolitho gripped his arm. 'It takes longer than you think to move an army, Adam. My instinct tells me that they will shift from there, and perhaps from other islands, when they know our Martinique attack has begun. They will likely have better intelligence in these waters than I do.' He dropped his voice. 'We will be together soon, Adam. Cochrane is not the admiral to deprive me of an extra fifth-rate when I need her so badly!'

Adam forced a smile. Just being close to Keen had brought the raw memory back to torment him. Himself with Zenoria. Zenoria giving herself to Keen, as she had to him.

He touched his hat and climbed swiftly down to his bobbing gig.

Bolitho said quietly, 'Still a wild one, Val. He risked everything to bring us news.'

Keen glanced at his troubled face. 'He has his ship, with prospects higher than he ever dreamed.' He saw the first lieutenant staring at him intently, like a keeper's hound. 'What he needs is a good wife, someone who'll be waiting for him when he has the sea at his back.'

He said to Sedgemore, 'You seem all eagerness to get under way. So carry on, if you please.' He watched the immediate tide of seamen and marines, the small islands of blue authority which were his lieutenants and warrant ranks as the hands were urged to halliards and braces.

Bolitho turned to Jenour. 'I shall require Yovell to produce two letters for me, Stephen. We will not waste time by stopping for a captains' conference: we will drop a boat, and send my orders to *Valkyrie* and *Relentless* in that fashion.'

'Shall we attack the island without *Tybalt*'s support, sir?' He saw that Jenour was watching him anxiously, probably thinking of the time when he would be ordered elsewhere.

'*Tybalt* will find us. Herrick must have opened his despatches by now. After that it is anybody's guess.'

Perhaps, Jenour thought. But it will be your responsibility.

Someone called above the din of billowing canvas and creaking blocks, '*Anemone*'s setting her courses!' Another group of idlers gave the frigate a cheer as she heeled over with the wind in her flapping sails.

Bolitho paused to watch her as she gathered way like the thoroughbred she was.

He said, 'God care for you, Adam.' But his words were lost in the bustle around him.

Later in the day, when a rising north-easterly had found and filled their canvas and thrust the flagship over until her lower gunports were all but awash, Bolitho sat alone in his cabin, covering his injured eye with one hand while he flattened her letter yet again on the table.

'My darling Richard, dearest of men, how I wonder where you are today, and what you are doing . . .' With great care Bolitho held up the pressed ivy leaf, crimson with winter, which she had sent in the letter. 'From our home . . .'

Bolitho replaced it in the envelope, and stared with shocked disbelief as a tear splashed on the back of his hand.

It was as if she had sent him one of her own.

18

Ghosts

Captain Valentine Keen waited until Bolitho had completed some calculations on his personal chart near the stern windows, and said, 'Nothing to report, sir.'

Bolitho studied the chart, the curving line of scattered islands in the Windward and Leeward groups. Places he would never forget, Mola Island, the Saintes, the Mona passage, confined waters and rugged fragments of land, their names written in blood. Great sea battles won and lost, and the rebellion which had cost them America. How could a nation as small as England have endured so much, standing alone and fighting France, Spain, Holland and then America all at once? And they were still fighting, although at long last it looked as if the tide might be on the turn in Europe. But here in the Indies the odds were as before, with the chances of running the enemy to earth more a matter of luck than knowledge.

Keen ventured, 'We can make another sweep to the nor' west, sir. It may be that Captain Crowfoot has taken his ships up towards Nevis in the hope of discovering the enemy.'

'I had thought of that. He is a resourceful man.' He straightened his back and stared at the chart, which seemed to mock him. 'It is what I myself might have done. You can lose a whole squadron amongst those islands.' The persistent worry returned. 'But he knows nothing of what Adam faced at Bird Island. If only Thomas Herrick had opened those despatches. They might reveal nothing, but . . .'

Keen said, 'Their lordships would not release a frigate like

Anemone to no purpose.' He sounded bitter, as Adam had been.

Bolitho said, 'Make to *Relentless* and *Valkyrie*. *Form line abreast of the Flag*. While there is good light, keep the distance five miles apart. That will give us a broader span of vision.' He listened to the wind through the rigging. It was still fresh, so they should make a few knots more before it eased off again. He waited for Jenour to scribble on his pad and hurry away to find his signals party.

He went on, 'They are both experienced captains – that is something, Val. I do not know Kirby of the *Relentless*, she had Captain Tabart at Copenhagen. But he has a good reputation. Flippance I have known for years.' He gave a distant smile. 'Governs his ship with the Bible and the Admiralty Fighting Instructions. The mixture seems to work well in his case.'

Keen made for the door. 'I shall shorten sail to allow the others time to work into position. Also, I must tell the first lieutenant to select his very best lookouts.'

Bolitho had returned to his chart; he was rubbing his eyelid again.

He said, 'Our master lookout from the jolly-boat, William Owen – what of him?'

Keen was surprised. How could he even find a moment to recall an ordinary sailor amongst so many?

He replied, 'I cannot speak too highly of him. I intend to rate him up to petty officer shortly . . .' He stopped as he saw Bolitho watching him, as if someone had just called his name.

'Do it now, Val. There may not be time later, and we shall need every experienced hand.'

Keen closed the door very quietly and hurried up the companion ladder.

'Shorten sail, Mr Sedgemore!' He shaded his eyes against the fierce light to look at Jenour's flags streaming from the yards, the signals midshipman with his raised glass calling out as each of the ships acknowledged.

Julyan the sailing-master shouted, 'As before, sir!'

Keen nodded, his mind busy. 'When we get under full canvas again we shall continue to the nor'west. Your noon sights will have to be your best today, Mr Julyan, for afterwards we will change tack and steer for the islands, Bird Island in particular.' Their eyes met and then Julyan said, 'Tomorrow, then?'

Keen turned away as the calls shrilled to muster the watch on deck for shortening sail. 'Master's Mate, find the seaman named William Owen for me.' *Do it now, Val,* Bolitho had said. Was it the same instinct which Keen had cause to respect? How did he know? But he did know, as Julyan accepted it without question.

He saw Owen striding along the lee gangway, completely at ease, as he had appeared even after the *Golden Plover's* loss.

He stepped on to the quarterdeck and knuckled his forehead. 'Aye, sir?'

'Everyone has spoken well of you, Owen, although I already knew your abilities.' He tried to smile. 'I shall have it logged immediately that you are to be promoted, with pay and victuals accordingly.'

Owen stared at him. He had an open, homely face which reminded Keen of Allday, when he had first met him aboard the frigate *Undine* under Bolitho's command. All those dangerous years ago, when he himself had been a young midshipman, like the one on watch nearby: De Courcy, who was pretending not to listen.

'Well, thank ee, sir!' Owen seemed genuinely pleased. 'I've been at sea in one ship or t'other for fifteen years. Never thought this would happen!' He repeated with a grin, '*Thank ee, sir.*'

Keen thought of the man in the great cabin below his feet. *How did he know?*

'Mr Sedgemore will explain your duties, at his leisure, but for the moment I am putting you with my cox'n. Together you will assist Mr Gilpin the bosun, should I need the boats to be lowered.'

Just for the briefest moment Keen saw his eyes flicker. 'But keep it to yourself.' He turned as Sedgemore hurried towards him. 'Something wrong?'

'I heard a mention of boats, sir.'

'And you will know why.'

Sedgemore stared round as Masterman, the sergeant of marines, exclaimed, 'Gawd, look at the old *Relentless*! She's gettin' a bustle on, an' no mistake!'

Sedgemore persisted quietly, 'But the sea is empty, sir.'

'We are informed that our combined attack on Martinique by Vice-Admiral Cochrane's ships and the army under General Beckwith is due to begin at any time. Weather permitting, in a matter of days. If I were the French commander of the ships and men at his disposal, I would move against vital bases – Antigua, for instance. If taken, it would leave our fleet like a headless chicken.'

Sedgemore found himself looking at the place on the quarterdeck where his predecessor Cazalet had died. Smart cordage, spotless decks, the men at the helm watching the compass and sails as they had always done. It was hard to imagine the hell it had been.

He said tentatively, 'But what if we came against them, sir, I – I mean without support?' It was rare to see him at such a loss for words.

'Then the people will fight, as they have never done before. Hereabouts the sea is a bottomless cavern, a place of total darkness, I believe. It is not much of an alternative, do you think?'

Sedgemore hurried away, needing something to do to stay his mind.

'*Relentless* on station, sir!'

Keen walked to the weather side and watched *Valkyrie*, under every stitch of canvas, clawing away towards the horizon to complete their line abreast, then he saw the vice-admiral's coxswain making his way aft and called, 'Memories, Allday?'

Allday squinted up at him and gave his lop-sided grin. 'Few more o' them shortly, I shouldn't wonder, sir!'

He vanished beneath the deck, going to the great cabin, knowing in his own private way that he was needed there.

Keen turned to the officer-of-the-watch, the third lieutenant. 'I am going to my quarters, Mr Joyce. Call me at noon so that we may compare sun-sights.' He paused. 'Earlier if you need me.'

Joyce smiled. He had served captains he would never dare to call, even if the ship seemed to be falling apart; afterwards they would blame an uncertain lieutenant with equal passion. To his midshipman he said, 'Remember all that you see and hear, Mr De Courcy. It might stand you in good stead, in the unlikely event that you stay alive long enough to be given a command!'

The midshipman, who was fifteen, was not too troubled by Joyce's manner. His father was a rear-admiral, and his grandfather before him.

'Aye, *aye*, sir! I will take heed of *everything!*'

Joyce turned away, hiding a smile. Cheeky little bugger, he thought.

Shortly after the ritual of shooting the sun with their sextants, and the murmured comparisons around the chart table, *Black Prince* and her two consorts crossed the eighteenth parallel, and came around towards the western horizon.

Lieutenant Stephen Jenour noted Ozzard's dour expression as he passed him at the cabin screen doors; the little man was carrying away Bolitho's breakfast, the one he had come to know was his favourite at sea. A slice of fat pork, fried pale brown with biscuit crumbs, and black treacle on a separate ship's biscuit. It was untouched, and only the coffee had vanished.

He saw Allday running a cloth up and down Bolitho's old sword as he must have done a thousand times, while his gaze rested on the broad panorama through the stern windows. Even allowing for the salt stains on the thick glass and the hazy dawn light, the view was breathtaking. The eastern horizon coming to life, the sea choppy and milky under the steady pressure of wind. Birds too, gliding back and forth below the ship's counter waiting for scraps, screaming away occasionally as some fish or other rose too close to the surface.

Jenour saw Bolitho on the bench seat, one foot on the checkered deck covering, his other knee drawn up to his chin; he saw too that his heavy uniform coat and hat lay on a chair, like the garb of some actor waiting in the wings.

He rather wished he could try his hand with his sketch book, but there was no time, and he told himself he could never capture the tension and the curious intimacy of this private moment.

Bolitho turned his head. 'Look at the birds, Stephen. If only we knew what they had seen in their flights amongst the islands. Perhaps nothing.' He glanced at a line of serried wave crests as the wind sped amongst them. 'If I am wrong this time, and with the wind still pressing, it may take days to beat back again and search elsewhere.'

Jenour said, '*Relentless* is in sight abeam, Sir Richard. She is on perfect station, it seems.'

Somewhere far ahead of *Black Prince*'s tapering jib boom lay the islands. They would still be in shadow, but daylight, when it came, would be swift.

'How is Captain Keen?'

'He was about early, Sir Richard. I could sleep very little too.'

Bolitho gave a quick smile. 'At least you do not have to stand watches with the others, Stephen. Maybe I do not work you hard enough.'

He let his mind drift with the spray against the stern windows, the hollow boom of the tiller-head as the rudder took the strain of sea and wind.

There is nothing more I can do. I am in a dark room. I cannot even rely on circumstances, for I do not know them.

Suppose the enemy attacked Antigua? What would Herrick do? Face another hopeless battle like the last? Or would he order a withdrawal until help arrived? *He would fight*. To punish himself, or to cast scorn on those who had wanted him guilty.

He thought of Adam's anger and sense of betrayal, and tried to picture how it had been between him and his old friend. Something else was troubling Adam; maybe he would share it, given the chance.

Jenour said, 'That was a hail from the masthead, Sir Richard.' His face was both troubled and excited.

Bolitho saw Allday's polishing cloth pause on the keen old blade. He had not heard it either.

'Be easy, Stephen. We shall know soon enough.'

Jenour watched him, fascinated, envious of the way he could contain his inner feelings, especially when so much depended on today. Or tomorrow. But he knew it would be today.

The sentry bawled, 'Midshipman-of-the-watch, *sah*!'

Midshipman M'Innes entered timidly and peered around the semi-dark cabin. 'Captain Keen's respects, Sir Richard, and . . . and . . .'

287

Bolitho prompted gently, 'We are all agog, Mr M'Innes, so please share it with us.'

The youth flushed under his sunburn. 'A sail is reported to the west'rd. The lookout says she may be a frigate.'

Bolitho smiled, but his mind was like ice. A frigate. She would be able to see *Black Prince*, if not the others, set against the brightening horizon. A friend then? She must be *Tybalt*. He tried to quell his rising hope. Even with a frigate it would take days to search amongst these islands.

'My compliments to the Captain. I shall come directly.'

He picked up his empty coffee cup and stared at it. 'Little boys and old men. Good ones and felons.'

Allday grinned. 'Nothing changes, Sir Richard.' He picked up the sword and thrust it into its fine leather scabbard. It must have worn out many of those in its lifetime, he thought. But only the one sword.

'Not yet, old friend.' Bolitho looked towards his flag-lieutenant, and there was something like pain in his grey eyes. 'Are you prepared, Stephen?'

Jenour said steadily, although he did not fully understand, 'I'm ready, Sir Richard.'

'Come, let us go up.' He touched his arm impetuously. 'They are not always the same thing!'

Allday watched them leave and sat down in Bolitho's chair. The wound was aching badly. A sure sign. He laughed harshly. *Nerves? An old Jack like you! Blast your eyes for a fool!*

Ozzard had entered silently. 'What is it, John?'

'Do something for me. Fetch my jacket an' cutlass from my mess, will you?'

Ozzard reacted predictably. 'I'm not *your* servant!'

Allday felt the tension draining away. It always did when you knew. 'I'll be needed in a minute or two, Tom.' He saw Ozzard's sudden anxiety and added kindly, 'We're going to fight today. So be off with you, eh, matey?' He seized one thin arm as Ozzard began to hurry away. 'I'll speak my piece, then close the hatches.' He felt fear through the little man's sleeve. 'If the worst happens . . .' He let the words sink in. 'I want no more o' that madness we had in our old *Hyperion*. Like it or not, we're mates. We stand together.' He watched the gratitude in Ozzard's eyes and added roughly, 'Fetch me a wet too, eh?'

Unaware of the private drama in the great cabin, Bolitho stood beside Keen and Jenour at the quarterdeck rail, his arms folded as he watched the sea opening itself on either beam in the first feeble sunlight. He saw *Relentless* directly abeam, perhaps a mile away until daylight made signals readily visible. Beyond her he thought he saw *Valkyrie*'s pale pyramid of sails, and wondered if Flippance had also sighted the far-off ship.

Bolitho glanced at the many figures moving along the upper gundeck and in the rigging overhead. The work never ceased. Splicing and repairing, tarring-down and caulking, and always the guns which dominated their daily lives. On the crowded messdecks the seamen who lived with them saw the guns when they were piped from their hammocks, with a touch of a starter for the last ones out, at their messdeck tables, where they took their too-often crude meals and drank their daily tots, or beer if any was still drinkable. The guns separated them like silent guardians. When they were off watch and repaired their clothing, 'a bit of jewing' as the sailors termed it, or made models and yarned of ships and places they had seen, so too, the guns were always with them.

And as a result of all the drills and the demanding discipline, the guns would wait for the ports to open, and be run out, and would turn those same messdecks into a smoke-filled hell.

'A glass, if you please.' He took it from Midshipman M'Innes and trained it abeam. The nearest seventy-four was sharper now, and he could even see tiny figures moving along the gangways, covering the hammocks which had been packed down hard in the nettings for another day.

Midshipman Houston stood with, but apart from, his signals party, his telescope raised, his face almost disdainful. He was probably thinking of his hoped-for promotion to lieutenant: the first rung on the ladder.

'She's *Tybalt*, sir!'

As men chatted and discussed what it might mean, Bolitho levelled the glass again and wanted to cover his injured eye with his hand, but the telescope was too heavy. And those around him might see, and suspect.

How grey it looked beyond the flapping jib, but that would

soon change. He found the frigate's pale topsails and saw the tiny, bright flags, the only true colour against the horizon, suddenly dip and vanish.

'Another signal, Mr Houston!' Keen's voice was unusually sharp.

'Aye, sir!' His voice was sulky, like the time he had been ordered aloft for bearing down on the seaman Owen.

Jenour read it first. 'Signal, Sir Richard. *Enemy ships bearing north-west!*'

Bolitho was aware of the sudden silence around him. *Tybalt* must have been searching for him and had run down on the enemy formation without knowing what it was. They were lucky to be alive.

'Acknowledge. Tell *Tybalt* to take station to windward.' He ignored the bright flags soaring aloft to break from the yards, the other bunting strewn around the midshipman and signals party like fallen standards on a battlefield.

Jenour was waiting with his book. 'General – *Prepare for battle.*'

Then as the flags soared up again and were acknowledged by the other two ships, Bolitho said, 'Then another, Stephen. *Form line of battle ahead of the Flag.*'

Keen understood. Bolitho was saving the flagship's massive artillery until he could estimate the enemy's strength and intentions.

Bolitho turned and saw Allday carrying his coat and hat across the old sword like an offering.

He slipped his arms into the coat, and knew the sailing-master was watching as he took his hat also. Remembering their last fight together, when he had worn Bolitho's hat into battle.

He raised his arms and allowed Allday to fasten the sword into place. Allday was wearing his best jacket, the one with the special gilt buttons he had given him. Their eyes met and Bolitho said quietly, 'So, old friend. It will be warm work today.'

Keen saw the exchange, but was thinking of Zenoria. He would never go home if he was maimed or disfigured. Never.

When he looked again he was surprised by the intensity of Bolitho's gaze. It was as if he had read his innermost thoughts.

Bolitho smiled. 'Are you ready?' He waited, as if to share his strength with him. 'Very well, *Captain* Keen.' He was still smiling, excluding all those nearby. 'You may beat to quarters!'

In the confusion of shortening sail yet again to allow the other ships to form line ahead, the sudden rattle of drums from the marine drummer boys, the muffled calls between decks were almost drowned. Then as men stared at each other, while others ran wildly to their stations at the guns or high above the decks in the fighting tops, discipline seemed to hesitate as full realisation came to those men who had never before faced an enemy.

Petty officers and boatswain's mates chased the laggards with blows and curses, while beside those guns visible on the upper deck, gun-captains were already selecting the first balls from the shot garlands.

Sedgemore peered aft anxiously. 'Ready, sir!'

Keen tore his eyes from the hardening shape of the approaching frigate and called, 'Faster this time, Mr Sedgemore!'

He glanced at Bolitho for confirmation. 'Clear for action!'

There was less turmoil, or so it appeared from the quarter-deck. This was mainly because the ship's company was separated into smaller groups, men were known to one another, and even their stations for battle were familiar to them.

Jenour watched over his signals party and then started with alarm as Houston called, 'Signal from *Tybalt*, sir! Repeated *Valkyrie* and *Relentless*. *Estimate six sail of the line to the nor'west!*'

Keen said, 'Alter course two points to starboard. Steer west-nor'-west.'

Bolitho did not have to think about Keen's actions; he had proved his skill many times. But he had seen the men on deck peering at one another as if for answers to their fears. The odds remained the same. Two to one. He had faced such odds before, but most of the people had not.

'Acknowledge!'

Up and down the line the pendants rose and dipped again, while with their yards braced round in response to Keen's signal, the others headed up closer to the wind.

Bolitho called, 'Will you go aloft with a glass, Stephen?'

Jenour made for the shrouds but paused as Bolitho called after him. '*I must know.*' Unconsciously he was touching his eyelid again, his face set with grim determination.

Allday folded his arms and nodded to Tojohns as he hurried to join the boatswain by the boat-tier. Here we go, he thought. He rubbed his chest and saw Bolitho watching him. He gave a slow grin. 'Just a habit, Sir Richard.'

Bolitho turned away as Jenour yelled from the crosstrees.

'From *Tybalt*, sir! *One frigate in company!*' Eventually it would be clear enough to see the enemy from the deck. But not that soon. Bolitho shaded his eyes to look at the masthead pendant. Noon then. He saw Julyan putting extra hands on the wheel, the marines trooping to poop and forecastle, and up the quivering ratlines to the fighting tops where they would try to mark down the enemy's officers, or rake them with swivel-guns if they drew close enough together.

Other patches of scarlet marked each hatchway and ladder: sentries to prevent terrified men from running below to hide. To cut them down, if necessary, to maintain the others' will to fight.

Bolitho heard Julyan murmur, 'Less the wind backs a piece, them buggers'll hold the advantage, sir.'

Keen nodded, dismissing what he already knew.

The breeze was a lively one and showed no sign of falling. If the enemy held the wind-gage, it was just possible they might be unable to run out their lower deck artillery with the ports almost awash. *Black Prince* on the other hand would keep the advantage with her main armament as the ship heeled over to the sail's demands.

It was little enough. Bolitho walked to the tightly packed hammock nettings and rested against them while he levelled his telescope like a musket. He saw the ornate gingerbread across *Relentless*'s counter and poop reflecting and holding the flicker of feeble sunshine. *Valkyrie* led the line, and he was thankful. He knew Flippance; he would be like an extension of his right arm and would likely be the first to engage the enemy. So they had a frigate with them. In his heart he knew it was the Dutch-built one which Owen had described. The other ships, whichever they were, must have slipped through the blockade during the foul weather or even earlier. At the second attack on Copenhagen several had broken out, and not all had been recovered or brought to battle. They would be from different ports, perhaps with captains who had never fought together before. The man who commanded such a mixed squadron would have had to travel fast and independently in order to rally the ships he must lead.

It struck Bolitho like a fist. *Why did I not think of it before?* There was one French officer who stood head and shoulders above the others, a young frigate captain when they had been fighting out here, in these same waters. A voice seemed to mock him from the past. *Were a frigate captain, Bolitho . . .* He held flag rank now, having survived the terrible bloodletting of the Terror. A brilliant man, and one who would certainly use a frigate, no matter who had built her, to restore the pride which had been lost at the Nile and Trafalgar.

'André Baratte, Val. That's who we are facing today.'

Then he remembered that none of those around him had been here in that other war. Except for Allday, and he would not have known. *We Happy Few.* All gone, wiped away in time if not memory.

Keen tried to understand, sensing his sudden depression. 'What is it, sir?'

'Baratte was a very daring frigate captain, Val. I have no doubt of his equal ability as an admiral.'

He glanced down at the spitting crests alongside. 'Make a signal to that effect to *Valkyrie* through *Relentless*. Spell it out with care. It may be useless to Captain Flippance, but he should be prepared.'

He stepped aside as midshipmen and seamen ran to the flag halliards again.

The name seemed to taunt him. Thomas Herrick would know, and it had likely been in the despatches he had refused to open. The Admiralty would send a frigate to carry such news. It sickened him to think of Herrick refusing to act; and it was impossible to see him as he had once been. Or was he himself the only one who still trusted in their old friendship?

High above their heads, perched on the main crosstrees and watched with curious amusement by a pigtailed seaman, Lieutenant Stephen Jenour watched the sea's face shining, and felt the first heat on his skin. With great care he adjusted his telescope and waited for the ship to heave herself upright again from a long trough. He could feel the mast and spars trembling beneath him, hear the wind moaning through the rigging and into the booming canvas. Unlike Bolitho he had a good head for heights, and he never grew tired of being this tall – above everything.

'Oh, my God.' He tightened his fingers on the telescope again. He could just make out the ships *Tybalt* had reported, and one, a frigate that stood apart from all the rest. She was even managing to stay on a different tack.

The lookout asked, 'Be it bad, zur?'

Jenour glanced at him. An old sailor. One of the few still left.

He said, 'Take this glass. Tell me what you see.'

The man squinted through it, the crowsfeet around his eyes creasing his leathery skin.

'Beyond them ships, zur?' He shook his head, as if shocked that he could still be surprised. ''Tis a *fleet*, zur!'

Jenour lowered himself swiftly past and around the maintop, where the marine marksmen lounged against the barricades watching his descent with interest.

Bolitho listened to him without comment, then said, 'It will be an army of invasion. Adam saw only a part of it, but this is the truth of the matter.'

Keen said, 'Can they be stopped, sir?'

'Until aid arrives, yes, Val.'

He looked towards the horizon, still dim with mist, like the smoke of a silent battle.

'Get rid of the boats. The victors can recover them.'

He ignored the calls and the rush of seamen to the hoisting-tackles. 'Well, there it is, Stephen. I thank you for your eyes today.' He saw other men running to prepare chain lifts to rig from the yards, to prevent them from falling on the unprotected gun crews if they were shot away. 'What will he do, I wonder?'

'If . . .' Jenour shivered as he recalled what he had just seen. 'If it is indeed the same French officer, and if, as you suspect, he was in that frigate . . .'

Bolitho tried to smile, but he could not. 'Too many ifs, Stephen.'

'He will know you are here, Sir Richard. Know, too, that you have never run from the enemy.'

Bolitho touched his arm. 'Then I have lost one ruse before it is begun. But I believe you are right.'

He watched the first of the boats being lowered, then cast adrift and left under the control of a canvas sea-anchor. He thought suddenly of the *Golden Plover*. Was Fate so certain after all? Had death merely been postponed until today?

Yet again he seemed to hear her voice, *Don't leave me*, and he answered her, but only in his mind. *Never*.

He saw Keen staring around the orderly decks, where men stood or crouched to await the next command. Perhaps he was already calculating the cost, seeing these same decks strewn with the dead and dying as Herrick's flagship had been.

Bolitho said abruptly, 'Let us have some music to pass the while, Captain!' The formality was for those nearest to them. If they lived, they would remember.

Keen gave a faint smile. '*Portsmouth Lass*, sir?'

Their eyes met. Another memory. 'None other.'

So while the ships sailed slowly towards an unknown enemy, the small marine fifers marched up and down the deck, piping out a sailor's tune neither Bolitho nor Keen would ever forget.

Bolitho felt for the locket beneath his shirt and pressed it against his skin.

I am here, Kate, and you are with me.

Lieutenant Sedgemore had been watching Bolitho and the flag-captain, his mind as yet unable to grasp the enormity of the enemy's strength. *But once this was over* . . . He allowed his eyes to stray to that part of the deck where his predecessor had died so horribly. As if he expected to see him lying there, torn apart.

He felt cold, despite the strengthening sun. He had seen something which he had only known as a stranger. It was fear.

19

We Happy Few

Bolitho plucked the shirt from his skin and watched some ship's boys carrying drinking water beneath either gangway for the gun crews. It had seemed an eternity since *Valkyrie*'s signal, '*Enemy in sight!*' had been repeated down the line, and Bolitho knew that despite their superiority in strength and numbers it was probably much worse for the oncoming French vessels. *Black Prince* had her yards braced hard round and was as close to the wind as such a large ship could stand, but at least they were holding formation and staying in line, with only half a mile between each of them. The enemy had the wind striking directly across their larboard bows, so that they appeared to weave this way and that, leaning over one minute with their sails like metal breastplates, and the next caught aback in a confusion of thrashing canvas.

Bolitho shaded his face to look through the mass of rigging. Nets had been rigged to catch falling blocks or broken spars, any of which could kill a man as efficiently as an iron ball. It was like being sealed in a trap. Men, weapons of war, everything they had come to accept as their daily existence.

Bolitho sought out the frigate *Tybalt* and saw her beating against the wind with no less difficulty than the enemy. But once the liners were close enough to engage, Captain Esse would run down from his hard-won position to windward and attack the enemy's fleet of transports and supply vessels to scatter or destroy any which fell under his broadsides. He might have little hope of survival, but every frigate captain knew the risks of independent action. *Tybalt*'s hull was created and designed for just such operations, but her timbers were no match at all for the massive firepower of a line-of-battle. Bolitho took a telescope from Midshipman De Courcy and trained it with care until he had found the ragged formation of ships which lay far away across the starboard bow. *So slow.* He had been right the first time. It would be at noon when the first guns tested the range.

And for what? It might eventually rate a comment in the *Gazette* as had *Hyperion*'s last battle. That had been almost lost in the resounding echoes of Trafalgar, and the death of the nation's hero.

Ferguson would hear it first, either in the town or from the post-boy. Then Catherine. He glanced at Keen's handsome profile. One did not need to be a magician to know what he was thinking as the time dragged by and men leaned on their weapons, some already gasping for breath as the suspense wore them down like exhausted survivors from a battle still to fight.

After all, what did Martinique really matter? They had taken it from the French by force in 1794 but, typically, had handed it back during the brief Peace of Amiens. It was always the same, and Bolitho had often been reminded of the words of an embittered sergeant of marines who had exclaimed, 'Surely if it's worth dyin' for, it's worth 'oldin' on to?' Down over the years his lonely protest had remained unanswered.

Now, with the war changing direction in Europe, the prospect of throwing lives and ships away to no lasting purpose went against everything he held important.

Once again, they were faced with action, not because it was logical or unavoidable, but because war had started to outstrip the minds of men who planned its strategy from afar.

Keen had joined him. 'If the rest of the squadron finds us, sir, we could still win the day. But if Captain Crowfoot has no inkling . . .' He turned and stared into the bright sunshine as *Tybalt* completed another tack.

'I cannot send *Tybalt* to find him, Val. She is our only hope today.'

Keen watched the men at the helm, Julyan speaking quietly with two of his masters' mates. 'I know.'

Bolitho took a cup of water from one of the boys. And what

of Thomas Herrick? Had he rallied some of his local patrols, and was he already heading out to offer support? It seemed far more likely that he would take charge of the seventy-four *Matchless* under the command of his latest enemy, Captain the Lord Rathcullen. Her repairs would be almost completed, and in any case, the sight of just one additional sail-of-the-line might make a difference to an invasion fleet which would wish to avoid battle at any cost. It was unnerving: this constant comparison with the events which had led to Herrick's court-martial. In her letter Catherine had touched briefly on the sudden death of Hector Gossage, Herrick's flag-captain at that costly battle for the convoy. He had never recovered fully after losing his arm, and even the unexpected promotion to flag rank could not protect him from the onslaught of gangrene. Had he known he was doomed that day in the great cabin below, his version of the evidence might have been very different. Bolitho had his suspicions, but they were not something he could voice freely without proof. Either way, Gossage had saved Herrick's future and probably his very life.

The only constant factor had been in the presence of Sir Paul Sillitoe.

Keen said, 'They're forming into two lines, sir.'

Bolitho raised the glass again, knowing that as he did so, Midshipman De Courcy was watching him fixedly. Another admiral in the making. How different his navy would be, he thought.

He settled on the two ships leading the enemy's lines, sails writhing while they tacked yet again, with the frigate passing through them, the terrier between the bulls.

The masts and yards were bright with signals and the streaming Tricolour flags, just as the short English line had hoisted extra ensigns as a gesture of defiance. Or was it only a hopeless obstinacy.

Major Bourchier called, 'Royal Marines, stand-to for inspection!'

He gestured to his second-in-command, Lieutenant Courtenay, a veteran for one so young. Who but the Royals would have an inspection in the presence of the enemy and, perhaps, in the face of death?

Bolitho touched his eye. It was itching badly, so that it watered whenever he looked towards the sun.

'What is the range, do you think, Val?'

'Two miles, sir. No more.' He thought again of the jolly-boat, and Bolitho's desperate attempt to conceal his blindness from those who were relying on him.

He saw Allday loosening his cutlass, and Jenour peering up at the flags while Midshipman Houston listened to his instructions.

And there was the sixth lieutenant, James Cross, a boy dressed as an officer and in charge of the afterguard and the mizzen mast with its less complicated sail plan and rigging. He looked neither right nor left, and never towards the slowly advancing Frenchman. And Lieutenant Whyham, the fourth senior who had served under him in the old *Argonaute* six years ago as a cheerful midshipman. He looked resolved enough as he watched his division of guns, and the spare hands who would be employed on the mainmast, the true strength of any ship-of-the-line.

And down below in the darkened gundecks all the others would be waiting, straining their ears, trying to recall a home or loved ones, but finding nothing.

The Royal Marine lieutenant was saying, 'I've never *seen* such a turnout, Colour Sergeant! Give him extra work after this is done with!'

The other marines grinned. They were not new to the ship, and but for a mere handful of recruits were of one unit, the scarlet line that stood through thick and thin between officers and forecastle. In spite of the crowded world between decks they still managed to keep to themselves, in their own 'barracks', as they called their messes.

There was a dull bang, and seconds later a thin waterspout shot up from the sea to leave a wisp of smoke where it had fallen.

The first lieutenant forced a grin. 'They'll have to do better than that!' But his eyes were empty.

Keen said, 'I cannot see the sense in dividing their strength, sir.'

'I think I know what they intend, Val. Three will go for our two consorts.' He saw his words sink in. 'The other half will come for us.' All at once the plan was so clear he could almost see it in action.

'Shall I load and run out, sir?'

He did not reply directly. 'Pass the word to the Gunner and Lieutenant Joyce on the lower gundeck. We still have time. *Valkyrie* will be the first to engage.' He considered. 'Yes, there *is* time enough. The enemy will try to do as much damage to our spars and rigging as possible to keep us from supporting our friends. But our thirty-two pounders will outshoot them. How much bar-shot and anything for that very purpose do we have? We will race them at their own game.'

It was not hard to understand the French tactics. It was customary for them to aim for the rigging to disable their opponents, whereas the English put their faith in rapid broadsides to smash the hulls into submission.

Keen said, 'It is unlikely that we carry enough for more than a few full broadsides. But I shall pass your instructions to the Gunner immediately. Mr Joyce is a good officer – I shall see that he is instructed to point each gun himself. With the wind holding us over, we should be able to maul them badly.'

'After that, Val, pass the order to load and run out.'

There were a few more shots but nobody saw where they fell, probably ahead of *Valkyrie* in the van.

The three other French ships had shortened sail, preparing to fight the three-decker with a vice-admiral's flag at the fore. The first embrace would be vital. The wind's steady strength would carry the enemies apart immediately afterwards, and it would take more time to regain any sort of advantage.

Whistles shrilled below decks and as the port lids were hoisted, the whole ship seemed to hold her breath. Then, with her decks shaking under their tremendous weight, she ran out her guns, their crews busy with handspikes while they peered over the black muzzles to catch a glimpse of the enemy. More whistles. Every gun loaded, the great lower battery packed with murderous linked shot, some like bars which doubled in length as it screamed through the air, others shaped like iron spades which when fired spun around like the sails of a mill.

Keen said, 'Let her fall off two points. I want to draw the others away.'

It was at that moment that *Valkyrie* and then *Relentless*

opened fire, the pale smoke fanning through their sails and rigging like low cloud. Much of the broadside fell short, flinging up banks of broken water, some of which reached the enemy vessels. The air quivered as the French line responded, the long orange tongues spitting out along the gunports. As Bolitho had predicted it was not a powerful reply; the lower guns were cruising just above the sea, and it seemed likely that the officers could not elevate them enough to reach the two seventy-fours.

'*Steady as you go!*' Keen crossed the quarterdeck, his eyes everywhere as he stared from the set of the sails to the enemy formation. They were beginning to draw near on a converging tack, whilst beyond them he could make out the sleek hull of the solitary frigate. He turned to say so to Bolitho, but saw him smile.

'I've seen her. She flies a rear-admiral's flag. It would be exactly what Baratte would do. This way he can remain in control, but move between the formations without delay.'

Keen found himself able to smile back. 'What *you* might do, sir, if I'm not mistaken!'

Sedgemore was striding along the upper gundeck, his bared sword resting on his shoulder as he looked quickly at each crew. From the gun-captains with their trigger-lines already pulled taut, to the seamen on either side of the carriage, ready to sponge out the smoking muzzles and reload as they had done so many times in Keen's relentless drills. The boys had sanded the decks, while others stood ready to fetch fresh powder from the magazine so long as it was needed. Boys from the seaport slums, or unwanted children from families already worn down by childbirth. The same age as the midshipmen for the most part. A million miles apart.

Keen drew his sword and tossed the scabbard to Tojohns, his coxswain. He would not sheath it again until the enemy struck, or it was dragged from his dead hand.

The leading French ship was changing tack very slightly. Bolitho imagined Joyce and his subordinates on the lower gundeck, watching the square ports, the glittering expanse of water and then out of nowhere, the enemy's bowsprit and beakhead.

Bolitho glanced at the masthead pendant. It was pointing

301

stiffly, like a lance, and he felt the deck tilting even further to leeward. The shrill of Joyce's whistle was drowned by the first pair of guns, and another, and still more until the air was filled with choking smoke. In the confines of that great gundeck it would be far worse.

The leading Frenchman seemed to wilt, her canvas writhing as if torn apart by giant claws, and with a sliding crash which could be heard across the water her foremast and rigging fell over the side, taking shrouds, spars and shrieking men with it.

The second ship, another seventy-four, had been obeying a signal to close on the leader, and now because her consort was staggering out of line, her forecastle strangely bare with the mast gone, there was danger of collision.

Keen shouted, '*Fire at will!*'

Whistles again, the upper and middle gundecks roared out at the enemy. Bolitho saw wreckage fly from the second ship, and holes punched through her flapping sails as the iron raked her from bow to poop.

Allday gritted his teeth. 'For what we are about to receive . . .'

Every port along the enemy's side flashed fire and Bolitho gripped the quarterdeck rail as he felt the shots smashing into the hull like great hammers. But nothing fell from above, and already several of the gun-captains below him had their hands in the air, ready to fire again.

Keen yelled, 'On the uproll, Mr Sedgemore!'

'*Fire!*'

The long twelve-pounders flung themselves inboard on the tackles, their black muzzles streaming smoke and hissing like live things as the wet sponges were rammed into them.

'*Run out!*' Sedgemore wiped his sweating face. 'As you bear, lads! *Fire!*'

The third ship had dropped down wind to avoid the leading two and swayed over to the force of a full broadside as she fired directly into *Black Prince*'s quarter.

There were crashes and screams from below the poop, and the rumble of a gun being upended.

'Put your helm down!' Keen watched the leading ship swinging towards them, still out of control because of the great mass of rigging and spars hauling her round like some huge sea-anchor. He raised a glass and saw the gleam of axes as men tried to cut away the fallen mast, while others stood, apparently unable to move as *Black Prince*'s jib boom passed their own.

At this range Joyce's great thirty-two pounders could not miss. The enemy stood at barely thirty yards' range when his guns thundered from every port, and another broadside of screaming metal ripped through the remaining masts and spars or across the deck itself.

Major Bourchier watched with little more than professional interest as his lieutenant snapped, 'Marines! Fix bayonets! *Stand-to!*'

They stepped smartly up to the packed nettings and slid their muskets across the hammocks to take aim.

Smoke swirled over the deck. Bolitho felt Allday flinch beside him as a ball crashed through a port and splintered on the breech of a gun even as it was being run out.

The gun's crew were hurled in all directions, some cut to pieces to cover the men at the neighbouring twelve-pounder with blood, others smashed down where they had been standing in their fixed attitudes before they fell to the deck.

Midshipman Hilditch, one of the twelve-year-olds who had joined *Black Prince* at Spithead, had been running messages to and from the lower gundeck. He fell down the open hatchway, but not before Bolitho had seen that half of his face had gone. *Like Tyacke*.

'She's trying to cross our stern, Val!'

Bolitho watched men running to Keen's commands, hauling on braces and halliards to allow the ship to turn even further downwind. Their immediate danger was the third ship in the French line. If she managed to press astern, and at this close range, she could pour a full broadside deck by deck through *Black Prince*'s unprotected stern. Any fighting ship, once cleared for action, was open from bow to counter; a single carefully timed broadside would turn the open gundecks into a bloody shambles. But the enemy had left it too late, and was now coming about to overreach the flagship's starboard quarter.

'Marines! *Open fire!*'

Like puny pop-guns amidst the thunder of the main armament the muskets obeyed, while far away in an unreal war the other battle raged on unheeded. When Bolitho raised his telescope he saw with dismay that *Relentless* was drifting, her steering apparently shot away, her main and mizzen cut down like savaged trees as she continued to fire into the dense smoke. *Valkyrie*'s masts were still intact, and he could see her flag floating above the drifting pall as if detached from any vessel.

More shots hammered into the lower hull, and men screamed and fell dying as two balls burst through the nettings, killing gun crews on the disengaged side.

A terrified midshipman ran across the quarterdeck, his eyes wide, probably from seeing Hilditch's body on the ladder. If, mercifully, the iron splinter had killed him.

Keen shouted, 'Walk, Mr Stuart! The people are looking to you today!'

Bolitho winced as another ragged burst of firing exploded over the deck. Keen's remarks had been like hearing himself, all that time ago. He heard the boy gasp, 'No more bar-shot, sir!'

'Get below. Tell Mr Joyce to resume firing at the ship on our quarter.'

The boy left the quarterdeck, walking, a small lost figure not daring to look at the sights around him.

Some of the crews of the forward division broke away, cowering, as another ball screamed past them and overturned another gun.

Sedgemore was there instantly. '*Get back!* Fight your gun, you bastards, or fight me!'

They ran to the tackles again, the gun-captain watching them with a shame Bolitho could sense even from the quarterdeck.

The nettings above the deck were bouncing with fallen cordage, and a musket dropped by someone from the maintop. Some seamen were struggling up the lee shrouds with a boatswain's mate to try to repair dangling rigging. One fell almost at once as marksmen fired from the other ship to test their aim and prepare to mark down the officers.

'The second ship is closing, sir!' Keen's hand went to his head as his hat was knocked to the deck. The shot had missed him by inches.

In a brief lull Bolitho heard the sharper bang of *Tybalt*'s guns. She must be among the supply ships.

'Must concentrate on the last one, Val!'

He almost fell as a ball smashed across the deck and cut down two of the helmsmen.

Two more ran to replace them but the quartermaster yelled, 'She don't answer, sir!' His white trousers were splashed with bright blood from his two companions but all he could think of was the wheel. The ship was already going out of control.

More shots hammered the stout hull, and Bolitho found himself recalling *Hyperion*'s last fight. She would have been no match for this merciless bombardment. A great explosion made the air cringe, but the intensity of the crossfire from all the engaged ships soon recovered.

It must have been a supply vessel blowing up, like the one Adam had destroyed.

Bolitho lifted a glass and watched the men swarming across the forecastle of the French ship, some exchanging fire with the marines, others brandishing hangers and axes, preparing to board as *Black Prince* continued to fall downwind.

Keen stared at him with wretched eyes. 'If we had some *support*, sir!' It was like a cry of despair.

Major Bourchier shouted hoarsely, 'More marines down aft, Mr Courtenay!' But the lieutenant lay dead beside his sergeant, and Bolitho was reminded of those first terrible seconds when he had boarded Herrick's flagship. Herrick had still been calling out orders to his marines, who had been strewn across the bloodied decks like broken toy soldiers.

Allday drew his cutlass and said, 'Together again, eh, Sir Richard?' He watched narrowly as Tojohns hurried to give Keen his hat. There was a neat hole punched through its brim.

Keen felt suddenly at ease. The madness, then. He had seen some of the new men break and run from their stations when death had moaned amongst them. *But not I. This is my ship. They will take it from me on pain of death.*

Balls hammered into the deck nearby and he guessed that the French marksmen were shooting from the two-decker's foretop. Then he heard Tojohns cry out, and saw him lurch against an unmanned gun, blood spilling from his mouth. Jenour knelt beside him but shook his head. 'He's gone, sir.'

Bolitho shouted, '*Come here*, Stephen!' He had seen the tell-tale splinters spurting from the deck. The enemy marksmen must have seen Jenour's uniform even through the choking barrier of smoke.

Jenour had caught the same unreasoning madness: he lifted his hat in salute towards the enemy's foretop, and then strolled unhurriedly across the deck to join him.

Allday glanced at the other coxswain, glaring and ugly in death, and sliced the air defiantly with his blade. 'Never volunteer, matey!'

There was a shuddering lurch as the other ship's bowsprit drove into the mizzen rigging like a tusk. Men were falling or leaping down on to *Black Prince*'s chains and gangway only to be hurled off, screaming, by seamen with pikes who thrust them through the nettings, forcing them into the narrowing wedge of trapped water.

Lieutenant Sedgemore yelled, '*Two men! Over here!* Help train this gun round as far as . . .'

A heavy ball struck him in the chest, and he dropped very slowly to his knees, his face filled with disbelief. He was dead before he hit the reddened planking.

Keen shouted, 'I'll not strike!'

Bolitho drew the old sword and saw Allday's big shadow overlap his own.

'Nor I!'

Somewhere a trumpet wailed through the sporadic firing.

As if to a signal, every ship fell silent. It was like being rendered deaf, until the cries and screams of the wounded and dying betrayed the gruesome reality of the battle.

Keen wiped his mouth with his sleeve. 'What is happening?' He saw Midshipman Houston staring at him, his cheek laid bare by a wood splinter. 'Aloft with you!'

Bolitho heard Lieutenant Whyham taking charge of the upper deck, and wondered if he saw the corpse of his superior as his chance of promotion, as Sedgemore had once done.

He heard Houston's voice too, shrill above the other sounds, shocked perhaps by the torn corpses in the maintop, which had received a full charge of grape shot.

'From *Valkyrie*, sir! Ships to the north-west!'

Bolitho gripped Keen's arm until he winced with pain. 'He

came after all, Val!' He looked around the deeply stained decks, the sprawled dead, the crawling, sobbing wounded. 'If only it had been sooner!'

The French ships were making sail, and as the smoke began to roll downwind Bolitho saw the enemy's solitary frigate, a rear-admiral's flag at the mizzen truck, and then, slowly emerging through the smoke beyond her, *Tybalt*. Her sails were peppered with holes, and there were deep scars along her hull.

But Bolitho could only stare at the motionless enemy frigate. He rubbed his eye until the pain made him cry out.

'The *flag*, Val! Look at it and tell me I'm not insane!'

Keen forced a smile; the madness was draining away. Afterwards it would be worse. But now . . . He replied, 'It's *our* flag, sir,' and then, surprised. 'There's more to *Tybalt*'s captain than I realised!'

Houston's voice intruded. 'The leading ship is *Matchless*, seventy-four, sir! She flies a rear-admiral's flag!' A short pause as if the words had caught in his throat. 'The others are our ships too!'

Whatever else was said was drowned by a wild burst of cheering. Men spilled out of hatchways and from guns; others hung in the rigging and cheered as if the rest of the squadron could hear them.

Keen asked, 'Shall we give chase to the enemy, sir?'

Bolitho rested against the sun-dried woodwork. There was fresh blood on his sleeve, but whose and when he did not know.

'No chase. There has been enough butchery today, and the enemy's plans are broken in the Indies.' He wiped his face again. Herrick had not forgotten. But for him, *Black Prince* and the others would have been overrun. But they had scattered the enemy. To some the price would be seen as paltry. Whereas, if they had struck to the enemy to save lives, they would have been dishonoured, damned by those same politicians who would eventually give him credit.

He gazed at the tired, powder-stained faces he knew and loved – that was the only word to describe it.

Allday, massive and unhurt, turning to take a mug of something from Ozzard as he crept past the damage and the

307

gaping corpses. Keen, already thinking of his men, and the need to prepare his ship again for any challenge, be it from the enemy or the ocean.

And those he only knew by sight and name. Like the two midshipmen nearby who were sobbing quietly, not caring who saw their relief. Julyan the sailing-master, tying his favourite red handkerchief around the wrist of one of his mates.

And all those who were cheering still, at him and to one another. And here came William Coutts the surgeon, more like a slaughterman in his bloodstained apron. Bringing the bill to his captain, the price they had paid on this day in February. The names of those who would never see England again, or know pride in anything they had done.

Jenour said, 'Orders, Sir Richard?'

Bolitho reached out and gripped his arms, and said quietly, 'Over there – the captured frigate *Triton*.' He saw it shake Jenour even from the brutal reality of battle.

'I . . . I don't want to, Sir Richard . . .'

'You will take my despatches to London yourself, *Commander* Jenour. Their lordships will doubtless give her to another, more experienced or with more influence, but certainly not more worthy. Equally, they must offer you a command of your own.'

Jenour could not speak, and Allday turned away, unwilling to watch.

Bolitho insisted, 'I shall miss you, Stephen, more than you realise. But war is war, and I owe your experience to the men you will command.'

Jenour nodded, his face lowered. 'I shall never forget . . .'

'And something else, Stephen. I want you to see Lady Catherine yourself and give her my letter. Will you do that?'

Jenour could say nothing. His face was drawn and mask-like.

'Tell her what it was like, tell her the truth – the way only you can. And give her . . . my deepest love.' He himself could no longer speak; his eyes were distant, seeing her walking on that wintry headland.

Someone called, '*Matchless* is lying-to, sir!'

Her Irish captain, Lord Rathcullen, must have sailed her

like a madman, like the day he had all but dismasted her. The remaining ships of the squadron were still far astern of him.

Keen said, 'I can't make it out, sir. They've lowered the rear-admiral's flag.' Then he said sharply, 'Muster the side party – *Matchless* has dropped a boat!'

Bolitho said, 'That is to let me know that I am in command again – he wants no part in all this.'

But when the boat came alongside there was no Herrick aboard.

Bolitho greeted the tall Irish peer at the entry port and said, 'You arrived just in time, sir!'

Rathcullen looked around at the dangling rigging, the dull smears where corpses had been dragged away, the hanging smoke and lingering chaos he had missed.

'I thought we *were* too late, Sir Richard. When I discovered what . . .'

'But where is Rear-Admiral Herrick? Is he well?'

Rathcullen was shaking hands with Keen. 'It was a ruse, Sir Richard. I guessed that if the enemy saw an admiral's flag they would assume a far larger squadron was about to engage them.'

Keen said shortly, 'It succeeded. Nothing else would have saved us, and we captured the French admiral for good measure.' But his voice was dull; he was haunted by the disbelief, the deepening hurt on Bolitho's face.

His head still echoed to the crash and thunder of battle: men dying, others pleading for death rather than the surgeon's knife. But all he could think of was Herrick.

Rathcullen sensed his disappointment. He said in a dispassionate voice, 'I reminded Rear-Admiral Herrick that I came under *your* command, sir. I suggested he should hoist his flag over my ship later – it gave me the notion for my ruse.'

'What did he say?'

Rathcullen glanced grimly at Keen. 'He said, "I'll not be blamed twice", Sir Richard.'

'I see.'

Keen said, 'I'd be obliged if you would pass a tow to my ship, Captain, until I can have the steering re-rigged.'

He looked back only once, and Bolitho half-raised a hand to him.

'Thank you, Val.'

Ozzard had reappeared with a heavy goblet. Allday took it and held it out to Bolitho. In his fist it looked like a thimble.

'Not all wounds bleed, Sir Richard.' He watched him put it to his lips. He hesitated. 'Lady Catherine would tell you. Some people change. It's not always their fault . . .'

Bolitho emptied the glass, and wondered if it had come from the shop in St James's.

'I thank God you do not, old friend.'

Jenour saw them walking together, and pausing to talk with some of the seamen. Their world. It had been his; it was his no more. He looked across at the captured frigate, and seemed to hear Bolitho's voice again. *The most coveted gift.*

But Lieutenant, now Acting-Commander, Stephen Jenour, once of Southampton, England, felt that he had just lost everything.

All Pan books are available at your local bookshop or newsagent, or can be ordered direct from the publisher. Indicate the number of copies required and fill in the form below.

Send to: Pan C. S. Dept
              Macmillan Distribution Ltd
              Houndmills Basingstoke RG21 2XS
or phone: 0256 29242, quoting title, author and Credit Card number.

Please enclose a remittance* to the value of the cover price plus: £1.00 for the first book plus 50p per copy for each additional book ordered.

*Payment may be made in sterling by UK personal cheque, postal order, sterling draft or international money order, made payable to Pan Books Ltd.

Alternatively by Barclaycard/Access/Amex/Diners

Card No. | | | | | | | | | | | | | | | | | | |

Expiry Date | | | | | | |

_____

Signature:

Applicable only in the UK and BFPO addresses

While every effort is made to keep prices low, it is sometimes necessary to increase prices at short notice. Pan Books reserve the right to show on covers and charge new retail prices which may differ from those advertised in the text or elsewhere.

NAME AND ADDRESS IN BLOCK LETTERS PLEASE:

....

Name _____

Address _____

_____

_____

_____

6/92